The Queen Ascendant

If Frane were to drop a bomb on this place at this time, I thought, *all of her problems would be solved.* I had never seen so many politicians and dignitaries in one place. *We truly are still a world of clans.*

"We gather here today," Newton's voice rang out in the hall, "to discuss the most serious threat to the Republic since the last rebellion, five years ago. The reemergence of Frane. She has secured the Republic's most scientific facility. We are still assessing what instruments of war she has obtained and what she may do with them."

"The government is too weak!" came a thunderous voice from the back of the hall. It belonged to Senator Thell, of my mother's—and Frane's—clan. "The problems we have can be traced to one source. There is no head of government to which all these wonderful delegates can hold allegiance. This is not right!"

There were thunderous shouts of "Hear, hear!" and "He is right!" which threatened to become a din.

I remember little of what happened next—the administration of the oath, how the Assembly Hall broke out in cheers and celebration, how the bells in the clock tower chimed, I was told later, for a full hour. I remembered none of this. But I remember the bells chiming again at midnight as Newton, sensing my exhaustion, removed me from the festivities, and I remember falling asleep, thinking, *I am Queen of Mars.*

Ace books by Al Sarrantonio

HAYDN OF MARS
SEBASTIAN OF MARS
QUEEN OF MARS

QUEEN OF MARS

AL SARRANTONIO

ACE BOOKS, NEW YORK

THE BERKLEY PUBLISHING GROUP
Published by the Penguin Group
Penguin Group (USA) Inc.
375 Hudson Street, New York, New York 10014, USA
Penguin Group (Canada), 90 Eglinton Avenue East, Suite 700, Toronto, Ontario M4P 2Y3, Canada
(a division of Pearson Penguin Canada Inc.)
Penguin Books Ltd., 80 Strand, London WC2R 0RL, England
Penguin Group Ireland, 25 St. Stephen's Green, Dublin 2, Ireland (a division of Penguin Books Ltd.)
Penguin Group (Australia), 250 Camberwell Road, Camberwell, Victoria 3124, Australia
(a division of Pearson Australia Group Pty. Ltd.)
Penguin Books India Pvt. Ltd., 11 Community Centre, Panchsheel Park, New Delhi—110 017, India
Penguin Group (NZ), Cnr. Airborne and Rosedale Roads, Albany, Auckland 1310, New Zealand
(a division of Pearson New Zealand Ltd.)
Penguin Books (South Africa) (Pty.) Ltd., 24 Sturdee Avenue, Rosebank, Johannesburg 2196,
South Africa

Penguin Books Ltd., Registered Offices: 80 Strand, London WC2R 0RL, England

This is a work of fiction. Names, characters, places, and incidents either are the product of the author's imagination or are used fictitiously, and any resemblance to actual persons, living or dead, business establishments, events, or locales is entirely coincidental. The publisher does not have any control over and does not assume any responsibility for author or third-party websites or their content.

QUEEN OF MARS

An Ace Book / published by arrangement with the author

PRINTING HISTORY
Ace edition / June 2006

Copyright © 2006 by Al Sarrantonio.
Cover art by Matt Stawicki.
Cover design by Rita Frangie.
Interior text design by Stacy Irwin.

ISBN: 0-441-01411-9

ACE
Ace Books are published by The Berkley Publishing Group,
a division of Penguin Group (USA) Inc.,
375 Hudson Street, New York, New York 10014.
ACE and the "A" design are trademarks belonging to Penguin Group (USA) Inc.

PRINTED IN THE UNITED STATES OF AMERICA

10 9 8 7 6 5 4 3 2 1

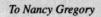

To Nancy Gregory

PART ONE

THE FIRST BATTLE

⊰ CHAPTER 1 ⊱

I WENT TO SEE FATHER AND GRANDMOTHER TODAY.

It had been a long time, but Newton insisted. I spent the morning practicing music (*tambon*), and the early afternoon reading (*The Runaway Kit*, fiction, which I did not like, and *A Short History of the First Republic of Mars*, which I greatly enjoyed—I must ask Rebecca, my lady-in-waiting, to bring me a meatier volume on that period), and then I was taken by airship and motorcar to the Arsia Mons Science Guild facilities. It was dusty, and old scarred Xarr was there, turning his head to look at me with his rheumy eyes. He always wears his military uniform, which is somehow endearing and annoying at the same time, but he gave me a wink and a slight sour smile and made an elaborate bow as I passed.

"Your *Majesty*!" he effused, with sarcasm.

I sniffed and walked on, leaving him to chuckle behind me.

"He is insubordinate," I said out loud, to no one in particular, but to my surprise Rebecca, at my side, answered me.

"He only seeks to bring you down to size, Princess," she said, with warm humor in her own voice.

I turned to glare at her, but her warm smile remained. "You are a wonderful young feline, Clara, but you are far too serious and far too young to be so. Your father was too young to assume the crown when he was forced to do so, and he was two years older than you. In many ways, you are still a kit—"

"Don't use that word!" I shouted, stamping my foot. I stopped in the corridor, and those behind us, old Newton and Thomas and a few others, halted also. I was infuriated by the smug look of tolerance on all their faces.

Filled with sudden rage, I turned on them. Even as Rebecca reached out to prevent me, I swatted her paw away.

"I will soon be your queen, and you will obey me!" I shouted. I was pleased to see the smiles melt from their faces—though Newton's ancient visage was inscrutable, and his eyes, as always, troubled me. They had seen much, more than I ever would, and sometimes I got the feeling that he saw straight through me and knew more about me than I did myself.

I turned in the corridor and began to march once again toward the far door, which led to what terrified me more than anything in the world. My fear was abated somewhat by the pleasure I drew from the sound of those following me in step, as if on command. I turned to Rebecca, but was surprised to see Newton in her place, staring down at me balefully.

"The princess and I will proceed alone," he said, and while it sounded like a suggestion, its result was a command, and the others, including my maidservant, withdrew immediately.

I wondered if their haste was leavened with relief.

I felt Newton's withered paw, which felt like a claw, descend lightly on my shoulder. Briefly he drew me toward him.

"Do not be afraid," he whispered.

I looked up at him, trying to put cold fire into my eyes, but instead burst into tears.

"I cannot go in there, Newton!" I sobbed, turning my face into his tunic. His claws patted my back. "I cannot face those . . . *ghosts*!"

"They are more than ghosts, Princess. You know that."

"But less than real! They haunt my dreams, every night! They frighten me!"

"Is it their images that frighten you, or what they represent?"

No adult had ever spoken to me so forthrightly, and at that instant my respect for Newton magnified. I pulled my tearful face from his tunic and looked up at him.

"Please explain," I requested.

A smiled touched his lips. "Always so serious!"

"What is there not to be serious about?" I replied. "I have a Republic to rule, great shoes to fill—"

"Ah!" he interrupted me. "Could this be the problem? Could it be that you fear that you will not measure up to your predecessors?"

Without my bidding, anger returned. "I have *no* fear of this!"

He bent down to gaze at me levelly. His face in old age was almost devoid of fur, now, his cheeks pink and wrinkled. His eyes looked even more enigmatic.

"Would it help," he whispered, "if I told you that you

have it in you to be greater than either your father or grandmother?"

I must have blinked, and again, against my will, tears filled my eyes. In a moment I had melted into his arms and was sobbing more uncontrollably than before.

"You are right . . ." I said. "I know I have great things in me. But I feel so *young*."

He patted my back, and let my crying jag, the first I had ever had, pass. "Poor Princess Clara," he said, wistfully, "always so strong, never showing weakness. Even as a little kit you were serious in play and in lessons. Hardly ever a smile, never letting anything more than the task at hand rule you. You never let yourself be a kit, Clara, and now that you are one no more it is too late.

"But I tell you this, and listen to me. You have in you qualities that are greater than either your grandmother Haydn, who was impetuous and headstrong, or your father Sebastian, who was, in the end, rash and too daring. You have a more solid head on your shoulders than either of them—and they were great felines."

By now I had stood back, noting the wet spot on his tunic, and stood staring at him.

"Do you mean these things?" I said.

He laughed shortly, which was not something he often did—though his eyes were not laughing. "Yes, I do. But can't you smile once in a while, Clara? It is the one thing you should work on."

"Then I will work on it," I said, seriously.

He smiled and then faced the door before us. "Shall we go in?"

My heart clenched, and I felt fear rise up in me, but I swallowed hard and said, "Yes, let's do so."

• • •

DARKNESS.

And then a silhouette of purple light, and another. They were side by side, as they often were, and seemed to be conversing, even though there was utter silence in the room. I held Newton's paw, and he drew me forward, to the foot of the dais upon which two dark thrones stood, and the violet figures, vague still, on them.

Behind my father's throne stood, as always, his ever-present manservant Thomas, who bowed.

"My niece Rebecca serves you well as lady-in-waiting, Princess?" he asked.

"Very well, thank you."

Newton announced, facing the two blue figures, "I have brought the Princess Clara."

Both silhouettes quickened in brightness—though the larger, that of my grandmother, flared more quickly. I could see her face, now, in scant outline, the smiling eyes and mouth. Then I heard an electrical hum from somewhere and smelled faintly the odor that wafted through my nightmares—a blue, cold smell like that during a storm, a strange, unnatural odor that had nothing to do with feline flesh.

"It is good that you brought her now, Newton," Grandmother Haydn said, and held her paw out. "Come here, Clara, and stand close so that I can see you."

I did so, holding my fear at bay.

She bent forward, a purple ghost, and stared at me with eyes that seemed to look through me.

"You have grown so!" she said, and something like a laugh issued from her spectral mouth. She turned to regard Newton, who had remained at the foot of the dais. "Do you know who she resembles?"

"I had rather thought her father, around the eyes."

"Yes, but her face is that of her grandfather, my husband, Sebastian's father. Kerl..." For a moment she stared at nothing, and seemed lost in memory.

I turned to regard my father, who had not said a word. He sat staring at me as if *I* were a ghost.

"As I said," Grandmother Haydn said, back from the past, "it is good that you have brought her. We have had messages from the far west, and they are not good."

I turned to regard Newton, who seemed to stiffen.

"What do you mean?" he asked.

"Apparently, Frane has been sighted."

At the mention of that name my blood ran cold. Frane was the monster who had caused not only my grandfather's death but my father's also. The last we had heard, she had been killed near Burroughs two years previously. A body had been produced, authenticated, burned, and buried.

Grandmother Haydn continued, "It seems old Frane took a page from my own book, and faked her own death."

"But the Science Guild did tests on that body—"

My grandmother held up a hand. "Remember, you had only an intact hand and arm to work on. The rest was horribly mutilated."

"She cut off her own limb?" Newton said incredulously.

"Apparently. The body was in pieces—it was claimed she was drawn and quartered . . ."

Newton stood in disbelief.

"It is true," Grandmother continued. "And she is gathering an army. She has been seen in the Solis Planum region."

Newton's nearly nude face went pale.

It was my turn to interrupt. "But, Grandmother, the F'rar have been loyal for more than five years! My mother is F'rar, and *I* am half-F'rar! Frane could not wrest them from the Republic a third time!"

She looked at me with surprise, and then a smile formed. "Well, I see that you have not only grown, but that your mind has grown, too, Clara." She looked at Newton, then back at me. "Frane is gathering an army of Baldies."

"What!" I blurted out.

"A vast one," Grandmother continued, while Newton remained silent. "In five years, and for years before that, even as she fought Sebastian, she has been forging alliances with the wild cats and their brethren. It is said that she cut off her own left arm in front of the four Baldie chieftains, and that they then pledged their allegiance to her. Even the more untamable wild cat clans have been brought into the alliance by force, threat, or assassination. And she has done this away from any prying eyes."

"Then let her stay in Solis Planum and rule over madmen!" I interjected.

My grandmother looked down at me with faint disapproval. "Your studies are not complete, Princess. She means to use this army."

I could not keep quiet. "Against whom?" My fear of being in this room was overcome by my self-confidence. I laughed. "There is nothing in that wasteland for a thousand miles to any compass point! They will be squabbling amongst themselves within the week—"

"Princess—" Newton tried to interject, but I would not be stopped.

"If they come within a day's march of any inhabited city, we'll destroy them from the air!" I continued, my confidence building. "We have the F'rar to help man our army this time. She has no hope! And she is one-armed, to boot!"

I looked first at my father, who sat stone still, and then my silent grandmother, and then Newton, whose faint look of hope faded as he watched Grandmother Haydn shake her head.

"The Science Guild facility at Solis Planum was attacked this morning. Reports from our gypsy friends are incomplete, but by all accounts the Baldie army completely overran it."

I looked at Newton, who said nothing, and then at my grandmother, who was silent. It was my father who spoke next, for the first time. Even though he was a ghost of sorts, his eyes bored into mine with a painful, close intensity, and I had the feeling that if he could, he would jump from his chair and enfold me in his arms.

His voice, when he spoke, was precise.

"How is your mother, Clara? How is my wife Charlotte?"

"She is . . . the same."

"I see. To other matters, then. What remains unsaid, Clara, is that the Science Guild facility at Solis Planum was the most important weapons-staging area on the planet. It was built there in secret to test, develop, and store the most advanced weapons on Mars, with technology produced from Old One discoveries. It is by far the most dangerous place on the surface of the planet.

"And now Frane controls it."

⊰ CHAPTER 2 ⊱

AS USUAL, THE CURTAINS IN MY MOTHER'S ROOM were closed, giving the room the quality of perpetual twilight. There was a breeze, bringing in the sounds and smells of the city of Wells far below this palace room, which, despite its height, I had taken to calling The Dungeon.

"Mother, am I disturbing you?" I asked, letting my voice show that, while I cared for her, there was business to discuss, and she would have no choice but to speak to me.

"How are you, daughter?" Her voice came faintly from the divan where she lay curled. As always she sounded as though she had been awakened from sleep.

"There are things we must speak about, Mother," I continued.

"I was having the most curious dream," she said, raising her head to look at me in the gloom. "In it, you were a little younger than you are now, yet your father was still alive."

"You've had this dream thousands of times, Mother. And Father *is* still alive. I've just been to see him."

I could see her visibly shudder. "That *thing* is not your father! It never could be . . ."

"Mother, I must ask you a few things about our family . . ."

"We have no family. It is just you and I."

"That's not what I meant. Your father, my grandfather, Senator Misst, was a traitor to the Republic, and sits in prison to this day. Is it possible he has been in contact with Frane?"

"Frane is dead . . ."

"She is not dead, Mother."

I sensed a sudden tension, a sharpening of interest, in the room. My mother raised her head to look at me with her still-beautiful eyes.

"What do you mean, Clara?"

"She is alive, and gathering an army of Baldies in the west. What I need to know from you is if there is any possibility in the world that our family would betray the Republic again."

She looked at me blankly.

"Mother!" I snapped. "Act like the queen you are!"

She lay back, and I knew that now the tears would follow.

"I am no queen, and never was. Your father was king, and he is dead. You know I have given over my regent powers, in deed if not in words, to the Senate."

"And it has been bad for Mars. You should have been . . ."

Again she raised her head.

"Stronger, Clara?" she said. "When my whole life ended before it began? I loved your father from our days as kits together. All my life I planned what it would be like when we were betrothed. And then my dreams came true, only to be snatched away by that . . . horrible *thing* Frane."

"Who is still alive."

"Yes . . ."

"Tell me, Mother: Is there any chance on Mars that Senator Misst has been a traitor once more?"

"I don't know. You would have to ask him. Frane is alive . . ."

Instead of weeping, which was what I expected, she swooned down onto the divan and was asleep in a few moments. I drew near, and saw the ever-present potions Newton had provided so that she might be kept out of the sanitarium and at least nearby. She was whispering under her breath, so I drew close to this mother I had barely known, who had been one step from mad since my birth.

"Ha . . ." she was saying, her breath sweet from the elixir, which smelled faintly of peppermint and more serious stuff.

I put my ear even closer to her whispering mouth.

"Happy . . ." she breathed.

I turned my face to regard her own, more beautiful than my own severe features would ever be, and kissed her once on the forehead, above her sleeping eyes, before leaving.

⊰ CHAPTER 3 ⊱

MY READING THAT NIGHT (FICTION HAD BEEN TO-tally abandoned for the *Short History*) was interrupted by a sound outside my window.

Ever wary of assassins, I slipped from my bed, dousing the light, and drew the blade I always kept (rather melo-dramatically, as Rebecca chided me) under my pillow, and drew myself quietly against the wall. The blade was cold against my side, but I held it tight. It had been Queen Haydn's own.

I edged my way toward the window on the far side of the room. This afternoon's breeze had increased to a steady blow, and the curtains were roiling wildly. Outside it was typical summer, hot and dry, with red dust in the air from the west which we Wellsians were used to as a constant presence. The curtains parted as one, giving me a view of the beautiful Assembly Hall nearby which my grandmother had built before her own assassination. There was only the flapping of the curtains now.

My hand relaxed on the hilt of the blade, and I was about to crawl back to bed and needed sleep, when the sound came again. A scrape, followed by a clang.

I kept edging toward the window.

As I reached it I was startled by a metal object that flew close by my head and fell into the room. Instantly it retreated, and then caught at the sill of the window, digging in. It was a three-sided hook, with a rope attached.

So . . .

I crept all the way to the window and peered out.

A figure, dark-cloaked, was climbing the long rope, which reached to the ground. I need only stand here and wait for him to reach a suitable height, then cut the rope and watch him plummet to his death.

I waited, as the cloaked figure scrambled up the makeshift ladder.

I reached out, blade between wall and rope, ready to slice the rope with a savage jerk as the figure drew closer, closer . . .

I began to cut through when he was six feet away.

He suddenly looked up—

"Clara, no!"

But the rope was cut, and I threw the blade aside and grabbed at the rope as it fell, watching in horror as it dropped below my grasping claws.

"Darwin, I'm sorry!" I shouted.

The rope slid through his fingers and he gave me a savage look as he tumbled down and away, grabbing fleetly onto the sill of the window below mine.

A light instantly shone out, and I heard a scream.

"Darwin, wait!" I shouted down, and by then there was commotion in the hallway outside my door. I heard a key rattle in its lock. It was thrown open, showing the night guard, who stared at me with wild purpose, drawing his sword.

"My princess—!" he began, advancing into the room, but I waved him off.

"It's all right! Everything's fine!"

"But—"

"Get out, Stapleton! Please!"

His oafish features finally relaxed, and he withdrew. "As you wish, Princess."

I looked down, and Darwin was nowhere to be seen. For a moment my heart caught in my chest, and I peered at the ground below, fearing to see Darwin's white, battered body lying in a heap.

"Boo," came a soft whisper over my head, and I looked up with a start to see Darwin hanging above me, upside down like a cave bat.

"*Dar—!*" I began to shout, but he had already pounced, landing lightly on my windowsill and jumping past me into the room.

"Thought you had me that time, did you?" he laughed.

"Not bad for an old coot," I countered.

"Who's old!" He made a mock show of looking around the room, under the bed, behind the curtains. "Where's your wet nurse, kit?"

Anger flared up in me. "I'm not a kit anymore!"

"Then prove it!" he laughed, and drew two wooden swords from his belt, tossing one nimbly to me.

"Be on guard!" he shouted.

I went into position, but he had cheated, thrusting forward at me before I had my footing and knocking me down with a blunt point blow to the belly.

"Cheater!"

"In battle, everyone cheats!" he laughed, and in the next

ten minutes he sprang from every piece of furniture at me, even swinging from the overhead lamp at one point.

Finally, he sat down on the floor, breathing heavily, and dropped his wooden sword beside him.

"You're right," he said, shaking his head as I curled on the floor beside him. "I'm not as young as I was."

"None of us are," I replied.

His eyes darkened. "My, you're serious tonight, Princess."

"There has been much news."

"I've heard." His eyes sparkled, and he smiled. "But there's *always* bad news—and always will be!"

"I wish I could be as sanguine as you."

He shrugged. "You have a more serious nature than I. Too serious. In fact, without me to lighten your moods, you would look like this all the time—"

He pulled his mouth corners downward with his paws and shook his head mournfully.

"I wish I could be like you, Darwin," I said, and I'm afraid my face must have looked much like his own exaggerated version of it. "But I'm afraid I have too much to worry about."

"Bah!" he said, brightening. "We all have too much to worry about. It just depends on how one deals with it. You brood. Me, I find something to divert me. In the end, we both have to deal with our troubles—but I'll bet I have more fun in the meantime!"

He threw back his head and laughed.

Retaining my dour demeanor, I shook my head, and said, "You're the older brother I never had, Darwin. Thank you for being such a good friend these last years. Without you I would have had no one to cheer me up."

He put his paw on my own, and his face grew serious. "I will be with you in that Assembly Hall meeting tomorrow, and I'll be with you whenever you need me after that. I watched you grow up from a skinny little sprite, into what you are now."

"And what *am* I, Darwin? Sometimes I feel like a skinny little sprite stuck in a slightly larger body."

"You're growing up, is all."

"And awkwardly, at that. I feel all out of proportion. My paws and feet are too big and my body is getting too long and my nose is too small and my eyes are too wide apart and . . ."

He drew back, looking at me curiously for a moment.

"What is it?" I demanded.

"Nothing," he said, and for the first time since I had known this jovial young man, this all white-furred fellow save for one roguish black stripe on his crown, this inventive, constantly moving clown, who never spoke about his own unhappy past but was always eager to share my own woes, he was at a loss for words.

"Are you blushing, Darwin?" I asked in astonishment.

"No, it's . . . just a skin rash."

I furrowed my brow and held a paw out to touch his face. "It doesn't look like a rash . . ."

He shrank back as if I had a disease and warded off my touch.

"It's nothing, Princess!"

"But—" I said, uncomprehending, taking a further step toward him.

"Please let it be!" he shouted, nearly backing to the wall.

"Very well." I shrugged, and lowered my paw.

His behavior was puzzling, because he had never acted this way around me before. But I carried it no further because he deliberately changed the subject.

"As to the Assembly Hall tomorrow, they will want you to be silent, but of course you must not be . . ."

LATER, WHEN I WAS ALONE CURLED UP IN MY BED with the window locked tight and Darwin long gone, through the window, I thought about what had happened.

And thought on it again, until sleep finally robbed me of all thought, and unfurrowed my brow, and the strange, unknowable stirrings in me were quelled for the night.

⊰ CHAPTER 4 ⊱

*IF FRANE WERE TO DROP A BOMB ON THIS PLACE AT
this time,* I thought, *all of her problems would be solved.*

I had never seen so many politicians and dignitaries in
one place. From my prominent position, wedged securely
between fat, scar-faced old General Xarr and the empty
seat that represented my absent mother, I looked out upon
a sea of expectant senators and ambassadorial representatives from the four corners of Mars. The tunic and pennant
colors were astonishing, and, among the twenty expected
hues of red from deep cranberry to a light pink, were bright
lemon yellows mixing with jade greens and blues as rich
and deep as the theorized oceans of Earth. There were pas-
tel shades and bold primaries side by side, a rainbow blur
that extended to the deepest recesses of the hall. Indeed,
the only empty seat was that beside me.

We truly are still a world of clans, I thought, and a slight shiver went through me to think that this Republic was still so fragile, held together with little more than . . .

Me.

Another shiver ran through me, and old Xarr leaned over and rasped, his breath still redolent of last night's wine, "Are you all right, Princess?"

"As much as I will be," I said, and he frowned.

"There is little for you to do today, missy. Just sit still, and pay attention."

"I'm not a kit, and don't call me 'missy,'" I ordered.

He sat up straight, as if an arrow had hit him. "Yes, Princess Clara."

I felt a pang of regret for the rebuke I had given him, but only a slight one because of the churning inside me.

Newton, at the dais to my right, called for order, and the shuffling and whisperings of the huge assemblage quieted.

"We gather here today," Newton's voice intoned, rather reedy but strong enough to ring out in the hall, "to discuss the most serious threat to the Republic since the last rebellion, five years ago. This may, in fact, be the most serious threat our planet has ever faced. Thankfully," he said, holding his paws out in an inclusive gesture, "we face it together, and not as a world divided clan against clan.

"But that does not decrease in any way the urgency, or the danger. You have no doubt read the literature distributed before this meeting began and know the basic facts of the reemergence of Frane in the far western wastelands. You have also been made aware that she has secured the Republic's most important scientific facility, which is located in that area. We are still assessing what weapons and instruments of war she has obtained and what she may do with them.

"But, believe it or not, there is a greater danger than Frane at this moment. Many of you who have kept up with our work in the Science Guild are aware of our warnings of the last five years that Mars is losing its atmosphere. Slowly, inexorably, the life-giving oxygen of our planet is leaking off into space. And to this point we have been able to do nothing about it.

"Today, rather than bring just bad news, I also bring good tidings. For the Science Guild has finally been able to bring one of the oxygenation stations that the Old Ones left behind back to partial life, and we are confident that we may soon go far beyond that and have all of these facilities—which in the dim past initially, we believe, provided Mars with its breathable atmosphere—back in operation. If this occurs, it will avert the single greatest danger our civilization has ever faced."

Though Newton held up his paws for quiet, the thunderous roar of ovation that broke out could not be quelled. He stood stoically while this outpouring of good will, a release, rolled over him and finally dissipated.

"Thank you, my friends, but there is much work for all of us to do. For with this new threat from the west, there is the possibility that Frane may interfere with this planet-saving work of ours. That is why I need all of you to make sure that your local governors secure their own territories, and patrol their own borders, and guard especially any of these oxygenation facilities that may exist nearby. Many of them are in ruins, but they must be protected at all costs. All of our lives depend on it."

A senator dressed in the resplendent robes of the K'fry clan, peacock blue and a deep, liquid yellow, stood and asked for recognition. Newton bowed and gave it to him.

"Newton," the senator boomed, holding a paw out clenched in a fist, "do you believe that Frane would be insane enough to destroy the entire planet?"

"We cannot assume anything. The woman is mad. It is a possibility against which we must protect."

The senator sat down, grumbling.

"We have only an outpost!" cried one of the ambassadors from the northern cold climes of Arcadia Planitia. Not as startling as the previous speaker's, his tunic was a plain, tasteful, light green fringed in gold. "There are two of these oxygenation stations within our borders, and we have nothing to protect them with!"

Newton held up a paw. "Protection will be provided, and troops will be sent to help you." He looked around the hall, forestalling any further outbursts. "This goes for all the stations. We will do everything we can to assist you, both the government and the Science Guild. This meeting was called merely to alert you to the danger so you could notify your localities of the threat."

"The government is too weak!" came a thunderous voice from the back of the hall. I knew that voice. It belonged to Senator Thell, of my mother's—and Frane's—clan, the F'rar. He stood up, a massive feline dressed in deep bloodred, his fur, like my own, black as night. Even from where I sat I could see the amber fire of his eyes.

"Senator—" Newton began, holding a paw out for silence.

"Let him speak!" came another voice, from the left of the hall.

"Yes, let Thell speak!" from the right.

"Yes!" just in front of me, the oily Prine, of the Sarn clan, clad in dark robes as viscious-looking as himself.

Newton bowed, and Senator Thell stood tall.

"The problems we have," he thundered in his basso voice, "can be traced to one source." After waiting a moment, no doubt for theatrical effect, he threw out one massive paw and pointed with an almost violent gesture at the empty seat beside me. "And that is it! There is no figure at the head of this government to which all these wonderful delegates can hold allegiance. It shames me to say that one of my own clan, and a distant cousin at that, spends her days unable to cope with her duties. Queen Charlotte grieves for her husband still, as do we all, but while she grieves, and while we wait for a *kit* to grow into a woman, Mars is run by committee! And in the meantime, the outer fringes of the Republic remain soft, and Frane—again to my greater shame, another of my clan for whom I once fought!—sneaks in and steals from under our noses the very things we need to say strong. This is not right!"

There were thunderous shouts of "Hear, hear!" and "He is right!" which threatened to become a din.

Without thinking, with a knot in my stomach the size of a fist, I slowly rose and walked to the podium. I heard nothing, until I realized that the Assembly Hall had quieted below a whisper. Newton stepped aside, and as I looked out I saw that Senator Thell, his mouth agape, was sitting down unsteadily.

I counted to five, thinking about the things Darwin and I had discussed. He had said I would have no trouble with my little speech, but he was not here now, and for a moment I went blank.

Then it all came flooding back to me.

"Esteemed senators, honored dignitaries and welcome guests," I began, wondering how strong my own voice sounded—surely a pip next to Thell's roar, "I welcome you today not as a kit, but as your *queen*."

I REMEMBER LITTLE OF WHAT HAPPENED NEXT—HOW Darwin, on cue, appeared with the administrator of the oath, how the Assembly Hall broke out in cheers and celebration, how the bells in the clock tower in Wells center city chimed, I was told later, for a full hour. I remembered none of this, nor little of the impromptu parties I attended nor the dignitaries I was introduced to nor the senators who kissed my ring. I remember briefly sitting on the throne and then, recalling that my grandmother Haydn had refused such pomp, sending it away with a wave of my paw. I remember dancing with Darwin before he was spirited away by another female, and his disappointed look when that happened. I remember dining on delicacies, and the receiving lines, and the blaring of trumpets, and playing (very briefly, and with mistakes) on the *tambor* while those around me clapped politely, and I remember drinking wine, though not for the first time (I had often stolen a sip at one function or other) and I remember the bells chiming again at midnight as Newton, sensing my exhaustion, removed me from the festivities with apologies all around and whispered in my ear, not without admiration, I thought, "That was an act of theater worthy of your grandmother!" and I remember falling asleep almost immediately with all of these things swirling in my head like those waltzing dancers, and I remembered last of all, amid all these dancing thoughts, *I am Queen of Mars.*

⇥ CHAPTER 5 ⇤

IT WAS THE NEXT DAY THAT OLD XARR DIED.

He took to his bed, I learned later, during the coronation ceremonies. Never one to pass up good wine, or bad for that matter, he had been thoroughly inebriated the last time I saw him, dancing badly with a senator from my own home district, Argyre. She was homely and stiff as a board on the dance floor, but that had not deterred the old general from circling her in a rough stumble that was anything but graceful.

But he had looked happy, and fit for his years—and then I was summoned to his bedchamber the next morning with the news that he did not have long to live.

Newton was there, scowling, and when I entered old Xarr fought to rise from his bed, and growled weakly.

"Let me address my queen!" he shouted hoarsely, and lay back exhausted but smiling as I stood over him.

"Your Majesty," he croaked out, his scar-ravaged face

even more grotesque, shrunken, the patchily furred features pulled back in a rictus of death.

I turned to Newton, and said, angrily, "What happened to him? This can't be some sudden illness. I saw him not ten hours ago fit and hale as ever."

"We don't know, Your Majesty," Newton said in a low, even voice, and by the hooded flat look in his eyes, and his grim visage, he told me that there was more to the story he would not tell me now.

I whispered, "Is there any hope for him?"

"No," was his curt reply.

A claw drew me around, and I turned to see the old general fighting off a spasm of pain, which bowed his body as his paw gripped me.

"Your majesty!" he hissed.

The episode passed, and he lay back, exhausted, and smiled weakly at me again.

"Come closer, sprite," he said.

"You may not call me that," I chided him affectionately.

"Of course I can." And for a moment his eyes closed, and I thought he was gone.

I bent closer, smelling a strange odor from his lips—a herb or medicine, vaguely weedy. It reminded me vaguely of another odor I knew . . .

He opened his eyes and looked straight into mine.

"Majesty," he rasped, "you must do your old general one final favor. I served your father, and his mother before her. I served the Republic with all my heart. I lost my son to the first war, but I . . . always . . . served. I only wish that I could have died on the field . . ."

He broke off into a weak coughing fit, and I swear that any normal feline would have been dead at that point. But Xarr fought death itself to finish what he wanted to tell me.

"I . . . have served well . . ."

"Yes, General, you have served well. No one has served better."

"Then grant me this . . . wish . . ."

Again he broke off, a spasm wracking his body from head to foot. He moaned and clenched his teeth until the fit passed.

"I . . ."

"Tell me what you want, General, and I will swear to do it."

"Find . . ."

His voice was barely a breath, and I leaned even closer, assaulted by the rancid, herblike odor.

His eyes drew wide, as if looking into the world beyond, and he grabbed me tight with both paws as if to take me there. For a moment I was frightened, but then his eyes locked on mine, and he roared, *"Find the one who murdered me!"*

And then his body went limp, and he was gone.

Shaking, I turned to Newton, and said, "Is this true?"

"Yes."

"He was *murdered*?"

"The same poison that was used to murder your grandmother Haydn. In her case it was put in gemel tea—this time into his last flagon of wine last night."

"Who did it!" I demanded.

Newton was staring past me, at the lifeless form of General Xarr. He seemed almost not to have heard me. I was about to repeat the question when I saw that a tear was tracking down the scientist's stoic face. I had never thought Newton capable of such sentiment.

"Who . . ." I asked, gently.

"We don't know, Your Majesty." And he looked at me, his eyes dry. "But it means we have a traitor and assassin in our midst."

• • •

XARR'S FUNERAL WAS ON A GRAND SCALE, AS I OR-
dered. His casket, draped in green and white, the colors of
his city of Burroughs, was lowered into the ground after
traversing a mile-long gauntlet of his troops. Though at attention, many of them were openly weeping. A plain white
tablet marked the filled-in hole. Later a monument, which
I had proposed and the Senate had immediately adopted,
would be erected on the spot, a statue showing the general
in his prime, arm raised to give orders, horrid facial scars
and all.

   "Good-bye, old friend," I whispered, and laid the first
red rose upon the white marker. I would be followed by ten
thousand of his closest friends, his troops. I could bear no
more and took my leave, nearly running to my chambers
so that others would not see their queen cry. This man, this
ancient warrior, had bounced me on his knee when I was a
kit and told me stories of the battles he had fought with my
grandmother and father. In these stories, he had never been
the hero, only a servant of the Republic, a humble soldier
who did the best by his men and gave his best for his Mars.
There would never, I knew, be another like him on the surface of the planet. He was already missed, and would ever
be so.

   My sobbing, self-indulgent, was short-lived.

   There was a message from my grandmother that I must
come at once, because war, once more, had broken out on
the planet Mars.

⊰ CHAPTER 6 ⊱

THE AERIAL TRIP THIS TIME WAS A GLUM AND LONELY
one. Newton's insistence that only those who could absolutely be trusted be allowed access to me limited my
companions to Newton himself and two bodyguards. Even
Rebecca, with whom I could at least play a spirited game
of Jakra, was left behind. It was not even certain that she
would be there when I returned to Wells, unless she passed
Newton's vetting. I had requested that Darwin accompany
us, but was told that he was busy elsewhere, doing Newton's bidding.

We found Thomas, my father's manservant, in his accustomed spot, next to the king's chair. But the chair was
empty.

"King Sebastian is being . . . regenerated," Thomas,
who always looked as though he was about to fade to a
ghost himself, explained, and this satisfied Newton.

"My niece remains well?" Thomas asked.

"Yes," I replied, and then I said, suppressing, as always, a shiver, "Doesn't any of this bother you?"

"What do you mean?" Thomas asked.

"These . . . *ghosts*," I said.

My grandmother, who was in a particularly vigorous state, her outline a vivid blue, smiled slightly, and said, "I've asked myself that often. When you think about it, Clara, it's better than the alternative."

"Is it?" I replied. I regarded Newton. "You may take this as a royal order. When I die, I don't want to be . . . *saved*."

Haydn chirped a laugh. "Are you sure, child?"

"Yes," I said adamantly. "You can have your One and Two, but there will be no Three."

"It is too bad this . . . process could not have been used for Xarr," Haydn said, her voice tinged with sadness.

"His poisoning was too severe."

"Yes . . . I do find it curious that his assassination came at an opportune time for Frane. According to the gypsies, and Quiff's people, who have been shadowing her, Frane is now at the head of a Baldie army ten thousand strong, heading north and east toward the Valles Marineris."

"She means to make a stand there?" Newton said, surprise in his voice.

"Apparently."

"Is she truly mad?"

"Perhaps. This is why Xarr's loss is so strongly felt at this time. It is curious that he was murdered just as Frane makes her first big move."

"I see no coincidence in it at all."

Haydn turned her steely blue gaze on the scientist. "Has it occurred to you that perhaps the F'rar clan will turn treacherous once more, and seek to destroy the Republic once and for all with Frane's help?"

Though I burned with sudden anger, I held my tongue as Newton immediately replied, glancing at me, "I would hope that would not be the case. But the timing is more than, as you say, curious."

Haydn was abruptly looking at me. "You must realize, Queen Clara, that even though you are half-F'rar, this may not be enough to stave off the F'rar appetite. Why have half a loaf when you can have it all?"

"I will not let it happen!" I shouted.

Her voice still even, Haydn replied, "You may have no say in it. There have been rumblings in the far provinces, and already violence has broken out between F'rar and the other clans. It is mainly incidental, because felines have good memories and the F'rar have been treacherous twice in the last fifteen years. I tried to heal the rift, your father tried to heal the rift, and now you will try. The record has not been a good one. These animosities go back centuries. The Republic, we both know, is the only hope of uniting Mars. But blood runs hotter than cold intellect."

"I said I will not let it happen!"

My own blood was running much hotter than my brain, and I spent the rest of the interview stewing in a corner, clenching my paws into fists, and listening to the mumbled strategy behind me. Out of the corner of my eye I saw my father's empty chair begin to fill with vague smoky blue light, which eventually coalesced into the shape of King Sebastian. Thomas, now filled with purpose, leaned over my father and whispered into his ear as he became ever more evident, an almost solid blue light.

Again I shivered, and vowed anew that they would never do this to me. When I was dead I would be dead, like old Xarr.

• • •

LATER, ON THE AERIAL RIDE HOME, NEWTON LEFT ME to my own thoughts and then, eventually, intruded on them.

"You must remember a few things, Your Majesty. And it's time you knew of others. There were things I thought best to keep from your father, and now I think it was a mistake. He did not know about Queen Haydn's . . . *regeneration*, because we in the Science Guild had no idea if what we had done would last. It was a difficult decision even to try. The technology had been gleaned, as most of ours has been, from the Old Ones. It is very difficult for me to admit, because I am a man of science, that most—practically all— of what I've accomplished has been by standing on the shoulders of those who came before me.

"We still know very little about the Old Ones, yet what we do know baffles us. Where did they come from? Why did they die out? Was there a time when our two races coexisted, and if so, why did we flourish while they were swept away?

"Their few books that have survived, along with a few of their fossils, have given us scant clues. It is through their machines that we know them best. We know, for example, that in their days on Mars there was an Old One named The Machine Master who built, or designed, much of what we have been able to make use of. We think that in that era the oxygenation stations had already been shut down and abandoned, because we find no mention in any of his records of any such devices. They must have been in use before his time.

"This lack, of course, hinders us now, because whatever records of The Machine Master haven't been destroyed are quite complete and useful. He was a meticulous engineer. There are hints of devices he made that are astounding. Your father and grandmother were regenerated using a technology that is incomplete to us—apparently a variation of it was used as a weapon. His notes mention 'plasma soldiers,' though we have been able to find no record of any such device."

"He sounds as if he was a horrible creature," I said.

Newton, as if broken from his reverie, looked at me blankly and then nodded. "Perhaps so. While much of his work was benevolent, there is a darker side to his engineering that is all too evident. There are hints that he was being driven to build destructive devices by a malevolent force—though we don't know what that was." He smiled faintly. "What it does tell us is that the Old Ones were not immune to war or cruelty, just as we are not." He eyes took on a faraway look. "There are hints at other storehouses of knowledge we have not yet discovered . . ."

"Let them stay hidden, then."

"Would you have creatures like Frane make use of such power, instead of the Republic?" he asked.

I pursed my lips because I had no answer.

"I fear we will miss old Xarr greatly. I know very little of military matters, and I don't much understand this move of Frane's, to fight a great open battle when she has a stolen weapon to draw on."

"What exactly did she obtain by taking over the Science Guild facility at Solis Planum?"

Newton's eyes darkened. "The last remaining concussion bomb on Mars, like the one that destroyed the city of Burroughs in the First Republic War. It had been kept for research purposes, and now it is in her hands. There was also an aerial machine, very fast, as well as a few ground transports. It is the concussion bomb that worries me most of all."

"What will she do with it?"

"I don't know, but she must be stopped before she has a chance to use it."

The rest of our trip home was spent in troubled silence.

XARR'S ABSENCE WAS ALREADY MAKING ITSELF FELT. There had been defections from the army, many of them F'rar. I was introduced to the feline who would take the old general's place, a much younger man in a crisp new general's uniform. He was prim and proper, with slicked-back black fur and pink eyes, and looked to me to be putting on an act, though I learned later that he had fought hard in the first two Republic Wars—on the side of the F'rar. I did not like him.

"And so," he said, for at least the tenth time, pointing to a spot on the chart, a map of the Valles Marineris region that I had to admit was detailed, "we will draw Frane like a magnet toward the great chasm, and merely"—he made a dismissive gesture with his paw—"push her in!"

"You make it sound so simple, General Reis. Tell me, how do your propose to, as you say, 'draw Frane like a magnet' toward the canyon?"

"It is simple, Your Majesty," he said, swelling up like a proud peacock. "She is already heading there!"

"And how long will it take her to reach Valles Marineris?"

"A matter of weeks, Your Majesty."

"And your army will be there, waiting for her?"

"Well . . ." He averted his eyes, pretending to study the chart.

"How large is our army, after recent defections?" I asked, keeping my voice level and businesslike.

"Those . . . figures are changing daily, Your Majesty."

"Today's figures, please, General."

Without looking at me, he pretended to shuffle through a stack of papers next to his chart. "That would be . . ."

"Let me give you today's figures," I said. "While Frane is at this point leading an army of ten thousand Baldies, with more arriving daily, the Army of the Second Republic stands as of this morning at eight thousand, seven hundred and fifty, with a defection rate of one percent per day. Does this sound correct?"

"I would say . . ." He nodded. "I would say that sounds correct, yes, Your Majesty." He turned from his papers to look at me hopefully. "But—"

"The word 'but' does not exist in this room, General. We both know that if you were to give the order this afternoon to march, with far garrisons joining you on the way, you could not reach Valles Marineris, or wherever Frane chooses to fight, in less than four weeks! And that's at a forced march pace, with defections bleeding away your army even as it's replenished. The defections we will work on. But the plain fact is that Frane will choose the battlefield, and will be there, entrenched, waiting for us."

" 'Us,' Your Majesty?" he said, his pink eyes widening.

"I will be leading the army, General Reis."

He began to blubber. "But—but—but—this cannot be!"

"What did I tell you about the word 'but,' General?"

His mouth clamped shut, and his pink eyes bulged.

"I will lead the army, and you will do everything in your power to assist me, and when the time comes we will win a great victory over Frane, and destroy her and her Baldie army. Yes?"

"As you wish, Your Majesty."

"Good. Now kneel, General," I said, holding out my right paw, "and kiss my ring of office in fealty to me and the Second Republic."

For a moment fire showed in his eyes, but he did as he

was told, going down on one knee and bowing his head over my outstretched paw.

I felt the lightest of kisses on my ring.

"From this moment on, you owe every ounce of your allegiance to me," I said. "You are F'rar, and I am half so, and we have a great duty to our Republic and to our planet. There can be no further treachery by our clan. It cannot and will not be allowed. Do you understand?"

He looked up at me briefly, before bowing his head again.

"Yes, Your Majesty."

"Good. With your help, I will stop the defections from the army among our people. And we will march tomorrow, at dawn. Yes?"

Again a brief, unreadable look.

"Of course, Your Majesty."

"Good. And if you do not prove yourself worthy to me, or your office, and betray either in any way, I will kill you myself."

⊰ CHAPTER 7 ⊱

"BUT THIS IS MADNESS!" DARWIN SAID, AS I KNEW HE would.

"I am very tired, Darwin, and I don't wish to argue. I have made my decision. Please be happy with it." I waved an exhausted paw, from where I lay curled on my divan. Its soft pillows felt like cool hands calling me to sleep. I wanted only to give myself up to them.

"But if you must go, take me with you!"

I shook my head, and yawned. "No."

"You cannot keep me here! You must take me so that I can . . . cook for you!"

I laughed. "You pride yourself too much on your cooking, Darwin. Just because you and my father were forced to become chefs in the last war doesn't mean you're any good at it. From what I hear, my father was the much better cook—"

"In all seriousness, I cannot stay here."

"I need you here to help Newton, and to keep an eye on the Senate and the assembly. I'm appointing you queen's representative. It's all in my grandmother's charter. You will have powers second only to mine."

"But you'll need me in the field!"

I was too tired, and did not want this conversation to go anywhere near the mysterious, frightening places it could easily go, so I feigned toughness, just as I had that afternoon with General Reis.

"It is my wish," I said simply. "Go now."

And then I closed my eyes until he was gone.

But sleep, of course, would not come, despite my exhaustion. I had done nothing but fight with someone or other the entire day. Even Brenda, the old cook, had to be reprimanded to keep her from marching to war with me—and she with arthritis and a bad hip!

I opened my tired eyes and watched the open curtains in my room flutter. It was a clear night, and over the top of the Assembly Hall the stars shone like diamonds on the blackest velvet. How soothing to be out among the stars, I thought—how much better to float among them and forget all the cares of running an entire world—one that might be destroyed either by war or natural catastrophe in the coming months.

How much better not to be me . . .

I dreamed then of my birth. Or at least what I thought my birth was like. I remember coldness from the beginning, descending a cold shaft, a mother devoid of warmth, lost in unhappiness and loss, incapable of transforming those feelings into a new, warm love for her only kit. My mother had a litter of one, which was unusual. Some—those given to superstition—said it was of special significance. I was given over to the care of nursemaids immediately and never wanted for anything except my mother's touch.

And then I dreamed of Darwin, barely out of kithood himself when he first played with me, always smiling and warm—in a way, I suppose, a substitute for my mother, as well as the brother I never had.

And even in the dream I knew that I had ordered him to stay behind not because I needed him to watch the government, which would do very well watching itself, I thought—but because I wanted him, above all other things, to be safe.

Because, I knew, he was in love with me.

And I with him.

⊰ CHAPTER 8 ⊱

"WHAT DO YOU THINK, REBECCA?"

In the mirror's reflection, I could see my lady-in-waiting's frown as she stood behind me, but her voice said sweetly, "Very becoming, my lady."

"Don't lie to me," I said.

"You do look rather . . . martial, Your Majesty."

"Yes. . . ."

I allowed myself a slight smile, which threw the entire look off. Head to toe in armor, a deep red, almost black, severe, with black leather boots. The outfit outlined my thin frame and made it look sharp and tight as a knife blade. From the table beside me I hefted my helmet, dark red with a thin plume of jet-black color trailing from the back like a ponytail. I fitted it onto my head and turned to stand full in front of my chambermaid.

"There!" I said, putting my gloved hands on my hips. "What do you think now?"

This time her frown was a full one. "It looks rather . . . *warm . . .*"

"Bah! It will be fine. I always knew I would need something impressive to go into battle, and it took me a long time to design this. Darwin said the same as you, but you're both wrong."

She bowed her head. "As you wish, m'lady."

"Help me fit on my sword."

She did so, and I discovered that, in its fancy scabbard, encrusted with rubies and sapphires and the occasional diamond, it was much heavier than I had thought it would be. In fact, it made me list slightly to the left, which I had to compensate for—which soon gave me a cramp in both sides as I strutted around the room.

I went to the window and looked down at the courtyard below, where my army awaited me. There was a sea of mounted men in ranks and files, and not a hint of metal armor among them. The day was warm, and the battle weeks away. Instinctively I knew that if I appeared among these felines in this garb, I would be an instant laughingstock. Not a good way to begin a campaign!

I removed my helmet, breathing heavily in the warm air, and wiped perspiration from my brow. I regarded myself in the mirror again, and a slow smile came to my face. I turned to Rebecca.

"Well, perhaps it *is* a bit much. Help me off with it, will you? I believe a simple tunic will do at this point. We can pack the light armor General Xarr gave me months ago. And Rebecca?"

She stopped in the middle of unfastening one of the hard-to-use buckles that were built into the frame of my warrior cage. "Yes, m'lady?"

"Let's keep this between you and I, shall we? I wouldn't

want the troops to think I was a fool. At least not yet, anyway."

Rebecca stifled a short laugh and nodded enthusiastically. "As you wish, Your Majesty."

When it was all off, a great pile of unwieldy heavy metal on the floor, I asked her sheepishly, "Would you do me the great favor of hiding this in a closet when I'm gone?"

WHEN I APPEARED, THERE WAS A STIFFENING OF BACKS and a hush. I rode slowly, inspecting the troops, nodding regally and keeping a steady pace. I had no idea what I was doing, but tried to remember Xarr's advice: "Look like you know what you're doing, and you've already done it." I hoped that my light crimson tunic, thinly fringed in a light shade of gold, was appropriate. The matching cape wafted behind me in the gentle breeze, and my sword, in its plain, lighter scabbard, felt good against my side.

When I reached General Reis at the head of the column his eyes flickered with either mild approval or disdain, I could not tell which. He sat stiffer and taller in his saddle than an officer should, I thought, but we would see his prowess tested on the battlefield, which was the most important thing.

"Good morning, General," I said.

"Your Majesty," he replied, bowing his head slightly.

"A good day to ride," I continued, taking my place to his right. "Shall we?"

"As you wish, Your Majesty," he said, and gave the firm order to march, waving his hand back and then forward.

"Onward, for the glory of Mars!" he shouted, and the great army began to move.

At the gates of Wells, which were open wide, I looked

for Darwin in the massive crowd, but was disappointed to see him nowhere. His distinctive white fur with the single stripe on his crown would have been visible anywhere, but was not to be found in that sea of faces, some shouting encouragement, some crying for a relative gone off to war, some shouting the slogans of war fever. It was magnificent and frightening—but without Darwin, I was a little more lonely.

I turned in my saddle to regard the Assembly Hall, already shrinking in the distance behind us. Darwin was there, no doubt, doing as I had asked, helping to run a world while its young queen went off to war.

"Something wrong, Your Majesty?" Reis asked in his unctuous voice.

"Nothing that victory won't cure, General," I said, turning back around to fix him with a steady gaze.

He nodded quickly and turned his attention back to the long road ahead of us.

I felt as alone as I ever had.

ODDLY, THAT NIGHT, CAMPING UNDER THE STARS FOR the first time in my life, was one of the happiest I had ever spent. And I didn't know why. Was it because I was finally fulfilling the destiny I had been groomed for my whole life? Was it because I was free of the constraints of Wells, the political infighting, the lying, the bowing and scraping? I had no idea. I only knew that I felt free for the first time ever.

It was a beautiful evening, with a purpling bowl of sky at the setting horizon darkening to deepest black overhead, with a billion twinkling stars accompaniment to the desert crickets of late summer. The gentle hills were still green with vegetation, but soon the flora would change to sparse scrub as we skirted south of the Great Desert west of Wells, which stretched almost halfway from the equator to the north pole. Luckily, routes had been carved below this sandy continent over the centuries, and it was not without water and rough-hewn towns. We would not be long out of sight of civilization on our march, which would eventually carry us away from the looming desert and into the plains of Margaritifer Terra, far north of my grandmother's homeland, Argyre, and then into the lowlands of Valles Marineris itself. I had only seen the massive gash in our planet once, by air, and even from a height of ten thousand feet it had astounded.

Phobos was up, casting its ghostly pink light. Unable to sleep, I wandered through the camp, always with my bodyguard of two, and listened to the night sounds of an army at rest. There was much cursing, most of it mild at the moment, the complaints of footsore infantry or riders whose derrieres were not yet formed to the saddle. There were many card games, most of them Jakra, which I longed to play, but, as instructed by Xarr, I was not to do because too much mingling was not proper. There was some singing, especially among one contingent of the Yern clan, who were known for their deep, melodious voices. Their reputation was not an exaggeration. I stopped to listen to a native song, from far to the north:

> And his homeland he missed,
> The young Yern soldier,
> And the true love he left behind,
> In battles he fought
> He became ever bolder,
> But he never forgot his homeland,
> Or the true love he left behind . . .

Imagine a deep tone of sadness and longing injected into these words, a lyrical bass voice that carried with it the hopes and dreams of a people, and you will have some sense of what I heard.

I walked on, nodding to these soldiers as I passed, and, suddenly, I had walked out of camp.

Only I had not quite run out of soldiers. For there was a solitary fellow off in a field, running hither and yon, aiming a small tube at the sky.

"I wouldn't bother with 'im if I was you, Your Majesty," one of my guards said, with deference.

"Why not?"

"He's balmy, is why," the guard replied.

I looked at the other guard for confirmation, but he was stone-faced.

"I should like to speak with him," I decided.

The first guard shrugged and said, "He's balmy, but he ain't dangerous."

"Very well, then. Stay here."

I walked on alone, into the field.

The fellow did not see me at first, and kept up his strange dance, moving from one spot to the other, aiming his instrument at the sky, then quickly moving to yet another spot. As I approached I heard that he was mumbling to himself: "Yes . . . oh, yes. Fine. Yes," as he went about his work.

"Excuse me?" I said when I was nearly upon him.

He jumped as if an electric charge had been run through him.

"Don't ever do that!" he squealed, panting and looking about him as if ready to be attacked.

"It's only your queen, and I wish you no harm."

His eyes fixed on me like a mad colt's, but eventually his breathing evened and he calmed down.

He continued to stare at me.

"Is it really you . . . ?" he asked.

I said nothing, and he made a jerking motion forward, stepping closer to me. He tripped over an unseen stone, and went sprawling at my feet.

I heard the tinkle of glass.

"My telescope!" He shrieked, as if he had been stabbed.

He pulled himself into a sitting position and retrieved the broken instrument from beneath him and examined it.

He began to sob gently, rocking back and forth, before suddenly remembering my presence. He held the instrument up, a movement which caused broken glass to slide down the useless tube.

"You'll forgive me, Your Majesty," he said, issuing hitching sobs. "It's just that I've had it so long, and took so much pleasure in it, and now it's . . . *useless!*"

Unable to continue, he broke into a fit of uncontrolled weeping.

I waited a proper amount of time, then asked, "You're an astronomer, then?"

My question calmed him somewhat, though his nod was a tentative one. "Of sorts. Not the proper kind, mind you, but I do love the sky so."

"What is your place in the army?"

"Whu—?"

This seemed to throw him, and I was about to repeat my question when he answered, with a bitter laugh, "Just a foot soldier, Your Majesty. And not much of one. I grew potatoes, you see, but now I'm to fight Baldies. This"—he held up his broken telescope—"is just a diversion. Something to keep me from, well, thinking about fighting Baldies."

"What is your name?" I asked.

"Copernicus, Your Majesty."

"Are you very good at astronomy?"

"Oh, yes!" He stood up. "I know the sky like I know the back of my hand, or every furrow in my far field."

"How did you learn?"

"By looking at the sky, of course! Every chance I can!" He regarded the broken tube in his hand, and let it fall to the ground. "I did, that is . . ."

"I'll tell you what, Copernicus. I have a beautiful instrument back in Wells, a telescope that belonged to my father. It was made by the Science Guild, designed by Newton himself, and has been collecting dust for years because I have never showed the interest in the heavens that my father did. It's less than a day's ride back to Wells. What would you say if I sent back for it and gave it to you?"

His eyes widened, as if I had told him that giant harlows were bearing down on him.

"You can't mean that."

I nodded. "Consider it done, Copernicus."

He fell at my feet and began to weep again. "You don't know how happy you've made me!"

Embarrassed, I drew my paw away as he slobbered over it. "Don't worry, Copernicus, I may need you to do me a favor someday."

"Anything!" he wept. "Anything, my queen!"

I left him there, drooling and gathering the pieces of his broken instrument. I gave the order to one of my bodyguards, who left to find a rider, while the other one stood shaking his head.

"Like I told you, Your Majesty: balmy."

"He may be balmy, as you say, but I have the feeling we may need him before all this is over."

• • •

THE MORNING DAWNED BRIGHT. I AWOKE REFRESHED,
dressed quickly in my tent with Rebecca's assistance, and
emerged to find General Reis waiting for me. A map table
had been set up in front of him.

"We have news from the west," he said.

I noted the drone of an airship overhead and looked up
to see one of Newton's fleet lazily circling the army. It,
and as many others as could be spared, would accompany
our march from now on. I found its motor's purr comforting.

"What have you heard?" I said, turning my attention to
Reis.

He spread out the map before him and pointed to the
great gaping mouth that was Valles Marineris, to our north
and west. His claw traced the extreme southeastern edge of
the canyon.

"Frane's army is concentrating here," Reis stated. "We
have aerial reconnaissance to prove it, as well as advance
scouts who have not been able to get very close. A few
spies have been trying to infiltrate the Baldie army, but you
can imagine the difficulties. We will continue to work on
it."

"Why this particular spot?" I inquired, studying the
map.

"It is close to their supply lines," Reis answered, "and
the ground to the south is level. I propose we approach
from the west, skirt the tip of the canyon, and attack them
where they are camped."

"Is it high ground?"

His face showed a puzzled look. "That's what disturbs
me. It is suitable ground, but there is better land for en-
trenchment to the north or west." He looked at me blankly.
"It's almost as if they can't wait to fight us."

"Perhaps they are overconfident."

"Let's hope so," he said, rolling up the map.

"It's time to break camp and find out."

THAT DAY'S MARCH, AND THE NEXT THREE, WERE EASY.
The weather was mild, late-summer breezes mitigating the
heat, and the nights were cool and clear. Copernicus's telescope arrived, and I fended him off as long as I could before finally giving in and exploring the night sky with him.

"You know," I cautioned, "this is something I've never
been much intrigued by. My father, and my grandmother
before him, were greatly interested in the planets and stars,
but for me they're only something to fill the night sky."

"How wrong you are, Your Majesty!" Copernicus en-
thused. He had trained the instrument—a sleek white tube
on a sturdy mount made of junto wood, on Deimos, which
just then was passing overhead. When he moved aside,
squealing with delight, I looked into the eyepiece.

"It looks like a pockmarked potato," I said, with little
enthusiasm, as the moon quickly moved across the field of
view.

"Yes! But isn't it beautiful?"

I gave the eyepiece back to him and studied the beautiful night with my naked eyes.

A blue dot, which I knew to be Earth, was just rising in
the east.

"Now that's something I've always found quite interesting," I said in passing.

"Hmmm?" Copernicus took his eye from the instrument and noted the direction of my pointing.

"Ahh!" he cried, immediately swiveling the telescope
that way. "It's up!"

After he had had his look, he turned the instrument over

to me, and I saw a tiny blue and brown world floating like a child's play marble in the heavens.

"It's where the Old Ones came from!" Copernicus said brightly behind me.

I took my eye from the eyepiece. "Who told you that?"

He became suddenly quiet in the dark.

"Speak to me, Copernicus."

"I have . . . proof," he said quietly.

"What sort of proof?"

He reached into his tunic and withdrew a single sheet of paper, many times folded. It looked fragile.

With a trembling hand he held it out to me.

"Will this get me in trouble, Your Majesty?"

"Why would it?"

"Heresy, perhaps?"

I laughed, taking the folded sheet from him. "It's not heresy to think that the Old Ones came from the stars, or Earth, or anywhere else, Copernicus. The truth is, no one knows where they came from. Growing up, I heard all kinds of stories. To tell you the truth, I found the stories much more interesting than the night sky. I've always been greatly interested in history, and the origins of the Old Ones is the greatest mystery of all, isn't it?"

"Not if you believe that paper," he whispered reverently.

I carefully unfolded it, and, holding it delicately by two corners, angled it toward the weak light of Deimos. It was a ruled sheet, and very old, but well preserved. There was handwriting on it, a bit of a scrawl, but after tilting it this way and that I was able to read the writing. It was a journal entry of some sort.

"The last ship leaves tomorrow, and I'll be on it," I read out loud. "Despite all our time here, we have failed. If only we had put our efforts into saving home, instead of remaking Mars."

I looked at Copernicus in the dark. "But there's no mention of Earth! It could be anywhere it's talking about!"

"Turn it over," he said, in a near whisper.

I did so, and squinted at a final sentence, which I could barely make out in the weak light: "Tomorrow we return to Earth."

"Where did you find this?" I asked.

"In my potato field, when I was plowing. It was in a very old box, made of metal that didn't rust, with a seal on it that hissed when I broke it open. There were some trinkets, and that paper, which was the last page of a journal."

I carefully refolded it and handed it back to him.

"Take good care of that paper," I said. "When we return from battle Newton will want to see it."

"I've never told anyone before, because I thought I would be beaten, or worse."

I laughed. "What was the rest of the journal about?"

"Whoever wrote it was a scientist," Copernicus said, "and mentioned cats once or twice."

"And?" I urged.

"That they were thriving, and would be left behind, along with the other . . . *animals.*"

"Animals?" I laughed again, but stopped when I saw the seriousness of Copernicus's demeanor.

"You just take good care of that piece of paper, all right?"

"I will," he said.

"Now let me have one more look at Earth."

LATER IN MY TENT, BY THE DIM LIGHT OF A LAMP, I pulled one of my own most precious possessions from its place in my traveling trunk. It was an Old One book, very old and brittle, with the names and pictures of Old One composers. It had originally been my grandmother Haydn's book. I had often wondered what their music had sounded like, and had even, when alone, written a few of my own little tunes on the *tambon*, trying to re-create what those sounds might have been like. The results had not been pretty.

I turned the pages with care, noting the missing or disintegrated entries. I came to my father's namesake, the beginning long disintegrated, only part of a fat old face visible above the partial name, SEBASTIAN BACH. My aunt Amy, whom I had never known, named for the Old One composer AMY BEACH, came next, and then the most intact of all the pictures in the book, FRANZ JOSEPH HAYDN, for whom my grandmother was named. The naked, severe visages of the Old Ones had often frightened me as a kit—they looked forbidding and massive, without humor or mercy. Only the picture of my own namesake, CLARA SCHUMANN, whose brother or perhaps husband ROBERT's portrait faced hers in the book, held a strange beauty for me. Though she was hairless save for a bun of black hairs on the top of her head, and her ears were strangely shaped and low, and she was devoid of whiskers and her naked paws, folded in her lap, had strange flat claws at the end of too-long fingers, there was something about her I found attractive. I had often thought I saw some of my own demeanor in her elegance, despite her weird ugliness.

I slowly closed the book and put it away, and lay back on my bed with my paws behind my head. I stared at the roof of the tent, undulating gently in the cool night breeze, and listened to the crackle and snap of distant and near campfires.

The Old Ones from Earth?

I smiled at the fantastic nature of it.

What would Newton say?

Or, perhaps, did he already know?

My mind, filled with fantastic thoughts, spiraled slowly down into sleep.

⇥ CHAPTER 9 ⇤

"ATTACK!"

I awoke with a start, the desperate voice I heard mingling with a dream of the Old Ones. For a moment I stared at the ceiling of my tent, bleached by faint light. Dawn?

"Attack! *We're being attacked!*"

The dream dispersed, leaving waking reality.

The flap of my tent was thrown open, showing a wild-eyed Rebecca. Outside I heard shouts and alarms, the clanging of armor and sword.

"What is it, Rebecca?" I asked.

"They—!" she said, unable to speak.

I threw myself from the bed and pushed past her.

A scene of chaos met my eyes. General Reis was nowhere to be seen, but his lieutenants were desperately trying to form their troops into some sort of order. In the distance I saw a mass of white bodies—Baldies?—at the edge of the camp and drawing closer. Within the camp was a huge and at first incomprehensible mass, charging like a roaring, bellowing machine from right to left.

"It's a *h-harlow*, Your Majesty!" Rebecca stammered, clutching at me.

"Merciful Great One," I breathed, my eyes fixed on the largest beast on the planet, a wild, raging monster, unstoppable.

It charged ahead, throwing bodies into the air, then suddenly turned its bulk toward me. I saw behind it a running horde of white.

"They're herding it!" I shouted, more fascinated than frightened. "The Baldies are guiding it!"

It was charging straight for us.

I pulled Rebecca away from the tent and broke into a run as the beast hurtled at us. Its eyes were wide and flat and black, filled with dark, mindless wild hate, and the unthinking brute suddenly leapt into the air—

I pushed Rebecca down as the beast roared over us, flattening my tent before galloping on. In its wake came a score of screaming Baldies, bearing whips with which they urged the harlow. Two of them split off and ran straight at Rebecca and me, snarling, their fanged mouths wide.

My sword was in the ruined tent, and I covered Rebecca with my body and turned to take the blow as the Baldie in front raised his whip to strike.

He was cut down as his hand came forward by a rush of my soldiers, but the other Baldie was able to lower his whip arm before he was taken down.

I felt the hot lash of the whip across my face, and then the Baldie fell dead at my feet, struck by a score of blows from rushing soldiers.

"Your Majesty!" Rebecca screamed, pulling herself from beneath me and kneeling to attend to my wound.

"Is it that bad?" I said, trying to keep my voice light and at the same time trying to ignore the hot, searing pain.

"It may scar!" Rebecca cried, dabbing at the streak of blood with her own tunic.

"Then it will scar," I answered, levelly. "I will look like General Xarr, perhaps."

I was being helped to my feet by a score of paws, and already my tent was being remounted. As I was helped inside I said, "What of the rest of them? And the harlow?"

"Most of the Baldies were killed," a young captain who strode up reported. "The harlow is gone into the hills."

"Send out parties after it, and when we set up camp this evening use the perimeter defenses that Newton supplied us with. Isn't it odd to find a harlow this far south?"

"More than odd," General Reis said, striding into my tent. "My apologies, Your Majesty—if we had had any indication of a harlow in the area, we would of course have used the perimeter defenses." He studied my face, which was still being dabbed at by Rebecca, who had retrieved a first-aid kit.

"Do I remind you of anyone?" I teased, but he did not, or chose not, to understand.

He asked, "Shall I give orders to march?"

"Of course. What of injuries?"

"One soldier dead, trampled by the harlow. The attack was deliberate."

"We may expect more of the same?"

"Perhaps. I've already doubled scouting parties."

I nodded, and after a moment he turned on his heel and left, marching out as he had marched in.

"Strange . . ." I said, to no one in particular.

"Your Majesty?" Rebecca answered, halting her ministrations.

I waved my paw. "Nothing, Rebecca. Thank you for your help. It feels much better."

There were sudden tears in her eyes. "You saved my life! And were hurt because of it!"

I took her paw in my own and squeezed it. "You would have done the same for me."

She snuffled, looking away, and continued to attend to my wound, which stung greatly but that I was already forgetting.

Strange, I thought.

Strange that the Baldies seemed to be in control of that harlow, when normally they would have been wild with lust for the beast's tusks, which they valued above all else. I had never heard of a harlow being controlled before, by anyone.

Did Frane now have power over all the beasts of the world?

And how was she able to control the Baldies to such an extent? Even with forged alliances, they were notoriously wild and untamable.

Strange . . .

⊰ CHAPTER 10 ⊱

WE BECAME A MORE CAUTIOUS ARMY, MORE VIGI-
lant, more ready, with more probing tendrils ahead, to the
sides, and behind us, more careful reconnaissance by our
aerial companions—and yet for the next two weeks, as we
drew nearer to Frane's army, all was quiet. There was a
brief sandstorm, whipped down from the desert to the
north but petering out almost before it began. In a way its
dispersal was a disappointment, for we had barely secured
our equipment and locked ourselves in our battened down
tents than the skies cleared and it was time to move again.
Copernicus explained to me later that we were too far
south to feel the real wrath of any such storm, and that we
had felt the farthest edges of it.

"Another hundred miles north, though . . ." he said,
shaking his head, "and it would have been a different story
indeed."

He did not share my disappointment, and spent that night in rapture with his telescope under the stars.

I had spent the previous three evenings alone in my tent, trying to compose a letter to Darwin. There was no doubt now in my mind that I loved him, and I thought it only right that I express that love. But every attempt—

My dearest Darwin . . .

Darwin, my love . . .

—had ended with my crumpling the offending sheet of stationery in my paws and throwing it to the ground.

Finally, I decided to be direct:

> *Darwin,*
>
> *I trust this letter finds you well. We are about to engage in a great battle, and I find that I must tell you certain things now, since there may be no other time. I don't know how this happened or why, but the fact is that I love you. This is a mysterious thing to me, but it is a fact that must be faced. When I return, if you feel the same, as I think you do, I propose that we be betrothed and that you be my king.*

I signed it *with all my love*, then read it over again and nearly tore it up. It was lame and ineffectual, but at that moment the evening courier arrived, and, almost without thinking, I folded and shoved it into an envelope, closed it with my seal, and gave it to him. There would be no other chance before battle, and I put the letter into his paw.

He bowed and left, and I took a great, deep breath and walked out to look at the stars with Copernicus.

TWO DAYS LATER A GYPSY ARMY OF NEARLY TWO hundred joined with us, led by a fellow named Corian, claiming to be a cousin of the great gypsy leader Miklos, whom my father had known. A day later, we met the forward edge of Frane's army. At dusk the perimeter alarms went off, and three harlows were spotted by far scouts. There was plenty of time to prepare, and an aerial bomb dispatched one of the beasts, along with its attendant contingent of wailing, herding Baldies, before it reached the fringes of our camp. The other two were dispatched closer in, by the weapon which Newton had given us, consisting of a ground analyzer, which picked up the beast's tread, and a heavy box on a tripod with a muzzle, which was aimed at the animal and issued a blast of blinding light that felled the monster. The other got closer, but was brought down before it had reached the perimeter.

There were two other attacks that night, and as dawn broke we prepared for our last march. General Reis pointed to the northwest, our direction of travel.

"Just over that ridge is a low plain, and then Valles Marineris will come into sight."

An unnatural thrill went through me.

"There are Baldies in the plain," the general continued, filling me in with scouting reports, "with the vast majority waiting at the rim of the canyon."

"Let's meet them, then."

He nodded, and we spurred our horses forward.

THE BALDIES ATTACKED FIRST WITH HARLOWS, AND then in packs consisting only of their own number. But we had anticipated this and spread our army to either side so that we could not be outflanked. The canyon, a tremendous cut in the ground that grew ever wider as we approached, seemed to swallow all sounds and echo them back in a ghostly fashion. The hair on the nape of my neck stood up as we grew near, and the battle intensified. It was as if we were marching toward a giant hole in Mars.

The harlows were dispensed with in short order. But the Baldie horde grew in front of us into a keening mass of mad beasts armed with tooth and claw. Some held weapons, swords, and even an occasional shield. And yet we plowed through them methodically, hacking at their wild, hissing faces, their pink and impossibly light blue eyes, their thin strange whipping tales, long claws, nearly hairless bodies with patches of dirty white fur covering their genitals and beneath their armpits with the occasional tuft on their near-naked heads. And still they came at us, and more of them, and we cut them down like stalks of wheat. We had armored our legs against their claws and teeth, and the foot soldiers wore light body armor, which made the beasts' advances nearly ineffectual. It was only a stupid or inattentive feline who fell to the brutes.

"This is too easy," I shouted to General Reis, above the din of wailing Baldies and the clash of battle.

He looked at me steadily, and nodded, pausing to hack down at a screeching beast who sought to gnaw at his boot and scratched madly as he was felled with a sword blow. The beast fell to the ground, its last breaths tramped from its body by the general's horse.

"There must be more than this!" he shouted, then turned to meet two Baldies who sought to strike at him from behind. They were dispatched.

I moved off, wading through the bodies of dead or dying Baldies, bringing my own sword into play when one of the brutes tried to tear my mare's leg armor off with its teeth. There was a curious odor that pervaded the battlefield, mingling with the copper smell of blood. I thought I had smelled it before . . .

I looked into the distance, where Baldies filled the

world from horizon to horizon, pressed against the rim of the Valles Marineris chasm. We were already nearing the cliffs.

I sought the bloodred armor and banner of Frane herself, and soon spied it to the left, amid a sea of her mad protectors.

I began to move that way, hacking through the mass of Baldies around me, which parted like a dying wave. I almost felt sorry for the brutes.

Frane's banner drew closer—and now I saw what looked to be the fiend herself, her left arm raised high with a sword, urging the Baldies onward, her helmet crimson in the sun.

The right arm was missing, and I was sure I had found my prize.

For my father, and my grandmother before her! I thought, my vision filling with bloodlust.

I spurred my horse on, riding through a sea of crazed white bodies as if they were water parting before me.

My prize drew closer—and now Frane's head turned to see me. Behind her, at the cliff's edge, Baldies were being pushed over into the nearly bottomless pit, flailing and screaming as they fell. I saw a harlow, crazed and trapped by the mass of bodies around it, hurl itself over the edge rather than be hemmed in.

Ahead of me, Frane turned, studying the terrain behind her. She tried to move to the left but was blocked by her own mad army, who were being pushed in great numbers to the ledge and over. To the right there was room where the harlow had been, and she drove herself into that spot even as more Baldies filled it.

I drew closer, brandishing my sword, and sought to meet her eye. Two Baldies, howling, jumped on my mare and tried to scratch its eyes out. I dispatched them, left and right, in quick succession.

Frane looked straight at me, even as I came within hailing range.

"Prepare to die, fiend!" I shouted, raising my sword.

Raising her own in mock salute, the one-armed monster turned quickly—

—and jumped into the chasm behind her, followed by a score of white-bodied acolytes.

"No!" I screamed, driving my mare to the edge of the chasm and rearing it up. White bodies pressed around me and I drove them off, down, hacked at them screaming, "It cannot end like this!"

The bodies thinned out around me, as others of my army advanced toward me, slaying Baldies in droves until their numbers dwindled and then disappeared.

I dismounted and stood panting, filled with impotent rage, staring down at the immense pit gouged in the surface of Mars and the tiny unmoving white bodies littering its bottom like specks of dust.

I spied the single spot of red among them and screamed in rage again.

"My queen," General Reis addressed me, riding up and quickly dismounting. He took my arm. "My queen, please move away from the edge of the chasm."

"She cheated me, even in death," I spat.

"She is dead, that is all that matters," he answered, trying to soothe me.

I turned on him, fury in my eyes. *"She cheated me!"*

He drew back, perhaps alarmed at my rage. Suddenly he bowed. "I will have her body brought up from the pit," he said.

"Do that." I rammed my sword viciously into its scab-

bard, and strode past him to mount my horse and trot slowly away, trying to calm my own ire.

The sounds of battle had died around me, leaving a field of white carnage and red blood. The moans of the dying and wounded were like a judgment on me.

Frane is dead, I thought.

The architect of so much unhappiness on my world, the murderer of my father, the sworn enemy of my grandmother, had been vanquished, and was no more.

There would be true peace on the planet.

Why did I feel so empty, so unsatisfied?

It had all seemed almost too easy—was that it?

Yes . . . something was wrong, out of place.

What was it?

Later that day I was to find out just how wrong things were.

⊰ CHAPTER 11 ⊱

THE BODY HAD BEEN TOO SHORT. I'M SURE THAT HAD been in the back of my mind, even during the battle. It was not a F'rar body, and not Baldie, but of some indeterminate clan, possibly from the far north.

"Perhaps a follower she picked up on her flight," General Reis said. "She was bound to have a few fanatics still close to her."

"But how many?" I asked.

On the slab before me, stripped of its armor and helmet, the body looked little like Frane. The missing left arm, hacked off at the shoulder, was the most telling part of its bodily disguise.

"Do you think . . . ?" I asked, pointing at the healed wound.

Corian, who had joined us, laughed. "Whether she hacked it off herself or Frane helped her, it makes no difference. It was a bold stroke—pardon the pun." He smiled, a thin gesture on his leathery face. "The fact remains, it was a daring disguise. It had my spies fooled, certainly."

Reis asked the nomad, "When was the last time Frane herself was in this area?"

"That is hard to say, General." Corian shrugged. "A week, two perhaps. She was seen and identified at one point, most assuredly."

Reis's cold eye lingered on the gypsy before turning to me.

"It seems you may have your chance at her yet, Your Majesty."

"Yes . . ."

It was then that a messenger arrived, white as a Baldie with fright, and handed Reis a note, which he quickly opened and read.

His own complexion paled.

"What is it?" I demanded.

Without saying a word, he handed me the dispatch. "The concussion device," he said, his voice cracking with disbelief.

I read the note, and my own heart turned to stone in my chest.

"The . . . city of Wells is . . . gone," I whispered, dropping the note to the ground.

I DO NOT REMEMBER MUCH ABOUT SPEAKING TO THE assembled army, only that I said the words that were expected of me. I told them what they already knew, that their families, their loved ones, their way of life, their government, everything they treasured, was gone. Everyone they had known in the old city was dead, every shop they had loved to frequent, the gardens, the byways, the streets, the certain slant of light between two buildings, the house where one was born, the Assembly Hall, the Senate chambers, and the senators themselves—all were no more. I told them that my heart wept for them, and did not lie—what I did not, could not, tell them was that my own heart was broken and would never mend. I told them what I could, and then I turned away and spoke no more, but went to my tent, alone, and wept.

I thought of the note I had agonized over writing to Darwin, and calculated the days it would have taken our fast rider to get back.

Yes, I concluded, he had seen it before he died, along with almost everything else in the world I loved.

Only Newton, I knew, had been spared, because he had been on his way north to one of the oxygenation stations near Bradbury. It was his people who had sent the message.

Frane had camouflaged her stolen aerial machine to look like Newton's own, and dropped her only great weapon on the finest city the face of Mars had ever known.

And my beloved Darwin, whom I had ordered to stay behind, was dead.

In effect, by my own hand.

I threw myself on my bed, curled up, and wept like a kit. "Oh, Darwin, Darwin . . ."

The day went away, and it became night. There were stirrings in the camp, but I paid no heed. I was like one half-alive, uncaring. I would neither eat nor attend to my duties. I would stay in my tent forever, and mourn, and berate myself for my own failings and oversight.

You should have known.

You should have seen.

How could I be a great queen, when my first act had been to be fooled into losing almost everything that was worthy in the world?

• • •

IT WAS ONLY HOURS LATER THAT COPERNICUS STOLE
into my tent, crawling beneath the back wall, his eyes wide
as saucers, that I came back to the world.

"What is it, Copernicus?" I asked. "I am not interested
in the stars tonight."

"Your Majesty," he huffed, nearly petrified with fright.

"What is it?"

"You must come with me now. They are coming to kill
you. General Reis is dead."

"*What—!*" I hissed.

I heard a growing commotion, cries of alarm, outside. I
lunged for my sword.

Copernicus swatted my hand, and I lowered the
weapon. "Too many! Come with me *now!*"

"Where is Rebecca?" I shouted.

"She is with a contingent fighting off the enemy—we
must go!"

Something in his urgency made me follow him, grabbing only my bag with important state papers and my most
precious possession, my book of the Old Ones, crawling
beneath the back of the tent, then moving off into the night.

I looked back and saw what seemed to be a hundred figures closing in on the tent from all sides, swords and daggers drawn. A torch was lit and thrown at the tent, which
went up in a great and instant blaze.

"What . . ."

"Corian's men, they weren't gypsies at all! Please follow!" he hissed, pulling at my arm.

WE WENT DEEPER INTO THE DARKNESS, PAST THE FIELD
where Copernicus had set up his telescope on so many
nights.

"I still don't understand—" I said, stopping again to look back at the camp—too many lights, not enough of my own soldiers, loud noises and exclamations.

"Please!" Copernicus hissed, frantically.

I stumbled after him deeper into the darkness, until we reached a little copse of junto trees. The night was cool, and the leaves swayed as if to music.

There were two horses there, eating grass, loaded with provisions.

I looked at Copernicus, but he pushed me toward the less-burdened one.

I mounted, secured my bag, and, after a second attempt, he mounted his own.

"Ride with me!" he urged, in the most frightened voice I had ever heard, and, numb with grief and disbelief and my own fright, I followed him into the night.

⊰ CHAPTER 12 ⊱

AS DAWN BROKE TENTATIVELY IN THE EAST, A BLOT of purple against the horizon of a black sky, Copernicus allowed that we could slow our horses down to a canter. We had galloped nearly the whole night, keeping at first to the northern edge of the chasm of Valles Marineris, where various outcrops and the occasional stand of trees hid us. For a while Copernicus considered climbing down into the chasm by one of the wide switchbacks and perhaps hiding for a time in one of the numerous caves set into its side, but in the end decided that it was essential to put as much distance between us and our assumed pursuers as possible. So we turned sharply north sometime long after midnight had passed. Strange echoes and soundings had come from the great chasm, as if it was filled with spirits, and it was a relief to leave the monstrous cut in Mars behind us.

But soon we met with other strange wonders, a forest the likes of which I had never seen. As daylight rose, I saw that the bark of many of its trees was a light pink in color, and peeling as if shedding skin.

"Rinto trees," Copernicus explained. "They only grow in this region, and still are very rare." He seemed suddenly interested in a particular stand of these trees, the lower bark of which was totally absent. He dismounted, studying the denuded specimens closely.

"I'm not surprised," he mumbled, half to himself.

"Surprised at what?"

He waved at me as if in dismissal and set to scraping carefully one of the denuded spots, letting the shavings fall into a pouch. "Later, Your Majesty," he explained, in effect telling me nothing. I must have shown disapproval because he quickly added, "It is a theory, and I will want to be sure."

As he had not been wrong to that point, I let him have his way and changed the subject.

He remounted his horse, which, I now saw in the daylight, had been packed with many things—bundles and pouches and tools and, of course, his beloved telescope, mounted along the horse's flank, its tube peeking from one end of a sheltering blanket.

"Stay here and rest, Your Majesty," he all but ordered me. "I want to backtrack a bit to that last ridge we climbed and make sure were are alone."

"We must be at this point."

He nodded briefly, but turned his horse sharply and rode off.

I dismounted, stretching my bones and letting my horse crop at a sparse clump of grass. I heard the tinkle of running water nearby and led my mount to it—a thick gurgling stream, silver-blue in the morning light. The trees overhead made a filtering canopy, letting the early sun peek through. I was suddenly chilled and pulled a wrap from the bundles on my horse. I did not want to think, but only to live. As the horse drank I sat down and tried to empty my mind.

A useless endeavor, but before long my weariness overcame me, and I curled into an unrestful sleep on the banks of the stream, with the fresh smell of morning in my nostrils. I dreamed of horrible things, a battle all in blood-red, a graceful black ship floating in the sky, letting loose a device that floated down like a spent leaf, falling, falling, falling into the center of my city, and I watched from afar as Wells burst into hot flame and was consumed alive, and no more . . .

I awoke from this horror with a start and heard mumbling beside me. For a moment I was disoriented, and reached into my tunic for my hidden blade, but then the sound resolved into Copernicus's voice, and I relaxed my grip on the handle of my weapon. The horrid images leaked out of my thoughts, and once again it was a beautiful late-summer day, growing warm.

I threw off my coverlet, which Copernicus must have arranged around me, and sat up, yawning.

"Are you hungry, Your Majesty?"

"Yes," I said, without thinking, because, though last night I had thought I would never be hungry or care about anything again, the growling in my stomach was something real and had to be attended to.

He was hunched over a makeshift workbench, constructed of a few fallen timbers laid across two piles of rocks. Something the deep color of blood was bubbling in a beaker, and another held a clear liquid, which gave off a sinister sharp odor.

He turned and grinned at me quickly. A makeshift pair of goggles occluded his eyes. He pointed to his mount.

"Lunch is there, not here," he said brightly. "You would not want to drink either of these, oh no . . ."

"What are they?"

"It's what they will be that's important," he answered.

"I'm in no mood for riddles," I snapped peevishly, and went to the open pack on his horse. It contained something that looked like roots and tasted like . . . roots.

"What is this?" I said, making a face.

"Hard tack," he answered. "Much of your army carried it, Your Majesty—though I doubt you ever had to endure it."

"It's horrible."

"It would keep you alive for weeks on end—and probably will."

I sighed heavily and went to sit beside him while he worked. There was a rock that proved to be a suitable stool, and I made use of it.

"It's time for you to explain everything to me, Copernicus."

He cocked an eyebrow, but kept working, mumbling over his two beakers, going from one to the other and counting off numbers.

"For instance," I said, "where are we going?"

"We'll continue north," he said. "It's the one place they won't dare to follow. Otherwise, I'm afraid we'll be caught."

"Are we still being followed?"

"Yes and no."

"No riddles, Copernicus."

"No riddle involved. There is a band of five heading northeast, and another heading due west. About twenty miles distant, but because of their line of march, that distance will only increase away from us."

"How do you know?"

"I watched them."

My silence must have been like a scoff, for he turned to regard me.

"The telescope," he explained. "It's as useful in the day as at night, is it not?"

My face must have shown my admiration.

"And our ultimate destination?"

"My home. It is to the north, and then the east a bit. They will not think to look there, because they do not know I am with you. For all they know you fled alone."

I could find no argument with that—besides myself, no one in camp had taken the slightest interest in the little fellow.

He had resumed his counting, and when I asked another question he held up his paw for silence.

"Twenty-nine . . . thirty . . . thirty-one, thirty—ah!"

The bloodred liquid turned clear, and the clear turned bloodred, as if a magic trick had been performed.

He immediately lost interest in the experiment and grabbed the two beakers, emptying their contents onto the ground. They hissed like snakes.

"That's that," he said, satisfied. "It's as I thought. They were drugged."

"Who was drugged?" I asked.

He took off his goggles and dropped them onto his workbench. "Practically everybody, except myself, your maidservant Rebecca, and a few soldiers who were on duty and hadn't eaten." He gave me a sober look. I opened my mouth but he plowed on, as if I were a science student in his own lecture hall. "It is called mocra, and it's culled from the bark of the rinto tree. It is one of the most dangerous substances on Mars. I doubt you've ever heard of it because, long before you were born, nearly every rinto tree on the planet was cut down and destroyed. This was before even the First Republic was formed. Because it is such a dangerous and unstable narcotic, mocra never became a large problem, but the potential for disaster was there, and so King Augustus, your great-grandfather, decreed that all the trees be destroyed, thereby eliminating the problem. But here . . ."

He spread his hands out, highlighting our own copse of rinto trees.

"And," he continued, "that's how Frane controlled the Baldies—before she sent them to their deaths against you."

"She drugged them . . ." I said.

"Oh, yes, no doubt. She must have experimented for months or years before she found a dosage that would make the Baldies malleable. But there's no doubt she did. It is usually made into a paste from dry powder, and is always red in color. It dissolves quickly in liquids of any kind. Do you recall smelling a particularly spicy odor on the battlefield yesterday?"

"Yes, I do."

"That was from the drug. It's ingestion produces that almost minty smell."

"And—"

He held up a paw. "I haven't finished, Your Majesty. That same smell permeated the army's camp last night. It's what alerted me to trouble. It was put into every chow bucket over every campfire, and eaten by nearly every soldier in the army. Enough to produce complete disablement of your troops. They became disoriented. Then, at that dosage, they went to sleep. I doubt many of them ever woke up."

"Merciful One," I swore. "And the others, the officers, they were merely slaughtered. And I trusted the gypsies . . ."

"Gypsies? There were no gypsies in camp," Copernicus said with conviction.

"Corian and his men were a gypsy band, sent from Miklos."

Copernicus shook his head. "Most assuredly not. I grew up dealing with gypsies, and that group that joined up just before the battle looked more liked raiders to me. In fact, I assumed that an alliance had been made, for this battle alone. They follow nothing but coin. They are mercenaries."

I was stunned by General Reis's incompetence—even though his failure to vet our allies had cost him his life. Ultimately, though, the responsibility still rested with me, and my mood became even darker.

Copernicus must have sensed this, because he said in a soothing voice, "You must remember, Your Majesty, that twenty/twenty hindsight is the clearest vision of all. It would have been very easy for those raiders to fool you. If only I had not been so caught up in my own studies, and had sought to ask . . ."

His own mood darkened.

"Well," I said, "we can sit here and brood on our stupidity, or we can move on and live."

He looked at me, and a small smile lit his brown-furred face. "I agree, Your Majesty. If we follow my plan and get to my home, there are inquiries I can make there, even as you hide from those who would destroy you."

"I will defeat Frane yet, if it is the last thing I accomplish on this world."

"That's the spirit!" he cried. He set about cleaning and packing all of his chemical apparatus, then broke apart his table, scattering the assembled pieces so that they were once more part of the natural landscape.

"We have food for a week, and two good horses, and two good riders, and all the will in the world!"

"What do you mean?" I asked.

"Only that we have a very good chance of living through it!" he answered, trying to stay cheerful.

"Living through the ride north, of course?"

Seeing my continued incomprehension, he added, pointing ahead of us, "The ride north, where no one will follow us! Across the Great Desert!" His laugh sounded almost mad. "Don't you remember, Your Majesty? When we got just a kiss of the dust storm from the north? I told you how harsh and forbidding it is—and now we're heading straight into it!"

Again his half-mad laugh. "Actually, there's very little chance we'll survive!"

⊰ CHAPTER 13 ⊱

THAT MAD LITTLE LAUGH OF COPERNICUS'S STAYED
in my mind as we headed down into the forbidding bowl
that was the Great Desert. From the sparsely grassed
heights of the last plateau it didn't look too forbidding—
the sun was shining and there was only a hint of increased
heat picked up from the hot sands below. Under the pink
late-summer sky it looked merely daunting, a giant version, to three horizons, north, east, and west, of a child's
sandbox. There were rolling dunes and dark patches that
promised oases and, under the summer sun on that gentle
day, it looked no more horrid than a ride across a huge valley. *Substitute sand for countryside*, I told myself, *and you
would have this quick trip*. In the distance were a few dark
patches above the sand that seemed to undulate.

"What are those?" I said, pointing them out to Copernicus, who was engaged in tightly tying down everything on
our two mounts, double- and triple-covering everything he

could, especially his precious telescope, which had disappeared under a bulge of blanket layers.

"Tornadoes," he said simply, returning to his work, which I helped with in my clumsy way.

Then he sat down beside his horse, crossed his legs, and closed his eyes.

"Now what?" I asked.

"We wait."

"For what?"

"For nightfall, of course. Only a madman would head into the Great Desert during the day."

In a moment his chin lolled forward, and he gently collapsed onto the ground and curled up into sleep.

I tried to follow but could not, and sat instead contemplating the subtle play of sinking sunlight on the sands, and the changing colors of the landscape, from severe pink to shades of russet and dark brown, as dusk approached and finally fell.

Just as I was nodding off to sleep, Copernicus rose from the ground, stretched, and cried, "Ah!" He shook me gently awake, and said, "Time to leave!"

"But I had no sleep," I complained, seeking to find the ground and slumber.

"All the worse for you, then, Your Majesty," he said, and jostled me until I stood and mounted my horse.

It was cloudy, and pitch-dark when our mounts made the first sifting steps into the sands.

A hot breeze assaulted us from the west, as more stars overhead were eaten by mounting cloud cover.

Copernicus sighed. "This is not good," he said. "Our first night, and we're to be welcomed with a storm."

But it never materialized, and as we pushed our way down into the bowl the clouds magically dispersed above us, and Phobos and then Deimos rose and set. Dawn found us surrounded by hot sand, and pitching a poor man's tent, which Copernicus had packed and now unpacked. It stood chest high at the apex and five feet wide at the floor, but could be sealed on all sides.

"The smaller the better," Copernicus explained, "since it gives the wind less area to work on."

I stretched, feeling hot and ill-tempered.

"There isn't even a breeze," I snapped. The sky had remained cloudless, and the sun stood out like a hot, angry coin against the pale and otherwise empty sky.

"Wait an hour," the little fellow said patiently, and crawled into the tent.

While I stood regarding the empty landscape, hill upon rolling hill of nothing but bright pink sand, he added, "I suggest you stay out of the heat as much as possible and get some sleep this time."

For a moment I stood pat, until I heard him snoring inside.

Then, angry and tired, I crawled in after him, to find that for such a small feline he took up a lot of space. I had to conform my own curl to his sprawl, leaving me with little room to sleep and his boot precariously close to my face. But I was suddenly exhausted, and finally slept—

—only to be awakened soon after by the wind, which had begun as a background hiss for my bad dreams, but steadily increased to a whine and on to a howl before I was awake, watching the walls of our poor structure rattle and shake like a dying man, and buckle toward me with each pounding fist of gusting wind.

Copernicus slept blithely on through it all, and when I briefly unzipped the tightly closed front flap to look out, I was instantly blinded by rushing, pelting sand. I could see nothing a half foot in front of my face, and pulled my head back in immediately.

The wind only increased, and all that day, try as I might, I gained no more sleep.

When at last darkness was falling, tinting the walls of the tent with darker light, the wind subsided, and then fell to nothing.

Copernicus awoke, stretched, and cried his habitual, "Ah!"

I looked at him balefully when he asked, "Did you sleep well?"

"The sandstorm kept me awake."

He frowned, then said, "Oh! You mean the wind, of course. That was no sandstorm. You'd best pray to your benefactor that we don't run into a real sandstorm, Your Majesty."

He pulled out hardtack from his tunic, and after a while I did also, and almost treasured its dry, brittle taste in my empty stomach, which I then washed away with a few bitter sips from my canteen.

Then we packed, pulling our tent free from the sand walls that had built around it and breaking it down, pulling the hoods from our horses before feeding and watering them, and riding off, once again, into the night.

THE NEXT NIGHT AND DAY WENT MUCH AS THE ONE before, and the one after that, also. I began to think, as fools often do when offered repetition, that this Great Desert wasn't so great at all and had nothing to show me that I could not handle. When the clouds rolled in on the third night, and Copernicus began to make noises of alarm, I laughed and waited for them to disperse as they had on the first night. But they didn't and only thickened. Then a fierce hot pelting rain began, with drops as big as a knuckle, which at first refreshed with their wetness but then began to assault.

"Tie the horses down and get the tent up as quickly as possible!" Copernicus shouted, jumping from his mount and yanking the tent poles from their makeshift scabbard. I followed with the tent itself, and soon we had secreted ourselves inside, pushing our way through a thickening mixture of sand and water that resembled not so much mud as a kind of semiliquid rock. Around us the landscape was turning to something resembling lava, rivers of water and viscous sand where only dry dunes and hollows had existed twenty minutes before.

"I hope we drove the tent stakes deep enough!" Copernicus fretted, as the floor beneath us undulated with a flowing mixture of sand and rain. It felt like we were floating on a river, when in fact the river was flowing beneath us.

"Pray it doesn't last long—they seldom do," Copernicus said.

"And if it does?"

His doom-laden look told me all I needed to know.

But as quickly as the pelting rain had come it stopped—as if a giant switch in the sky had been violently turned off. One moment there was the roar of watery fury on our roof, then it disappeared.

Already the ground beneath us stopped moving, and then settled.

"Quickly!" Copernicus cautioned. "We must break the tent down now or we'll never get it out of the sand!"

We crawled out into a bizarre landscape of scudding clouds, dark patches of deep star-studded night overhead and a landscape altered around us—a hiss of drying sands arose, sending clouds of steam into the again-dry air. Already the sand was drying out underfoot, clumps held together by water falling and flaking apart. Our tent was mired in a pool of the stuff, and we dug around it madly before the sheer weight of drying sand kept it as a souvenir of the desert.

"I don't understand," I said to Copernicus as I furiously scooped sand away from it—it seemed to be sinking beneath us.

"The water goes back into the air, but the first rains went deep enough to be retained by the desert. Some of it will end up in underground aquifers. Some will form quicksand pools that won't dissipate for days. The violence of the change when the hot sand once again takes over from the temporary water is such that anything on the surface will be sucked down into the ground—including the horses!" he cried, abandoning the tent for a moment to run to the horses, nearly ankle deep in sand and slowly sinking as I watched. He slapped them on their flanks and they reared up, then moved their hooves and were free.

As I stood watching them I felt my own boots sinking into the ground and had to yank them up, one after the other, before falling to the work of reclaiming the tent.

Copernicus rejoined me, and before long, with a mighty heave, we pulled the collapsed structure free of the pit in which it had been mired.

I looked down to see a retreating pool of water, which cracked and dried as I watched, then broke apart, with a sighing sound, into a plain and level measure of desert sand.

We laid the tent out on the now-dry sandy surface nearby and collapsed exhausted next to it. The horses were safe, and the night was once again clear and beautiful and full of stars, which Copernicus regarded with clear lust.

"If I wasn't so tired, I would set up the telescope," he

remarked, craning his head high to regard a red star overhead.

But a moment later he was asleep and snoring, and before long I followed his example and enjoyed the first extended sleep I had claimed since the beginning of our journey.

⊰ CHAPTER 14 ⊱

"AS YOU'VE SEEN," COPERNICUS REMARKED THE FOL-
lowing night, one crystal clear and free of even a hint of
breeze, "the desert has its own set of rules. It has its own
weather, its own way of tending to itself."

I nodded, in a slightly better mood than I had been. I
had slept nearly a whole day and deep into this night, and
my belly was full of hardtack, and my thirst, which was not
as great now as it had been at the beginning of this journey,
had been sated with a mouthful of water from my nearly
empty canteen.

"I've heard that there are tribes of nomads who never
leave the desert," I said, and I saw him, under the faint
light of Deimos, shiver.

"The Sandies?" he said. "We can only hope this desert
is wide enough that we don't come across a Sandie."

"Why? I've heard that they are cousins to the gypsies,
and of a like temper."

"Hardly. They boil kits alive, so happy are they to find meat of any kind—never mind what they would do to a full-grown feline."

I laughed shortly. "That sounds like an old wives' tale."

He brought his horse around to face me and stopped in his tracks. "It is no myth," he said. "You must remember, I live on the other side of this desert. When I was a kit, one of my playmates was spirited off in the middle of the night by Sandies and never seen alive again. His bones were found years later, half-covered by sand at the bottom of a dune. His skull was never found."

"How do you know it was him?" I asked, eager to play devil's advocate. "And how do you know he was spirited away by Sandies? Every community has stories about beasts and outsiders, whom they demonize and ascribe with powers and foul rites. Look at our concept of the gypsies, before my father fell in with them. He found them to be moral and even patriotic. Darwin told me stories that he had heard while growing up about gypsies that would curl your facial hair. And they turned out to be one hundred percent untrue. We always demonize the 'other.'"

Copernicus merely shook his head, unable or unwilling to change his mind. "Believe me, we do not want to meet up with a Sandie."

I shrugged. "As you wish."

He was studying the now-dawning horizon, a mottled band of red and brown with strange patches. One of the tornadoes we had witnessed periodically from afar was whipping its way from east to west, leaving a high brush-stroke of dust behind it.

"We will travel a bit during the day, today. We need to find an oasis, and water, even if it takes us out of our way, and they are much harder to come across at night."

I said nothing in answer, trusting his judgment, and we

mounted, heading northwest toward one of the darker patches of landscape, a ruddy red blot in the distance.

It proved not to be an oasis but rather an outcropping of red rocks thrust up through the surrounding sand. We passed this strange sculpture and went on.

Our next destination was a fortuitous one, a dark patch that resolved itself from brown to dark green as we approached, and proved to be what we sought. There was a deep, bubbling pool of water surrounded by tiny desert flowers of blue and yellow. We filled our canteens. Our horses lapped greedily at this bounty, and it proved to be so cool and refreshing that I resolved to take a quick bath.

Copernicus, filled with modesty, moved off to examine the flora at the edge of the oasis while I removed my tunic and undergarments and slipped blissfully into the pool. The water was almost cold, and I happily submerged myself, feeling the dust and sand slide out of my fur.

Something tickled my foot and I looked down into the murky deep, just making out a huge shape—

With a yelp I was out of the pool and shivering on the bank, pulling on my underthings. I watched in wonder as a long, thin tentacle, mottled and dark blue in the sun, snaked up out of the water as if testing the air. It grew impossibly long, five feet, six feet, seven—

"Amazing!" Copernicus cried, appearing beside me. "A Gigantus! Here in the middle of the Great Desert! That pool must lead to an underground ocean or deep river!"

I continued to shiver.

"You're lucky he didn't pull you down," Copernicus said gravely, as the tentacle formed a loop at its tip, then slowly sank back into the water, leaving a tiny splash behind.

In a moment the pool was smooth and inviting as it had

been, but I was putting on the rest of my clothes and turning my back on it.

"WE HAVE WATER TO LAST US THE REST OF THE TRIP,"
Copernicus announced happily an hour later, as we left the oasis behind and headed due north once more. He was studying the horizon and sky, paying particular attention to the west, which was now suffused with a line of mist or sand that rose high into the sky.

"I don't like the looks of that," Copernicus said. "But it may blow south of us."

We pitched our tent in the early afternoon, after leaving the oasis, and any Sandies ("Where there is water there are Sandies," Copernicus had declared) and sought to sleep, but Copernicus rose every half hour to check the approaching line. It did indeed move to the south, behind us, he reported, but was still growing in the west when night fell. We went on, and as the night wore on I heard, very faintly at first, a distant keening sound that grew incrementally.

"I'm afraid we're in for it," Copernicus said, just before dawn. The keening sound had become a high, whistling howl, and the entire south and west were lost in a high, roiling cloud of disturbed sand. Copernicus brought us to a halt in a small valley. To my surprise, after securing our tent and filling it with our food and water supplies, he slapped the flanks of both horses, driving them away to the north. Needing no more encouragement, they galloped away, bearing with them the rest of our provisions and Copernicus's beloved telescope.

"Why did you do that?" I asked, already half-knowing the answer.

"If they stay the storm will kill them. This way, without

our added weight, there is a chance they will outrun it. If so, I will see my telescope again. If not . . ."

He shrugged, resigned to fate, and we crawled into our meager shelter and secured the flap after us. The howl outside was becoming a scream, and Copernicus had to shout to be heard.

"We will get no rest, I'm afraid," he said. "Soon, you will not be able to hear yourself think. You will believe you are going mad, with the roar of the storm. We must pray that our stakes are deep enough to hold us in place—otherwise, we will be blown away. And we must pray that the storm does not last too long, or we will be buried alive, too deep to dig our way out."

"Cheerful thoughts!" I replied, trying to smile and show him the courage I did not possess.

He shook his head. "There are no cowards or heroes in sandstorms, Your Majesty. Only the dead, and the survivors."

As if in answer, the wind kicked up another screeching notch, and I could no longer hear what the little fellow was saying when he opened his mouth.

And so the storm went. I did not think that any sound could be so loud, and yet it became even louder. I pressed my paws over my ears and gritted my teeth against screaming, and still it grew louder. Sand flew at our tent in slapping sheets, like water without wetness. This thumping and shearing sound only added to the din, which became unbearable. I looked at Copernicus, who was rolled up on the ground, his ears covered, eyes wide, his mouth open—I could not hear his cries. And still the storm mounted. I watched in horror as one of our tent poles began to vibrate like a plucked string. It broke suddenly, and one end of our structure collapsed. The other pole, nearer to our heads, also began to vibrate and, as I reached out to steady it, it broke in my hands and the tent collapsed completely on top of us. I felt a weight of sand pressing me down from above, and the wind keened higher and yet higher.

The din seemed to go on for hours, as the weight of sand steadily grew above us, pushing us down. It became difficult to breathe. I reached out for Copernicus, who was shivering like a leaf.

"I can't breathe! I can't breathe!" he screamed, a snatched whisper above the wind. I tried to push up the tent above us, but the weight was too much, and I could not budge it. It was as if a giant hand was pushing down on us, telling us to succumb.

We waited for the end.

Then there was another sound joined to the wind, now, a strange thumping and then scraping. I could no longer believe my own senses. The scraping went on and on, unidentifiable, and then suddenly the tent was ripped open above my head. The tear grew until both Copernicus and I were uncovered. The night was black, and sand beat against us mercilessly, and then a shape in the dark, a wrapped figure with dark eyes, which looked huge, reached down for me.

Before the world went away I heard Copernicus screech once, a mighty fearful sound above the wind:

"*Sandies!*"

⊰ CHAPTER 15 ⊱

I AROSE FROM BLACKNESS.

I could hear nothing but the inner beating of my own heart. I was in a dark place, but the dire howling of the wind was gone. No, not gone—but distant, muffled, quieted.

I reached up and my paw instantly hit something, a smooth wall or ceiling, not a foot over my head. Behind me was another wall, and the toe of my boot found another at my feet. To my left my paw found fur, an arm, a face which, I determined by gentle probing, belonged to the sleeping form of Copernicus. To my right—another body, this one awake.

A low chuckle was followed by a rasping voice: "Sleep. That is all there is to do, now. Sleep through the storm."

"Who—"

"I said sleep." The low chuckle again. "We will discuss *eating* you after the storm is over."

Again the chuckle, joined by other voices giggling elsewhere in the box.

I tried to sleep, but could only think of those last words . . .

FINALLY, I DID SLEEP, BUT WAS AWAKENED BY A rough hand. I opened my eyes to brilliant sunshine. I closed my eyes against the harsh light, but they were immediately forced open by an ungentle paw. A wrapped face lowered itself over me and piercing eyes looked into my own, back and forth.

"There is no damage," the voice, lilting, reported.

"The corneas are clean?" a second voice, the one I had heard in the box, inquired.

"Yes," the lilt said.

"Good. They were not caught outside, which means at least one of them is not a fool."

The face over me retreated.

"May I get up?" I inquired.

The rasping voice replied, "Of course! Get up! Dance if you wish! The storm is over and it is a brand-new day!"

The lilting voice laughed.

I sat up, blinking, and saw that there were two of them. Copernicus was nowhere to be seen. The two, wrapped from head to foot in brown cloth, looked to be man and woman, and the woman looked to be with kit. Her belly under the cloth was huge.

"Where is . . . ?" I began, but before I could finish, the gruff male, who was thin, replied, "We did not eat him, do not worry. He is using the . . . facilities, as he said, or he has run away. It is nothing to us."

Noting the humor in the voice, I said, "You saved our lives. Thank you."

"It is what is required," the thin figure said, making a slight bow with his head. "It is nothing more than the courtesy of the desert."

"Nevertheless, thank you."

Again he bowed his head, as did the female.

"Are we your prisoners?" I asked, and now the two of them laughed out loud.

"We are all prisoners of the desert," the thin one said. "As to whether we hold you, the answer of course is no. You head north, I take it?"

"Yes."

"Then you will reach it in a matter of days. You will fight no more storms. Your ponies are safe, tethered at an oasis an hour from here. We will show you the way."

"That's very good to know."

Another bow.

I stood and stepped out of the box we had been in, a red wooden coffin some six feet on a side, set into the desert floor.

"We are lucky a takra was nearby when we found you," the male said. He lowered the lid of the box and began to kick sand over it with his foot. The female joined in and, out of courtesy, so did I, until the box was covered. I noticed a thin red pole with a red flag on it, which was attached to the back of the structure that stuck out of the sand and made the structure identifiable.

"Are there many of these?" I asked.

"All over the desert. One learns their locations as one learns the oases. It is a matter of survival."

"You're not really cannibals, are you?"

"Oh, yes," the lilting voice said, with mock seriousness. She patted her stomach. "We also eat our own young when they pop." She uncovered her face for a moment, showing a wolfish smile. "They are particularly tasty!" The smile broke down into laughter.

"She jokes, of course," the male said.

"You two are betrothed?"

The term seemed to mean nothing to them, so I amended, pointing on to the other, "You are . . . mated?"

The male threw back his head and rasped laughter. "By heavens, no! She is my sister!" His laughter dissolved. "She carries the litter of our chieftain, as do all females. This makes all of us sons and daughters of the chieftain."

"I see . . ."

He pointed to himself, then his sister. "I am Tlok, and my sister is Fline." He pointed to me. "And you are . . . ?"

I hesitated, then said, "My name is Clara."

"Clara . . ." Tlok seemed to roll the name around in his head before deciding that it was acceptable. "Clara, yes. Very good."

His sister said, with a note of sarcasm, "And you and the chubby one, you are . . . as you say, betrothed?"

It was my turn to laugh, as a very disturbed and unhappy-looking Copernicus appeared, trudging toward us.

"No," I answered, "we are not—"

I was interrupted by Tlok, who said to Copernicus in a mocking voice, "You had a nice walk?"

Copernicus at first ignored him, then said, "No."

"He did try to escape! Ha! And what did you find, little man?"

"More of you. Kits. They taunted me."

"Ha!" Tlok laughed again. "Perhaps we will let them *eat* you!"

Copernicus's demeanor didn't change. He offered Tlok a quick, sour look. "Perhaps you will."

Fline touched my arm lightly—I saw that her claws did

not retract but were out and very sharp. "We will not harm you," she whispered.

But the look in her eye was mysterious, filled with laughter, and something else unreadable.

COPERNICUS'S OUTLOOK BRIGHTENED A BIT WHEN WE were presented with our horses, unharmed, a few hours later. The trek to the oasis, where the mounts were feeding and watering themselves, was uneventful except for the cavorting troop of kits who accompanied us. They moved so fast, bouncing and jumping and cartwheeling in the sand, that it was hard to count their number, but I finally settled on seven. They, like their adult counterparts, were dressed head to toe in brown cloth coverings, and there were rough-hewn sandals on their feet. Every once in a while one of them would throw back his head and yip or yowl, and his face-cloth would slip, showing a variety of markings: white and black stripes, one jet-black, many shadings of brown, and one curious mix of pure white and brown, each color on one side of the face split exactly down the middle. He or she seemed to be the leader of the band, and directed them on their games, suddenly running out away from us, followed by the others, and then bringing the line of racing fellows back at top speed. They seemed to particularly enjoy bedeviling Copernicus, who made the mistake of letting them get under his skin. By mostly ignoring them and, occasionally, smiling at their antics, I was soon deemed boring and left alone. But poor Copernicus became the center of their universe and the butt of their pranks.

"See what he has on underneath!" one of the rascals squeaked, and for the next ten minutes Copernicus was swatting the devils aside as one ran under his legs, trying to dislodge his tunic, while another attacked from a different angle.

I held my tongue as long as I could, and then broke into laughter.

"Don't encourage them!" Copernicus brayed, pulling one away by the scruff of the neck while yet another darted between his boots.

Finally, he was sprawled in the sand, covered by a mob of pecking kits trying to tear the tunic from his body.

A single sound from Fline, a kind of high-pitched yelp, and they instantly left Copernicus alone, running off to reassemble into a dancing ring thirty feet away.

"I don't trust them," Copernicus whispered fiercely, as I helped him to his feet. "I tried to get away before, to get help, but those little monsters herded me like a heifer back to camp. They'll eat us yet, I tell you."

"They seem hospitable enough, if a little strange," I answered.

"There's nothing strange about them," Copernicus nearly spat. "They'll find our bones in the desert, I tell you. They'll make a meal of me, then you."

"Why you first?" I teased.

"Because there's more of me," he said, and, perhaps realizing the silliness of what he was saying, he nearly smiled.

"Sorry," he said. "It's just that I'm very worried."

"About what?"

Tlok and Fline had stopped ahead to wait for us, and Copernicus's words were rushed.

"Cannibalism aside, what they might do with us," he said.

• • •

BUT THERE WERE OUR HORSES, CONTENT AND SAFE, and there were our provisions, untouched, and Copernicus's demeanor lightened.

Once we had taken our fill of water, I found Tlok marking a stone with a flint knife. The markings were strange to me. When he was finished he placed the stone at the bank of the oasis's pool (this one shallow, and not inhabited by a Gigantus!).

"What are you doing?" I inquired.

"This is Bleen oasis, owned by that chieftain, and though we may partake, we must leave thanks and a message of reciprocity."

"Reciprocity meaning that if he or his people are in need of an oasis owned by your chieftain, he may partake in kind?"

"Exactly!" He seemed pleased that I understood the concept.

"You . . ." he began, sitting down by the edge of the water.

"Yes?"

His face was serious. "You are intelligent. We were told . . ."

My ears pricked up. "You were told what?"

He shook his head and stood up. "Nothing. Please, we must go. We have already overstayed our welcome in this place. And we have another place to be by nightfall."

He walked away, gathering the kits together with a loud whistle, and soon we were on our way, Copernicus and I mounted, and, mostly, out of reach of the scampering, jumping kits, whose energy had not flagged a bit, but Tlok's words stayed in my mind.

We were told.

And I thought, *Told by whom?*

⇥ CHAPTER 16 ⇤

. .

WE STOPPED THAT EVENING, AND TO MY SURPRISE,
Tlok announced that we had found another underground
shelter and must use it for the night, which was clear and
starlit.

"But why?" I asked.

He hesitated for a moment, then said, "We are in the
Valley of Tornadoes, and must guard against the possibility. Though the weather is clear, a tornado can appear at almost any time. One moment the air is still and clear as
water, then the winds come, seemingly from nowhere, and,
well, one is lost."

"I see . . ."

I glanced at Copernicus, who looked very unhappy indeed. But he held his tongue and instead busied himself
with his mount.

The kits had found the red flag in the sand and were

making a great game of uncovering the big square wooden coffin that lay beneath it.

When the lid had been pried up, Tlok indicated that we should climb in first. "Please . . ."

I lay down in the box, and so did Copernicus, who was breathing heavily. When we were comfortable, Tlok began to lower the lid over us. I saw Fline and the seven kits looking at us soberly as the cover dropped upon us.

"But what of the rest of you!" I shouted, my words already muffled.

I heard a clang of metal, followed by a loud click.

"I am sorry," came Tlok's voice, muffled through the wood.

"What are you doing!"

"We must leave you for others to find. This is what we were ordered to do. It was ordained by all the chieftains. I see now that they may have been wrong in agreeing to this. There is nothing evil about you."

"What are you doing!" I pleaded.

"We know who you are, Queen Clara. But it was ordained and agreed by our chieftains that you would be turned over to Frane of the F'rar. Pacts were made, sealed with blood, which cannot be broken. It saddens me, and I will speak with our chieftain Klek when we return to him, but if I would act now otherwise, it would mean that his own word would be broken, and he would be an outcast among all the chieftains. It would bring shame and ruin on us all."

Fline's saddened voice added, "I am truly sorry."

Some of the kits were crying, and one of them, their squeaking leader, was pleading, "What will happen to them?"

"I don't know . . ." Tlok's receding voice answered.

Barely heard, the little sprite pleaded, "But the fat one was fun!"

And then we heard no more but the silence of the night.

AFTER AN INTERVAL, COPERNICUS SPOKE UP. HE breathed a huge sigh.

"Thank the sky Tlok was so upset by his task that he didn't see me taking my tools from my saddlebags and hiding them in my tunic."

I heard a rattle and metallic clunking, and Copernicus moved away from me in the dark space.

"And thank the sky that there's room to work. This may take a while, Your Majesty, if you'd like to take a nap."

He began to pound on the door overhead, and I heard a chewing sound of metal on wood.

"I couldn't sleep if I wanted to, with that racket. What are you doing?"

"I'm going to drill a series of holes, and then saw between them and make us a door to escape from. I imagine it will take most of the night."

"What if our new visitors from Frane get here before then?"

"I hadn't thought of that."

"Had you thought of merely removing the hinges?"

There was silence for a moment.

"That's brilliant!" Copernicus cried, finally. "And I have just the tool to do it!"

He crawled off in the dark, and I followed, and before long he had removed the pins from the metal hinges, and we heaved up with our backs, throwing the door up and over and away, where it broke the lock Tlok had secured it with, and we were free.

Our horses stood tethered nearby.

Without a word, we left that place, galloping on our well-rested mounts, and before morning the sands began to recede and thin, and the air lost its arid feel, filling with humidity and a thicker warmth, and as the sun rose on our flank, the new day, and a world dominated not by sand and dry heat but by greenery and rolling hills, spread out before us like a heavenly vision.

Copernicus, filled with pride, pointed at a distant valley, which looked as lush as anything I had ever seen.

"My home," he said.

⊰ CHAPTER 17 ⊱

AND SO I SPENT THE FALL AND WINTER HIDING IN A place called Hammerfarm, and became a farmhand.

Autumn was brief, with junto trees shedding their leaves almost by the calendar, on the season's first day. The air turned from warm to chill, and smelled colder. The nights, which Copernicus invariably spent with his telescope, became downright cold, and if I hadn't carried a shawl out to the little fellow on occasion, I'm sure he would have frozen. But he was happy as a man could be with the turning of the season, which meant the coming of the winter stars. To me they were but a new set of bright dots in the sky, but to Copernicus they were old friends seen a new way.

"Come look at this nebula, Your Majesty!" he would gasp in pleasure, and my eye was met with yet another faint cloud of gas.

Which would invariably lead to argument when I told him so.

The one thing that continued to spark my interest was Earth, which I made him turn the instrument toward whenever it rose. It was a strange blue and brown ball in the eyepiece, showing its various landmasses and polar caps to great effect.

"It's strange, but I feel an affinity with that place," I remarked one night.

"Why?" Copernicus asked, taking over the instrument. "It's just another rock in space. Great Jupiter shows as much to us—more, even."

I shrugged and, feeling the chill of night, soon went in. To my surprise, little Copernicus followed me.

"What's bothering you, Your Majesty?" he asked, as I made gemel tea on his ancient stove. The farmhouse was older than the stove but cozy, a wood structure with a bedroom loft Copernicus had given to me. It rattled when the wind blew but always managed to be warm inside. The main room was filled with Copernicus's many lab tables and experiments, but there was a single cozy chair which I now sat down in to face him.

"I'm restless. I should be doing something!"

He frowned. "Didn't we decide that the best thing to do was wait until spring? By then the search for you by Frane's people will surely lessen. There haven't been inquiries in almost a month, after that frantic first week."

Indeed: I had spent almost a week hiding in Copernicus's root cellar, while a strange band of gypsies or pirates—we were never sure what, exactly—came through the area asking questions and worse; only the fact that everyone in the area looked exactly like Copernicus, and that they had no specific name for the "little fellow seen traveling with a thin black-furred girl named Clara" had

saved us from detection. That and the fact that no one else
in the area knew of my existence, since, as Copernicus had
said, "Coin can make a betrayer of a friend in less time
than it takes to clap your paws."

I looked at my little friend. "I thought it was a good
idea, but now I'm not so sure. I should be trying to reach
my grandmother and father. Or Newton—"

"That would be the worst thing you could do! There are
spies everywhere! You've heard the news, that Newton
controls the cities in the east and Frane has tentative control over the badlands in the west and north. But neither
has a real army!"

"Then I should be gathering one!"

"How? This whole area is under Frane's control! You
would be caught in a minute or less!"

"Still . . ."

He took a step forward. "Please, Your Majesty. Give it
time. Let me continue to make my own quiet inquiries.
We will get word to Newton, eventually. But it will take
time."

I looked at him and sighed. "You are right, Copernicus.
Of course you are. But I am going mad doing nothing! I
need something to do!"

AND SO I BECAME A FARMER.

That late in the year there was not much to do but get
the fields ready for spring planting. But I threw myself into
this task of preparation with everything I had. I found that
I liked working with the soil, getting my paws dirty, watching calluses form on them. I became good with the plow,
learning the needs and moods of Copernicus's pack mule,
Tessie, when to push her, when to give her water, when to
do nothing because that was what she was going to do. I

learned how to use a hoe and a shovel, a spade and a rake. I learned how to bundle and burn refuse, how to feed chickens, gather eggs, milk a goat. These simple tasks served to lessen, over time, my sadness. When I thought of Darwin it was from a strange, faraway place, as if he had been in another life.

But I could not learn to get along with Copernicus's dog.

"I don't understand how anyone could have one of those *things* as a pet," I said to Copernicus one night at dinner, as a late-autumn rainstorm howled coldly outside. The fire was warm, the vegetables well cooked and tender. I felt like any domestic farmwife, proud of her full day.

But the dog was constantly under my feet, with its cow-like eyes and its mournful brown face, floppy ears, short useless legs, and wagging tail.

"Come here, Hector," Copernicus cooed, but the animal insisted on following me around wherever I went in the house.

"I won't pet you!" I growled at it. I stood at the sink, and the creature nuzzled up to me, making a needy noise in its throat and looking up at me expectantly.

I turned on Copernicus. "How could any one creature need so much love?"

He shrugged. "It's their way."

I shivered, and nudged the beast away with the toe of my boot, which only made him beg louder.

Suddenly he gave a mournful howl.

"Oh, all right!" I spat, throwing down the carrot I was peeling and bending to give the creature a pat on the head. He rolled over happily and showed me his belly.

Copernicus laughed as I knelt to scratch the beast's stomach, and the dog chuffed happily and squirmed back and forth like a river eel.

"Disgusting animals!" I said, standing up.

But the dog had not had enough, and continued to mewl and beg, still on its back, looking up at me.

"He'll win you over yet," Copernicus said, getting up to help me finish the kitchen chores, before he spent the night with one experiment or other, or out under the stars with the telescope.

"He'll win you over yet," he repeated, scratching the dog behind the ears, which sent it into further paroxysms of ecstasy.

"I doubt it," I said, and shivered again.

AND SO AUTUMN TURNED TO WINTER. THE SNOWS came early but gently, in blanketing white storms with almost no wind. It was cold, but warm in the farmhouse. And, I was happy to discover, work on a farm did not end when the winter came. There was always something to do, good hard labor that made the days go fast.

Hector the dog became, naturally, my constant companion. And while I liked the beast no better, I did come to value his company, especially on those days when Copernicus stole off to the village down the hill to make a subtle inquiry for news both local and broader, or to post one of the letters that might eventually bring word to Newton, and through him to my father and grandmother, that I was safe. Rather than becoming more frequent, as the hand of Frane was pulled back from our area of Mars, that hand seemed to be tightening into a fist, as Frane took advantage of the reported disarray in the east to, miraculously, begin to build yet another army to dominate the planet.

And there began to appear in the sky at that time a strange, black airship, which flew very high overhead, and sent me hiding whenever it appeared.

• • •

"THAT'S IT, THEN," I SAID, AFTER THIS LATEST NEWS OF Frane was delivered. "I can wait no longer, Copernicus. I must leave, and try to pull the remnants of the Republic together."

"But you'll be caught! I told you, Frane now has permanent 'representatives' in the village. It's the same everywhere, from what I hear! It would be madness to leave now!"

"Then I'm mad. But I won't sit on my heels any longer. I must go. If I stay here, how long will it be before I'm finally discovered?"

"Only a matter of time, I'm afraid. Even today, old Roost was asking about the new worker he saw from the road . . ." He shook his head sadly.

It had begun to snow again, another storm with just a hint of wind. Gentle drifts were kissing the farmhouse and the barn.

"I will go with you," Copernicus said. Hector sat at his feet, looking at me with his needy eyes.

"You will not. I will do as we planned months ago, and follow the route you set out for me. But if you remember that plan, you had to stay, to divert attention from me."

He nodded, resigned. "I will continue to try to get word to Newton. If he contacts me, I'll tell him where to find you. But remember, you must keep to the route."

"I will."

We spent the rest of the night with packing and provisions, while poor Hector, for whom I finally did admit affection, bayed as if the two moons overhead were no more.

THE SNOW HAD CEASED WHEN I STEPPED OUT OF THE farmhouse and bade Copernicus good-bye. He did not hide his weeping, and I barely contained mine. I bent down to rub Hector behind the ears, then kissed Copernicus quickly on his furry cheek and turned and walked away.

To my surprise the dog followed me, and would not be convinced to turn back.

"It seems he has made his decision, too," Copernicus said.

"But he's your dog!"

Copernicus shook his head. "Only as long as he wanted to be. He wants someone else, now. Treat him well, Your Majesty."

Before I could protest, Copernicus had closed the door.

I looked down at the beast, whose tongue lolled and eyes were filled with anticipation and love. I had to admit that over these months he had, in his own strange way, helped me heal. I shrugged, and turned to the path that led from the farm and down the hill away from the village, to the rolling hills beyond.

"It seems I have a dog." I sighed.

⊰ CHAPTER 18 ⊱

THE SNOW RETURNED THAT NIGHT IN GREAT FORCE.

We had trudged barely five miles from the farm when the storm hit. It was sometime after midnight, when my horse immediately turned his flank to the wind, I knew we were in for it. Hector, who began to howl, tried to claw me from the saddle, but he needed no help. I climbed down as a sudden avalanche of snow hit us. The sky had whited out, and I could not see a foot in front of me.

"No chance to turn back, eh, boy?" I said, hugging the shivering dog, and I yanked my horse to the right, toward where I thought I had seen a clump of bushes.

I found the bushes by walking into them. They were thick tacra trees, with thin denuded branches that twisted together tightly. In the spring they would blossom with tiny red buds, but in the snowstorm they formed a sheltering canopy over us, though it was a tight fit.

As soon as we were settled, Hector insisted on running

off. I saw the faint and disappearing tracts of a rabbit or stoat, and he was compelled to investigate.

He returned sometime later, mournful at his failure to hunt properly.

"That's all right," I said, petting his head. It was amazing how soothing to me the motion was. The branches shook above us, but we were effectively in a little cave, snug if not warm. I pulled some food from my saddlebags and fed my two animals, then myself. I was suddenly weary. Overhead, and not three feet from where we sat, the storm raged, but I spread a blanket on the ground and curled down onto it.

In an instant I was asleep.

I AWOKE TO BLINDING LIGHT, REMARKABLY RE-freshed. Overhead, the snow caught in the branches of the tacra tree had partially melted and refrozen into mottled ice, throwing a prism of colors around our little cave. I pushed past the horse, who snuffled with impatience, and made my way outside.

The world was beautifully white.

Except by the sun, there was no way to tell north from south, east from west. There were no discernible landmarks. As quickly as the storm had come it had gone, leaving a thick blanket of white on every hill and valley to all horizons. I put my boot down into it and estimated that nearly a foot of snow had dropped during the night.

It would be impossible to travel cross-country with so much snow on the ground.

"Well, that's it," I said out loud. "We'll have to go back to Copernicus's farm and take our chances."

At that moment a tiny dot appeared in the sky in the east, and quickly grew into an airship. It was the strange craft I had seen over the farm in the past weeks. Almost jet-black in color, it looked like a huge, sleek, metal bird.

I shrank back into the mouth of my shelter and waited for it to pass on. But, instead, when it was almost overhead it began to circle, dropping down with each lap until I could plainly see its unmarked surface, and the darkened windows along its side and in its nose.

It drew lower, lower, circling like a bird of prey, and I suddenly felt certain that it was searching for me. A hundred thoughts flew through my brain—Copernicus had been taken prisoner, tortured, made to give up my position and heading; Frane had bribed and terrorized her way into finding out where I was . . .

The black bird swooped lower, and from its underbelly, long black skis descended in lieu of wheels, as the plane straightened and swooped down to a landing.

I retreated to my horse and drew my weapons, a sword to go with the dagger beneath my tunic.

I would not go without a fight, and Frane would not have me alive.

Hector began to growl as the black plane touched down at the far end of the valley and headed straight for me. On the ground it looked even more like a carrion bird, its black beak pointed at me.

It churned up vast amounts of snow in its wake and came to rest, its engines spinning down, not a hundred feet away.

There came a mechanical whining sound, and a door snicked open on its left side behind the cockpit, and lowered itself to the ground.

I stepped out of my hiding place to meet my enemy, my sword clutched tightly in my right hand, dagger in my left.

A figure descended the steps of the lowered gangway,

obscured for a moment by a burst of wind that threw its tunic across its face.

I moved forward and waited.

The figure stepped to the ground and stepped toward me.

My heart went into my throat.

I dropped my sword and dagger and began to run.

"Darwin!" I shouted, with every ounce of feeling in my body. "You live!"

PART TWO

THE SECOND BATTLE

⊰≣ CHAPTER 19 ≣⊱

"IT ISN'T MUCH OF A MYSTERY AT ALL," DARWIN IN-
sisted, his paw resting in both of my own.

We were truly snug and warm, a half mile off the
ground and flying like birds. The airship was comfortable,
but that had not kept Hector from raising holy hell when I
tried to get him on board. I would not have thought that
such a creature, weighing no more than fifteen pounds,
could exert so much backward pressure. It took both Darwin and I, laughing madly, to push the dog into the plane,
and to keep him there. He was sitting now on a seat in front
of us, making angry, sad noises in the back of his throat
and staring out the window with his big, moony eyes.

"Why didn't you let it be known that you had left Wells
before the concussion bomb was dropped?"

"To put it simply," Darwin answered, in a much more
patient manner than I remembered his having—he looked
older and, yes, a bit wiser than he had the last time I saw

him—"I was on a diplomatic mission with seven senators and had just reached Bradbury when the bomb struck Wells. In fact, nearly half the Senate and a third of the Assembly survived the attack. Many were in their home districts solidifying support for your monarchy and preventing any repeat of F'rar defections. We thought it best not to let Frane know just how much of the government had survived, Your Majesty."

"You must call me Clara!"

"As you know, *Your Majesty*, there are certain proper ways of address that must be adhered to—"

I squeezed his paw. "But when we are wed . . ."

He grinned. "Then you may call me 'King'! Or 'Mr. King,' if you like!"

I gazed into his eyes, his face, which I had thought never to see again.

"You must never leave my side, Darwin," I said. "Consider that a royal order."

His grin widened, then clouded. "There were times these past months when I thought I would never see you again, too. And then when word reached us from Copernicus that you were hiding in his home, and that sooner or later Frane or her monsters would find you . . ." His paw, still resting in the cup of both of my own, clenched into a fist.

"We will defeat her, Darwin," I said. "This time she cannot win."

His eyes had a faraway look.

"How is Newton?" I asked brightly, to bring him back.

Darwin sighed. "He is an old man and has become even older. He sees the destruction of Wells as the fault of the Science Guild. It weighs heavily on him, and I'm afraid you may be startled by his appearance."

"I will try not to show it. He is a great man."

"Yes, and the Republic may not last without his help."

Again he had that look—as if he was in another place.

I tightened my grip on his paw. "What is it, Darwin? What's wrong?"

"There are . . . other developments, Your Majesty."

"Tell me."

He shook his head. "I will let Newton tell you. It is his place."

For the rest of the flight we talked of many other things, some of them happy, such as our betrothal, and, of course, our coming nuptials.

Even Hector was content, barking at a flock of keesel birds, huge white-feathered beasts with wide, deep red beaks, flying in formation below us. The dog had finally found as much wonder in the sky as on the ground.

❧ CHAPTER 20 ❧

TO MY GREAT SURPRISE WE LANDED NOT IN THE CITY of Bradbury but at the base of Arsia Mons, the Science Guild stronghold. It seemed like five years had passed since I'd last been here, but it had only been a matter of months.

"Is Newton here?" I asked hopefully.

"Yes," Darwin said, averting his eyes.

When I sought more information he would only say, "You will see soon, Your Majesty."

The drafty corridors were as I remembered them, the various rooms the same, and when I traversed that last passageway with Darwin by my side the same old knot in my stomach formed.

"Must we see them?" I asked.

Darwin, his eyes still holding that strange look, said, "It is imperative."

Taking a deep breath, I pushed open the door to the blue chamber and went in.

At first I thought the two thrones were empty, but then in the gloom I could just make out two ghostly figures.

Then the voice of my grandmother called out, in strong if faint tones, with the usual faint air of amusement, "Come close, Queen Clara."

I nodded automatically and climbed the short steps to stand by her.

She was smiling, but I could almost see through her. On his own dais, my father looked even more insubstantial, staring into nothingness.

"What's wrong with you?" I asked.

"We're dying, child," Grandmother Haydn said, smiling sadly.

All of my fear of what they had become was gone in an instant, and I dropped to my knees in front of her. I tried to throw my hands around her legs, but my paws went right through the simulacrum.

"It is true," Newton's voice rasped from behind me. I turned to see his face shockingly wizened and wrinkled. He cleared his throat and coughed. "They will soon be gone. The regenerations are no longer working, and this will be their last time among us."

Something broke in me, a deep well I did not even know was there, and I began to sob.

"This cannot be!"

"Shhhh," Grandmother Haydn soothed, and for a moment I felt the faint touch of her paw on my head, as if a feather had brushed across it.

I looked up, and she was still smiling. I could not stop weeping. "As much as I've always dreaded coming here, I've always *loved* you! You're all I have!"

Again I felt the feather touch of her paw and looked

over to see my father staring at me, concentrating, a slight smile on his face.

"It's all right, daughter," he said, his voice sounding a thousand miles away. "This will be better for your grandmother and me."

"But you can't go! I'll be all alone!"

My father's eyes flickered toward Darwin for a moment. Again his ghostly smile. "That's not true, Clara."

He seemed to go away for a moment, but then the blue cloud that held his essence slowly coalesced once more.

"You're my family!"

"Soon you'll have your own family," Grandmother Haydn said gently. Her voice hardened, ever so slightly. "Now act like a queen and stand up. We have things to discuss."

I did so, banishing my tears.

Once again my father was staring at nothing, a beatific smile on his face.

Even as he weakened, my grandmother seemed to strengthen, her form becoming substantial.

"Newton will discuss this with you later, but Frane is making preparations for one last battle, in the north, near the ice cap on the plains of Arcadia Planitia. It is where she was all along, while you fought her shadow army at Valles Marineris. Her army is not huge, and it is a ragtag of outlaw clans, mercenaries, and criminals, most of them mad with mocra root. She has gone mad with it herself, we are told."

She took a deep breath and for a moment was unable to speak, and Newton, behind me, cleared his throat and continued, in his old man's voice, "The good news is that at the moment she has almost no F'rar backing. With some careful moves on your part, there will be no insurrection from within. She is making her last stand, Your Majesty. This time we can finally destroy her."

Something hardened within me.

"Then we will do it."

Grandmother Haydn resumed: "There are no more concussion bombs on all of Mars. She will fight a conventional battle. She can be beaten."

I saw the same hope in her own tired eyes that I held in my breast.

"Then this will be her last battle."

"Good."

As if all of her strength had gone into this meeting, she suddenly faded, looking even more insubstantial than when I had come in.

"There is one other thing," my father said. Even as my grandmother faded he seemed to draw that strength to himself.

I stood before him, and, to my surprise, he would not meet my gaze.

"What is it, Father?"

"Your mother . . ."

"What of her?" A sudden horrid thought came to me. Almost desperately I asked, "I was told she survived the attack on Wells."

"Yes, she did."

"What, then?"

"She is with Frane."

It was as if a thunderbolt had gone through me. "This cannot be!"

"Her own . . . madness was caused by mocra root, administered to her by we know not who, a confederate of Frane within the palace. The same spy, we believe, poisoned General Xarr with an overdose of the same drug.

Before the capital was bombed, your mother was spirited away, and we know that she is now in Frane's hands."

Rage grew within me, but I held it in check as I saw my father's spectral form begin to weep.

"I loved her so . . ." he said, covering his face with his paws.

"I will bring her home safely," I said.

"If you were to do that," my father said, reaching out—and through—my own paw with his own, "what is happening to me would be a peaceful end."

"I will get her back, Father," I said, gritting my teeth. "I vow it."

My father's form faded, flickered, came wavering back.

Newton was behind me, his paw drawing me gently away.

"You must let them rest," he whispered.

"No! Leave me alone with them for a moment!"

As if my command had been a gunshot, both Newton and Darwin withdrew from the room, closing the door gently behind them.

I faced the only two forms who had dominated my nightmares and my waking life since I was a kit. As much as I had always dreaded the place, I had longed desperately for the company and wisdom of these two beings. And here before me they were fading, dying, forever.

"I will never forget you," I said, and again tears threatened to come.

My father said nothing, only nodding. My grandmother mustered all of her strength and, for just a moment, became substantial. She reached out with her paws and drew me to her, holding me. I could have sworn I felt her beating heart against my breast.

"You are the hope of all of Mars," she said, "and I leave

knowing that everything your father and I hoped for, and my father before me, will be fulfilled in you."

She kissed the top of my head, a substantial gesture.

"Go now," she said, and I felt her embrace melt away around me.

At the door, I looked back, and they were nearly gone, only flickering shades inhabiting their thrones and staring into nothingness.

I walked out, and met Newton and Darwin in the hallway waiting for me.

"Isn't there anything you can do?" I pleaded.

Newton shook his wizened head. "Very soon they will be gone. I am sorry, Your Majesty."

I fell into Darwin's arms.

"This burden is too much!" I said.

He let me cry for a few moments, then he whispered in my ear, in as light and tender a voice as he could muster, "But you will have me at your side. Always."

THAT EVENING, AS WE PREPARED TO TAKE OFF FOR the city of Bradbury, word came from Newton that my father and grandmother were gone forever.

⊰ CHAPTER 21 ⊱

NO COMMITTEE GREETED US AT THE OUTSKIRTS OF Bradbury when we landed, nor was one expected. As Darwin had explained to me, Frane had put a mighty price on my head, and money did strange things even to staunch loyalists. We were spirited from our black airship into a black motorcar, its windows darkened, and taken to the heart of the city, much less grand than Wells but still a pretty place, where the government-in-exile had been established.

When I entered the hall, a smaller, drab version of the grand Assembly Hall, I was happy to see so many familiar faces. I was greeted from both sides of the aisle by senators and Assembly members alike, some close friends whom I thought I would never see again. As I climbed to the dais to speak I looked out at many unfamiliar faces, also, but immediately sought to make them feel at ease.

"It may sound strange, in these troubled times, to say

that this is a happy day for the Republic," I began, "but that is exactly what it is. For free government does still exist, a united Mars still does exist. Many of you are newly elected to your posts, having come to office under sad and dire circumstances, but do not think that you are in any way 'substitute' senators or fill-in members of the Assembly. You have been appointed, or, in some cases, elected, by the people of Mars—and it is the people of Mars we represent. As long as the people exist, a free Mars will exist. And, after this final battle, Mars will, once and for all, be free of the forces that seek to destroy it.

"As I said, these are happy times. Many of you lost loved ones in the dastardly bombing of Wells, as did I. These losses should make our resolve even greater. And even with such a dire blow, we still sit here today and plan our future, and that of our kits. Soon we will embark on a great mission, but today, I say yet again, is a happy day.

"For it is the day your queen weds."

My words had the desired effect. I had known this first meeting with the women and men who were the backbone of my rule was important, and what better way to present myself to them—to many, for the first time—than as a betrothed queen.

I left the dais, then, and a page announced that there would be a wedding ceremony followed by festivities that evening—which meant, of course, that I immediately went into a kind of shock.

That afternoon was a bittersweet affair. Darwin, making his own preparations, was nowhere to be seen; but Thomas, who had accompanied us back from Arsia Mons, was a great help and comfort. He joined me with his niece Rebecca, my lady-in-waiting, who had happily survived the last melee at Valles Marineris and made her way with the remains of the army to Bradbury.

"You know," Thomas said, and for the first time I noticed that he was a half pace beyond middle age, his fur greying and his step not quite as brisk as it had always been, "I was at both your father's and your grandmother's wedding—though I was only a kit when Queen Haydn was married. My uncle, Rebecca's grandfather, who later betrayed Haydn"—and now, for a brief moment, bitterness entered his voice—"was her closest adviser, and I was allowed to attend the ceremony, which was with an army on the march." He smiled at the distant memory. "I had my first taste of wine that evening, and my first dance—with the fat cook Brenda. She was a wonderful woman."

"It was a shame she was lost when Wells was bombed."

"It certainly was," Rebecca chimed in. She was aiding the bevy of seamstresses who buzzed around me like sand hornets as I stood on a box, putting pins into my white gown and taking them out again.

"Many good people were lost when Wells was bombed," Thomas said. He shook his head. "I look at Newton and see myself in a few years. There has been too much strife for too long."

"I agree."

Thomas caught the irony in my voice and looked up from his own thoughts. "I'm sorry, Your Majesty. Of course you know these things." He put a claw to his chin, pensive. "You father's wedding was a fine affair. We were at Olympus Mons, and the gypsy kings Radion and Miklos were present, and there was much wine drinking and dancing, I can tell you! Your father and mother were so happy. And now when I think of what's happened to your mother, her own betrayal . . ."

He shook his head.

"We will save her and find out who the betrayer is," I said.

His face darkened. "I have made it my personal mission, Your Majesty."

And then, as if by an act of will, he lifted his gloomy thoughts from his shoulders and told me only happy things about my grandmother, and, especially, about my father and mother in happier times.

When the seamstresses were finished I struck a pose, and said to Thomas and Rebecca, "Well?"

"It is a magnificent gown, Your Majesty!" Rebecca said brightly.

"It certainly is," Thomas seconded.

"I think so, too," I replied. "You are finished, ladies. No more pins. And I thank you."

The seamstresses bowed and withdrew, and so did Thomas and Rebecca, and I stood regarding myself in the full-length mirror before me. I certainly did not look like myself, all curves and white flowing lines with a chaste veil. The scar I had suffered on the way to Valles Marineris had faded. In a way I was disappointed, since I had worn it in Xarr's honor. I longed to return to my tunic and boots and stretch my arms, but I lingered for a moment on the strange vision before me.

I actually looked like a queen.

All you have to do now is act like one, I thought.

Then I did remove the gown, and let the seamstresses back in to work their magic with needle and thread where pins had been.

THE CEREMONY, THE CELEBRATION, THE ENTIRE evening went by in a blur. I was handled like a prize horse, pulled around by the reins from here to there and back again. There was much wine drinking, but I did not much like the taste of the stuff; and much dancing, though I already knew that I could not so much as take a step in time to the music; and many paws to shake, and many lips to kiss my ring, and many presents I would never open but give to the poor, and much pomp and formality, which I discovered—as I had feared—that I had no taste for. The festivities were not as I had imagined them. As for Darwin, I saw him barely at all, for he was mired in his own bog of formalities as the new king. There were papers to sign, and wax seals to be pressed with a signet ring—though we were not even together even for that!

It was with a very happy heart that I was finally able to steal away from my own wedding party, long after midnight, as the music and wine were still in abundance, but my own patience was not. I had not seen my husband for more than an hour, and would not have been surprised to find him in one of his famous hiding spots, just to get away from the noise and bustle.

In my white gown, which felt more constricting by the moment, I stole out to the gardens behind the Assembly Hall, which had been cleared of its chairs for the party. The laughter and drunken bravado faded to a washing murmur behind me, and the stars were out in abundance overhead. The air was filled with the perfume of flowers. I looked up at the sky and thought of Copernicus, and of our adventures together. I hoped he was well, and resolved to send for him when it was safe.

I felt rather than heard a movement behind me—and had been grabbed before I could react.

Paws encircled me, pulling me tight and forcing me to turn around.

I began to fight, then saw Darwin's face before me, grinning from ear to ear.

"My queen!" he whispered, kissing me fiercely on the mouth.

It was as if hard stone had suddenly melted, and I turned to a soft thing in his arms. We dropped to all fours and nuzzled, and then we kissed.

The heavens were forgotten, and a new kind of heaven opened up for me, right there in the garden, with the night's perfume around us.

Later, as I gathered the ruins of the white gown around me and stole to our wedding chamber for a proper sleep and more, I caught sight of blue Earth high overhead, a beacon.

It still had that strange pull on me, and I thought again of Copernicus, and his paper that claimed Earth as the origin of the Old Ones—but then Darwin whispered fiercely in my ear, "To bed!" and all thoughts of others were banished to the wind.

◄ CHAPTER 22 ►

TWO DAYS LATER FOUND ME ON THE MOST BIZARRE trip of my life. Partway by airship and then by motorcar, through gates of thick iron and massive stone towers to either side manned by grim gunners, across a courtyard where we parked and I left the motorcar, attended by five burly guards who brought me through another, smaller but even thicker iron gate, which protested on its rusted hinges like a yowling feline, then yet a third gate, where a stone-faced guard, fully the tallest and widest feline I had ever seen, looked down at me and bowed, saying in a rumbling voice that sounded like caught thunder, "Your Majesty. He waits for you."

I thanked him, then was let into a stone building, cold and damp and nearly without light, and led down a long corridor passing empty cell upon empty cell until I stood before the last one on the left, which was narrow and dim.

Somewhere there was a steady, slow drip I already found annoying.

My massive companion turned to me, and said, "We will stay with you," indicating the five guards and himself.

"No, you will leave me alone."

"Then you must not enter the cell, Your Majesty."

"Nonsense. Open it and let me in."

"But—"

"This moment, gaoler."

He gave a deep sigh. "Very well."

With a low growl of disapproval in the back of his throat that sounded like a breaking storm, he unlocked the barred door with a great key, which made a huge *click*, and pulled the door wide.

Before I could enter he stuck his head into the gloomy space and said in an unfriendly, deep hiss, "If one hair is disturbed on her head, I will break you in half myself."

A low chuckle came from within, and I saw a figure shift in the dimness.

The gaoler stepped fully aside and let me enter.

To my surprise he locked the door after me.

"Rules," he explained in his basso rumble.

"Of course. Now let us be."

"As you wish."

The gaoler moved off, and five guards following reluctantly.

I turned to the figure in the gloom.

"Hello, Grandfather," I said, trying to make my voice sound without inflection.

The low chuckle came again, and now my grandfather, Senator Misst, traitor to the Republic, rose fully out of the dimness into sight.

To my surprise he looked much as I had remembered him on my one and only other visit there, when I was a kit.

My mother had taken me, before the onset of her madness and over the objections of my father, of course. But she had wanted me to meet my grandfather, as much for his sake as for mine. He had been severe, well-groomed—but when he saw me then there came a glint to his eye, and he had smiled, something my mother later told me he never did.

He was smiling again—still well-groomed, still severe even in his prison rags. He had moved to the end of his cot and sat looking up at me expectantly.

"You look a little like me," he said, not without some self-satisfaction.

"I always thought so," I replied.

He patted the cot next to him. "Come, sit beside me. I won't bite."

"I know that. I've come for your help."

"Oh?" He cocked an eyebrow. "I thought you came merely to visit your old grandfather on his birthday."

"Is it your birthday?"

"No." The low chuckle again. "It's just that, I thought you might come."

"Why?"

"Because you need me to keep the F'rar in line, while you finish Frane off once and for all. I may be in gaol, Clara, but my mind isn't."

"I was told you were one of the sharpest senators ever to walk the floor of the Hall."

"Oh, yes."

"You were also a traitor."

"Yes, again."

"Why?"

His smile faded. "Do you have to ask that? Is there so little F'rar blood in you that you have to ask?"

"I want to hear it from you."

He stood up, and the veins in his neck stood out, and he pounded one clenched paw into his open one.

"Because we are the natural rulers of Mars! The F'rar were the first great race of felines! All other clans were inferior, and always will be!" He turned to me and his face was filled with pleading.

"Don't you see this, Clara? You have done a great thing—become Queen of Mars—but now you must use that position to make the F'rar the true rulers of Mars—now and forever!"

I stood. "I thought I could speak with you," I said, trying desperately to control my inner rage, "but I see that you still don't understand."

He took hold of me. "Listen to me, granddaughter! You are queen! All you need do is declare your F'rar blood, to the exclusion of all else, and the deed is done! All the F'rar will rise to support you! Frane is history—you are the future!"

"Is that madness in your eyes I see?" I asked.

"It is allegiance to my race!"

I pulled away from him, and walked to the door of the cell.

I turned around, and said, quietly, "Frane has kidnapped my mother."

"What!"

"It is true. One of Frane's confederates slowly poisoned her for months, driving her mad with mocra, and now Frane holds her."

He was pensive. "You know I hate your mother for putting me here."

"I know that."

"But I love her, and always will, because she is my daughter."

I waited, and finally, in the gloom, he spoke again, quietly. "I will help you, of course."

"That's what I thought you'd say."

His coarse chuckle returned. "You know you remind me too much of myself."

"I was counting on that, Grandfather."

He broke out into a loud cackle of a laugh. "Oh, I do believe I both like *and* love you, Clara!"

"Thank you." I approached him, and held my signet ring out in the dimness. "From now on you will address me as 'my queen.'"

His eyes were steady on me, unwavering in the twilight of his cell.

"And," I continued, "once you kiss this ring, you will have pledged fealty unto death to me, and to the Republic I stand for. You do realize that, Grandfather?"

"Yes," he said. His eyes had not left my face, and he made no move to bend his head and kiss my ring.

"And you realize that if you were to break that oath of fealty, your death would be swift, and certain?"

"I have never broken an oath."

"I know that."

He bent his head, and kissed my ring.

"I have never broken an oath until now," he continued, lifting his head. His smile, a hard one, returned. "I once swore allegiance to Frane—but now, for what she has done to my daughter, she will die."

"I know that before becoming a senator you were a great general, is that not true?"

"It is true."

"Then I will ask you to be a great general again. We will march against Frane within the week, and you will be at the head of my army with me."

"It will be my pleasure to serve you. And, of course,

you sought my fealty knowing that it would quell any lingering unrest in the F'rar clan. By securing me you have secured the F'rar. Clever girl."

"Gaoler!" I shouted, and at once the huge lumbering feline, jangling his keys, returned, standing before me expectantly.

"Let us out," I said. "This man has been pardoned."

⫷ CHAPTER 23 ⫸

A LONG WEEK OF PREPARATION. MY GRANDFATHER proved to be even more able than I had hoped, and wasted no time in getting our army of three thousand ready for war. Ours would be a cold-weather campaign, and each feline was outfitted with proper clothing and schooled in the arts of winter fighting.

I left the army in General Misst's capable hands and traveled to the east with Newton by motorcar to examine one of the revived oxygenation stations. My king came with us, and we made the trip a honeymoon of sorts. It was beautiful country, farmland and junto tree forests all in the first bloom of spring.

"It's odd that we'll be leaving spring behind to fight in perpetual winter," I remarked, and Newton concurred.

"I've been to the pole, and it's a horrid place," he replied. "At the height of summer the temperature never rises above twenty degrees Fahrenheit. At this time of year it will be even colder."

"It's a fitting place for Frane," I said.

Gloom descended on our party until we stopped an hour later for a picnic lunch. We were on a hill overlooking a green and red valley. A thick wood sat at our back. The pink sky was dotted with wisps of clouds, and the noon sun was warm. There was the faint smell of newly bloomed flowers in the air. I thought of the night of my wedding, when that same odor had wafted through the garden, and how Darwin found me there . . .

He must have been thinking the same thing, for he was grinning at me. "Would you like to take a walk, Your Majesty?" he asked slyly.

We stole off, leaving Newton and our guards to set a lunch, and found a spot in the woods.

"Listen," Darwin whispered, and I heard nothing but the rustle of new leaves overhead and our own breathing.

"Isn't it marvelous?" Darwin said. "Nothing! No barking orders of generals, or the drone of airships or motor-cars . . ."

"I wish it was always like this."

"Yes . . ." Darwin said, and took me in his arms.

Later, before we returned to Newton, Darwin looked into my eyes, and said, "I love you more every day, Clara. I don't know how, but it's true."

I kissed him once more, and we held hands like the young lovers we were.

WE CAMPED THAT NIGHT UNDER THE STARS, WHICH once more made me think of Copernicus, and the next day, before morning was spent, when we topped a sandy rise, having left the dotted green pastureland and forests of

Daedalia Planum for the rougher, redder, rockier landscape of Arabia Terra, who did I see waiting for us at the gates of the oxygenation station but little Copernicus himself!

I ran to him and drew him into my arms, which embarrassed him greatly.

"Copernicus!" I cried. "How did you get here!"

Newton, who had seemed younger and happier since the beginning of this happy trip, chimed in, "I wanted it to be a surprise, Your Majesty."

"It is! And a wonderful one!"

"Well, I must say I'm pleased myself," Copernicus added, and I laughed.

"How did you get away?"

"Actually, Newton sent his black airship for me," Copernicus explained. "It was my first ride, and I must say it was fascinating."

"After hearing about his aptitude from you, Your Majesty," Newton said, "I decided that Copernicus here was much too valuable not to have with me."

Copernicus threw out his chest proudly. "I'm now a member of the Science Guild!" he boasted.

Newton smiled kindly. "Though self-taught, he has a remarkable aptitude for just about anything he puts his mind to. And I must say I was fascinated by the paper from the Old Ones that he found."

"Is it genuine?" I asked.

Newton scratched his chin. "It may be. It is a fascinating idea, that the Old Ones came from Earth."

Copernicus broke in, "I have a few ideas about the station here, to improve the efficiency . . ."

He and Newton went off, arm and arm, nodding over technical terms that meant nothing to me, while Darwin and I followed them through the gates under a stone archway and into the station itself.

It was a huge, dilapidated structure made up of many other elements: rows of what looked like bunkhouses and other freestanding buildings. Towering over everything were three huge stone smokestacks, one of which was intact, the other two crumbling. They pointed to the sky like broken fingers. There was debris and an air of quiet abandonment. But from somewhere I heard the faint whine of hidden machinery and a vague chuffing noise.

Copernicus turned and gestured happily. "Come into the main building!" he said, skipping ahead with Newton in tow.

They disappeared into the largest structure, which looked like a gigantic warehouse or hangar.

We followed, our boots echoing on the debris-strewn floor as we entered under another archway and open door. The space was filled with offices, machines of every sort, pillars that disappeared through the high ceiling overhead.

Newton let Copernicus run on ahead, and waited for us. He was studying the floor around him, his eyes roving over a pile of what looked like a makeshift fence or fortification.

"Your grandmother and I fought a battle with Baldies here," he said to me, when Darwin and I had joined him. "It was Haydn's first battle." He pointed behind us to an open door. "We all almost died in that room, barricaded against the horde after our line was broken here. Your grandfather Kerl saved us."

He looked as if he were seeing ghosts.

"That seems as if it were two lifetimes ago," he said.

"Newton!" Copernicus called, his voice echoing from the other side of the building. "You must see this! I've gotten eight more percent out of the main generator!"

Newton's eyes brightened, and he ambled off to consult with his new protégé.

• • •

LATER, AS WE MADE CAMP FOR THE NIGHT IN THE same room in which Newton and my grandmother had fought their battle so long ago, Newton explained the importance of the structure.

"This station," he said, his face looking even younger in the glow of our lamps, as we sat in a circle as if around a campfire, "and the others like it, must be brought gradually back into operation in the next two years if life on Mars is to survive. I am already heartened by the progress we've made. And Copernicus, here," he said, as Copernicus's chest once again swelled, "is proving invaluable in the effort. Already this station is putting out twenty-five percent of the oxygen it needs to. The repairs of necessary equipment have gone slowly, but, importantly, we are learning the technology. We will be able to fabricate the new parts we need, and, eventually, I think we will be able to manufacture new oxygenation stations as needed. But it is imperative that these structures we have now be put into operation, or we will never have the chance to build new ones. My one concern is that, because of war, we have not been able to guard the major stations as I had hoped. If even one of them were destroyed, we would be doomed."

He took a deep breath. "But I am happy to report this evening, Your Majesty, that the dire news I gave you months ago is dire no longer. Copernicus and I have come up with a schedule and a plan this afternoon, and, if things go as I now think they will, we will indeed be able to replenish the atmosphere of the planet."

He beamed—looking for the first time since I had returned like his old self.

"That's marvelous!" Darwin said. He produced from somewhere a bottle of wine, and we opened it and drank a toast to Newton, and to little Copernicus, and to ourselves and our planet. Overcoming my own distaste for wine, I even joined in the celebration.

That night we slept peacefully, in a place free of Baldies, content in our accomplishments, a little lighter of heart, safe in the bosom of a place that would save our world.

It was a last peaceful interlude in what would be, all too soon, a very dark time.

⊰ CHAPTER 24 ⊱

AND SO WE PREPARED FOR WAR.

Once again I stood before a mirror, but this time not in my wedding gown but in a ridiculous full-length white fur cloak, which made me look huge and weighed as much as I did.

"It's hot as blazes in this thing!" I protested.

"You won't complain when the temperature drops to ten below zero," my grandfather said, smiling knowingly. "It's designed for movement as well as utility. And with the red F'rar sash—"

"I told you before, Grandfather—I will wear no symbol of any clan! Only the colors of all Mars."

He tilted his head in a bow. "As you wish. But you cannot fault an old man for trying."

Growling with displeasure, I pulled the monstrous cloak off, as General Misst withdrew to attend to other matters. I saw Thomas, an almost constant presence these days, glowering in the mirror's reflection across the room.

"What is it now, Thomas? You never smile anymore."

"That is true," he said enigmatically.

"You see demons in sunlight. Trouble where there is none. You skulk around the halls like a wraith during the day, and Creator knows what you do at night. You're like a live ghost, Thomas. You worry me."

He moved his head in a "whatever-you-say" gesture.

After a moment he asked, quietly, "Will my niece Rebecca be along soon?"

"Yes, of course. It is time for my noon meal. Will you join me?"

"No, thank you. I have business to attend to. But I will stay until Rebecca arrives."

As if on cue, the door flew open, and my lady-in-waiting arrived, bearing a tray. This was a new duty for her. She also led Hector by his leash. She gave a cursory nod to her uncle and set the tray down on the table set by the window.

At the sight of the dog I dropped my white fur on the floor and rushed to greet his slobbering form. He was straining at the leash and whining, and when Rebecca let go he leapt into my arms and nearly knocked me over.

"Good heavens!" I shouted, holding him up by the front paws and examining him. "What have they been feeding you! You're twice the size you were at Copernicus's farm!"

His fat belly was proof of that, and when I dropped him to the floor he walked around dragging it as if it were a pouch beneath him.

"There's no way on Mars you can travel with me now!" I said, laughing. "You will have to stay here and get even fatter!"

He barked, and pawed at the ground, his ears flopping, and looked up at me with his sad eyes.

"No, I'm sorry, this is how it must be!"

"Rebecca," Thomas said quietly, "remove the dog, please."

"But I've just seen him!" I protested. "Here, let me give him something to eat—"

Thomas was there, gently staying my hand. "Please see Hector later, Your Majesty. We have important matters to discuss."

"Very well . . ."

Reluctantly, I allowed Rebecca to remove the whining beast, who pawed and yowled as he was put outside the door and given over to a guard.

"You are tasting and handling the queen's food now, I understand?" Thomas asked innocently, as Rebecca returned. He stood beside his niece at the table.

"Oh, yes," Rebecca said brightly. "Her regular attendants are being outfitted to ride with her, so I offered—"

Thomas reached around her and put an extended claw into my tea, bringing it quickly to his lips.

"It is mocra," he said, his voice filled with sadness, and before I could protest, he had drawn his dagger and thrust it deep into his niece's breast.

She let out a startled cry, as blood flowed from the deep and fatal wound.

Her uncle lowered her gently to the floor, his eyes never leaving hers.

"Why did you do this?" he asked gently. "Was there not enough shame already on our family?"

"I—" Rebecca gasped, her eyes suddenly bright with fury. "I did it to avenge my grandfather! To avenge his murder!"

"Jeffrey was not murdered, he was rightfully executed. As you have now been."

Thomas shook his head slowly, even as she closed her eyes, and her last breath escaped. He laid her body flat on the floor and stood up, his dagger dangling from his hand.

"She was a fool among so many fools," he said, his voice suffused with melancholy. "She drove your mother slowly mad with poison, and assassinated poor old general Xarr. She was in league with the mercenaries at Valles Marineris, and provided them with the mocra that incapacitated your army. I began to suspect when she returned unharmed from the battle. And then, when she did all she could to become keeper of your food, I knew. She was a gentle soul, and could never use a blade. Poison was her way. And today she would have assassinated you." He sighed heavily. "All for a fool's idea that her grandfather was some kind of patriot! He was a traitor who assassinated your grandmother for a foolish idea, and brought a curse upon all of us."

He paused, and his eyes were filled with infinite sadness. "This is a burden that cannot be borne, Your Majesty. My family is now forever in disgrace. Her grandfather was an assassin, and she the same. Her father and mother, as you know, are long dead, and I brought her into your service. I am as guilty as she. King Sebastian is gone, so there is no need for me. I am the last of my family. It must end here."

"Thomas—!"

Before I could stop him, he thrust his dagger into his own breast, at the heart, and fell instantly dead at my feet.

For a moment I stood frozen in shock. Then I knelt and smoothed the fur from his troubled brow. His face relaxed into a kind of peace I had never seen in him.

"Fear not, old friend," I said quietly. "Because of you,

because of your dedication and the service you gave my father for so long, your family name will always be remembered with pride on Mars."

He had fallen onto my new white fur cloak, which I had dropped on the floor, and there were now the red stains of his blood on its pristine surface.

I would wear that cloak, I resolved, with pride, and with the blood of this great and tragic feline intact.

⊰ CHAPTER 25 ⊱

WE MARCHED ON THE LAST DAY OF SPRING. THOUGH it was warm, and I sweated like an ox in my white fur, there was a smell, the faintest of odors, of cold climes to come. My grandfather, resplendent in red and, after much arguing, without his F'rar crest, rode beside me. He had done wonders with a makeshift army, turning a mass of cynical old veterans and new recruits—farmers and manufacturing men who had never held a sword, fired an arrow, or handled a scarce firearm—into a cohesive fighting force. There was discipline in this trained army, and I now led them proudly.

My initial thoughts of cold were, of course, an illusion, and we spent the first week marching north through one of the worst early heat waves on record. My white fur was packed away in favor of a light pink tunic. Even that was too much in the heat and, on the seventh day of the heat wave, I abandoned it in favor of a simple white cotton blouse. Many of the soldiers were stripped to their skivvies, and the usual army complaints were in order:

"Cold my arse! Feels like hell it does!"

"I doubt there'll be any ice cap when we get there. Must be melted clean away by now!"

"You don't need to cook your food—just hold it in your hand, and the sun'll do the job!"

And so on.

But the heat did not last, and somewhere in the middle of the second week the unusual temperatures began to give way to the inevitable cool of the northern spring. Skivvies were covered with tunics, then neck wraps, and, finally, coats and cloaks and random wrappings. By the third week of march the complaints had changed:

"Cold as hell it is!"

"The whole bleeding planet must be one damned ice cap!"

"Look! My dinner's frozen before it reached m' lips!"

And as the climate changed, so did the landscape. What had been gentle dunes spotted with green hills and blue lakes turned to windswept red vistas, white-frosted ponds and an angry, bare pink sky streaked with thin, high, cold-looking clouds. The air huffed vapor when I breathed. My fingers felt stiff, and the glare off the occasional patches of ice hurt my eyes.

By then there were ice hills in front of us, which proved slippery to our mounts, and farther on the Northern Cap itself, which grew gradually in the distance from a line a bit higher at the horizon to a climbing wall of glaring blue-white, which ate up more of the northern sky every day.

It snowed once at the beginning of the fourth week, a gentle reminder of things to come, and again a bit harder two days later. There was no wind to speak of, which was a blessing; but it came during the third storm, which drove us to our tents. Scouts reported that Frane's army was a week's march away, entrenched on the cap itself, and that we would either have to make a perilous climb to reach her, or go out of our way by marching for four days to find gentler slopes to the west. I resolved that we would cross that bridge when we reached it.

It was well that Darwin was a good Jakra player, for we spent nearly three days entrenched while the wind howled and intermittent snows blew. The temperature had dropped precipitously, and I blessed the white fur cloak I wore for keeping me as warm as I wished.

"Bah," my husband said, losing his third game in a row and throwing his cards on the ground.

"You're sick of Jakra?"

"I'm sick of waiting. Why don't we march?"

"You're always too restless, Darwin. And why do you disappear for much of the day while we *do* march?"

He looked at me slyly. "I'm looking for a new wife."

"I doubt it." I laughed.

"You know why I disappear," he said. "It's what I do. I'm always looking for a place to hide. It's what I've always done."

"Have you found anything interesting?"

"Always," he said. But he did not elaborate, for he had jumped across the mass of Jakra cards to wrestle me to the ground and kiss me.

FINALLY, A DAY LATER, THE STORM LIFTED AND WE resumed our march. The sky had cleared, and it was a fierce bracing cold day, with no wind at all. We traveled up a long, gradual snowy slope that led to a ledge. Below us stretched an ice valley whose blue glare was startling in the sun. We moved down a series of switchbacks to reach the floor.

Once again Darwin had left my side, which always made me uneasy. But that was his way. Sometimes he might be gone for a day or two at a time—but always, when he returned, my heart leapt like a mare's. Often when I asked him where he had been he would shake his head, or mumble something about "hiding spots, just in case,"— but that day he returned in midafternoon with a wide grin on his face. With him was an impossibly tall feline, nearly as wide in girth as the gaoler from Robinson prison.

"This is Miklos, a real gypsy king!" Darwin announced. Even at full-grown height, my husband came up barely to the fellow's chest.

"And this is *little fish*!" Miklos cried, lifting Darwin as if he were a bundle of clothes and holding him high in the air.

My husband laughed like a kit, and explained to me, "He used to do this to me when I first met him, when I was barely out of kithood!"

"He tried to run and hide from me, the scamp, but I caught him up— just like a fish—ha!"

Miklos put Darwin down, and the two of them wrestled and hugged in a most affectionate manner.

Suddenly Miklos was down on one knee before me, and kissing my ring.

"As a gypsy king," he said seriously, "and like my brother Radion before me, land rest his soul, I pledge myself and my people to you, my queen, just as we did to your father King Sebastian. Long live Queen Clara!"

Before I could protest he had stood up, taken me by the scruff of the neck, and held me high in the air, showing me like a rag doll to my own troops, who howled with laughter, and his own people, who had materialized behind him and began to cheer.

I could do nothing else but laugh, and when the huge gypsy had set me down, saying, "I hope I have not embarrassed you, my queen—it is our way," I merely adjusted my cloak, and said, "Of course not. Welcome, King Miklos."

"He will fight with us!" Darwin announced. "He has a hundred men, but they will fight like a thousand. He's been tracking us for days!"

"You knew this?" I said to my husband in surprise.

"Oh, yes. But Miklos didn't know I was following *him*!"

"Ha!" Miklos said again, and lifted Darwin up once more. "Little fish has always been quiet, and sneaky, and wise!"

SUCH AS COULD BE PREPARED, WE HAD A CELEBRAtion that night. Doubly so, when Miklos learned that Darwin and I were wed, and he took the two of us by the scruffs of our necks and marched around the entire camp, announcing our good fortune. Darwin, when let loose, introduced me to the gypsy band's cook, named Tyron, a sour-faced fellow who beamed in my husband's presence.

"I taught him everything he knows about cooking, when we both traveled with Radion," Tyron said.

At the mention of Radion—who I knew had died fighting by my father's side—both of them went silent.

I lightened the mood by saying, "Then it is you, Tyron, whom I have to blame for my husband's bland preparation of meals?"

"Bah!" he said, beginning to get angry before he saw the joke, and Darwin broke into laughter.

"She loves my cooking—and all because of you!" he said, slapping the gypsy cook on the back.

The sour-faced man smiled. "Then I will prepare a special feast for you tonight, my queen!"

"I shall look forward to it," I said, and left the two cooks to plan their meal.

I found Miklos, or, should I say, he found me. He loomed up before me as I was entering my tent, and I invited him in. He readily agreed, and produced, when we were comfortable inside, a huge skin of wine.

"I don't like wine," I declared, when he offered me the skin, which looked to be made of goatskin.

"What!" he cried. "Then you have never been offered real wine. Taste this, please."

I could not refuse a king's offer, and so brought the skin's tip to my lips and tried it.

It was like honey in my throat.

I took a second sip, and a third.

Miklos nearly grabbed the skin from my paws and took a great long drink, pulling the skin's tip away from his mouth so that the golden red wine squirted in from nearly a foot away.

"*That* is how to drink wine!" he announced, handing the skin back to me. "Try it!"

My first try resulted in wine everywhere but in my mouth, but soon I had mastered the trick, and the concoction, like melted butter in the throat and warm in the belly, had begun to work its magic on me.

"Enough!" Miklos said, taking the skin gently from me and putting it aside. "There will be more later. Now we talk."

I felt slightly light-headed, and happy.

"By all means, talk," I said, dreamily.

"Your Majesty, I am serious now," Miklos grumbled,

and I pushed the effects of the wine aside and met his eyes squarely. "These are the facts as we know them. There will be others to meet up with us in the coming days, including the pirate Pelltier and his men from the west."

At this news I was startled, for no one had even sought to call on the old pirate's allegiance. To me his was a picture in a history book. He had helped my grandmother Haydn when she was hiding from Frane after the destruction of the First Republic, and I was surprised to hear that he was still alive.

"This is marvelous news."

"He brings troops and supplies, and his men have already been harassing Frane's outward positions. He is a scamp, but he will be a great help, and has pledged undying friendship to you."

I nodded my pleasure.

"There are others, also, who will fight with us. The Quiff, who have been friends to the gypsies for ages past, have been patrolling the underground caverns that lead to this place. Many of them are beneath us as we speak."

As if prodded, I looked down at the floor of my tent.

"And then there are also remnants of Mighty's people, the nomads from the middle and northern latitudes, who will fight, though they are not many these days, I'm afraid."

Another history lesson—Mighty had held my grandmother for ransom and ended up dying in her cause.

"There are also," Miklos continued, "the local clans, some of them outsiders but most already pledged to the Republic, who will naturally join the cause and lend support."

"This is very gratifying."

"Yes," Miklos said, but the joyless tone of his voice made me listen to his next words very carefully.

"That is the good news, Your Majesty. All of Mars, except the evil raiders, who as you know are mercenaries and have taken to Frane's army for coin, and the mad Baldies, are on your side."

"How many raiders does Frane command?"

"Two thousand. And there are two thousand more Baldies, held in thrall by mocra root and wild beyond madness. She commands upwards of five thousand troops all told. We will approach that number, easily."

"Then what is your concern, Miklos?" I asked.

He was silent for a moment. "Two things . . ."

I waited until my patience ran out, and then said, "And they are?"

"Yourself, for one, Your Majesty."

"Ah," I said, leaning over to pull the wineskin to me. I took a short quaff and wiped my lips. "You talk not of the danger to me, but rather of my . . . let us say, ineptitude in battle at Valles Marineris?"

Still studying the floor, he nodded. "Let us call it . . . inexperience."

"My grandfather, General Misst, commands the troops now, King Miklos. I have learned my lesson and am here mostly to inspire."

"That is good," he mumbled, and, realizing the possible insult, looked at me in apology. "That is to say . . ."

I held out the wineskin and smiled.

He took a long drink and gave it back to me.

"And the other thing?" I asked.

"The deviousness of Frane," he said without hesitation.

"What do you mean?"

"She has . . . made this all look too easy. She sits on a sea of ice, with little high ground, and waits for us."

"You're sure she's there? The last time . . ."

"She is among her troops. The Quiff have spotted her, and kept track. Her bloodred tent sits behind the lines, and every day she marches among her army, distributing money and mocra. It is said her severed arm is hideous, a ragged stump uncovered by any cloth. She is as mad as the Baldies, and takes mocra herself in vast quantities."

"Then what is the problem? If she has grown that mad, then perhaps she has also grown stupid."

Even as the words left my mouth I knew they were foolish, for his own concerns had tapped some of my own inner fears.

What have we forgotten?

He slowly shook his head. "Frane has never been stupid."

It was my turn to nod, and we both drank.

"Then what can we do?" I asked the gypsy king.

"I don't know," he said. "If we meet this insane army of hers on the ice, whether by frontal assault or by stealth, we will easily defeat it. She must know that."

"Perhaps," I said, choosing to continue in the role of devil's advocate, "her madness has reached the point of self-destruction—"

"No! There must be something else . . ."

He sighed, and drank long and hard. When he rose he was a bit unsteady.

"We will continue to keep vigilant, and continue to think. There will be no repeat of Valles Marineris. Begging your pardon, Your Majesty."

"That's quite all right."

"I will speak with your grandfather and make battle plans."

I held the wine up to him, but he refused it.

"It is for you, Your Majesty. Think of it as a gift."

"Thank you," I said, admiring once again the intricate

etching design on the sides of the skin, the skillful construction.

"This is very beautiful. It is goatskin, yes?"

"Dog," he said, turning to leave, and it was a good thing he did because I thought of Hector and gagged, and the wine rose in my throat like bile.

⊰ CHAPTER 26 ⊱

THERE WERE MANY HANGOVERS THE NEXT MORNING, my own among them (though I did refuse at dinner, which was excellently prepared by my husband and Tyron, any gypsy wine contained in a skin), but that kept no one from the matters at hand. At noon, in my tent, I met a representative of the Quiff, another historical character from my father's travels, whose people resided mainly underground and were, up until a number of years ago, completely unknown to the typical Martian land dweller. He was an odd-looking fellow with long, fanglike teeth, but pleasant enough; the other quirks I noticed were his penchant to stretch words when speaking and an extreme fondness for fish. In fact, it had already been noted that where you found a Quiff, you were likely to find an ice-fishing hole.

"Thank you for joining us," I said to him, and he bowed.

"Your father was a wonnnnnderful mannnn," he replied.

"You knew him?" I said, startled.

He shook his head. "My owwwn father was his guiiii-ide. But I did seeee him when I wassss a kit. My father has passsssed on."

He then went on to explain to me that the Quiff had explored many of the underground passages near the pole, but that much of it remained uncharted.

"We have seeeeeen some strange thingssss," he said, citing among them caves that looked feline-made, and some tunnels that led nowhere.

I thanked him again for his assistance, and he bowed and left. He was immediately replaced by the most ridiculous character I had ever seen, dressed in a red undershirt beneath a frilly white bodice, short breeches and long boots. On his head was a cocked hat with a long yellow feather in it.

"Girlie!" he announced, and for a moment I thought he was speaking his own name. But then the memory of my grandmother's adventure placed him for me, and I smiled.

"You must be Pelltier."

"Indeed!" He struck a pose. "Da pirate, his self! And you look little like Haydn, I say."

He was squinting at me as if I was a new cabbage, to be inspected and bought.

"You still run your lake camp near Sagan?"

"You know of me, den?" His preening only increased.

"Why, you must be quite old by now!" I blurted out.

He deflated a little. "So you see tru my makeup, den? Yes, I am old, but I want to look good for the grand-girlie of my ol' fren' Haydn, so I—how do you say—'doll it up' a bit."

He abruptly stepped forward and grabbed my paw and kissed it.

"You are beautiful, yes, but in a diffren' way dan Haydn!"

"Thank you."

He went to one knee, still holding my paw. "I pledge mysel', and my men, and my material to you, den."

"Thank you, again."

He stood up. "Good. And I bring some-ting for you."

He drew a packet from beneath his white shirt and thrust it into my paw.

"It is tobac, like your gran-muder used to li'!"

"Tobacco? Cigarettes?" I said in wonder. I had never even seen the stuff, it had become so scarce. Never mind the negative health effects Newton and the Science Guild had claimed for it for so many years.

The faint, strange odor wafted up to my nostrils.

"Thank you, Pelltier. For . . . everything."

"Anyting for my girlie-girl!" he said, and turned on his heel and walked out. It was only then that I detected a bit of frailty, in the lack of spring in his step.

There were other dignitaries of other wayward clans and groups who had become allies. By the end of the afternoon my paw was weary of kisses. But it seems our army had almost doubled in size.

My grandfather joined me for dinner in my tent, though Darwin, not surprisingly, was nowhere to be seen. General Misst was gruff but confident—a little too confident, I thought.

"Forward scouts report absolutely no movement in Frane's army."

"That's good news?" I said, cautiously.

"Of course! She has a plan, and she's sticking to it. I doubt she knows the true size of our army." His rasping voice grew calmer. "Miklos's spies say that Frane spends all of her time in her tent, administering mocra to herself. She mumbles and fumes, and acts mad as a whippet. She had an aide executed yesterday just for asking her if she wanted to eat."

"Could it be an act, for our benefit?"

My grandfather seemed taken aback. "Why?"

"To lull us into complacency?"

"I don't think so, Your Majesty."

"There's no need for the condescending tone in your voice, General. Doesn't this all look too easy—like Valles Marineris all over again?"

"Everything we know and see indicates—"

"I don't care about what you can see, General! There's something about it that doesn't feel right!"

"We'll leave your feelings out of it, granddaughter. If I may be so blunt: You had your chance at Valles Marineris. I took charge of this army on the condition that I wouldn't be second-guessed and meddled with. Correct?"

I nodded, though I still frowned.

"And what of my mother?"

His ebullient mood lessened considerably. "That is the one thing I am not sure of. She has not been seen anywhere in camp. My own guess is that Frane has secreted her somewhere else, for use as ransom."

I nodded. "But where?"

"That is a mystery at the moment. But with luck, we will soon know."

Again I nodded.

"Then will you leave me alone to win this battle?"

I now saw some of the fierceness my grandfather was known for—as well as some of the arrogance. I wondered how much of that was in myself.

"Of course, General. Just, please, think on these things."

His anger had not diminished. "Of course I will. As I

think of another hundred things a day. We will march at dawn, Your Majesty."

"Very well . . ."

When he had gone I tried to put my finger on the feelings I had, but was unable to point to any one spot and say *there*.

But something was not right. Though I had yet to come face-to-face with my bitter enemy, Frane, I felt I knew something of her. She had outwitted my grandmother and my father, two very smart felines. She had easily outsmarted me, even when she wasn't present. And now . . .

I drew out the packet of tobacco that Pelltier had left with me and examined it. Removal of the outer wrapping revealed a frail paper box, red in color, and topped with foil. I opened it carefully. The odor became very strong.

Inside were twenty thin white paper bars, each containing tiny brown flakes of tobacco. I opened one up with a claw. The dry flakes spilled out.

I brought my open paw to my nostrils. The scent was, in a way, alluring.

I took another of the white tubes and placed it in my mouth. I found a taper and put it to my meager fire, lighting it.

I brought the taper to the far end of the cigarette and sought to light it, but nothing happened. Then, remembering my grandmother Haydn's description of the process in her scant memoirs, written in the year after her assassination, I gently drew breath into my lungs while lighting the far end.

It hissed into flame, burning the paper tube.

My mouth was filled with smoke, and then my lungs.

It was not as sweet as it smelled or as I anticipated it would taste. It was, instead, harsh and, well, like having a mouthful of smoke.

I coughed, then coughed again, throwing the cigarette to the ground.

I snuffed it out with my boot, still coughing.

One of my attendants burst into the tent, her eyes wide.

"Your Majesty, are you all right?" she asked.

"Yes," I said, hacking out words between coughs. "I'm . . . fine. Just learning another lesson is all."

And then I coughed again, and put the packet of cigarettes away as a memento, nothing more.

⊰ CHAPTER 27 ⊱

THE MORNING WAS BRACINGLY COLD. A LIGHT WIND put a bite into the chill, and the horses' huffing breath put clouds of artificial smoke into the air. There was something about a packed and just-moving army that invigorated me. I loved the sounds: chuffing horses, clanking harnesses, the stretching protest of saddle leather and the clatter of cook's wagons, pots and pans making music, the grumblings of feline soldiers not yet awake. Leaving nothing behind and going somewhere new. A just-moving army meant change, and promise, and the hope of victory. A camping army was a dead thing, without life or vitality— but an army on the march was exactly the opposite.

The wind was in our faces, keeping the crispness in the air as the sun rose to our right. Before us was a wall of blue-white ice as far as the eye could see from west to east. As we drew closer it resolved into a series of steppes and bluffs and switchbacks. We had been placed well, and though the climb would be a good one, it would not be hard.

The late afternoon found us halfway up and stopped on a vast level plain invisible from below. We saw our first Baldies, two lone scouts, above us, looking nearly insensate. One was dispatched with an arrow and the other with one of our precious rifles. When their bodies were recovered they appeared nearly emaciated, their teeth bared in permanent fiendish howls of madness and hunger.

"Frane wasn't starving them at Valles Marineris," I remarked.

"But she is now," Miklos replied. He, along with General Misst, examined one of the scouts where he lay on a table. We had been joined by our surgeon, who concurred.

"Look at the area around the eyes," he said. "See how the eyeball is protruding? That's a sign of advanced mocra poisoning. It's not so much that they are being starved as that they lose all interest in eating. This fellow has been living on nothing but mocra for weeks. He would have been dead in another month, if we hadn't killed him. In many ways, you did him a favor."

"What kind of opposition will we face if they're all like this?" General Missst inquired.

"None," the surgeon said flatly. "This Baldie couldn't fight if he had to. The only thing on his mind was mocra."

The general's chest swelled, and he gave me an "I told you so" look.

I frowned.

"This will make our work easy," Miklos said, though I detected a note of doubt in his voice. I made a note to speak with him alone later.

"If there's any doubt," the surgeon continued, "look at this poor fellow's claws."

The doctor held up one limp paw, and pressed the pad so that the claws would appear.

They were brittle and blood-caked, two of them broken off completely.

"That's like no Baldie claw I've ever seen," General Misst proclaimed. "What can they possibly fight with? Ladies and gentlemen, though I hesitate to proclaim victory now, I do think we will very soon be in that camp."

There was silence, but my grandfather broke it by laughing harshly and slapping the dead Baldie on the chest.

"Thank you, young fellow, for giving me the battle!"

"I NOTED YOUR HESITANCY TO CELEBRATE SO EARLY," I said to Miklos later in my tent.

He smiled wryly. "I fear the general is too sure of something that is not sure enough. Frane has the blood of my two brothers on her hands, and they were both very smart fellows. We gypsies just do not believe that anything in this life is easy. There is a saying, 'The hard path is the true one.'" His smile widened a fraction. "I believe that applies here, Your Majesty."

"So do I, Miklos."

"And yet," he continued, "I can see nothing but an easy victory before us. If Frane is truly in the throes of this drug, then our work has been done for us. And with no useful army to assist her . . ."

We both sat, brooding, and not knowing why.

"Like you, Frane took two of my family. And they were anything but stupid. I do not intend to be reckless."

"That is good to hear."

"So I will have your support on this . . . caution?"

His smile widened yet another fraction. "Gypsies are always cautious. Especially with their own hides."

• • •

TWO MORE OF FRANE'S FORWARD SCOUTS WERE EN-
countered that night, one killed, the other captured. The
captive Baldie proved quite mad, and, at the first opportunity, threw himself from the nearest ice ledge. His cries
echoed in the cold night.

My grandfather's self-satisfaction only grew.

And yet . . .

⇥ CHAPTER 28 ⇤

AT DAWN, ONE HIDDEN BEHIND HILLS OF ICE AND snow to the east, we continued our climb.

General Misst was in an ebullient mood. His horse snorted contemptuously at the morning chill, straining against the reins.

"He wants to be running," the general explained, then turned to pat the horse. "There, Champion, be patient. You'll run soon enough through a battlefield."

As if the horse understood him, it huffed, showing its teeth.

My grandfather laughed and patted the horse again.

"He's ready for the slaughter!"

"What do you have in mind for a battle plan?" I asked, trying to sound innocent. I looked round at Darwin, who rode just behind me. He had a scowl on his face and shook his head.

The general snorted, a sound not unlike that of his

horse. "We won't need one, Your Majesty. We'll charge through 'em like a hot blade through new butter."

"A nice analogy, but I think we should hold some troops in reserve."

"For what?" he cried. "The more the merrier!"

"I'd like to hold the gypsies and Pelltier's men in reserve."

He looked at me and waved a hand in dismissal. "Do what you like. If they don't have the stomach for a fight let them stay behind."

"That's hardly the case—"

Again he snorted, as did his mount. "I'll have plenty of men without them."

"Thank you."

His contemptuous look all but said, *Bah.*

WE TOPPED THE LAST RISE IN MIDAFTERNOON. THE sun was lowering toward the west, throwing lengthening shadows from the ice hills in that direction. But ahead of us was a white expanse flat as any soiled plain.

And there, three hundred yards in front of us, was our prize: the army of Frane waiting patiently, her own banner, bloodred with a yellow stripe, waving lazily in the slight breeze. I thought I could spy Frane herself, a distant figure gazing at us unmoving across the field of ice.

There was a commotion to our left, and I saw a band of wild Baldies charge at our flank. There were only fifty or so of them, and they were easily dispatched. My grandfather, sitting high in his saddle, watched the ruckus and grinned.

"Imbeciles," he said.

Another mad band hit at our right flank and, similarly, was easily taken care of.

"Can you think of any reason to hesitate?" General Misst asked me, triumphantly.

As he gave the order to advance, I reined my horse around and fell back to Miklos and Pelltier. Darwin followed me, and a few Quiff. I passed many expectant faces and many confident words:

"We'll give Frane hell today, Majesty!"

"This will be for you and your poor father, my queen!"

"A bloody cakewalk, that's what it'll be!"

But when I reached Miklos he was not smiling, and neither was the pirate.

"I *smell* some-ting bad, girlie-girl," Pelltier nearly hissed, as I reached him. His old senses were all awake, and he sat forward in his saddle sniffing the air. "I don' know what it 'tis, girlie-girl, but . . ."

I told him to keep his men back with me, and he did so. Miklos and his hundred joined us also, and we observed, a tiny army watching more than three thousand ride confidently forward.

Miklos studied the line and shook his head. "At least he should form a claw," he said, making a U with his paw. "He isn't even flanking, now!"

"He doesn't think he has to," Darwin said.

A ragtag band of five Baldies, screaming madly, ran at us from the direction of the setting sun. I drew my sword, but they were cut down before they got within two horses of me.

"This is madness," Pelltier said, sheathing his own sword after making use of it. "I tell you, some-ting is no' right."

Far back in my brain, something began to tickle, a faraway noise like distant thunder.

"Do you hear it?" I asked, but my two companions were both alert now, sitting stiff and straight in their saddles.

The lowest, faintest of rumbles, which incrementally grew.

A horrid realization blossomed in me.

Ahead of us, my grandfather gave a loud order of "Charge!" and the line of men and horses, roaring as one, forged ahead as the great mass of Frane's Baldie army rushed forward to meet them. I noted that Frane, with perhaps five hundred non-Baldie troops, stayed behind.

The low rumble grew, overcame the shouts of the army.

All at once there rose a sheath of ice in front of the army, and another behind the oncoming Baldies, and the entire plain they inhabited began to collapse, as if in slow motion, into the ground. There was a roar that filled my ears, and a geyser of snow and ice flew impossibly high into the sky as the ground opened completely beneath them and swallowed the army whole.

Miklos was shouting, and Pelltier was gesturing madly, but I could hear nothing above the howling ungodly roar as the ground shook beneath us. There was a cloud of blue-white powder where our army had been, but already it was settling to the ground and into the huge chasm that had been formed.

One of the Quiff drew up beside me. "That devillll hollowed out the plainnnn beneath the icccce!"

I heard another sound above these—a keening wail. The hairs on the back of my neck stood out, for at first I thought it was the sound of the dying in the massive pit. But that was not it. As the cloud in front of us dissipated we saw a mass of charging bodies moving around it, coming straight for us.

"Frane!" Miklos shouted. He quickly gave orders, and we formed into a chevron. There were little more than one hundred of us against five times that many.

"D' queen mus' get away," Pelltier said.

Before I could speak Darwin nodded. "Stay close to me," he whispered to me fiercely.

"It is important for you to go," Miklos said.

"I won't leave any of you!"

"Fight, den," Pelltier said, and looked at Darwin. "But if d' opportunity to flee come, take it."

Darwin nodded.

Through the settling cloud of snow, I saw Frane, her one arm held high clutching an impossibly long blade, her mouth open in a shout as she charged toward us, her horse leading an army that looked focused and keen.

"Look at her," I said. "These will be her true diehards. All of the rest was a ruse. All of it!"

"She is the devil his self," Pelltier said.

Frane drew closer, closer, and her eyes were locked on mine with a fierce hatred that made me go cold inside. I was suddenly very frightened, but determined not to show it.

As if to drive the fear away, I suddenly kicked at my horse, drew my sword, and, shouting, charged straight for the fiend.

Behind me, with shouts, the others followed.

Frane, unblinking, galloped straight at me, her mouth open in a cry of rage. Her face, ravaged by time and hate and the drug mocra, was a death mask with patches of fur. Her eyes were huge red slits, her teeth bared like fangs.

"Dic today!" she screamed, bringing the sword down toward me.

Our horses passed, and the blow missed. We quickly turned and went at one another again. Around me were the full sounds of battle, and I saw Miklos take down two of Frane's minions with a mighty blow. Darwin was nearby, trying to fight his way toward me, hacking and pushing madly.

I faced Frane once more, and our horses drew toward one another like magnets.

"Die!" Frane screamed again, and I saw her sword fill the sky above me. Then it drove down at me, filling my vision—and suddenly the day went black, and I heard and saw no more.

⊰ CHAPTER 29 ⊱

THE SMELL OF COLD.

Yes, cold *did* have an odor—a bracing, clean, empty fragrance.

Cold.

I shivered and opened my eyes. Someone or something moved against me as I did so, adjusting weight.

I sat up in white glare and almost immediately swooned.

"Don't move," Darwin's soothing voice said.

I closed my eyes and moaned, then opened them again. As long as I didn't move I was fine, it seemed.

"Where are we?"

"Underground." He was adjusting blankets and furs around me. The movement itself sent a cold chill through me and made me shiver.

My teeth chattered when I spoke again.

"Wh-where are the o-o-others?"

"Nearby. That was quite a nasty bump you got on your head. For a while I was afraid . . ."

"W-what?"

"That you wouldn't wake up."

Ever so slowly, I reached up to feel at my forehead with my paw. Something knotted and raw sent a bolt of pain through me when I touched it.

"It will go nicely with my face scar. What h-happened to me?"

"Frane's blow glanced you with the hilt of her sword."

The chattering had stopped, but I lay still, trying to draw warmth from the coverings and my husband's adjacent body.

"It's very cold in here."

"Yes. We thought it best not to start a fire. Many of Frane's soldiers are still in the area, and I'm afraid we're not up for another battle at the moment."

"Tell me everything."

"Well . . ." I could feel the reluctance in his body, hear it in his voice.

"We were beaten badly?"

"Frane made only one charge, which cut us up pretty well, but then she and her troops rode through and away. It was quite smart, because we were in no shape to follow, especially with you down."

"Why didn't she kill me?"

"Miklos and I fought her off after you fell from your horse. If her men hadn't pulled her away, I believe she would have jumped from her own mount and tried to fight through us. She was screeching like a madwoman."

"How many did we lose?" Very slowly, I turned my head to regard my husband, who looked at the ground before meeting my eyes.

"More than half. Many of the Quiff died, and many of

Miklos's people. He's attending to their burial now, in the snow."

"Take me to him."

I tried to rise, but once more found myself in a faint.

When I woke up it was darker, as if the sun had set above us, and even colder.

IN THE MORNING I COULD SIT UP. OUR LITTLE CAVE seemed to spin around me, but if I kept very still everything steadied, and I could speak.

I was warm now—too warm—and threw off some of the cloaks and blankets that had been covering me. Darwin was asleep at my feet, looking very young in his slumber, his hand on his sword, which lay next to him. He looked cold, and I covered him.

Slowly swiveling around, I surveyed the space and saw that it was an ice cave with an unseen opening behind us. I could hear low talk and assumed it was guarded by at least two of our soldiers. I wanted very badly to climb out into the sunlight but was unable to stand up.

After a while I gave up and curled next to my husband, letting sleep take me once more.

WHEN I WOKE DARWIN WAS GONE, BUT I HEARD voices closer, and spied two soldiers bearing a tray making their way down the long grade to where I sat.

One of them raised a hand in greeting—and at that moment the roof above him collapsed. A sheet of white came down on the two felines, whose screams were cut off as if with a knife.

Forgetting my disability I rose and hobbled to the spot

where a new wall of snow and ice blocked the way. I called out but was met with only silence.

Darwin appeared behind me.

"Merciful Great One!" he cried.

"Two poor fellows were caught in this. Can the others dig us out?"

"It would take days, perhaps a week or longer. This new material will be hard as rock before you know it."

I looked at him for an alternative.

"We have a little food, and water will be no problem. I've surveyed this passage for a good couple miles, and it continues downward—but there may be a side passage that leads us out. It's better than sitting here and waiting for starvation and cold to claim us."

"All right."

"How do you feel?"

"Woozy, but much better."

"Then we'll make a go of it."

We returned to our sleeping place, and Darwin made an inventory. "Two swords, two daggers, a bit of hardtack, a box of matches, an oil lamp. I suggest we wrap ourselves with as many layers of clothing and blankets as we can. It may warm us too much now, but we may need them later."

We did so, and then wasted no time, heading into the cave, which sloped down into the bowels of an unknown world.

⇥ CHAPTER 30 ⇤

EVER SO GRADUALLY WE LOST THE LIGHT, AS THE
mass of ice above us filtered the sun away. Then darkness
fell, making our blackness utter. Darwin lit the lamp, and
it threw eerie blue ice shadows on the walls.

After a while I began to feel as if we had made no
progress. Our little area of illumination never changed: the
same white ice walls, ceiling, and floor. Though we
walked, I was beset with the illusion that we were walking
in place.

"I must rest," I said, the pain in my head finally overcoming me. I fell to the floor, and Darwin attended me.

"Your bump is less noticeable," he said, gently probing
the wound.

"It feels as though someone is rhythmically beating me
with a closed fist," I said, feeling suddenly faint.

He put water to my lips from his canteen.

"Then we'll rest here for the night."

"How will you know when it's day?" I asked, and he laughed.

"We won't," he said, "but we'll guess."

He must have laid me gently down, for when I awoke I was swaddled in blankets on the floor of the ice tunnel.

I sat up, glad that the pounding in my head was gone and I could move my head without a stab of pain shooting through it. The lamp had been turned low. Darwin's even sleeping breath marked the only sound.

And yet—

There was another sound, very faint, and very far away. Another kind of breathing, it sounded like, but so light that it might almost be an illusion.

I thought of all the fairy tales I'd heard about mythical ice monsters, huge horrid white worms that lay in the bowels of the ice caps sucking intruders into their terrible round mouths and mashing them with row on row of tiny pure white teeth—

I had managed to frighten myself, and sat most of the rest of the night in vigil, listening to that ever-so-faint breathing, letting my imagination run riot.

WHEN DARWIN WOKE (IT *WAS* MORNING, BECAUSE A whisper of light from above illumined the walls light blue around us) he stretched contentedly, then studied my face.

"You look like you haven't slept at all!" he remarked.

"Very little."

"Is it your head—?"

"My head is fine, now." I considered telling him of my night worries but thought better of it.

Besides, I could hear nothing now in the long, endless stretch of tunnel that lay ahead of us.

"Shall we march?" Darwin said, offering me a bit of hardtack, which I gratefully accepted.

I stood up, and we gathered our meager things and walked.

LATER IN THE DAY, WHEN THE WALLS HAD DARKENED for good, the angle of our descent began to increase sharply. Darwin turned up the lamp, trying to peer into the distance, as our feet began to slip on the ice, drawing us down.

"I have an idea," he said. He peeled a blanket from each of us and laid it on the ground. "Sit on this," he explained, "and we'll slide down. It's too steep to walk. If you start to go too fast, just dig your boots into the ice to slow yourself down."

"Like a kit's sleigh!" I said, and he laughed.

"Exactly."

But as with many good plans, the execution did not match the inspiration. As soon as we sat down on our respective blankets we began to slide forward, at first at a manageable pace, but then faster and faster. I tried to dig my boots into the ice to either side of the cloth but the slope had become so severe that there was no stopping. With or without blanket we were going down the slide, with no slow-up. Darwin, holding the oil lamp high, raced past me, peering intently into the gloom ahead. With no choice I followed him, my stomach lurching. There was a turn to the left, another to the right, then we straightened out again.

And then, suddenly, the ride was over and we slowed to a halt as the pitch of the tunnel leveled out and became flat.

Darwin stood up and gave a sigh of relief. "Are you all right?"

I could not help but laugh. "That was quite a ride!"

And then my laugh died in my throat—because, as plain as day, I heard the breathing sound I had heard the night before, only now steadier and much louder.

"You hear that?" I whispered, but Darwin had already heard, and was holding the lamp out to the right, moving slowly down the passageway.

He made a silent motion for me to follow, and I gathered up my blanket and did so.

There was light ahead of us, pulsing and faint. The tunnel bent slightly to the right, and widened. The light grew slowly stronger, and the breathing became a steady pulse—*chuff, chuff*—that grew.

"That's not a white worm," I said out loud, in relief, for the sound was too mechanical and unnatural.

"A *what*?" Darwin asked, looking at me with a frown.

"Nothing," I said. "Just the fairy tale that kept me awake last night."

He shook his head and walked forward.

The slight curve to the right continued, and the light grew brighter ahead of us. Darwin doused our lamp.

CHUFFFF-CHUFFFF

We passed an artificial barrier from white ice to hard, white, artificial floor.

Our boots echoed on the spotless tile of an anteroom, and ahead of us were two tall, metallic silver doors.

I put my paw on one of them and held my breath.

Beside me, Darwin drew his sword.

"Go ahead," he said, nodding.

I pushed at the door, and it opened—

—but not into the bright cave of machines and wonders I had expected. The room within was dimly lit and not large. If fact, it reminded me of . . .

An old familiar knot formed in my stomach, and I drew back.

"What's wrong?"

"My . . . grandmother and father. This room . . ."

"It can't be the same place."

In the middle of the room was a familiar dais, with a not-quite-empty thronelike chair upon it.

As we watched, a vague form took shape, a ghostly violet image that grew and filled in . . .

"I must leave," I choked, not able to face my dead relatives, my grandmother Haydn or father Sebastian, once more drawn back to life from the realm beyond.

I turned, but Darwin blocked my way. His sword was at his side. "Turn and look," he said gently, taking hold of me and forcing me around.

I turned, and looked at the shaped form on the chair on the dais.

My breath turned to a gasp in my throat.

"An Old One!" I whispered, in wonder.

⊰ CHAPTER 31 ⊱

IT WAS, INDEED, AN OLD ONE DARWIN AND I BEHELD.
There could be no doubt. The stature—more than a foot
taller than either my husband or I—the naked facial features, a flaxen, limp mane of hair covering only the top of
the head and drawn down over the low-placed ears, the
long limbs, skinny paws and overly elongated fingers and
blunt claws—this could be nothing less than one of our
mysterious, near-mythical ancestors come back to life.

The figure sat wan and tired-looking, its blinking gaze
unfocused. It was still solidifying, already more solid than
my grandmother or father had ever been, not a blue ghost
but an almost real thing. It wore a strangely shaped tunic
and sandals on its overlarge feet; the toes, again, were
elongated and blunt-clawed, altogether alien.

The room was brightening, too, the dimness dissipating,
making the specter in front of us less ghostly. Darwin

sheathed his sword and, at the sound, the Old One turned its wizened head slowly in our direction.

"You have come to see me?" it said, its voice weak and broken by static, but decidedly female.

Her eyes were also strange, large but sunken, pupil and iris malformed compared to a feline eye.

The Old One blinked and seemed to take on even more form.

"Yes?" she said, her voice louder, stronger.

We stepped forward, and I said, "I am Queen Clara of Mars."

"Indeed?" The Old One took a deep breath, which seemed to refresh her. She looked down at me with a more piercing gaze.

"You are a feline!"

"Of course."

"I am told . . ." She held up a long digit, for silence, and closed her eyes. "My word . . ." she breathed.

She opened her eyes again and regarded us. "I am told that I have been in stasis for almost one and three-quarter million years."

"To us, the Old Ones are nothing but a fossil record," I stated.

"I see." Again she closed her eyes and breathed deep. "This comes as a bit of an adjustment. I certainly did not plan on staying 'in the bin' for so long—nor to waking up to . . . another species."

She regarded us closely, and I became uncomfortable at her stonelike gaze.

"Are there none at all like me then?"

"You are the first live Old One who has ever been seen by a feline."

"'Live,'" she said, issuing something like a chuckle, "is

a relative word. Reconstituted, more like. I stayed behind by my own choice, but I thought they would return."

I must have looked at her quizzically, for she continued, in a tone as if she did not quite believe it herself, "They all went back to Earth. The terraforming went fine, and for hundreds of years, even after the time of the Machine Master and the wars among the Five Worlds, there were humans on Mars—but then, when Earth was once more habitable and the wars ended . . ."

She shrugged, as if I would understand, and when I said nothing she leaned forward in her chair and put her huge hands on her knees.

"Don't you see?" she said. "You were left behind. There was nothing on Mars when we came, and we made it habitable and brought the things we knew and loved from home.

"Cats, for instance. Our . . . *pets*."

I drew myself up with as much pride as I could. "Do you mean to tell me we were *hauled* here, like so much cattle?"

"As I said, pets, my . . ." She thought better of what she was going to say, and addressed me instead as "Your Majesty."

I was filled with indignation and rage, but, unaccountably, Darwin beside me was holding his sides and laughing. The Old One had begun to laugh, too.

"You find this *humorous*?" I shouted in the little room, but my self-important rage seemed out of place and was drowned out by the laughter around me.

The Old One held her hands out in supplication, but she was still chuckling.

"Doesn't it make sense, Clara?" Darwin said. "Our own fossil record, the evolution from dog size to our present stature, Copernicus's paper . . ."

"I'm afraid it's true, Your Majesty." She gave another

laugh. "If it makes you feel better, my own kind also evolved from lower animals! It is the natural way of things."

It was my turn to laugh, and Darwin joined me.

"It is the natural way of things," the Old One repeated. "But still, to see two felines fully developed into sentient creatures. You were left behind when men returned to Earth, and now, well, you have inherited a world . . ."

She shook her head.

"You mentioned Five Worlds?"

"Oh, yes, Earthmen colonized Venus and Titan and Pluto besides Mars, and then, of course, there were great wars among them. And at the end of those wars Earth, which had been decimated by plague as well as conflict, became livable again. And also, there was a messenger of sorts from beyond the Solar System . . ."

She seemed to be trying very hard to remember.

"There were many things that happened in my time."

"Why did you stay on Mars?"

"I was too frail to make the trip home, so I consented to be turned into . . . this," she said, indicating herself with her strange, large hands. "I loved Mars, so it was not a difficult choice. It was thought that Earthmen would return before long and try to live here again. I was to welcome them back. But I see that it has never happened.

"So tell me," she continued, her hands on her knees again as she leaned over us eagerly, "what has happened in the last one and three-quarter million years on my beloved Mars? How has it fared in the Age of Felines, as opposed to the Age of Humans, when war and strife and hatred were rampant upon this land and others?"

So we told her, and as our story unfolded her eyes became misty, and her face clouded over with dismay and sadness.

⊰ CHAPTER 32 ⊱

WE STAYED THERE FOR TWO DAYS, UNTIL OUR HUNGER overcame us. There was nothing to eat in Stella's (for that was her Old One, or "human," name) domain, and only water, which Darwin produced by melting ice, to drink. The hardtack was gone, and hunger began to gnaw at us like a living thing.

Stella could rise and walk around her room, but was unable to leave its walls. She explained in essence how she was preserved, and it was in line with what Newton had known, and deduced, when my grandmother Haydn and my father had been saved—only, in their case, as Stella surmised, the equipment had not been as well protected or preserved as hers had been. It turned out that Stella had a secret, but she would not tell us what it was.

She was curious about my name, and that of my father and grandmother. When I showed her my most precious possession, the Old One book of composers, she was delighted.

"Ancient Earth composers!" she cried. "I loved their music!"

"All they ever were to us were pictures. My great-grandmother loved music in general, and that's where the naming tradition began."

"Wait," she said, and closed her eyes.

In a moment a sound wafted from the corners of the room, and then built into a full-blooded roaring of instruments, some of which were unknown to me. But the sound was beautiful.

"That's a symphony of Haydn, one of his later ones," Stella said with delight.

We sat and listened to this strange cacophony, which, in its own way, made delightful sense.

When it was over, there was a pause while Stella once again closed her eyes, and then a single singing instrument, which sounded as though there were strings involved, came into the room, followed by others of the same. The sound was sweet and ethereal. A glorious chill went up my spine.

"That's Johann Sebastian Bach, his 'Air on a G String,'" Stella explained. The look of happiness on her face was surely mirrored on my own. "It's nice to see that he can still have such an effect after almost two million years."

When it was finished she said, "And now to your own namesake," and produced a piano (which sounded much like the *tambor* I had labored over since I was a kit) work by Clara Schumann, whose husband, I was informed, was also a musician.

• • •

AND THEN, ON THAT LAST DAY, AS WE PREPARED TO leave, she gave us her secret. I had sensed a growing fondness for her, and I could tell at this last audience that she had made some sort of decision.

"If what you have told me is true about Mars losing its atmosphere, and I have no reason to believe it is not, then you must do everything you can to preserve life here. And every tool must be made available to you. If humans have indeed abandoned Mars, then it is up to you felines to protect what you have inherited here. It is obvious to me that your technology is in the primitive stages. What advances you have made have been through the haphazard discovery of what we humans left behind. This 'Newton' you have described sounds like a brilliant fellow, and I will be happy to meet him. But in the meantime, I have decided to turn over to you my storehouse. You must pledge to use it for good, and to eradicate this Frane creature you have spoken of once and for all. We humans have always periodically had to deal with evil forces bent only on destruction, and it is an art learned only through blood and sorrow. Any help I can give you I must."

And then she told us where to go to find her treasure.

AS WE TOOK OUR LEAVE OF HER, I WAS OVERCOME by affection and drew her large body to my own. She put her long fingers into the fur on my head and petted me there as if I were a dog.

Suddenly she laughed, and pulled her strange fingers away. "I'm so sorry! It's just that the last time I saw a cat, it was my own pet!"

⊰ CHAPTER 33 ⊱

HUNGER WAS CATCHING UP WITH US, AND I WON-
dered if we would reach our goal, still deeper into the polar
ice cap, before it overcame us completely. But Darwin
proved hardier than I, and with his encouragements we at
last stood before the doors of the fortress Stella had described. Being white, they nearly blended in with the surrounding ice walls.

Taking a deep breath, we pushed the doors open.

At first we saw nothing but a huge empty room. The
ceiling and floor were also white. It looked like a massive
empty warehouse.

And then there was a shimmer, and the camouflage unit
we had been warned about deactivated, revealing the true
contents of the space.

We stood with our mouths open.

There in the center of the room was something long,
sleek, and wedge-shaped. It vaguely resembled the airships

that Newton had constructed with clues from Old One technology—but this machine was not meant to fly in the atmosphere of planets alone but between them.

"With this, we could visit other worlds," Darwin said dreamily.

"And save this one," I said, trying to sound practical as I sought to find the entry port, which Stella had described to me. The underbelly of the craft seemed to be of a seamless design, with no crack or gap—

But then my claw scratched across the slight recess I sought, and there was a hiss of ancient mechanisms and a doorway pulled in and away, leaving an oval opening.

"Darwin," I called, and he retreated from the aft, where he was studying the monstrous propulsion tubes.

We entered together.

It smelled flat and stale, but even then another hidden system was activated and I heard the *ssssss* of air being freshened and circulated.

Lights, recessed in the walls and ceiling, went on as we walked, our boots echoing hollowly on the deck of the ship.

An animated voice crackled into life.

"What is it you wish?"

"Guide us to the main cabin," I ordered.

"As you say," the voice commented, and the wall and ceiling lights dimmed as a row of lit lines formed beneath our feet.

We followed them through a huge lounge, a sleeping area—one of three as it turned out—containing twenty comfortable big bunks, an eating area and attached galley, rows and rows of storage lockers, and, finally, the cabin. A thousand lights and gauges and switches were arrayed around two contoured chairs, with a third chair set behind them. The front windows were thick but clear, floor to ceiling, showing the white room we had just left.

Darwin sat easily in the captain's chair on the left.

"What is it you wish?" the animated voice asked.

Darwin looked at me, and I sat gingerly down in the companion chair.

"Shall we?" Darwin whispered to me, then, without waiting for an answer, he said, out loud, "Take us out of here."

There was no response.

Darwin frowned, then he looked at me and held out his paw.

"The code Stella gave us," he said, and I suddenly remembered and dug the written numbers out of my tunic and handed the paper to my husband.

Darwin read the numbers out loud, and immediately there was a subtle shift in the machine. "As you say," the mechanical voice intoned. I heard a faraway snicking noise, which must have been the hatch being closed. A humming began deep in the ship and built to a rumble, then a roar.

A bright light filled the white room outside. There was a monstrous rumbling sound. I looked up and out of the front port to see two white doors hinging open above us, letting in sunlight from an impossibly high distance.

"Are we going up—?" I started to say as we did, the ship lurching forward and upward at the same time, diving up into the atmosphere even before I had finished my words. We were blinded by sky.

"Where are we going—?" I said, but again my question was answered before it was asked as the ship came to an abrupt stop.

It was dark outside.

I stood and looked through the front port.

"Great One in heaven, Darwin. Look."

"Stasis position reached. Instructions?" the mechanical voice asked.

"Stay where we are," Darwin ordered, his eyes already feasting on the view outside.

"Very well," the voice replied.

"We're in space," I said in wonder.

"Above Mars," Darwin said.

Below us was spread our own planet, seen from a height from which no feline had ever beheld it. The north polar cap was far below us, a tiny insignificant thing, and beyond it in all directions a red and green world with pale blue patches of lakes and oceans, a million shades of red, from the lightest pink to crimson and russet and the darkest brown rust. The green patches were vivid in the midst of these colors, and now I spied Arsia Mons, its massive caldera looking, from that height, small and lonely. The world was split into night and day, and in the dark area was a weak patch of illumination that marked the city of Robinson. I saw another in the far distance that marked Bradbury, and its lights were even more wan.

And enveloping it all, the thinnest blanket of pink-yellow, the merest smudge against the edge of the world, the atmosphere.

"It looks like a toy, so fragile," I remarked.

"I could stay up here forever," Darwin said.

It was then that my stomach spoke to me, announcing my hunger with a pain that doubled me over, and when next I awoke we were on the ground and dawn was breaking in the city of Bradbury, and I was being helped from the marvelous machine that already Newton was eyeing with delight, and brought to a place of rest and refreshment.

PART THREE

THE LAST BATTLE

⇥ CHAPTER 34 ⇤

A DAY LATER FOUND ME RESTED, AND RESTLESS. THE
court physician, Mandrake, tried to keep me in bed, citing
my still-healing head wound and recent bout of malnutri-
tion, but I overruled him and called a council meeting for
that morning.

"But at least hold court in bed!" he begged.

Darwin, I learned, was in even worse shape than I,
which meant his protestations of fatigue and hunger had
been a feint for my benefit. I wanted to kiss and kick him
at the same time, but Mandrake wouldn't let me see him.

"Get out," was my reply, and only after he had left did
I admit my own frailty and called for the meeting to come
to me.

Even then I felt silly, propped up by a dozen white silk
pillows and attended to by a bevy of servants bearing trays
of potions and sweetmeats. The only thing I had been able
to keep in my stomach were bits of dried bread and water.

Even so, I was ravenously hungry. The dichotomy of want impossible to satisfy was maddening, and added to my ill temper.

Finally, I cried, "Get out, all of you!" to the servants, as Newton, looking sprier than I had ever seen him, no doubt because of the stimulation of his new toy, looked on wryly, and the other ministers pretended not to notice.

When the trays and their bearers had left, Warton, war minister since my grandfather's death, reported the last sighting of Frane, which had been to the north and east of Bradbury.

There was something else, I could tell, and I ordered the rotund feline, who had a brilliant scholarly mind but had never buckled on a sword in his life, to tell me what it was. He hemmed and hawed, pulling his claws through his whiskers nervously, until I exploded with him the way I had with the tray-bearers.

"Tell me immediately, or resign your position!"

His light brown fur blanched, and his eyes widened.

"Your mother . . . is with her," he said.

I went cold, and said to no one in particular, "As we thought, Frane had her secreted away during the battle." I turned specifically to Warton. "And you have no idea where they are?"

He shook his head ruefully. "Only that they are north and east of here."

"Then that is where we will look."

Warton began, "We are scouring the hills and towns with—"

Impatiently, I cut him off and turned to Newton. "Can we utilize the spaceship?"

The old scientist shook his head. "It is too fast for use in the atmosphere, and its tracking instruments are strictly for navigation. We are using every airship at our disposal,

of course, and are checking on reports from local farmers
and townspeople—but, as you know, Your Majesty, Frane
is crafty, and sometimes locals are loath to talk to officials.
We do know that the area she is in is free from underground passages, which means she is somewhere on the
surface. But the going is hard—"

"Then we will find her ourselves," came a weak voice
from the doorway, and I turned to see my husband, Darwin, standing pale and weak. He was smiling at me, and
winked, before he collapsed to the floor. Warton rushed to
his side and helped support him as he was removed, back
to his own bed.

I was feeling tired myself.

"Let me think on this," I said, adjourning the meeting.

Before the last of them had reached the doorway, I was
dead asleep.

⊰ CHAPTER 35 ⊱

I AWOKE WITH SOMEONE SHARING MY BED. A JOLT of alarm went through me, and I reached for the dagger by my bedside and the bellpull that lay just behind it, but a paw stayed me.

I turned to look into Darwin's grinning face.

"I meant what I said, you know," he told me, gently releasing my arm.

We lay back, our sides touching, and I said, "I missed you. How do you feel?"

"Like a new kit. Nearly a day has passed since I collapsed in your doorway. You will feel much better, too, when you've had something proper to eat."

"You should have told me you were in such bad shape."

"Why?" He laughed. "So you could feel even worse?"

I stroked his paw lightly with my claws. "What news is there?"

"This place is running without us. Newton has gone to

meet with Stella and draw out the rest of her secrets. Half the army is out crawling over the hills looking for Frane. The senators and the Assembly are acting like there never was war and are fighting with one another over anything that presents itself. And the architects are drawing up plans to rebuild Wells into an even grander place than it was before."

I nodded absently, and he pushed himself up on one elbow to regard me. "What? None of this pleases you?"

"She is still out there."

He nodded, and lowered his voice to a whisper. "That's why I'm here. You and I are going to find her."

"What!" I exclaimed.

"Shhh!" His put a finger to my lips. "Keep your voice low. There are minders and tenders and servants, valets, chambermaids, grovelers, scrapers, and watchers of every stripe just outside your door. If they knew you were awake, they would burst in here like a tide."

I sighed. "It will be my lot from now on. They'll keep me locked up like a doll in a glass case. Even if I insisted, or made it a royal order, they'd gang up on me and insist it was 'for the good of Mars.'"

"Exactly. Now that the danger to the Republic is perceived to be over, things are quickly reverting to normal. We will never see another exciting moment in our lives."

"True."

He sat up on the bed but kept his voice low. "Now let me ask you. What are the chances of finding Frane with army patrols bumbling about the countryside and looking under hay bales?"

"None. She will hide, using my mother until she is no longer useful—then, once again, will attack somewhere up the line."

"Exactly. But now let me ask you: What are the chances

of two lone trackers, one of them an expert at hiding and stealth, bringing Frane to ground and saving your mother?" He smiled.

I could not help it, my voice rose. "They would never let us do it!"

He continued to smile. "Of course they won't! That is why we will have to sneak out under their noses!"

And then he told me his plan.

I WAS PATIENT, THOUGH I FELT LIKE ANYTHING BUT. The better part of the week was spent in regaining my appetite (much of it thanks to Darwin's excellent cooking—which also enabled him to have the run of the kitchen and secrete away the provisions we would need), endless meetings with ministers and counselors, and public displays from my balcony to the cheering populace. All the while, Darwin and I planned. Besides food, he found the proper clothing and, in a final stroke of brilliance, enjoined Miklos, who had returned from the North Pole, to sneak us out of the temporary capital.

During that time the expected news was received that Frane was nowhere to be seen. It was as if she had dropped off the face of the planet, and my mother with her.

Finally, the day came. Both Darwin and I were fit and hale again, and when the final audience of the day arrived, a hulking gypsy whom I knew well, he strode into my chamber after his announcement with my husband under his arm like a sack of wheat.

"How we worried!" he boomed, dropping Darwin to the ground. He stomped forward to embrace me. "We dug and we dug and we dug—but always there was more ice! Finally, when a storm came, we were forced to leave! But never for a moment did I doubt that little fish"—here he picked Darwin up again—"would not let anything happen to my queen!"

He dropped Darwin again and went to one knee before me. He looked into my eyes.

"Are you sure about this, my queen?"

I nodded. "It must be done."

"Already my gypsies are moving over the hills and into the villages, and there is word that the evil one is farther east than was thought."

"Then that is where we will start."

"We will always be close by," he vowed, and I took his giant paw in my own.

"Then I will not worry," I said.

I HEARD AND SMELLED RATHER THAN SAW MY OWN escape. Dropped from the window of my audience chamber in a sack to the ground below, as was Darwin and then the dog Hector, who had been mildly drugged for the duration, I felt the quick descent and none-too-gentle transfer to the back of a wagon. The sack smelled of oats, which made me want to sneeze. Other sacks, which were piled around us, some of them atop my own, contained everything else we would need.

I felt the jostle and shake of the wagon as its ponies were reined into motion. We traveled for perhaps an hour outside of Bradbury, during which time, no longer caring for the dry smell of oats, I cut a slit in my bag to breathe the late-day air.

Instead, I smelled the manure sacks that Miklos's men had piled atop everything else to discourage close inspection—especially after our disappearance was discovered.

That didn't take long, because after perhaps another half hour the cart came to a grinding halt, and I heard the driver questioned in mumbled tones. The words became more heated until the driver said, "Take a whiff, then!" I felt one of the bags above me lifted away, and a grunt of disgust.

"Happy, then?" the driver snorted, and the bag was dropped back into place.

Soon we were on our way.

Though I still longed for the smell of oats, the odor of manure never smelled so sweet.

WE EMERGED IN STARLIGHT. A SMALL FIRE WAS BURN-ing, and Darwin immediately began to prepare a meal. Our driver would not stay to eat, but immediately mounted the extra pony that had been tied to the back of the wagon and rode off.

"Good luck! It was Miklos's wish!" he called, raising a hand in farewell.

The night was still.

"Where are we?" I asked.

"Not too far from the last sighting of Frane. From here we head due east. Miklos's people have to be careful because everyone is wary of strangers these days."

He handed me something roasted and spicy, and, thankful for my appetite, I ate.

I looked down at Hector, who was revived, and whose big eyes studied me greedily. He barked once, then sat there with his tongue lolling.

Darwin laughed and tossed him a morsel from his own meal, which Hector devoured.

"This isn't dog, is it?" I said, warily, holding up my meal.

"Of course not!"

I gave Hector a bit of my own meal.

"Can we rid ourselves of the manure at least?" I asked, joking.

"No!" he said, which surprised me. "For now, we are two traveling farmers who sell manure."

My newly returned appetite began to leave me.

"Perhaps in a few days, after we make a few sales, we can rid ourselves of it and become mere peddlers."

"Not soon enough for me."

AND THAT'S WHAT WE DID. WE MET A FARMER WHO— after Darwin allowed him to rob us in a transaction for the manure just enough so that he felt kindly toward us, but not enough so that he became suspicious—informed us over his table that two strangers had, indeed, been that way not the week before.

"Strange they were, too," the farmer said, smoking on his pipe and scratching his whiskered chin. I thought of Pelltier's cigarettes, and almost gagged. "One of 'em was plain mad, and the other never showed her face or paws. All bowing and thankee and good day. The mad one just stared into space. Then they were gone east."

"What's east of here?" Darwin asked innocently.

"Hills and more hills, until you get to the town of Opportunity."

"That's quite a name for a town."

The farmer smiled, showing a distinct lack of various teeth. "'There ain't no opportunity in Opportunity,' the saying goes here." His chest puffed out a little, and he leaned back, blowing a smoke ring. He waved his pipe stem at us. "And the thing is, you might want to watch yourselves in that town, yes indeed. They ain't as kindly in transactions to wandering peddlers as I." He leaned forward, resting his elbows on his table, and smiled.

"Now I believe we were going to discuss rent for a night's lodging?"

THE NEXT MORNING, A BEAUTIFUL CLEAR ONE, FOUND us on the road, climbing and descending hills. The countryside was pretty but monotonous, and soon I tired of what looked like the same bubbling brook or the identical grove of junto trees or similar clusters of ancient rock huts, shaped like beehives, and for the most part demolished.

"Did you know that ancient feline hermits used to live in these structures?" Darwin informed me, and I pretended that I did not already know. We were cresting yet another hill. Even Hector was bored, running ahead to scout, then, inevitably, stopping to lie down in the sparse grass by the side of the road to wait for us when nothing of interest presented itself ahead.

This time he began to whine excitedly and ran back to jump into the cart and sit up beside me.

"What is it?" I asked in a low voice, but Hector only whined with anticipation.

Darwin was finishing his history and anthropology lesson, and I pretended to listen.

The cart topped the hill.

"Wonderful!" I cried, and Darwin said, "Why thank you, I had no idea you were so interested in ancient monks—"

"Not that—look!"

Below us was the dirtiest place I had ever seen in my life.

⤙ CHAPTER 36 ⤚

OPPORTUNITY INDEED! MORE LIKE RED DUST TOWN, with plumes of airborne dirt hanging over the streets like permanent clouds. The residents of this shanty village wore a permanent layer of filth on their fur, which gave them a strange, almost insubstantial look. We felt as if we were beholding them through a crimson fog. I began to cough almost immediately, which brought little notice because almost everyone else was doing the same.

Between bouts of hacking, I turned to my husband. "Why is it so—*cough*—dusty here?"

He pointed to the street below us, as well as the surrounding hills. "This town—*cough*—could only have been built by fools. It's set—*cough, cough*—in a bowl, with a perpetual breeze on a bed of red silt. Madness!"

Every building was covered in a fine layer of dust, and I could not tell haberdashery from general store. In fact, there were no markings on any of the buildings, which puzzled me. But there was one large structure in the near distance that everyone on the street was either coming from or going to, so we headed there, wiping our eyes and sniffling.

Hector, his eyes closed, was snugged down between us in the wagon, making noises of complaint in the back of his throat.

The doors of this structure were huge and thrown open, with an aisle as wide as the main street leading in. We passed through strips of plastic sheeting that hung down from the top of the entry, and suddenly the dust and dirt were gone.

"Ingenious!" Darwin remarked, looking back. The strips kept most of the filth outside and allowed for a free atmosphere within.

We found ourselves in a huge indoor bazaar. To either side were booths and tables set with wares and food. Rich aromas filled the air. There was the sound of laughter and the shouts of vendors.

"Welcome to Opportunity!" said a little feline to our right, stationed in a booth. Before us was a lowered gate.

The little fellow smiled, showing even fewer teeth than our recent farmer acquaintance. "I'd say you'll need two spaces to fit that wagon. That'll be a tenner, please!"

Darwin paid him, and the little cat, red as the dust outside from head to foot, bowed. "Been here before?" he inquired, as if he already knew the answer.

"We're from out west, thought we'd try the waters here."

The little fellow cackled. "Waters! There's no water for miles."

"Why, may I ask, is there a town here at all?"

There was a smaller wagon behind us, the driver beginning to complain about our slow pace, but the little feline was only too happy to give us the short history of the town.

"Ever seen how rock candy grows, mister?" he asked. Before Darwin could answer he went on. "You start with a string in a glass o' sugar water. Pretty soon some of the sugar sticks to the string. Then more, and more. And before you know it you got a whole lot of candy."

"Move on!" the irate driver behind us shouted, but the toll taker ignored him.

"Fellow named String, of all things, camped here a hundred years ago. Then, he wakes up and there's another camper next to him, then another . . ."

He laughed and waved us through. "Lots Fifty-seven and Fifty-eight! End of Aisle Fifteen!"

As we moved through we heard him beginning to chat with the irate driver and charge him twice what he had us.

NEEDLESS TO SAY WE FOUND OUR SPOT AND BEGAN to interact with the populace of this, the real heart of Opportunity. For an indoor city it was. While Darwin set up our wares and pretended to be a peddler, I leashed Hector and we walked through this indoor wonderland which, as I could see once we were within it, was three times as huge as I had thought. The ceiling was lost in the glare of lamps and electric lights strung from poles, and I saw birds swooping and turning as if they were under any other sky. There were thirty aisles, and I found a directory, a huge flat chalkboard, set up like a nonpermanent grid, with markings for the day in each lot, which was represented by a small square. The grid itself was well organized into sections by type of wares—foodstuffs along the back of the building, weaponry clustered together, as well as clothing, trinkets (our own section), soaps, and entertainment such as jugglers, mimes, magicians, and the like.

Overtaken with the marvelousness of the place, I found myself rattling the coins in my tunic and observing wares closely. I found a hat I had to have, and a folding pocket-knife with eight different tools that Darwin would love. There was even a shop that sold sweetmeats for dogs, and I indulged Hector.

I was so taken with the loud, carnival atmosphere of the place that I barely noticed two cloaked figures who passed close by and walked on. I was admiring the talents of a conjurer, who was producing Jakra cards out of thin air, one after the other from his empty paw.

But then I heard a hissed whisper in my ear: *"You've found me, wretch. But you won't live out the hour."*

I turned, adrenaline coursing through me like an electric charge, and there before me, her death's-head face, now completely naked of fur, not inches from my own and grinning with madness, was *Frane*.

She moved even closer, sniffing, her eyes impossibly wide.

"You are not with kit. I can tell. Which means when you die there will be no heir."

I drew back—I could smell the mocra on her breath, a sour, sickly odor.

Behind Frane was my mother, staring through the two of us as if we were not there.

Even as I reached for my own sword, Frane's cloak parted and in her left hand was a long, evil-looking blade, tipped with crimson.

"I killed your father with this, and now you!" she screamed, and raised the blade high.

My own sword was out, and there were shouts around

us as patrons realized what was happening and shrank
away.

I saw my mother melt into the crowd, which pulled her
away with its momentum.

Screeching like a carrion bird in its dive, Frane leapt at
me, hacking downward.

I parried her thrust, feeling the strength in her, then gave
her a blow of my own, which she blocked.

She pushed my sword back with her own, her skeletal
face suffused with glee. Her two front teeth, the gums receded from mocra, looked like fangs in her mouth. Her
white parchment skin, devoid of fur, looked alien, too thin,
monstrous.

"Let's see if the kit can fight!" Frane cried, and now the
battle was joined in earnest, with blow and thrust and parry
in increasing number. She drove me back toward the
crowd, which parted for us. The conjurer was transfixed, a
card in his hand, and when we were forced into his lot he
dropped what looked to be a hundred cards and ran. Beside
him was a table holding his wares, cheap magic tricks for
kits, and I was forced up onto it, spilling his goods. Frane
below me chopped and heaved at me, screaming obsceni-
ties all the while.

The table collapsed, and for a moment I was on the
ground. I saw Frane's blade thrust down at me and rolled
aside, jumping to my feet.

We continued, down the length of one aisle and over
into another. Tables and wagons were damaged, goods
flew into the air as Frane and I traded blows and positions.
At first she had the advantage, then I did, then she did
again. I thought I had her but my sword cut through only
the front of her tunic, and then she was at me again. Back
and forth we went at it, the crowd running in chaos before
our progress.

Suddenly I found the tip of her blade locked not an inch from my throat, her strength driving it toward me—I knew that it was poisoned, and if pricked I would meet my end.

With all of my effort I pushed back, and the blade was forced toward her own skinny neck. Her eyes widened in a moment with fear, and she snarled.

Darwin appeared, thrusting his way through the crowd, and his blade was advancing on her, too.

She saw him, and suddenly all the tension was loosed in our joined battle. She pulled her blade back and ran off into the crowd.

"Darwin, don't let her get away!"

Darwin was after her, but she was like a wraith, jumping over tables and pushing screaming patrons aside, until she was out a side door.

We raced after, pushing through the strips of plastic.

"Soon we will *all* die!" she shouted at us, her voice swallowed by the wind.

Suddenly we found ourselves in a whirling dust storm, the air filled with a keening wail. We could not see two feet in front of us.

We pushed our way through, but it was hopeless.

Frane had disappeared.

With a sudden thought I turned and ran back into the mall. Pandemonium had given way to the aftermath of battle, with patrons milling and shopkeepers taking stock and checking damage. Into this swirl I flung myself, searching desperately, looking at faces, moving on.

I slowly traced my way back to where the melee had started, and there she was, standing just where she had been left, the lost look painted onto her face.

"Mother!" I shouted, but there was no recollection, only the blank, lost stare of the addict suddenly without drug or purpose.

I pulled her to me and hugged her, but again there was no response. I might have been anyone.

"I'll take care of you, Mother," I whispered fiercely into her ear.

There was no response, and then a single word, uttered with a kind of awe and need, as if a god had been summoned, escaped her lips.

"*Mocra,*" she said.

⇥ CHAPTER 37 ⇤

"I KNOW WHO YOU ARE," A KIND WOMAN IN THE crowd said, and before I could answer, she said, "Come with me."

Darwin rejoined me, after finding Hector crouched in fear underneath our wagon, and we followed the woman out of the mall into the dusty streets of Opportunity. "Stay close!" she advised, which was good because the storm had not abated. But she seemed to know the way, and took us to a small building with many floors.

Inside, the sound of the dust storm was muffled, but still we heard silt washing against the side of the building like water waves. She led us up a rickety staircase that swayed under our weight, and past one floor and on to the third. There were three doors, and she put a key into the lock of the middle one and drew us in. It was a small, spare room with a bed and sink and a single chair.

"It's not a rich man's place, but it's all I have and you're

welcome to it, Your Majesty." She bowed, pushing the key
into Darwin's hand, keeping her eyes down.

"I won't forget this kindness," I vowed, and Darwin
said, "But where will you go?"

"I will stay with friends. If you need anything, ask for
Anna in the shop next door."

"We will."

She shook her head, and then she was gone, closing the
door after her.

And then our vigil began.

AFTER A DAY, MY MOTHER BEGAN TO SWEAT PRO-
fusely, and see things that weren't there. She squirmed on
the bed like a sick kit, her paws thrashing. Hector, sorely
frightened by this activity, stayed in the far corner of the
room, cowering.

At one point my mother spoke to me by name but it was
only a phantom that she saw, another daughter Clara, perhaps when I was little. "Good girl!" she cooed, and clasped
herself as if embracing someone. "So good at your lessons,
and I love the way you play the *tambor*!"

At that point I began to cry, because she did not
know me.

The second day she began to scream, an almost constant keening wail that left her hoarse. Her body was
wracked with intermittent trembling that degenerated into
shaking fits requiring both Darwin and me to hold her
down, lest she hurt herself. Her legs kicked madly and her
arms flailed, and she screamed at demons only she could
see.

"Mocra! Mocra!" she screeched, as if beseeching a
lover. The skin had retreated around her eyes, and her lips

were pulled back over her teeth, making her look grotesque.

By the third day Darwin and I were exhausted, spelling one another to short naps, which were inevitably broken by my mother's hoarse wails. The good woman Anna appeared with food and drink, which we snatched at like fugitives. Though my mother had lost her voice, she had not lost her energy—but finally, thankfully, she fell into a rough slumber at the end of the day.

"The worst of it is over," Darwin said, then announced, "I will leave you now and go after Frane."

"Don't!" I protested. "When my mother is well we will go together."

"And in the meantime, the trail will grow cold. Stay. I'll be back within the week."

I could not hold him, and his words rang true, so he went. The dust storm had retreated, leaving only the normal choking conditions outside. At the door to the room I embraced my husband and bade him well.

"I'll be careful," Darwin said, then he was gone.

FOR ANOTHER TWO DAYS MY MOTHER'S CONDITION alternated between stretches of unsettled sleep and bouts of madness. She flailed at me when I tried to give her food or water, and only when she was asleep was I able to steal close and pat her fevered brow with a cool cloth.

And then, after five days, she suddenly opened her eyes and knew me.

"Clara?" she rasped tentatively, and held my paw in her own.

"Yes, Mother."

"Are you real? Is it really you, or am I dreaming?"

And then she fell into a sound and restful sleep, which lasted into the middle of the next day.

When she awoke she took food, which did not stay down, but it was a good sign. Her thirst returned, and she drank glass after glass of water, always needing more. Her sleep pattern became more measured, which meant that I was able to sleep, too. I began to worry about Darwin, and my worry became alarm when a report reached the town, and therefore Anna, who was a great gossip, that a caravan had been attacked not three days out of Opportunity. I met her in the shop next door, which turned out to be a saloon.

"Killed 'em all, they did—whoever did it, that is. Slit their throats. Two old gents and a younger one."

She looked at me and soothed, "There, there, don't you worry. That husband of yours can take care of himself, he can. He'll be just fine, Your Majesty."

"He should have been back by now."

Anna motioned the bartender, a great friend of hers, who drew two fresh ales and put them before us. It was a modest establishment, a makeshift bar lined with plain stools and a mirror behind it, a floor covered in red dust let in when the two huge swinging doors were opened and closed, which they often were. It was the middle of the day and the bar sparsely attended.

"He'll be back before you know it. And anyway, your Darwin was heading east, weren't he?"

"Yes."

"And this caravan, it was heading south it was, toward Spirit."

"What's in Spirit?" I asked.

She laughed. "Less than here, Your Majesty. They ain't even got a trading mall, and nary a saloon to be seen. It's a way stop, a crossroads of sorts. There ain't nothing else for a hundred miles in any direction."

"Nothing at all?"

She shook her head, then emptied her glass. "Not unless you count the Old Ruins, as we calls 'em."

"What are they?"

She shrugged. "Not much. Things left by the Old Ones. Covered with more dust than this town. Not even worth charging money to see, they is. The only thing of any value is the station there, like the ones everybody's been talking about."

"An oxygenation station?"

"Right! And the biggest one of them all. There's been talk about the Science Guild coming in here soon to get it up to speed again. Makin' air, as they say. But for now it's just dust and sand and broken machines, and a couple of soldiers guarding it."

She motioned the bartender but I stayed her hand, and pushed my own untouched ale over to her.

"I must get back to my mother," I said.

She grinned, and took the offered potable. "Thank you, Your Majesty! And cheers to you and your husband's safe return!"

She drank half of her ale down, and I took my leave of her, thoughts roiling in my head.

I thought of Frane's last words to Darwin and me as she ran off into the dust storm.

Soon we will all die.

IT WAS THE NEXT DAY WHEN THE REMAINS OF THE UN-fortunate caravan were returned to Opportunity and brought into the mall for display. With relief I saw that Darwin had not been among the victims, who were both older and younger than my husband. One of them had, indeed met his fate with a cut throat, but the other two were strangely unmarked. It was only upon closer examination that it was discovered that each had been pricked with a single, non–life-threatening thrust.

"Poison?" the doctor theorized, and then I knew it was Frane who had killed them.

There were two wagons returned, and one missing. The toll taker in the mall, who kept track of everything, reported that there had been three wagons in all. After examining the two remaining wagons, which contained surveying equipment and engineering supplies, he looked at his manifest, and said, "The missing wagon was filled with explosives. They were heading out to the Planitia Oxygenation Station, in advance of a Science Guild team."

I needed to hear no more.

"BUT YOU CAN'T GO ALONE, CLARA!" MY MOTHER begged. She had regained some of her color, though she was still very weak. "Wait for Darwin at least!"

Hector, who had taken to my mother after her condition improved, sat on her bed and made contented noises as she stroked his head.

"If Darwin comes back, tell him where I went. He'll know what to do."

"But daughter!" She began to weep and tremble, and I went to her and held her. No longer was she an automaton, staring into space. She was my mother again.

"I have no choice," I soothed. "Anna will take care of you, and you have Hector to keep you company. When I come back, Darwin and I will take you to Bradbury. You'll never be in danger again, I promise."

"But I don't want to lose you! I couldn't bear it . . ."

Her weeping turned to gentle snores, as in her weakened condition she still mostly slept. I laid her back against her pillows and rose, checking my weapons and hefting my saddlebag onto my shoulder. A good strong horse waited for me below on the street.

I patted Hector, and said, "Take care of her."

I looked down at my mother and smiled.

"I have no choice," I whispered to her sleeping form. "If I don't stop Frane, she will kill everyone on Mars."

⫷ CHAPTER 38 ⫸

MY HORSE PROVED STURDY AND ABLE. SOON WE
had left the dust bowl of Opportunity behind and climbed
a series of hills into blessed fresh air. It was a relief to
breathe freely again. Even my mount noticed the change
and snorted with pleasure.

The highlands before me were nearly featureless, scant
grasslands pocked with sand oasis and dunes. It was a
bleak crossing we made. That night the stars rose in a black
velvet sky, and I was glad for their company. I thought of
Copernicus and also of my husband, and wished them
well.

The next day was much like the first. I passed the town
of Spirit, skirting south of it, and it did indeed look as
bleak as Anna had described. But on the morning of my
third day something appeared on the horizon that broke the
static landscape. It was a jagged line that only grew above

the horizon as I traveled toward it, and by noon I was sure that it was the Old Ruins, the oxygenation station.

I KNEW I WOULD NOT MAKE IT BY NIGHTFALL, SO I made camp as the sun set. I resolved to set off at dawn, but the buildings were beset by weird flickering lights and far-off, faint noises, and something deep within me told me not to wait. So with only the stars and the quick-passing moon Phobos to accompany me, I rode toward my destination. The silhouette of the buildings was huge before me, and a mile out I tied my horse, patted his flanks, and made off on foot.

The gates were as rusted and unused as those of the station I had visited. But this one was on a monstrous scale. The main building loomed before me like a behemoth, and when I entered the yawning opening of its portal I felt as if I had been eaten. The flickering lights were gone, and I was assaulted by darkness within. Each footfall made an echo that might as well have been a thunderclap. If Frane was here she was aware of my entry.

I passed an empty wagon, and two dead soldiers without a visible mark on their bodies.

And then sudden light flared, and I saw Frane. High up on a catwalk she perched like a vulture, staring balefully down at me. A bolt of fear went through me. She had dyed her face and limbs deep crimson, and looked like a demon from the depths of the underworld. She smiled viciously.

A gust of wind flew off the desert and the huge doors behind me swung closed with a great clang.

"It ends here, Frane!" I shouted, my words echoing in the empty space.

"Indeed," she said. "It ends for all of us, *queen*." She

spat the last word down at me with such spite that I winced.

I edged my way toward the ladder leading to the cat-walk, and she followed me eagerly with her eyes.

She drew something from her tunic and threw it down at me. I jumped back but when it struck the floor nothing happened. I saw that it was a timepiece.

"Look at it," Frane ordered.

With the toe of my boot I turned the face of the minia-ture clock toward me.

"When the hands meet, this place, and eventually Mars, will be no more."

In less than ten minutes those things would happen.

I kicked the timepiece aside and began to climb the lad-der leading up to her. Already she was drawing her sword from its scabbard.

When I reached the top she was waiting for me twenty paces away.

"It will give me great pleasure to kill you before all of Mars loses its oxygen," she said.

I drew my own blade and advanced on her.

"Prepare to die, *queen*," she said. "Just as Haydn and Sebastian before you died."

"Where have you put the charges, Frane?" I asked.

She smiled madly. "Your king is minding them, of course!"

She extended her tongue and licked at a spot around her lips, removing a spot of the red color. Then she drew her tongue over her crimson forearm, making a streak. "This is pure mocra," she said, licking again. "It is all I have left, but it will be enough."

"What do you mean, my king—"

She cackled, a strangled sound, and indicated a spot below and to her right with the tip of her sword. I looked down to see my husband, bound and gagged, staring up at me, surrounded by the explosives she had taken from the caravan.

"Darwin!" I shouted, but at that moment Frane, shrieking *"Die!"* attacked me, slashing her sword down in a vicious arc. I blocked her, and she drove at me again and again, pushing me along the catwalk, which began to sway with our efforts.

She was insanely strong, and I felt myself losing to her. I was forced back, until she had me against a stanchion, and then crouching with it at my back. She rained blow after blow which I was barely able to parry. The fire in her eyes was madness itself.

"Die! Die!" she screamed, driving me down to the floor of the catwalk.

With a last gasping effort I thrust my blade up at her, and somehow found her breast.

Reeling backwards, she wailed in pain.

Fighting for breath, I pushed myself up and advanced.

A blot of blood appeared on her red tunic, and she looked down at it in wonder.

"The kit has claws," she said.

She leapt at me, finding strength, and we battled once more.

Again she drove me back, but that time I gave as well as I received and pushed her away.

Once more I cut her, below her arm.

Her crimson features blossomed in rage, and she brought her blade down, forcing me once again to the floor of the catwalk, which swayed like a kit's swing.

She stumbled for a fraction of a second, and with all of my strength I drove my blade up into her breast, a deeper and truer strike.

She gasped and dropped her sword, which slid from the catwalk and fell, rattling on the floor below us.

She staggered back, clutching at her breast, and I followed her, jabbing again and again, finding flesh.

She dropped to the floor of the catwalk and lay back, gasping.

"Come close," she begged, her voice a dying rasp.

When I took a step toward her she drew a dagger and sought to cut me with it, howling.

I moved aside, avoiding the thrust.

Then, suddenly, she dropped the blade.

I thrust my sword four times into her horrid, twitching body.

"This is for my grandmother, Haydn of Mars! And this for my father, and this for my mother! *And this is for Mars, which you would have destroyed!*"

Finally, her eyes clouded and went blank, and she lay still and dead.

Mars, the universe, and my life were free of her.

Quickly, I climbed down the catwalk. The timepiece indicated there were two minutes to spare. I went to my husband, cutting him free, and between us we quickly disarmed the explosives.

And then, panting, barely able to catch my breath, I sat down and wept. I wept copiously for all the felines who had died at the hands of the butcher Frane. I wept for my father and grandmother. I wept for all the wars and the years of hardship and pain my planet had endured.

My husband came, and held me.

"It's over," he said, soothing. "After all these years, it's all over."

And then, finally, I wept in joy for Mars.

⊰ CHAPTER 39 ⊱

ALL OF MARS CELEBRATED.

When we returned to Bradbury, it was in triumph. My mother, well now and attended to by her new lady-in-waiting Anna, was a new woman, and treated with the respect due her. Darwin and I were paraded like celebrities, to the point where I withdrew out of embarrassment. And still we had to appear at our window twice a day to greet the throngs who continued to come to the temporary capital, for if we did not, we were told, there was danger that the crowds would tear the building down in their joy.

Newton, with Copernicus at his side, went about with a permanent smile on his face. He talked endlessly about the things he had already learned from Stella and the things to come. He had already announced his retirement from the Science Guild, putting Copernicus in his place, so that he could devote his remaining years to the new knowledge from the Old Ones.

And Wells would be rebuilt, on the ruins of the old city. It would be an even grander capital than it had been, with a new Assembly Hall and a new palace.

"It's just as well," I told Darwin, during one of our infrequent quiet moments together, "because we'll need all the space we can get."

"What do you mean?" he said, charmingly dense to my meaning.

I patted my not-yet-swelling belly.

"You're with kit!" he shouted, a smile splitting his face.

I nodded. "Just." And then I laughed as he threw himself around the room, cartwheeling and whooping for joy, like a kit himself.

And all was happiness, until, a few days later, I learned of his plans.

"WHAT IS THIS FOOLISHNESS!" I SCREAMED, STORMing into a meeting of Newton, Copernicus, and Darwin. They looked up from their table as if they had been caught stealing.

"Your Majesty—" Copernicus began meekly, but I silenced him with a glare, which I then turned on my husband.

"When were you going to tell me of this?" I demanded.

"Soon . . ." he mumbled.

I turned my ire on Newton. "And you condoned it?"

"It was my idea, actually," he said evenly. A ghost of a smile played over his lips.

"*I forbid it!*" I screamed, and stormed out.

DARWIN WAITED AN APPROPRIATE NUMBER OF MINutes, then came into my chamber and stood before me.

"We're going," he said simply.

Newton was at the door, still smiling. "There's no real danger involved, Your Majesty," he said. "Stella has been in touch with Earth directly. There aren't many on the planet, most left long ago for the stars, and it would be a shame not to take the opportunity. They are fascinated by what has happened here, and extended the invitation. The spaceship is well equipped, and the trip will only take a matter of months."

"We have to do it," Darwin said.

"Let someone else go!"

"Clara," he said, taking my paw, "I would regret it for the rest of my life if I didn't go."

"Copernicus and Darwin will be safe," Newton said. "I would go myself, but I want to devote my remaining time to Stella and her wonders."

"If that's the way things are," I said, conceding, "I give my consent. I have only one condition."

⊰ CHAPTER 40 ⊱

IT WAS THE MOST BEAUTIFUL DAY I COULD EVER RE-
call, with Sol a perfect gold coin in a crystal-clear, bright
sky. Which was odd, because our destination was in darkness, visible only from the other side of the planet, hanging like a blue jewel in perpetual night.

Newton was already gone, back to Stella at the North
Pole, with whom he had formed an attachment that was at
least affection and seemed even more. He had already assured us that by the time we returned the new city of Wells
would be well under construction. In the meantime, Bradbury would continue as the temporary capital, with my
mother as chancellor. She would have the assistance of fat
Warton as protector of the government, under my appoint-
ment. He had proved so able as war minister that it seemed
a shame not to put his talents to work elsewhere. He would
be a good protector, and had the vote of the Senate and Assembly behind him.

Mars was at peace, the first it had known in generations, and the people had settled into it with relish. Whatever dregs Frane had commanded had melted into the hills and tunnels, never to be seen again. Without the head, the body of the snake quickly died.

The gypsies, under their leader Miklos, who would also accompany us, had been, by fiat, granted clan status. No longer would they walk in the shadows of Mars. The change made Miklos quite nervous, of course, which was delightful to see. But not too nervous, after the ceremonial tapping with sword, to lift Darwin up by the scruff of the neck and pronounce, "Little fish! I am one of you now!"

Also with us were members of the Science Guild, a few self-important dignitaries and others deemed important or curious enough to fill out the delegation of fifty.

It was a fine day, and a fine launch. With precise instructions from Stella, who assured us that the ship's controls, once set, were mostly automatic, our liftoff was a smooth one. Our designated captain was one of Newton's trusted airship pilots, and Darwin sat in the copilot's chair. I occupied the third seat, at one time used by a navigator, behind them. The rest of our Martian contingent were divided among the three set of spacious crew quarters behind us.

The launch went much as the first one Darwin and I had experienced. Our pilot was a lean fellow with small eyes that grew very wide when, in a matter of moments, we found ourselves high above Mars and hanging in space like an ornament. It was as if a switch had been thrown, turning light to dark. The sun, which had hung so serenely in the glory of a Martian midmorning, now hung in blackness.

We studied our beautiful planet, its reds and browns and whites and greens and blues, and I could hear the chorus of oohs and ahhs behind us, for the crew quarters were appointed with their own porthole windows.

Then the pilot pushed a button and the view began to fade behind us into a shrinking reddish ball, as the ship turned in space toward its destination.

I held in my hands my most precious possession, the book of Old One composers that had been my father's, and my grandmother's before that. It was a connection with them, and the past of my planet, that was vital to me. I was told by Stella, through Newton, that they were informed that there were musicians at our destination who still played the strange instruments for which the Old Ones had composed music, and that they would be happy to perform a concert in honor of the Queen of Mars.

I would make of the book a present to these strange Old Ones who had once regarded us as pets and now stood as our equals.

For that matter, what would they look like? Had evolution changed their own forms and features over one and three-quarter million years? Would they look like the pictures in my book—or something completely strange and alien? They had seemed particularly excited to hear that we had dogs as pets, and requested that I bring Hector, who slept peacefully under my seat.

Under the book was my other precious possession. In my swelling belly, I could already feel faint movement, which Dr. Mandrake, who was also on the trip to attend to me, assured me would only increase. Already I knew there were at least two kits, possibly more. The first two, whether male or female, would be named Haydn and Sebastian.

They would be born on the trip, making them children not only of Mars but of space.

The ship had completed its turn, and pointed toward the tiny blue planet that was our destination.

I felt a strange stirring, as I always had when contemplating this jewel in the sky.

Finally, I knew what it was.

As the spaceship accelerated, and the blue speck of Earth became ever so large in space before us, I understood at last the feeling I had always felt when looking this way.

We were going home.

Fantasy that Goes to the
Next Millennium and Beyond

Flights

edited by Al Sarrantonio
0-451-46036-7

This daring, all-new anthology showcases some
of the genre's biggest names and hottest
newcomers. Setting the standard for the
twenty-first century, this collection presents
fantasy that rocks the field of
science fiction.

Includes new stories from:
Neil Gaiman
Harry Turtledove
Dennis L. McKiernan
Joyce Carol Oates
Orson Scott Card
And others

A444

Run on the Wind

Jenifer Dalton

A DELL/EMERALD BOOK

Acknowledgments

A special thank you to Leslie O'Gwin-Rivers for the research on the Shoshone Indians, and on the many other parts of this novel that enabled me to keep the work historically accurate.

Also, I wish to express my appreciation to the Lander Chamber of Commerce, to Viola Garrett, Curator of the Riverton Museum, and to the U.S. Department of Agriculture, Forest Service, for the Teton and Yellowstone National Parks.

And to those wonderfully warm and friendly people of Lander, Riverton, Dubois, and the Wind River Mountain area of Wyoming, who gave of their time and knowledge of the rich history of the area they were born and raised in.

The Wind River area of Wyoming was actually settled in 1868–1869. I have taken the literary license of dating this novel prior to that time because I did not wish to accidentally offend any of those second, third, or fourth generations who still remember the original founders.

The historical references are true, but the names and the people used in this story are purely imaginary.

I have also striven to portray the role of the Shoshone Indians accurately. Chief Washakie did live. He was known as the white man's friend, and because of his great foresight, the Eastern Shoshone Indians lost no lives in a fruitless war against the expansion of the white man. Washakie made a lasting peace with the United States government that still stands today.

One further historical note seems necessary. Wyoming, in 1869, became the first government in the world to grant "female suffrage." The women of Wyoming were the first in the nation to vote, to serve on juries, and to hold appointed and elected public office.

Jenifer Dalton
December, 1981
Pomona, New York

PROLOGUE

June, 1867

Dusk was settling over the mountains as two men slowed their horses. To curious eyes, they would seem a strange sight. The small man was copper-hued, with long black hair falling straight to below his shoulders. His lean, bare chest was hairless. His only clothing was buckskin pants and doeskin moccassins. Around his neck hung four large bear claws on braided rawhide. The Shoshone sat astride a cream and brown spotted Appaloosa.

Next to him was a man of completely opposite complexion. Dark, wavy hair topped a tanned face that held almost cat-like amber eyes. Even though his face was covered with a week's stubble, his straight nose and strong chin were evident. The man's mouth was firm, not large but not small, either. His finely muscled chest and arms were covered by a worn Union army shirt, the golden braid of his captain's rank was faded by the sun. The man's waist was trim, and his thighs flared with muscle as they pressed against the horse's flank. His high brown riding boots reached passed midcalf.

His horse was a giant gray Andalusian stallion that pranced easily as the tall man guided him between the rocks of the ravine.

Soon the Indian signaled a stop. The white man nodded in agreement.

"Treemont, tonight will be our last night. Tomorrow I will be home, and you, my friend, will follow your path." Smiling, the Indian slipped from his horse's back. "I will start a fire," he said.

Kael Treemont dismounted and smiled at his friend before he began to unsaddle the stallion. Behind him, Two Wolves began to gather wood for a fire.

Suddenly, the Andalusian shied from Kael, forcing him to stumble.

Two Wolves froze as he heard the animal's snort of fear. From the corner of his eye, Kael saw Two Wolves drop the wood and draw his hunting knife. Only then did Kael look over his shoulder. A chill spread through him at what his eyes discerned.

Above him, on the reddish rock of the ravine's wall, was a tawny ball of death. Even as Kael reached for his rifle, he saw the cougar tense as it began its leap.

Kael felt a sharp pain in his back, then he fell forward as Two Wolves pushed him to safety. The Indian turned and met the golden cat in midleap. The flashing blade of the Shoshone's knife struck at the cougar's side as Kael watched the cat pull his friend into an embrace of death.

Rolling along the ground, Two Wolves and the cougar fought their deadly battle. Suddenly, Kael heard the mountain lion's scream of pained rage, as Two Wolves' knife raked along its side.

Galvanizing himself into action, Kael pulled the rifle and aimed it at the two bodies that rolled in battle. Kael did not fire at the constantly spinning pair, waiting purposefully until he could get a clear shot at the animal. Suddenly, he heard the cat scream, then watched as its rear paws drew under its belly. The powerful muscles of the cougar's haunches knotted, and the cat raked Two Wolves from chest to groin with razor-sharp claws.

Firing blindly, Kael tried to kill the wild beast.

Standing motionless above its victim, the cougar glared at Kael with glowing yellow eyes. Opening its mouth wide, the animal's loud growl of challenge tore into Kael's ears. Unexpectedly, the cat jumped free of the Indian, and ran from its victory. Kael watched helplessly as the tawny beast of death fled with Two Wolves' knife still deeply imbedded in its side.

Kael ran to his friend and knelt beside him. Lifting Two Wolves' head, Kael gazed into his eyes.

"Treemont, the cat . . . He will kill many people before my knife finishes him . . . He must be stopped." Two Wolves gasped, and Kael saw the pain that filled his friend's face.

"I will kill the cat," Kael promised.

"Good," Two Wolves whispered, as his body trembled within the hold of death. "Treemont. My village is half a day from here. Take me home . . ." he whispered as he died.

"I'll take you home," Kael said. Slowly, he carried Two Wolves' body and laid it next to the unlit fire. Then he took a blanket from his saddle pack, and wrapped his friend within it. Sitting through the night with his rifle beside him, Kael guarded the body.

Kael Treemont had found Two Wolves four weeks before in the Black Hills. He'd been riding for most of the day when he reached a small plateau. Deciding to make camp, Kael scouted for the best spot. Then he'd seen them.

Lying on the ground were the bodies of five Crow warriors. In their midst was the bleeding body of a single Shoshone. Of the six, only the Shoshone still breathed. Kael spent three days fighting the death that threatened the Indian. On the fourth day, the man had begun to come around. By the sixth day, Kael had learned Two Wolves spoke fluent English, and why he had been there.

11

The Crows had raided his village and had slain many people before they were driven off. Among them had been Two Wolves' sister. Two Wolves and three other Shoshone warriors had gone after the Crows, swearing an oath of vengeance, prepared to never return home until their people had been avenged. The other Shoshone warriors had lost their lives several days later in a second battle with the Crow. Two Wolves had been the only one to survive and to continue tracking the Crow. When he had found them, he used the high vantage point of a tree to shoot them down. All but two had been killed. Two Wolves faced them on the ground, and had won, but he had also been badly hurt.

Now, throughout the long, dark night of Kael Treemont's vigil, he pondered the fate that had led him to Two Wolves; at the coincidence that he, too, was on a trail of vengeance, and would not stop until his mission was complete.

When the sun rose over the mountain peaks, Captain Kael Treemont, now retired from the United States Army, secured his friend's blanket-wrapped body on the Appaloosa, and began to track the cougar by the light of the day. Slowly, on the thirtieth anniversary of his birth, Kael followed the telltale trail of scarlet patches of blood.

PART I

The Idaho Territory
Wyoming
June, 1867

Placing a small, booted foot into the leather stirrup, Lara Dowley grasped the pommel of the saddle and began to swing her light body up. Pausing momentarily, birdlike above the ground, Lara's ice-blue eyes surveyed the land around her. The morning's golden sun flowed down onto the lush green valley that sat like an oasis, surrounded by almost barren terrain. With a slight flaring of her shapely nostrils, Lara picked up the scent of pine, sage, juniper, and wildflower. Sighing with pleasure, a sigh that spoke more than words, she began to complete her upward movement.

"Lara!" came her stepfather's loud bellow.

Feeling a tinge of apprehension, Lara loosened her muscles and allowed her slim body to return to the ground. She had hoped to be gone before he'd finished his breakfast. Now she turned slowly, certain of what was about to happen.

"How often must I tell you that a lady does not dress like that?" Martin Dowley admonished as he completed his walk from the covered veranda of the too-large house. Although it was only a few hundred feet to the stables, he was breathing hard and sweating profusely. Martin Dowley was fifty-two, with a balding pate that was continually covered with a succession of different hats. His face had a mean, jowley look to it, and his body was shaped more like an egg than a man.

"Father, I'm going for a ride, not a social," Lara reminded him. Seeing the hardening set of his small mouth and the narrowing of his dark eyes, Lara reacted angrily. "I am not your property!" she spat.

"No? You are wrong, young lady. You most certainly are my property. You are bought and paid for, and I have the papers to prove it," Dowley replied with a grotesque fascimile of a smile. "Now, damnit, girl, you'll do exactly what I tell you. Look at yourself. Wearing buckskins and a man's shirt. You should be ashamed, I am!"

"Am I to ride through the sage with a dress and petticoats?" Lara asked sarcastically as she fought back the tears that his taunting reminder of her adoption summoned.

"No. You may take the carriage, or ride our property like a woman, with a woman's saddle and a proper riding dress. You're indecent the way you are."

"Indecent? I'm *indecent*?" Lara almost screamed her incredulous reaction to her father's hurting words. "At least all I do is ride in pants. I don't force women to travel across the country to chase my ambitions. I don't push people beyond their capabilities. I don't drive people to their deaths." Lara's nineteen-year-old eyes turned cold, her entire frame became tense with anger as she spoke. Suddenly, Lara realized just how far she had overstepped her bounds. Watching her father's face turn a dark shade of red, she wisely and quickly mounted the roan mare and, using her heels, commanded the horse to move.

"Never—never speak to me like that!" Martin Dowley yelled as he began to run after the burgundy-haired woman. "Come back here this minute!"

Ignoring his shouts, Lara forced the mare to a gallop in an effort to put her father, and their home, behind her. Through the rich green valley, and then over the small hills that led toward the Wind River, Lara sped toward freedom from prying eyes. She felt the breeze full in her face, felt the heavy mass of her hair being lifted and flung about as she let her buckskin-covered legs mold themselves to the horse's flanks.

The smooth movements of the roan's muscles as they rippled against her thighs gave Lara a sense of oneness with the large animal. She tried to block out all thought as she concentrated on the horse's gait, the wind in her face, and the warm sun above her. But she could not.

Lara's mind was in a rage; her heart beat heavily within her breast. The rising heat of the day and the heat of her anger made the young woman perspire freely. She felt the rivulets of moisture run between the valley of her breasts, felt the cooling effect of the perspiration beading on her brow as it mixed with the rushing air.

"Father!" Lara spat out the word as if it were a curse. Oh, how she wished she had known her real father. Not this fat obscenity who demanded so much but was unwilling to give anything in return. Not this miserable man who had forced her to leave Pennsylvania; to leave her friends, and to leave the man she had planned to marry.

Lara's light blue eyes softened and began to mist as she thought about Jason Grumman. They had grown up together. The Grumman family, who were Quakers, had owned a fine business and a house near her own. Jason and Lara had pledged an undying love for each other when she had been so harshly forced from her home to move West. She made him promise to wait for her. One way or another, they would be reunited.

Had it been only yesterday that she had received the letter? It seemed like years already. She had slept fitfully last night, dreaming of Jason, and of what she had read in the letter. Amelia Forman, her friend in Philadelphia, had written to her. It was the worst news Lara had received since arriving in the Idaho territories. Jason Grumman had married another. Although she had spent a miserable night, when the sun had risen, the pain of his treachery had dimmed, and the reality of her situation had entered Lara's thoughts. Now she was alone, forced to face her future as a grown woman.

Dressing, Lara had looked at the soft globe of the rising sun with a new sense of understanding and had forgiven Jason. Perhaps she had always known that he would not come for her, that he could not leave his family.

But how she hated Martin Dowley! How she despised this man who forced her to give up every dream she had ever built. Lara loathed her stepfather even more for making her realize Jason's weakness. Just thinking of Martin Dowley made her angrier.

The foliage that had been so lush and green was now becoming sparse. The changing land that had always warned Lara to turn back from the untamed wilderness of the Wind River Mountains went unnoticed by her misted eyes and enraged mind as she continued her own inward journey.

Lara had never known her natural father. He had died two months before she had been born. Eleven months after Lara's birth, her mother had married Martin Dowley. Kristen Fairwald had agreed to this marriage because she had felt that she and her baby daughter needed the protection and security of a man of Martin Dowley's stature. A rich and seemingly noble man.

But that rich and noble man had made her mother's life a living hell. He was demanding, self-seeking, and bigoted. Martin Dowley had treated her mother, and Lara, like chattel, to be used when he deemed necessary and forgotten until needed again. Dowley had killed his wife. Not physically, but through years of mental torture, blaming the loss of his fortune on her. Then the unanswered question of how he had regained his wealth, combined with their move to the Idaho territory, had brought Kristen Fairwald to death's door. The trip was hard, even for people such as they who had the means to afford more comfort.

Lara had watched her mother deteriorate every day of the trip, with each mile the wagons traveled. During the last days of her mother's life, Lara had held her continually, soothing her and pressing her close against herself. At the end, Kristen had died looking into the blue eyes of her daughter. Kristen had smiled, sadly, and had raised her hand and stroked Lara's cheek.

"I'm sorry, baby. I'm sorry I have to leave you. I can't stay any longer, I just can't. . . ."

Lara had cried as she had pressed her mother's still warm cheek against her own, rocking the dead woman as if she were a newborn infant. Lara didn't know how long it had been before the wagons stopped for the night. When Dowley found them, he'd pulled her away from her mother and had buried Kristen without even the smallest of prayers on his lips. The next day, he had acted as though nothing had happened, and Lara heard the whispers from the rest of the people in their wagon train. They had respected his strength in going on, in acting as the leader of the group. Lara had wanted to tell them that it wasn't strength. Martin Dowley had only one care, one love. Himself. From that point in her life, Lara's hatred for him intensified, and burnt deeply within her breast.

The harsh bellows of the roan mare's ragged, forced breathing returned Lara's mind to the present. Flecks of foam flew back at her from the horse's heavily sweating neck. Dismissing the mist that had been veiling her eyes, Lara glanced around her. Gently, she loosened the grip of her legs and drew back the reins. Lara was entering a deep ravine, and her whereabouts were a mystery to her. Looking over her shoulder, she sighted a familiar landmark. A bold, barefaced mountain that signaled the start of the territory of the Shoshone Indians.

The mare began to snort fiercely, prancing about nervously. Suddenly, the roan reared hard, throwing an unprepared Lara from its back. Everything seemed to move slowly before her eyes as she flew from the saddle. She saw the mare's head and fear-filled eyes, a swirling of blue and white sky, the yellow ball of the sun. Landing on her back, Lara felt one brief instant of relief. Then her head slammed against a jutting rock and she knew only blackness.

※   ※   ※

The rifle felt like a dead weight strapped across his back as he climbed another outcrop of rock. The tall man stopped to wipe away salty sweat so that his eyes could search, unimpaired, the area before him. His body moved quickly and gracefully as he spotted another splash of wet red against the gray-brown rock.

"Close," he said to himself as he moved forward again. When he crested the large outcropping, Kael Treemont froze. As silently as a fish swimming underwater, he pulled the rifle over his shoulder and head. The movement took an eternity as his muscles sang tensely and his eyes never wavered from the tawny golden form of the crouched mountain lion.

As Kael leveled the rifle into position, he could not help but admire the feline, and mighty, beauty of the wounded animal. The cougar's muscles were corded with tension and power, the cat's breathing was hardly discernable, betraying nothing of the pain it was in. Kael stiffened as he saw the animal's tail twitch once, then lower its belly against its rocky perch.

The cougar crouched, perfectly still yet ready to spring. Then a new sound came to Kael's ears. The sound of a horse scenting danger and venting its fears. Kael knew he had little time as his finger began to pull the trigger. As the great cat started its leap, Kael's finger eased back. Cougar and bullet collided in midair with a whining, screaming impact. The beast's leap continued, but Keal knew he'd hit his mark. At the end of the cat's arc would be death.

Without thinking of anything else, Kael sped from his position, carrying the rifle carelessly in one hand as he ascended the rocky terrain. When he reached the animal's perch, Kael Treemont froze. The tableau that unfolded below held him transfixed.

The horse he had heard, a roan mare, stood trembling, its forelegs pawing the ground nervously. Eight feet in front of the mare was the dead cougar. Behind the horse, a limp figure in buckskins lay motionless.

He jumped down from the rocks and the mare snorted its fear again. Walking slowly toward it, Kael began to speak softly to the horse. Carefully, and with a steady flow of words, Kael reached the mare and caught the reins with his free hand. Then he walked the horse to the side of the ravine and secured the mare to a leathery brown vine. Only then did he turn to the unconscious figure on the ground.

Walking toward the sprawled body, Kael's first sight was of long, burgundy hair splayed out beneath the head. Kael realized that it was a woman who lay before him. As he got even closer, he felt his breath catch in his chest as he noticed the clear, bronzed skin of her face, and the delicate line of her mouth. Slowly, Kael knelt beside the woman, lifting her head gently to examine her scalp for head wounds. The mixed scents of horse and soap assailed his nostrils as his fingers probed beneath her hair. He lowered the woman's head, having found no injury other than a now rising lump. He studied her, watching the rise and fall of her chest as she breathed slowly and evenly. As he gazed at her, Kael knew he was looking at one of the most beautiful women he had ever seen. Her peach-colored lips, small, straight nose, and well-defined cheekbones blended into a picture of soft beauty that ensnared him. Suddenly, her breathing changed, and she began to stir. A small pink tongue licked at dry lips; her eyelids fluttered lightly. When they opened, revealing blue eyes the color of a mountain lake, Kael Treemont smiled.

Opening her eyes slowly, Lara saw an unfocused shadow hovering over her. As her vision cleared, she made out the leering face of a scruffy, hatted man. Trapper! her mind screamed. Instantly, Lara realized her peril. She had strayed far from the quasi-civilized area of her home, and a wandering trapper had found her. Summoning all her strength, she began to fight the inevitable. Hitting the man with the balled fists, kicking out and upward with her small, booted feet, Lara Dowley struggled against what she knew would be a horrible fate. Before she could do more than land several futile blows, she felt the man's ironlike arms surround her

21

and crush her against him, effectively stopping all her resistance. Her chest heaved with exertion as her breasts were pressed flat against the stranger's torso. Desperate, Lara opened her mouth, trying to find his neck in order to bite the vulnerable skin. She felt her head jerked back, the man's hand pulling cruelly on her hair.

"Stop fighting, dammit! Stop fighting and I'll let you go," he ordered through clenched teeth.

For some reason, the man's voice, not his words, made her believe him. Her mouth was still open, ready to bite his neck, her eyes fixed on the vein that pulsed along the corded muscles of his neck. Lara felt the stranger's iron lock lighten, and she pulled her head back to stare into his firey eyes. They were only inches from her face and Lara was able to see floating islands of brown and gold in an amber sea. Slowly, she nodded her head and relaxed her body. As she did, his arm loosened on her back, and his fingers released her hair.

Lara's gaze held his for a long moment as she studied him. Silently, he stood and backed away. Before she could stand, the man's hand went out and one long finger pointed. Her eyes traveled the length of his arm, following the finger's aim. Not far from her was the body of a dead mountain lion.

"I'll accept your apology now," he said.

Lara's head whipped back to face him, instantly taking in the relaxed smile on his lips and the laughter in his eyes. "My apology? For not letting you maul me?" she asked sarcastically as she stood. Then she smiled, too. "I'm sorry. Please accept my apology, thank you."

"Accepted," he said with a slight bow.

It was then that Lara recognized the faded uniform and the sunbleached gold brain that decorated each shoulder. Taking in his appearance quickly, she also noted the way the man filled the old uniform. He was tall, wide shouldered, with a strong chest that tapered into a narrow waist and slim hips. The tight-fitting pants accented the powerful muscles of his thighs, and Lara realized that if he had not released her, she would never have been able to fight free.

"But if you saw what I see, you would understand why I fought you," she said.

The man's hand went to his face and rubbed across his chin. They both heard the rasping sound of whiskers against his fingers. Then, as he lowered his hand, his large mouth formed another smile, revealing even white teeth.

"I shouldn't think it was that bad, its only been a week since I've shaved." With those words, the man lost his smile. "Permit me to introduce myself. Kael Treemont at your service."

"Why is an army officer out here alone?" she asked, not bothering to introduce herself yet. She was still suspicious. Even though he seemed gentlemanly, and gallant, he could be anyone, or anything. A deserter, or worse.

"Retired, ma'am. I'm here to visit some family. I guess you're lucky I happened along," he said with another smile. "May I check you over?" Lara's widening eyes and suddenly drawn lips warned him of his mistake. "For injuries. You were thrown pretty badly." Then, without waiting for her permission, Kael took one of her arms and began to run his fingers along it. "How does your head feel?"

"Like I've been hit. How should it feel?" she snapped. Lara shook her head, wondering why she was being so waspish. He did seem to be considerate.

"Would you walk about, see how your ankles are."

"They're fine, Mr. Treemont," Lara declared as she took several steps.

Kael watched her move, taking in the figure she presented and silently applauding her. She was a full head shorter than he, and she filled her buckskins wonderfully. Flaring hips, slim legs, and he sensed that beneath the loose-fitting man's shirt was a small waist.

"What are you staring at?" Lara asked, as she turned and found his eyes inspecting her.

"It's hard not to stare at a woman in pants."

"Well, try not to. There's nothing wrong with pants."

"I agree," Kael replied with another smile.

"Well, you're a majority of one."

"I always was," he replied without a smile. Then Kael looked upward, checking the angle of the sun. "How far away do you live?"

"Farther than I should. About eight miles. I . . . I guess I was daydreaming. I shouldn't have come into Indian territory."

"I'm glad you did. It gave us a chance to meet, but I still don't know your name." Kael's eyes fixed on Lara's, and held them tightly. She felt caught within his gaze, and a tingling sensation coursed through her.

"I'm Lara Dowley. I live ouside Valley City," she finally told him. "I would like to thank you properly for helping me. Would you like to escort me home and have dinner with my father and myself?"

"I'm sorry. I would enjoy dinner with you, but I've some business that must be attended to. But you should go now, the sun's high, and you won't be able to ride the mare too hard." Nodding her head in agreement, Lara walked up to Kael and extended her hand.

"Thank you again," she said as his hand grasped hers. She felt the heat from his skin pour into hers, sending little shocks of flame through her arm. They gazed at each other for another long moment before Kael finally released her palm.

Lara could feel his amber eyes on her as she walked to the mare and untied her. Slowly, Lara mounted the roan, and turned back to Kael. Walking the horse up to him, she smiled. "Perhaps the next time we meet, you'll have shaved, and I won't be frightened that you are about to ravish me." With that, Lara started out of the ravine.

Kael's eyes followed her until she passed from view. He stayed like that for several minutes as he tried to sort out his thoughts. Something had happened to him that he hadn't expected. When he'd first looked at her still form and had seen the beauty that was there, he'd wanted to touch her, to stroke the smooth skin of her cheek and to feel the sun-bronzed skin against his fingers. When she'd awakened, fighting and kicking like a spitfire, he'd felt an unexpected flash of desire blaze up in him. When he'd held her pressed against his chest to prevent her from escaping, the heat emanating from her body had added even more fuel to his passion. It had taken all his willpower to release her, and to appear calm.

Kael knew it had been a combination of things—the sight of her quiet beauty, the womanly smell that surrounded her, and the feel of her softness against him—that had ignited the emotions he'd kept dormant for so long.

Forcefully, Kael tried to push the vibrant image of Lara Dowley from him, thrusting it into the place that he had put everything and everyone that had mattered to him. He must push away all feelings until he had finished what he'd come to Wyoming for. When his job was done, and if anything could be salvaged, then he would try to bring his emotions out again.

Finally, Kael turned back to the dead mountain lion. Pulling a knife from his belt, he knelt next to the mighty engine of death and began his grisly work.

It was past midafternoon when Lara arrived home. She cantered halfway through the green valley, then slowed to a walk for the final mile. The day had turned blisteringly hot, as she had learned it would become every year at this time. The Wyoming area was a contrast in everything: lush valleys, arid plains, cool mountains; hot, searing summers, and cold, blizzardy winters.

Without fully knowing why or understanding it, Lara had grown to love this country. She felt equally at home in the mountains and on the plains. She felt a freedom of spirit, a oneness with everything around her. It was only when she returned home, after a long and peaceful ride, that she began to feel trapped again.

Lara's anger of the morning was gone, replaced by the stoic acceptance she must have in order to survive her life with Martin Dowley. Even though she was not his natural daughter, she was his charge. Her biggest worry was that he might fulfill his pledge to see her wed to whomever he desired. Up until yesterday, Lara had planned, somehow, to wed Jason Grumman. Part of this morning's anger had been fear of her diminishing options for control of her future.

The sharp pain she'd felt when she had woken in the ravine had eased to a dull but constant hurt. Lara explored the back of her head, wincing as her fingers felt the large bump. At the same time, Kael Treemont's smiling face seemed to dance before her. Lara smiled back at the image her mind had produced, until the smile faded as she thought about the stranger and what he would look like clean-shaven and properly dressed. But she already knew, somehow, that she would find a strong, well-rounded chin beneath the scruffy whiskers. Adding to this his glowing eyes, and the strong white teeth that had showed through his wide-mouthed smile, Laura had no doubts that Kael Treemont was handsome.

"Enjoy your ride, Miss Lara?" Lew Cross's grating voice jarred her from her thoughts. She looked down at the foreman and repressed a shudder. His brown eyes roamed her face, and his mouth was held in a sneer.

"I always enjoy my ride," Lara responded as she dismounted and haughtily handed Cross the reins. "Is my father home?"

"No. He went into town."

"Good," she replied as she turned her back on the foreman and walked to the house. Throughout the entire walk, Lara sensed the foreman's eyes on her back. She knew that he was watching her, as he had done a hundred times before. She could almost feel his eyes undressing her.

Kael Treemont sat straighter in the saddle as he glimpsed the first wafting wisps of smoke in the distance. Stopping his horse, Kael swiveled. Behind him, Two Wolves' spotted Appaloosa stopped also, its nostrils flared as it picked up the familiar scents of home. Across the horse's back lay Two Wolves. A low sigh escaped from Kael's lips as he turned forward again and urged his mount on.

He knew that many eyes, although unseen, were watching his approach to one of the main villages of the Wind River Shoshone. When Kael reached the first tepee, several thin and rangy dogs began to yap and run near his horse.

Nowhere was there a sign of an Indian.

Stopping the Andalusian stallion in the center of the village, Kael dismounted and went to Two Wolves' pony. Without haste, he freed his friend's body and gently lowered it to the ground. Then he sat next to it and waited.

Although he did not betray any emotion as he sat under the sweltering sun, his well-muscled body was tense, ready for instant action. Then, from the corner of his eye, he saw a movement. One lone Indian walked out to face this stranger.

By his headdress of two large gray and white eagle feathers, Kael knew him for one of the tribal chiefs. The man was tall for an Indian, broad shouldered and finely muscled. His face was expressionless, but alert black eyes studied Kael with a deep-seated look of intelligence. The man's finely chiseled features were smooth and aquiline, and Kael felt a pinprick of recognition as he looked at the Indian's face. There was a vague familiarity about his features that tugged at Kael's mind.

The Indian spoke four words in his own language. Kael shook his head, and stood slowly.

"*Parlez-vous français?*" the Indian asked.

"*Non. Anglais,*" Kael stated.

The Indian nodded his head once. "I am called Painted Hawk," he said in clear, well-enunciated words that were heavily accented with both British inflections and his own strange way of speaking.

"I am Treemont, friend of Two Wolves."

"You speak truthfully. Only a friend would return a warrior's body without fear." Painted Hawk nodded once more, then lifted a sinewy arm high. Within seconds, the village erupted. Voices called out, and people moved forward.

Suddenly, a high, keening wail cut through the air, and a young woman came forward, her eyes held forcefully on the still body that rested on the ground.

A path opened for her and she walked slowly to Two Wolves. She bent, her long, braided hair falling down the sides of her face as she lowered herself to the dead warrior's body.

Kael watched as a knife flashed in her hands. Quickly, the woman cut off each of her long braids, never once stopping the lamentation that ripped through Kael with every primitive note.

Painted Hawk's eyes pulled away from the clawed body and fell again on Kael. "The lion?" he asked, and this time the sounds of deep emotion were evident in Painted Hawk's voice.

Kael turned to his horse and pulled free a small pouch that was tied to the pommel. He turned to Painted Hawk and handed him the bag. The Indian opened it. Looking quickly inside, he grunted as his eyes saw the bloodied ears of the cougar. His gaze went back to Kael, and Painted Hawk nodded.

"Two Wolves' spirit is indebted to you."

"No. My spirit will always owe a debt to Two Wolves. The lion was for me. Two Wolves saved me from its attack."

"You and Two Wolves rode the blood path together?"

"We did," Kael answered, not bothering to go into the details for how he'd found the Shoshone, half dead, lying next to the bodies of the five Crow braves he'd tailed for almost a year.

"His vengeance was achieved?" Painted Hawk asked.

"Two Wolves slew many. He was satisfied."

"That is good," proclaimed the Shoshone chief. "I would not have my brother's spirit float away, always searching."

The high wail died as the young Indian woman draped the body of the dead warrior with a ceremonial blanket.

"Come. We talk. When the moon is high and rides the heavens, we will send Two Wolves into the arms of our ancestors."

Kael looked at the strong-faced Indian and understood his familiar look. Kael nodded to his dead friend's brother, and followed the man to his tepee.

Lara luxuriated in the warm water. She always bathed in the late afternoon, when the house was peaceful, occupied only by herself and Anna. Anna was the half-breed woman who cooked and cleaned for the Dowleys. Her father had been a trapper and her mother an Indian.

When the Dowleys had arrived at the newly born town of Valley City and had registered their property as a government grant, Dowley had immediately hired many men to build the main house and to set up a corral for the breeding horses that would be arriving later in the summer.

At the same time, Martin Dowley had come across Jacques Betrait and his daughter, Anna. Lara wasn't sure exactly what had transpired, but that evening Anna had come to them. From that point on, Anna had taken care of the cooking and the newly built house. Whenever Lara brought up the subject, Anna would avoid it, but Lara believed that her stepfather had bought Anna, as an Indian would buy or sell one of their women.

"Ees late," Anna said as she walked over to the tub and held a sheet for Lara to step onto. "Your fazzer, 'e come now." Anna spoke with a peculiar accent, half French, half unknown.

"Thank you," Lara replied as she smiled at the woman. Anna nodded but did not change her serious expression. Anna never smiled, Lara thought as she watched the woman leave the room. And Anna never cried, either. "Perhaps she is better off than I," Lara said to herself.

Drying herself thoroughly, Lara walked to the large oval mirror that her mother had made Martin Dowley bring with them. It had suffered little damage from the trip, only a small chip on the top corner. She turned her back to the mirror and dropped the sheet. Looking over her shoulder, she saw the scratches from the rough ground that traced their path across her back. Only near the shoulders did the ground do any real damage. Her lower back, curving softly inward before rising into the pliant flesh of her buttocks, was unmarked.

Lara turned again and saw her full reflection in the mirror. She judged her breasts to be smallish, but they rode high and were perfectly shaped. The darker-tinted tips hardened now as she felt the chill of the sun's departure. Her stomach was smoothly muscled, and her waist dipped inward before it flowed outward to pleasantly curved hips.

She knew her body was good, although not as spectacular as her friend Angela Crimmons's. Angela had the full breasts

30

and narrowed waist that made most men seem to step all over themselves to get next to her.

What Lara didn't know was that the sensuality she exuded with her confidence, and the way she carried herself, more than made up for her not having the large proportions that seemed to be the style of the times. More than one head had been turned her way, and Martin Dowley had to turn a continuing string of young men from the door. An action that Dowley was well suited for. After one confrontation with him; most of the young men of the area never thrust their attentions at Lara again. They understood that her father had already made plans for his daughter.

But Lara did not know all of this, and so she felt that most men preferred full-figured women.

Hearing the front door open and close, Lara began to dress quickly. Tonight she must dress properly, in order to lessen the damage she'd done that morning.

Three layers of petticoats went on first, followed by a blouselike chemisette that she buckled at the waist. Finally, Lara slipped on the organdy and taffeta dress and adjusted it in the fading light of the day. When she was satisfied that she looked as proper as her father would want, she went to the dressing table and began to brush her hair. After the thick Titian mass was smoothed out and shining, Lara reached up and wrapped the hair into a knot on top of her head. Taking one of her mother's favorite hairpins, Lara placed the white-capped metal pin through the knot and tested it once. Satisfied, she put on her silk slippers and left the room. She knew that her covered shoulders and half-sleeved arms would show nothing of her earlier accident.

As she reached the head of the stairs, Lara could hear Martin Dowley's voice in conversation with another. Adjusting the bodice and readjusting her breasts to fall more comfortably, Lara took a deep breath as she began to descend the stairs.

Dinner went smoothly, with her father keeping himself busy in conversation with his guest. For all of Martin Dowley's

Jenifer Dalton

faults, Lara understood that he was a great man, one who was much respected in the Idaho territories. He was the government's agent for the home office, in charge of Indian affairs, and was considered by almost all of the settlers as their leader. It was rare that a night passed without someone having dinner in their home. Lara always played hostess, and did it well. Tonight's guest was an important man, important to Dowley because he had also started a cattle company. Dowley would soon become the largest and the most prosperous landowner in the territory. This was only one of her stepfather's schemes. He also invested in the businesses of, or loaned money to, the majority of Valley City's population. Martin Dowley was Valley City's unacknowledged banker.

The guest, Johnathan Setterley, her father's business associate from Kansas City, was the man who had supplied Dowley with the cattle to start his small herd.

When they finished the meal, Setterley wiped his lips and smiled at Lara. "Both the meal and your company were wonderful," he said with a nod in her direction. "Martin, I'm always amazed when I come here. It's like I'm back East. Your food is always perfect, and your home is like a bastion of civilization in the wilderness."

"I could not stay in Philadelphia and do what I do here, so I brought some of the East to Wyoming," Dowley declared as he moved his hands expansively. And he had, Lara thought, brought a lot of the East here.

Her father enjoyed every compliment that was made about their home. A china cabinet, filled with her mother's fine porcelain, stood proudly against the paneled wall. The dining room table was made of hand-hewn rosewood and had matching chairs with deep velvet cushions. No expense had been spared on the furnishings in this room and the others, making this house in the rugged West a landmark of wealth and opulence.

Lara felt someone watching her, and pulled her mind back to the present. Turning her head slightly, she saw Setterley's flat gray eyes appraising her. She felt herself flush at his open stare, and pushed her chair back.

"Father, Mr. Setterley, would you care to take your brandy and cigars in the library?"

"Very good," replied Setterley, who kept his eyes locked with Lara's. "Martin?"

"Yes, let's," he agreed as he glanced at his associate's expression, and at the obvious recipient of it.

Watching the two men walk out of the dining room, Lara felt a shiver of apprehension at the way Johnathan Setterly had been looking at her. But even that feeling couldn't stop the smile that played at the corners of her lips. The two men presented a strange picture. Her father was short and squat, and Setterley thin and lanky, with a too-large head upon his shoulders, seemed like many of the drawings that had been in the books of fables which her mother had read to her when she was a child.

Shrugging away both the apprehension and the picture they invoked, Lara went into the kitchen to get the coffee that she knew her father would want before his brandy.

Carrying the coffee tray, Lara neared the closed library door. Before she entered, she heard her name mentioned and stopped. As she listened, the apprehension she had felt only minutes before surfaced harshly as the men coldly discussed her.

"Yes, she is of marriagable age. In fact, I am looking for a suitable match."

"Would you consider me?" Setterley asked.

"Johnathan, my dear friend, you're twenty-five years older than she. What would you do with a mere child? I always thought you preferred the experience of older women."

"For play, Martin, for play. But Lara intrigues me. I would marry her," he declared.

"But, Johnathan, I've planned on marrying her to a man in the Dakotas. He has a large ranch, and he's made it plain that it would be to my benefit if Lara were to be his wife."

"Martin," Setterley began, his voice turning hard and cold

33

as he spoke, "I have desired your daughter since I first saw her. I want her for my wife. Between the two of us, we can own the entire West. Martin, I can supply you with all the cattle you'll ever need. I can arrange for every wagon train that leaves Kansas City to pass through your lands, to buy those cattle, and to make you wealthy beyond your imagination."

Lara, unable to restrain herself, but also knowing that to admit she had been listening would cause her harm, pushed the door open and tried to act as if she'd heard nothing. She poured the coffee expertly, then stepped back.

"Gentlemen, I'm feeling tired, I shall wish you good night." Without waiting for a reply, she turned and started out.

"Wait!" her father called. Lara froze, then slowly turned. "Johnathan will be staying with us tonight, and tomorrow. I would like you to show him our property. Good night, Lara."

"Good night, Father, Mr. Setterley," she replied, forcing away any roughness from her voice. Then, with a nod to her stepfather, Lara left the room. After she closed the door to the study, she fled to her room, and in the confines of this relative safety sat at her dressing table. Staring into the small mirror that was framed in brass webbing, Lara spoke to herself.

"I will not marry him! I will marry no one that I do not choose!" she vowed. Then her eyes turned as hard and cold as a frozen river as she built the determination within herself to resist her father's plans.

During the four days following the morning she'd been thrown from her mare's back, Lara confined herself to the ranch to appease her father. The first day she had spent with Johnathan Setterley. Riding in the carriage that morning, Lara showed him the vast lands that her father owned.

In the beginning of the day, Setterley had been quiet, smiling almost pleasantly as he made warm comments about the property and about her father. Wisely, Lara did not let on that she already knew what he wanted. By lunchtime, they had covered the south range. She'd shown him the cattle pasture there, and the now fast-multiplying herd of heifers. On the way back she'd taken Setterley by the breeding corral and had shown him their prize stallion, sire to most of the ponies of the property. Those ponies were now being gentled for sale to the army. Another range held the lower-caste horses that would be sold to passing wagon trains, to supplement and resupply them before they crossed the Continental Divide.

By the time they returned to the house, Lara was hungry and had Anna serve them immediately. After lunch, she had two horses saddled, her roan mare, Camilla, and a dappled, buckskin gelding for Setterley. While the horses were being readied, Lara changed her clothing for the afternoon's ride.

Because Lara did not want to do anything that would arouse her father's anger, or intentionally lead Setterley on, she chose a modest riding dress. The bodice covered her from waist to neck, and the skirt fell to her ankles. The petticoats had been slit along the front, as had the dress, to accommodate the saddle. The light brown of the riding dress almost blended with Lara's tanned face and hands.

Once they were on the horses, Lara took Setterley to the north and west ranges, showing him the area that her father planned to expand the cattle herds into. When they were finished but before they started back, Setterley stopped his horse near a small creek, and called Lara to join him.

"I want to talk to you," he said. As he helped her dismount, his hands lingered on her waist for longer than was necessary. Lara pulled away, fighting her fast-rising anger as she tried to smile.

"Lara, I've asked your father for your hand. He's told me he will think on it." Setterley smiled at her and then stepped closer.

"And what of me?" she asked, her words short and clipped.

"I would hope you'd want to marry me. I can take you away from this hopeless life. You're a beautiful woman who should have everything that is due you, not be hidden away in this godforsaken wilderness. Your father was a fool to take you here, but his foolishness is working for me." With that, Johnathan Setterley closed the distance between them. Grabbing her, he pulled Lara against him. Before she realized what he was doing, she was trapped within his arms. His lips were against her throat, and his hands began to travel over her body.

"Stop it!" she ordered, trying to free herself. His only response was a guttural laugh. Then Lara felt the hot wetness of his lips on the skin of her neck. Her revulsion grew as his hands pawed her buttocks and she felt his hardness grow against her.

"No!" she said through tightly clenched teeth. Using the toe of her booted foot, Lara kicked him in the shin. She heard his sharp grunt of pain, and his grasp loosened. Lara stepped back, her breasts rising and falling rapidly in anger. "Don't ever touch me again!" She felt even more disgust as she looked at his face. Setterley's gray eyes were filled with naked lust.

"Soon, my dear Lara, you will not spurn me."

"You will never live to see the day I come willingly to you."

"I'll see that day within the year," he declared confidently, stepping toward her again. "Within the year, you will be mine."

"In hell! But not here," she swore. Turning quickly from the evil in his eyes, Lara mounted the mare.

"Lara," Setterley called in a growling command. Swiftly closing the distance between them, he grabbed Camilla's reins and held the horse fast. "Your father is a greedy man. There is much he wants, and much he sees for himself. I have what he wants. Therefore, you will be mine. That is a fact."

Ripping the reins free of the cattlebroker's hand, Lara wheeled the mare around. "As much as I would like for it to happen, Mr. Setterley, if you don't get on your horse and follow me, you may never find your way back."

"I always find my way, and I always get my way," he said pointedly.

Without another word, she urged Camilla into a smooth canter, challenging Johnathan Setterley to follow.

Setterley left the next day, with a sly smile and a searching look that told Lara he expected to get what he wanted.

The following three days were spent quietly, with a rare absence of houseguests, and the peacefulness of riding alone. Each morning, Lara would saddle Camilla and ride the mare to the very borders of their property. Once there, Lara would sit for hours, and think of the man with the iron-muscled arms, and the deep, amber eyes.

The first lazy tentacles of light were hesitantly reaching over the eastern mountains when Kael heard footsteps behind him. Turning, he saw the smiling face of his cousin, John Crimmons.

" 'Tis a good feeling, watching the day begin," John said.

Kael nodded his head and found a smile of his own. He had arrived last night at suppertime, bringing confusion, laughter, and memories with him. Kael hadn't seen his cousin since before the start of the war, and after the great battle had started, he'd been too busy fighting and trying to stay alive to keep in touch. When he finally realized that he would have to go to Wyoming, he knew he would stop to see his cousin.

"I have to tell you you gave me quite a shock last night, lad. Constance, too," said the transplanted Englishman. "The only one who acted as if nothing special had happened was Angela, and I think she was just too tongue-tied to speak."

"She's grown up a lot since I saw her six years ago."

"That she has. She's a woman now. You'd be surprised at the number of men that come calling."

Kael shook his head silently. He wouldn't be surprised at all. His younger cousin had grown from a gangling little girl, all hair and eyes, into a beautiful young woman who at seventeen was ready to break many hearts.

"But," John said, interrupting Kael's thoughts, "I know

you've not come just to visit. Don't misunderstand me, lad, but nobody rides a horse fifteen hundred miles to pay a family call. Though, truthfully, I'm glad you're here. And now, if you please, I'll have the real reason you've come.

"John, when you first came to America, when I first met you, I remember thinking that you were just like my father. I still think so."

"Your father was a good man. He never let his kin, or his friends down. I owe him a lot," John said.

"Owed," Kael corrected. A deep bitterness filled his words.

"Owe, lad, owe. Whether it be on this earth, or any other place, my debt to him and my love for him will always be with me. You know it was your father who brought me over from England, who paid the way for me and my family to come to Pennsylvania. You know it was he who sent us out here when the war started. No, lad, the debt and your father will always be alive in my mind."

Kael turned away from the force of his cousin's emotions, and let his eyes go to the now light-filled sky. Forcing the tightness in his throat away, Kael began to speak.

"John, you know my father was murdered. I wrote the sad tidings to you myself. Now I'll tell you what really happened." As Kael began to speak, the living memory of what had happened three and a half years ago flooded his mind. As he spoke, he relived it.

Kael had been wounded in one of the early battles for Atlanta. His commanding officer had sent him home to recuperate. But Kael had arrived in Philadelphia at the wrong time.

Heavily bandaged, Kael left the carriage that brought him home. He stood outside the house he'd grown up in and gazed at the dark wood door. After an eternity, he reached for the handle. The door had swung open effortlessly, and Kael walked in.

He was about to yell out his greeting when he felt an all-pervading silence surround him. Quietly, and as quickly as he could, Kael went from room to room, until he reached his father's study. The door was slightly ajar, and suddenly he felt a chill run along his spine.

The wound in his chest was sending rippling, shooting pains with every breath he took, and just the effort of walking from the carriage and through the house had weakened him badly. Pushing the pain aside, Kael gripped the door handle. As his fingers tightened on the cool brass and the door opened slightly, he heard his father's voice. Intuitively, Kael froze.

'You will make full restitution to everyone you've swindled!" Ryan Treemont ordered. "You will repay everyone, and then, if they and I are satisfied, you will not be prosecuted. But when it is done, you will leave Philadelphia."

"You are an old fool!" the other man said, in a coarse, distinctive voice. Kael had never heard the voice before, but in that instant, it became etched in his memory. Forcing the pain of his wound from his mind, he listened warily to the men in the room.

"I am beyond prosecution, Treemont. I am beyond the law! You and the others are idealistic fools who think the world should be what you want it to be. It's not! The world is made for people like me, to take and use and enjoy. Goodbye, old man."

Then Kael heard the explosion of a firearm, followed by his father's surprised cry.

"No!" Kael yelled, ignoring the tearing lance that burned through his chest as he opened the door fully. Kael saw his father sprawled across the large mahogany desk. His pain-blurred vision wavered as he stepped into the room. His mind was still dulled from the effects of the laudanum the doctor had given him earlier in the day, and his reactions were slow.

Without thinking clearly, Kael took several steps toward his father before he realized that the other man was not within sight. Before he could turn to seek out his father's murderer, his head exploded with pain. And then there was only darkness.

Groggily, Kael began his trip back to consciousness. Pain assualted him from his chest and head. He could feel the wet, sticky bandages on his chest, signaling more damage to his wound. Gently levering himself up on his arms, Kael tested his head. A wave of dizziness washed over him, but he fought it until it receded. Slowly, Kael stood, his ragged breathing loud in the still room. Then his eyes went to his father's desk, and he saw the same scene that had been there before he'd been hit. With small, unsteady steps, Kael went to his father.

Before he reached him, Kael knew that Ryan Treemont was dead. Thrusting aside the hurt, he pulled his father back, and saw his lifeless eyes stare out unseeingly.

The world wavered again as Kael drew his father into his arms and stared at the open door of the study.

He would find the man responsible for this. He would avenge his father's death no matter what the cost.

"And that was how my father died," Kael finished. He took another deep breath and continued. "While my wound was healing, I spent the days searching for anything that would lead me to his murderer. I found what I was looking for in my father's papers. What had happened was simple. My father was an abolitionist. This man, Malcome Dupont, was supposedly the leader of a group who smuggled slaves from the South to the North.

"My father, and several of his associates, funded Dupont's efforts. It had been going on for several years, when my father became suspicious of Dupont and began an investigation. He discovered that the organization that Malcome Dupont supposedly headed had never heard of him. Apparently, my father confronted this man at the time I came home. Dammit, John, I should have been faster!"

"Sweet mother of God," John Crimmons swore as Kael finished his story. "I'm sorry, lad, I'm deeply sorry. But 'twas no fault of your own that you were wounded."

"The man who did it will be sorry also," Kael promised in a cold voice.

"Do you know where this Dupont is?" John asked.

Kael shook his head slowly. "Malcome Dupont was the name this man used. The real Malcome Dupont had been dead for ten years before my father met his killer."

"How will you find him?"

"His voice. And something else I was lucky enough to find."

"Then that's why you're here," John Crimmons stated.

Kael nodded. "I've thought about that voice every day for three years, John. Every day. In the middle of a battle, I would hear it. When I was wounded again and sent back home for good, I thought about it continually. I spent a year trying to find out who the man is, going through my father's papers repeatedly, looking for something I might have missed. I found it, finally, in a special file that Father had hidden away. In it was Malcome Dupont's name, and a note saying that mail had been sent to him at General Delivery in South Pass City, Wyoming. Now I mean to find the killer."

"Why would an abolitionist have his mail sent to South Pass City?" John asked thoughtfully.

"He never was an abolitionist. He was a thief! He probably used the Idaho territories as a false escape route, knowing that no one would be able to check it. But I know he's around here somewhere. John, I feel it!"

"It sounds like it, lad. Then you'll be staying a while?"

"For as long as it takes, if you'll have me."

"For as long as it takes, or longer," John agreed. "You'll be coming into town with Angela and myself today?"

"If I may. I'd like to take a look around."

"Good. We'll leave after we've had a proper breakfast," John said as he turned and began walking to the barn.

Kael followed his cousin, wondering what Valley City might hold for him, and for his future.

Saturday arrived with sunny warmth. It was the day everyone went to town to take care of the weekly shopping and whatever business could not be handled from home. Lara could taste the dust from the dry road as her father drove their carriage into Valley City. Martin Dowley had several business appointments today, the usual ones with the small landowners who would seek his favor and help. He ruled this area almost as a sovereign, and the local populace courted him as such. He also owned a fair percentage of many of the businesses in Valley City. While her father conducted his business, Lara would do the shopping. She was looking forward to it, and to her freedom from the ranch.

She also knew that her friend, Angela, would be in town, and that they would go to the café later, to talk over tea.

Valley City was a town in progress. It was fresh and small, but expanding rapidly. Evidence of its growth surrounded Lara; three new buildings were in the works, adding stature to the eight that now stood there. There were already several small homes on the main street, housing the local merchants, a saloon, the hotel that had been built last year, the general store, a feed store, the stables, and the café. Martin Dowley's offices were in a building of their own, the most prestigious in the town. It was two stories high and was the official government office for the territory. Dowley was the territorial official in charge of Indian Affairs, and the town's sole governmental representative. He was by far the most important man in Valley City, and possibly in the entire region.

Driving slowly along Main Street, both Lara and her father, his usual frown missing, smiled and nodded to the people that called out in greeting. Dowley stopped the carriage in front of the general store and turned to his daughter.

"When you're finished, come to the office. Cross will drive you home."

"Yes, Father," Lara said as she stepped down. She stood still as her stepfather pulled away, then shook out the long skirt of her traveling dress. This particular dress was one of her favorites. Mauve in color, its long, flowing skirt fell smoother than most, and its bodice was more comfortable, moving separately as she walked, never binding her waist. The silk camisole that she wore under it felt soft against her skin. The sleeves of the eggshell underblouse were full, and were caught at her wrists by a single band of silk. At her neck was another band of silk that seemed to mold itself along the lines of her neck, opening at the center to show the valley created by her high breasts.

Turning from the departing carriage, Lara walked slowly along the wooden sidewalk until she reached the entrance to the general store. As she opened the door herbs and spices assailed her senses, the aroma of chickory and sweets flew to her like a magnet. After spending a week at the ranch smelling the outdoors, the horses, and the sweat of the men who worked there, this place was like a paradise to her deprived senses.

"My goodness, I thought you'd never arrive," called a light voice with a crisp British accent. Lara smiled as Angela Crimmons rushed up to her and pulled her into her arms.

44

Angela was the same medium height as Lara, but all resemblance ended there. Angela had wheat-blond hair, fair skin that she had to keep shaded during the summer, and shining blue eyes, many shades darker than Lara's, set in an almost round but sultry face.

"Come to the back, Lara. Mrs. Smithers just received a new shipment from St. Louis. She has the most beautiful gowns . . ." Angela said she swept Lara along with her.

Lara was glad to be with her friend. She enjoyed the feeling of being a woman with another woman. Anna, the housekeeper, could hardly qualify as a friend.

Before Lara had a chance to protest, Angela hefted one of the new silk gowns and pressed it against Lara.

"Perfect!" she declared. "Don't you think so, Mrs. Smithers?" Angela asked as she turned to the older woman who had come from behind the counter to assist them.

"Absolutely," the storekeeper agreed as she smiled at the two friends, and nodded at the luxurious brocaded gown that would show much of Lara's bosom because of its deeply cut bodice. The sleeves, too, seemed to be almost nonexistent, just two small puffs that would barely cover her shoulders.

"Not today," Lara said with a slight frown. "Mrs. Smithers, I've a list to be prepared. Mr. Cross will be by later to load the carriage." She handed the woman her order. Mrs. Smithers nodded her head and turned away, but not before Lara saw a sorrowful look flash across the woman's face. Mrs. Smithers thought Lara should be married, and wearing the fine dresses that were imported from St. Louis and Boston. Lara, too, wanted to wear such clothing, but now, more than ever, would not become further indebted to her stepfather.

"What's your hurry, lovey?" Angela asked. This time it was she who was swept along by Lara.

"I'm parched. And I'm dying to sit in a comfortable seat, and to talk to someone who can understand me." Lara smiled at her friend's gaping mouth as she pulled Angela out of the store. Though the girls looked about the same age, Angela was actually two years Lara's junior. The fact that Angela was the only woman in the area who was even near Lara's age would have been enough to make them close, but Angela's inherent intelligence and sense of humor had overcome any differences between the two and turned their friendship into something special.

As the women walked to the café, they passed the town's only saloon. Although it was barely ten in the morning, the voices of many men came out to the street. Lara noticed one man walking toward them. She assessed him as a drifter; one of those aimless men who traveled everywhere, worked for a while, then spent their money on drinks and whatever women they could find. There seemed to be a lot of these wanderers about lately as a result of the war that had ended, leaving them nothing to return to. This one was tall and thin, and looked as if he had just come into town. Lara and Angela were almost at the café's entrance when he reached them. They could smell the odor of weeks on the trail as he stopped and leered at them. A gaping smile split his face, showing stained yellow teeth.

"Hello, ladies. Care for some company?"

"You're docking at the wrong port! What you want is in the saloon," Angela yelled in a voice loud enough to cause several of the townspeople to stop and stare at them. The man nervously stammered an apology before quickly passing on.

"Oh, Angela," Lara laughed, "the wrong port? In the middle of landlocked mountains? Where did you get that from?" Lara had to hold her side to force herself to stop laughing.

Angela smiled shyly as she looked at her friend. "My mother's been a bit worried about all the new men coming into Valley City. She told me to just yell whatever came into my head, and it would probably scare them away. I guess it works," she ended proudly.

"I guess so," Lara agreed with another laugh. "Come on, let's have some tea." The women entered the busy little café and walked to the rear, where a table was available. Within moments, their order was taken.

When the tea arrived, Lara opened her heart to her friend.

"Angela, I'm worried. No," she corrected herself, "I'm afraid."

Angela looked at her, the flowered porcelain tea cup halted halfway to her mouth.

"Afraid?" she asked. Lara Dowley was the one person, aside from her parents, that Angela looked up to. Lara was her friend and confidente.

"My father is going to marry me off," Lara said in a hoarse whisper.

"He wouldn't!" Angela declared, but she, too, had heard the rumors of Martin Dowley's plans for his daughter. Angela shook her head sadly. She knew that Lara was one of the most desired women in the territory, and although everyone said it was because her father was rich and powerful, Angela knew it was because of her friend's graceful, stately bearing and the aura of femininity that she exuded.

"He would," Lara replied sadly.

"Did he tell you so?"

"No. I overheard him talking to Johnathan Setterley. Oh, how I loathe that man! But I guess it doesn't matter, there doesn't seem to be anyone else breaking down the door to take me away."

"Oh, ta-ta . . . you can have the ones that are trying to break down mine, lovey," Angela said with a falsely broad English accent and a smile. Her dark blue eyes danced mischievously as she looked at Lara. "But I'll tell you what. I'd trade all of them for one."

"Just one? Who?" Lara asked, smiling along with her friend. Angela always seemed able to make Lara laugh at her problems, and to forget about her father for a little while.

"Oh, he's a great one, he is. Big and strong, handsome as . . . I can't even begin to tell you how handsome he is. Lord, what I'd give—"

"Angela!" Lara admonished in a sharp voice. "What are you talking about?"

47

Angela smiled secretively, her eyes still dancing with amusement, and something else, Lara thought.

"I'm talking about my cousin. He arrived yesterday. Lord, I haven't seen him in almost six years, and back then, why, I was only a child."

"You're certainly not a child any longer," said a deep voice from behind her. Angela jumped, spilling a few drops of the tea. Lara's eyes, which had been fastened on Angela's, drawn in by her friend's animated conversation, flew upward to meet the smiling face of Kael Treemont.

"Kael, you scared me silly," Angela said, as she tried to regain both her poise and the teacup. The deep flush that suffused Angela's face was receding as she smiled at him. "Kael, I'd like you to meet my friend—"

"We've already met. Good morning, Miss Dowley."

"Good morning, Mr. Treemont," Lara returned as she forced herself to break away from the hypnotic hold in which Kael's eyes held hers. Lara, too, felt the first stirrings of a flush threaten to cover her, and quickly forced herself to calm down. She had been right: beneath the scruffy beard had lain a smooth, strong chin. His lips were no longer hidden, and Lara could see their fullness. Seeing him again, she could once more feel his arms around her, could feel the heat of his body as if she were again held against it.

"May I join you?" Kael asked, breaking the silence, and freeing Lara from her thoughts. Throughout this, Angela had been watching both of them, and was puzzled by it all. She was also aware that Lara was acting strangely.

"I hope you're feeling better, Miss Dowley," Kael said in a concerned voice. "That was quite a spill you took. Have you had a doctor look at you?"

"Mr. Treemont—"

"Kael."

"Kael, there isn't a doctor within a two-day ride. Besides, I'm fine." Lara picked up her cup of tea, not because she was thirsty, but because she needed something to do to mask her confusion. She felt as though she were a little girl again, and feared that she was making a fool of herself. The very nearness of this handsome man seemed to make her heart pound loudly enough for everyone in the café to hear. Stop it! she told herself silently.

"Would one of you like to tell me what you're talking about?" The confusion that was so plainly written on Angela Crimmons's face made Kael smile.

"I did something rather foolish," Lara admitted. "I was daydreaming while riding, and I ended up near Eagle Face Mountain." As Lara explained what had happened, both she and Kael watched Angela's already large eyes widen further.

"Lord . . ." Angela said when Lara finished her tale. "But, Kael, if that was four days ago, where have you been?"

Kael looked at his cousin, and then at Lara. "Are you sure you want to know? It's a long story." Both women nodded immediately, and he took a deep breath. His eyes fastened on Lara, and he paused for a moment to force away the emotions that her presence brought out.

"Then I'd best start at the beginning, hadn't I?" he asked. Both women nodded again. "The reason I was there when the cougar attacked you was because I was hunting him. It had started the day before. I was with Two-Wolves, a friend and a Shoshone warrior . . ." As Kael spoke in his rich voice, both women became lost in his vivid descriptions. None of them noticed the stout man who had seated himself at the next table.

"Lord," Angela said again as Kael stopped for a minute, "but what about after you killed the cougar?"

"Oh, I was with Painted Hawk and the Shoshone until yesterday," Kael said offhandedly.

"That's what I want to hear about," Angela probed impatiently.

"That was a brave thing to do," Lara cut in, gazing at Kael. "I'm glad you did it."

"So am I," he replied, his face serious as he returned her intense look.

"But what about the three days before you came to us?" Angela asked again. Her persistence and open, honest curiosity forced Kael to smile, making crinkling lines of crow's feet dance around his eyes.

"The Shoshone burial rights for one of their chiefs—and Two Wolves was a chief—are magnificent and beautiful. It took three days of ceremonies to complete. If I were to try to tell you what happened, we would be here for hours." Kael stopped talking for a moment, his eyes locked on Lara's face.

Just then, a shadow covered the table. Lara looked up, and Kael saw a flash of annoyance across her beautiful features. He turned his head and saw a stocky man of medium height, with dark brown eyes and hard, lined face.

"Sorry to interrupt, Miss Lara, but your father told me to fetch you and to take you and the supplies home."

"I'll be right out, Mr. Cross. I'll join you at the store," she said in dismissal.

Kael watched the man begin to walk away, but noticed that he was in no hurry.

"That's Lew Cross, my father's foreman. I'm afraid I'll have to go, Kael. Perhaps you can finish your story another time?"

Kael looked into Lara's light blue eyes and read the interest within them. "It would be my pleasure. When?"

"Why . . . I don't know," Lara replied, surprised at his eagerness.

"A week from tomorrow," chimed in Angela. "A picnic at the river."

"Wonderful," Lara said with a smile, "I'll see you both then. I'll ride over myself." With that, she turned to leave.

Before Lara could take a step, she felt a hand grasp hers and turn her around again. Once more, Lara felt searing heat leap along her arm as Kael's strong fingers held hers.

"I'm glad you're all right," he said in a low voice.

Lara nodded her head, her mind filling with confusion as she pulled free and left to meet Lew Cross, who was still standing by the door, watching everything.

Lara swept past the foreman and out onto the wood-planked sidewalk. Walking quickly, she forced herself to calm down. She didn't understand the emotions that were singing through her body. The heat she'd felt travel along her arm had driven deeply into her entire being. She was concentrating so hard that Cross had to speak to her twice before she heard him.

"What?" Lara asked as she stopped to face him.

"Who was he?" the foreman demanded.

"It's not your concern," she snapped.

"I'm sure your father would be interested to know you spent the morning with a stranger." Lara did not like his threatening tone or insinuation.

"Mr. Cross, it is not your business to spy on me. What I do is my own concern. Tell my father whatever you'd like. And, I'm sure he has no objection to my talking with John Crimmons's cousin." Turning away from Cross, Lara picked up her pace and led the foreman to the general store.

If Lara had turned back, she would have seen the look of desire, and of hate, that filled Lew Cross's face, but her mind was still too filled with the sight, sound, and touch of Kael Treemont for her to even bother glancing back.

The setting sun was like a burning disk that slowly fell behind the western mountains. Holding her breath at the sight of its beauty, Lara wished she could capture this instant and hold it forever in her memory.

Even after two years, she never tired of watching the sunset. For her, it made the day worthwhile. The beauty of the red-capped mountains always lifted her spirits. After a long day of riding, of checking on the newborn calves, of the record keeping that she did for her father, and even the hour she always managed to spend working in the small garden she had started this past spring, Lara accepted the reward of the serene beauty of the day's end as her due.

Tonight's sunset was not only magnificent, it was private. All but three of the ranch hands had gone to town, and her father had also decided to stay there. She was alone, with Anna, and that made her happy.

Saturday evenings were special to Lara. She enjoyed the peace and quiet, without the raucous goings-on that came nightly from the two bunkhouses. The men were hard workers, and spent twelve hours a day at their jobs. Lara knew they were entitled to let off steam, and accepted it well. But tonight was peaceful, and it was hers.

As Lara stepped off the corral fence, Camilla whinnied and came over to her. Smiling, Lara opened her hand and let the mare take the small ball of molasses and oats.

"Good girl," Lara said as the horse nuzzled her cheek with affection. "Tomorrow we'll ride: tomorrow you'll have your head," she promised.

The horse drew back and threw its head up and down.

Lara laughed. "Sometimes I think you really do understand me." For an answer, the roan whinnied again, and pranced away.

"Eez cool," came Anna's voice as she stepped next to Lara." I bring you wrap."

"Thank you, Anna," Lara replied as she took the Indian shawl, a smaller version of a blanket, and draped it aross her shoulders. Early summer evenings in the mountains of Wyoming had a slight but comfortable coolness to them.

"You are 'appy zat your fazzer eez not 'ere?" Anna asked, her dark eyes looking intently at Lara. Lara stared at Anna, not believing the woman was actually talking to her. If Anna had said more than three words in a row over the past year, Lara could not remember when.

Lara nodded at her, unable to hide the truth.

"You need good man. You need get away from 'ere. Eez not 'appy place."

"If my mother had lived, it would have been much happier," Lara said in a low voice.

"Your fazzer, 'e treat you like squaw. 'E order you everywhere. Eez not so wiz ozzer white peoples." Lara knew that Anna's words were comment only, and kept her silence.

"Cross man, 'e bad. You watch out. You watch out for eem." Without any further clarification, Anna returned to the house.

Lara was stunned. Anna had lived with the Dowleys for over a year, and Lara had always felt that the half-breed was devoid of emotion. Now Lara had learned better. Cross man? Suddenly, Anna's strangely accented words made sense. Lew Cross!

Lara had always been aware of the foreman, she couldn't help it. Wherever she was, Lew Cross seemed to be there, too. She always felt his eyes on her, and could read the lust that seemed to be a permanent part of his expression. Lara shivered, even in the warmth of the wrap, as she thought about Lew Cross.

Taking a deep breath of the cool night air, Lara started back to the house. She paused, thoughtfully, at the steps that led to the front door, and looked up. All but three windows were darkened, two on the main floor, and the third, her bedroom, glowed with a welcoming warmth. The house was large. Overly large for just two occupants. It was, of course, Martin Dowley's showplace, and a smaller duplication of the grand mansion that he had left behind in Philadelphia. This ranch was what her father jokingly called his Royal Palace of the West.

In comparison to every other home in the territory, it was palatial. A formal dining room, a sitting room, a music room, Martin Dowley's library and study, and even a necessary on the main floor. The kitchen, at the rear of the main floor, was the most modern in the West, containing one of the new, large cast-iron stoves that were becoming popular in the big cities of the East. Four bedrooms filled the second floor, each having its own small sitting room. Martin Dowley had told Lara many times that he'd built his home so that important men in the government would be impressed when they visited.

Entering the house, Lara shook her head as she thought of the lavish expenditures that were necessary to run the household. Because of her father's need to impress people, she had been forced to order the most expensive and impressive items from all over the country. That, too, aside from the bookkeeping of her father's many businesses, was her responsibility.

Lara entered the music room and went to the small piano that sat in the middle of the room, resting its finely carved legs on the intricately designed carpet that her father had ordered from an Oriental importer in San Francisco. The piano had been Lara's since she'd turned seven. Her mother had given her music lessons, and Martin Dowley required her to play when he entertained.

Lara grew sad at the memory of her mother, and forced herself to forget, again, the pain of losing her forever.

Trailing her fingers along the ivory keys, Lara produced a low, tinkling sound. When she reached the end of the keyboard, she shrugged, and moved toward the staircase.

As she walked up the steps, Lara could detect the faint scent of cedar that emanated from the walls. Two years, and the aromatic pine still filled the air.

She paused inside her room to look around before she undressed. Of all the rooms, hers was the most muted in decor. White gauze curtains covered the windows, and those in turn were framed with heavy, scalloped blue drapes. The three landscape paintings that hung on the walls had been done by her mother many years before. A large white lacquered chest of drawers stood between two of the paintings, and her matching white dressing table, with its brass-framed mirror, stood proudly on another wall. Her bed was white also, with four thin pencil posts that stood solemnly at each corner.

After several seconds of gazing again at one of the paintings, her mother's garden in Philadelphia, Lara undressed. She put on a cotton nightgown, then sat at the dressing table and began to brush out her abundant waves. As she absently stroked her hair, she focused on the miniature of her mother. Eyes the same color as her own stared back. The artist had captured Kristen's small, patrician nose perfectly, even to the light band of freckles that spread across its bridge. The delicate lines of her mother's mouth were identical to her own. The biggest difference between mother and daughter, was the color of their hair. Lara's, a dark burgundy, as was her father's, contrasted to her mother's pale blond.

Lara had never seen her father, and Kristen had never had a portrait. They'd only been married a short time before James Fairwald had died. Pirates had taken his ship and killed the crew.

Lara shook away the thoughts that always produced sadness and moved to her bed. Blowing out the tallow candles, she climbed beneath the heavy woolen blanket. She welcomed the comfort of the feathered mattress, and closed her eyes to await sleep.

Unbidden, a face floated up before her. Its taunting smile and bright eyes called to her. Deep within her, she felt the stirrings that she'd cast away from her earlier in the day when she'd talked with Kael. Who was he that he could have such power over her emotions? Rolling waves of heat flowed through her body. She felt the tips of her breasts harden, even under the warmth of the blanket, and she tried to force the vision away.

Finally, Lara admitted to herself what she'd been fighting. The attraction she'd felt that first day she'd met Kael Treemont had taken a swift hold within her. The emotions she felt were new to her, resembling nothing she'd felt with Jason Grumman. What now seized Lara was a raw, deep need to be held within Kael's strong arms. To be crushed against his chest, and to taste his lips upon hers. In truth, Kael Treemont was the first man that Lara truly desired.

With that admission came the release of her pent-up emotions. A soft sigh escaped from Lara's lips as she fell into a dreamless sleep.

The small pond glistened in the summer sun like the facets of a beautiful gem. Kael Treemont and John Crimmons stood at the edge of the man-made pond and stared into it. Running off the pond, in three directions, where wheat, beets, and potatoes, in small but evenly spaced rows.

"I still can't believe you did all of this," Kael said, shaking his head in wonder.

"What was I supposed to do, lad? Hope there would be enough rain to keep the crops alive?" John smiled at his younger cousin, but felt proud inside. The extra work that was required to maintain his crops had been a burden, but one he welcomed. John Crimmons grew enough beets and wheat to supplement the stock and keep his grain and feed costs low. It was worth all the effort it had taken to dig, mortar, and fill the pond with water so that he and his family could enjoy having corn and potatoes to grace their dinner table.

"How did you get the water to stay without seeping into the rock bed?" Kael asked.

"My grandfather was a mason. Your great, great uncle, James Crimmons, taught me ways to make mortar from almost anything, including the sand and rock I found in this area."

"You must be proud."

"I am," John said with a smile. "Especially in dry times. Everyone thought I was crazy. They told me what a waste it was to haul all that water from the river. They laughed when they thought about the pond running dry and myself having to spend another two months carting water. They didn't realize that once the pond was filled, it would be almost self-perpetuating. Every rainfall fills it again, and each winter's snow adds more." John stopped talking after that little speech, and studied Kael for several long moments.

"How did it go in South Pass City?" John asked. Kael had just returned from four days in the newest boomtown of the Idaho territories. Gold had been discovered in South Pass City, and with it had come hordes of seekers. Kael knew that the strikes were not great, and that the gold boom would die out soon. But he had gone to the most likely place that a greedy man would be found.

"Nothing," Kael responded as he swung his eyes around to stare out at the hazy mountains. "I talked to everybody I could. I listened everywhere, but he wasn't there. Maybe I missed him, but I'll go back another time."

"Maybe he moved on?" John ventured.

"No! I don't know why, but I feel it. I feel he's around here somewhere." The expression that filled Kael's face left John Crimmons no choice but to believe him.

"Lad, I wish you'd come with me to meet Martin Dowley. I told you how fine a man he is, and Kael, he's the most powerful man in Wyoming. I'm sure he can help you," John pleaded. Kael had shown a strong reluctance to speak with anyone about his mission, and John felt certain he trusted no one.

"I will not let anyone know what I'm doing. I can't take the chance that my father's murderer will find out."

"Kael, Martin Dowley's an honorable man. What you tell him in confidence will be kept that way."

"No!" Kael said stiffly, as his eyes returned to his cousin's. "John, I know how much you respect him, but this is private. No one is to know. You gave me your word."

"I did, and I'll keep it. I just feel it would make your life easier. Will you think on it? Besides," John said with a slow-spreading grin, "from what Angela's told me about your meeting with Martin's daughter, I should think you might be interested in calling on the Dowleys."

A strange look passed across Kael's face, causing John to wonder if he'd spoken foolishly. He saw many things that his words opened, and then as quickly saw Kael mask them.

"John, Lara Dowley is beautiful. But before I can think of any woman, I must do what I've promised myself."

The hard sound of his voice jarred against John's sensitivities. He did not like what his younger cousin was doing to himself, what he was denying himself. If it went on too long, John knew Kael might be destroyed in the process.

"And this Sunday? Are you not planning to join us for our picnic, and impress us with your Indian story?"

Kael smiled at his cousin, but before he could answer, Angela Crimmons rode up to them, her face flushed as she reined her horse to a stop.

"Papa," she called breathlessly, "one of the new lambs is down." Without another word to Kael, John Crimmons went to his own horse and jumped on its broad back. Angela led the way and John followed his daughter. Kael mounted the gray Andalusian stallion and started to follow. In his mind, John's words echoed as tauntingly as did the vision of Lara Dowley.

Saturday night had come again with another magnificent sunset, and with it came the quiet peacefulness of the empty house. Lara's father had again stayed in town, and she luxuriated in her solitude. Throughout the long week, she had maintained an even composure which did not betray the turmoil that was a constantly running stream through her mind.

Urging the recurring of Kael Treemont away whenever it threatened to enter her thoughts, Lara forced her mind into other channels. Each morning since she had spoken to Kael in the café, she rode her horse hard, forcing Camilla to gallop through the level terrain of the countryside in an effort to purge herself of the nightly dreams dominated by the visage of the handsome man. Lara applied herself to her duties as she never had before, heaping one upon the other without resting, without pausing to give her mind a chance to be free.

Yet whenever she stopped for a moment, Lara would find herself wondering what Kael Treemont was doing just then. Now, with the sun bedded and the pale sliver of the crescent moon rising into the sparkling blanket of the darkness, she could no longer hide from her thoughts.

The cool, clear, and cloudless sky held a promise of the day to come. Lara knew the weather for the picnic would be beautiful, with a warm sun shining down and gentle breezes that would sweep from the mountains surrounding the area like the wall of a fortress.

Losing herself in the beauty of the western night, and in the vision of the tall, muscular man she would see tomorrow, Lara was unaware of the eyes that stared at her from a short distance away. The eyes that watched her with unconcealed desire.

"Painted Hawk and I sat in his tepee until the sun was down. A small fire burned in the center, and smoke rose in a small stream through the hole in the top. When the night had settled, three Indian women entered with food. We ate silently, and when we were finished, Painted Hawk stood and looked at me."

" 'It is time, friend of my brother, to begin to send Two Wolves' spirit to rest.' " Kael took a deep breath as he paused and looked at his listeners. Angela stared at him, wide-eyed. Her mother and father sat next to each other, listening intently. Lara Dowley sat a little apart from the three Crimmonses, and closer to Kael. Her light blue eyes had locked with his the moment he'd begun his tale, and had not wavered since. Kael tried to ignore the hunger that surfaced each time his eyes met hers. With every sun-reflected sparkle of her wine-colored hair, his concentration wavered. Then, as he spoke, a veil seemed to cover his eyes, and he, too, became lost in the story he was telling, the memory of it still alive within his mind. Although he spoke in a rich, deep voice, his words seemed to come from somewhere else.

When Kael and Painted Hawk emerged from the tepee, they found the entire tribe waiting. Kael realized that there were at least fifty warriors standing there, and half again as many women and children. As Painted Hawk led the way for Kael, the Shoshone opened a path for them that led to the body of Two Wolves, surrounded by burning torches which illuminated the body in a shimmering glow. A blanket covered the dead man's torn chest, but his black hair glistened and fell smoothly on the litter. A headdress of eagle feathers sat on his head, and his face was painted in a design of multitudinous colors.

Reaching his dead brother's side, Painted Hawk turned to Kael. He signaled the white man to lift the back part of the litter as he bent to lift the front. When it was raised, five women dressed in antelope skins picked up the torches and began to lead the way. Ignoring the weight that pulled at his arms, Kael watched with wonder the procession that he was part of. Behind him, he heard the sounds of many feet and of wood hitting wood. At first it seemed to him to be a random sound, but after several moments he picked up the rhythm. Soon the entire tribe was singing in low, plaintive tones that tore through Kael's heart.

Painted Hawk stopped before a tepee. Signaling Kael, he lowered the litter. As Kael stood, Painted Hawk took one of the torches. Moving slowly, he walked to the front of the tepee from which an apparition of a man/animal emerged. A coyote mask covered his face, and an animal skin was draped over his shoulders. Painted Hawk faced the coyote man and bent his head.

The coyote man touched Painted Hawk's shoulder with a long medicine stick, then stepped back. With a loud, ceremonial wail, Painted Hawk threw the torch inside the tepee. The entire village began to wail, sending a chill coursing along Kael's spine. The collective keening, combined with the burning tepee, made Kael feel the deep grief of the people.

Painted Hawk turned and motioned to Kael. Again, the

two men picked up the litter, and began their slow march. The sounds of mourning dropped but never ceased. After a ten-minute walk, they stopped again.

Painted Hawk took Kael's arm, and led him away from the litter. At a distance, they watched and listened as the burial ceremony began.

Kael saw the woman who had cut her hair when he'd first brought Two Wolves' body to the village. She walked to her husband's body, and knelt. Taking her severed braids, she placed them across his chest. Then she stood. After her came a procession of others. As they went to the dead warrior, each Indian cut a strand of hair and placed it upon the body. They were all members of Two Wolves' family. When the procession ended, Painted Hawk went to his brother's side. Lifting a long strand of his own jet hair, Painted Hawk cut it quickly and let it fall to join the rest. Slowly, he returned to Kael's side.

"Treemont, every hair that is cut is part of us that goes with Two Wolves so that he will never be alone in the world of the spirits." Then, like a ghostly apparition from another world, the coyote man stepped in front of the body and began to speak. Kael felt as if he had gone back to the beginning of time. Painted Hawk translated everything that was said, and Kael learned much of the Shoshone religion.

"O, great spirits who watch over us, and you, Father Coyote, we send to you the spirit of Two Wolves. We follow, Father Coyote, what you have taught us." Then the medicine man in the animal mask turned and faced the people of the village.

"Again, one of us has left, and again we must remember our beginnings, and remember that we, the Shoshone, are the children of Coyote! We follow the lesson that has been taught. Oh, great Coyote, creator of our ancestors. O, great Coyote, who tricked the Sorceress of Life into marriage, and whose children became all the Indian nations, we remember that it was you who turned to us when our Great Mother was busy with her other children, and washed us clean. It was you,

Coyote, who made us Shoshone." The shaman paused, and Painted Hawk looked deeply into Kael's eyes. Only when the medicine man began to speak again did Painted Hawk turn from Kael.

"When one of your children dies, Coyote, we follow the lessons that you have taught us. We follow the path that you followed when your brother, Wolf, died through your jealousy. As you cut your hair, so shall we. As you did not bathe for a year, so shall we not bathe for a year. As you gave up to the fire your brother's possessions so that your greed would die with him, so shall we give up Two Wolves' possessions." Suddenly, a torch was placed into a pile of dried branches and, within seconds, a blaze shot skyward. Two Wolves' family began to march past the fire, throwing all of the dead warrior's personal belongings into it. When it was done, silence again covered the ceremony.

Throughout that first night, stories of the Shoshone were told. Lessons taught the children of warriors and the haunting wail of the entire village made themselves felt. The following night, the ritual was repeated, with more of Two Wolves' possessions thrown into the blaze. More and more of the Shoshone religion and legends were told, and Kael absorbed it all. Then, on the third night, Two Wolves' body was placed upon the fire. Again, the medicine man, still wearing the mask of Coyote, spoke.

"Now, Coyote, we give you back one of your children. He will live, always, with you, and as you have directed, from this moment on the name of Two Wolves will never pass the lips of a Shoshone." With the heavy beat of wood against wood, the shaman ignited the funeral pyre. As it burned, the people of the village began their dirge for the last time.

When Kael awoke the next morning, the village had resumed its normal ways, and by afternoon, Kael had given Painted Hawk his thanks and had begun his ride to the Crimmons ranch.

*   *   *

After Kael finished the tale, everyone was silent for a few minutes. Then John spoke.

" 'Twas a rare experience, Kael, something that few of us are permitted to see. They must have felt you were a good man."

Kael nodded his head as he looked at John's face. The heavy silence continued for a few seconds longer, until Constance Crimmons spoke.

"I'd like to remind you gentlemen that you've three hungry ladies awaiting your pleasure. We did come for a picnic, didn't we?" she asked with a warm smile. "So, if you two men would care to give us room to set out our fare, we'll be getting on with the business we came for."

Both tall men stood, and as the three women prepared the area for the picnic, they walked to the river's edge. When they reached it and stopped, John turned to Kael, his face serious.

"Lara likes you a great deal, lad," John offered in a low voice, pausing for a moment as he waited for Kael to speak.

Kael knew what his cousin was thinking, but his determination was strong, and once he made his mind up on something, it was the devil to change it. Besides which, Kael knew that to get involved with Lara before his task was done, no matter how much he desired her, would only bring hurt to her. "How can you tell?" he asked, only half-convinced that John was speaking the truth.

" 'Tis only a feeling. It's in the way she looks at you when you're not looking at her."

"John, she's a sweet thing, I'll admit that, but I can give her only a little of myself. I'd rather not do things that way."

As Kael spoke, he turned to watch the women. Lara stood out, radiantly. She wore a blue calico longskirt that rode her flared hips smoothly, falling in folds until it stopped a bare inch above the ground. Under the skirt, Kael knew, were no womanly slippers, but riding boots of soft leather. Her bodice had caused him to silently applaud her beauty. It was soft and white and blousey; barely covering her shoulders, yet falling modestly low enough to show the swell of her soft, lightly freckled breasts.

"Kael, you've got to stop thinking that way. If you're meant to find the man, you will. But you must live what life you have now. Lad, it's a sad thing to grow old alone. . . ."

Kael gazed at his well-intentioned cousin and nodded. Then the call of a bird in flight floated above them, and Kael raised his eyes to look at it. A large gray hawk flew lazily a hundred feet above them. Kael watched with admiration as the bird circled swiftly before looping down, only to rise again on the wind. Then the hawk seemed to pause in flight. Suddenly, it turned and dived. So fast was the bird's downward line that Kael found it almost impossible to follow. The hawk disappeared for a second, and a loud, high-pitched call was heard. A moment later, the bird rose with something trapped in its claws. As Kael followed the hawk's flight, its search over, he thoughtfully wished his would end as swiftly. Staring after the disappearing bird, Kael was unaware of the ice-blue eyes that studied him.

Lara felt another wave of emotion spread through her, like the rippling waters of a still lake after a stone had been thrown into it. She'd been watching Kael as he and John had talked, unable to keep her eyes from the man for more than a few moments at a time. The silhouette he formed against the backdrop of trees on the far bank of the river made Lara's breathing labored. She still did not understand what made her feel this way about him, and not the same toward any other man she had met.

Pulling her eyes away, Lara saw Angela and Constance staring at her. She blushed, and quickly placed a small basket onto the quilt.

As they ate their meal, sitting under the warm summer sun, Lara thought that last night had fulfilled its promise to her, and the day had, indeed, overflowed with beauty.

Putting her glass down, Lara turned her face upward. She tucked her legs under the full skirt of spun blue cotton and leaned back, using her arms for support. The sun kissed the exposed flesh of her shoulders and chest, making her feel even better. Smiling, Lara released her inhibitions of the past week. The voices of the others faded from her ears as her own thoughts turned inward. Lara felt a catching of her breath as she remembered arriving at the Crimmons ranch and finding Kael standing near his stallion. Without trying to, Lara had taken in every bit of Kael Treemont. He was clean-shaven again, and his tanned face was both handsome and rugged. He wore a lightweight shirt that hugged every contour of his broad chest without seeming to. His pants were a fine quality buckskin that accented his slim waist and outlined his powerful thighs and muscular calves. Suddenly, Lara felt eyes on her. Raising her lids and turning her head slightly, she found Kael gazing at her.

He, too, had finished the cold chicken, slaw, and baked bread, but he was holding his glass, still half-full of the wine Lara had brought from home. She smiled at him before forcing her eyes to move.

John, his eyelids heavy, stretched out full length on the ground. Constance sat next to him, her hand running through his hair absently, her hazel eyes distant.

"Goodness," Angela declared with a wide yawn that she tried to hide. "I guess I'm as tired as Papa. Lara, why don't you take Kael and show him the island?" Angela tried to hide the openness with which she was trying to maneuver Lara and Kael, and she hoped she was doing a good job.

Angela had been upset by Lara's news that Dowley was going to marry her off. That morning at the café, when she'd seen Lara's reaction to Kael, Angela had noted it well. She'd had an intuition that Lara felt more than she was admitting, and if possible, Angela was determined to help it along.

"Island? In the middle of Wyoming?" Kael asked with raised eyebrows.

"There's a small one in the river. It's really beautiful," Lara said. He watched as Lara's face grew thoughtful. "It almost reminds me of the countryside in Pennsylvania," she finished wistfully.

Kael watched her but paid no attention to her words. The depth of her eyes, as she spoke, had pulled him into them. Summoning up what strength he could, he tried to push his feelings aside. But his undoing came with his inability to take his eyes from hers. Softly, he spoke.

"Would you show it to me?"

Lara glanced at him, and suddenly she felt a charge leap between them. Rather than risk speaking with a voice she knew would tremble, she nodded her agreement.

Standing, Kael offered his hand. Lara grasped it and let him pull her to her feet. He did not release her hand, and she did not try to free it. "This way," she said after a long moment.

They walked silently, leaving the others far behind. Neither spoke, neither seemed to want to break the spell that had formed so comfortably around them.

Ten minutes later, they stopped on the bank of the river. Barely a body's distance across the water rested a small island, shaped like a triangle and covered with trees.

"Isn't it lovely?" Lara asked, as she turned to the tall man and looked up into his face. Her heart was beating faster now, as she waited for him to speak.

"Yes," Kael stated simply. Then, without warning, he bent his head and pressed his lips to hers.

Lara felt a fire sear downward, setting her insides aflame. Her breath was lost, and her legs weakened. Her arms went around Kael's wide shoulders for support as his tongue burned an entry into her mouth. Lara's mind went blank as she bathed in the intense pleasure of the kiss. Suddenly, she became aware of Kael's lean body against hers, and the pressure of her breasts against his hard chest. Lara felt trapped again in his arms, but this time she wanted no escape.

A moment later, the kiss ended. It took Lara another full second to open her eyes after his lips left hers. Her breasts heaved with the shortness of her breath, and fire raged within her. Opening her eyes languidly, Lara saw Kael looking down at her, his amber eyes glowing hotly.

"I wanted to do that when I first saw you, before you woke and turned into the little spitfire that attacked me."

Still feeling the soft heat of his lips on hers, Lara forced her mind to function again. She smiled slowly.

"Why didn't you?"

"I wasn't sure if you were alive or dead. Even though you're a beautiful woman, I don't like to kiss corpses." Kael smiled at her wide-eyed reaction to his words.

Lara pulled indignantly away from his arms and stared up at him. Placing her small hands on his chest, Lara pushed hard. His look of shock brought a silent laugh to her lips, but his expression, as the heels of his boots began to slip on the rocky edge of the riverbank, brought the laugh out. The sound echoed in the air as Kael, arms flailing, fought for balance and lost. His large body hit the shallow water with a resounding slap.

By this time, she was laughing uncontrollably. After another moment, she stopped. Lara had expected an angry, yelling man to rise from the river. Instead, all she heard was silence.

Carefully, Lara went to the edge.

Kael was gone.

Looking both up and downriver, Lara frantically searched for the tall man. But because she didn't look at her feet, it was her undoing.

Kael's hand snaked upward and grabbed her ankle. With a screech of indignation and surprise, she tumbled into the cool water of the mountain river.

Surfacing to gasp for air, Lara felt Kael's arm encircle her and pull her close. His burning lips found hers once again.

They stayed locked together, their bodies molding to each other's, oblivious to the cool water that tugged at their clothing. After what seemed an eternity, Kael pulled his mouth away.

"You're the most beautiful woman I've ever met," he said in a husky whisper. With his words came the knowledge that he could not let this woman go from him. No matter what! Again, Kael bent to feast on her lips.

The heat that radiated from Lara sent tendrils of desire racing through him. The touch of her breasts against him, of her belly pressing on him, drove all thoughts of revenge from his mind. For the first time in over three years, Kael Treemont thought only of the moment.

Swiftly, he ended the kiss and scooped Lara into his arms. He turned and, spotting a low edge of the bank, swung her up, depositing her on dry ground. Lara stretched out, letting the sun bathe her as Kael pulled himself out of the river.

Kael paused as he reached land. His eyes went to Lara, roaming every inch of her. The wet skirt was plastered against her thighs, clinging tightly to her slightly rounded stomach. The peach-colored tips of her breasts showed through the wet white material as if she wore nothing. Feeling his desire mount, Kael lay down beside her.

Lara's eyes went to his face, studying it intently. She traced a path with her blue eyes from his wet, glistening hair to the dark, full brows capping the amber fire that filled his gaze. Finally, her eyes stopped on his lips.

She had seen the desire in Kael's eyes, and knew that his look was mirrored in her own. She wanted him, fiercely, but at the same time she was afraid. Lara had thought she knew what love was. But she'd never experienced with Jason the intense feeling that one kiss from Kael had brought forth. She was afraid, not of Kael, but of her own reaction to him. Not of losing her virginity, although she knew she should fear that, but of losing her life and love to Kael, and being given to another by her father.

"Tell me more about Two Wolves, about when you first met him," she said, trying to free herself of the thoughts that were now haunting her.

"Do you really want to know?" Kael asked as his hand reached out to gently stroke her cheek. Lara nodded.

Kael told her again, in more detail, about his meeting with Two Wolves, of nursing him back to health, and of his own sadness at his friend's death only hours away from home. When he finished, Kael noticed that tears were unashamedly falling from Lara's eyes. His fingers went to her cheek, and he wiped the tears away.

"Why?"

"Because it was sad for him to die so close to home, but not be there. Because of the way you described the funeral, because an entire tribe of people loved and cared enough to grieve for one man." Lara blinked away more tears, then shook her head sorrowfully.

"They're supposed to be savages, unfeeling heathens who have no emotion. The people around here look on my father as a saint, because he was able to make a peaceful treaty with the savages. You've just proven all of them wrong. The Indians are as good as we are. They're noble, strong, and caring," Lara stated.

Kael couldn't help himself, as he became lost again in the deep, wet pools of her eyes. First desire came, then a softer warmth filled him as he gazed at her and listened to her words. Slowly, Kael bent his head and kissed the salty wetness that was on her cheeks.

Suddenly, he pulled away, and as he spoke, his voice turned rough and scratchy. "Come, its getting late, we've got to return to the others." Kael knew that if he stayed another minute, he would be lost completely, and so would she.

Lara looked at him, trying to understand his abrupt change. Silently, she stood and began to walk back with him. The burning embers of the fire that had started with his kiss glowed unchecked, undampened by the gruffness of his voice.

She felt him take her hand again, and felt the trembling pressure that he used. Lara bit her lip in response to both the pain she felt from his strong grasp, and the desire that his touch fanned even further upward.

When they came within sight of the others, Kael stopped. Turning to Lara, he gazed deeply into her eyes. "I want to see you again," he said in a voice that was barely above a whisper, but to Lara's ears, his words were deafening. "I've never desired anyone the way I do you."

"Kael, I have duties during the week. I have my responsibilities at home. I can't . . ." she said softly. If her father found out about them, he would become enraged. Martin Dowley would destroy whatever they would have. He might even have Kael hurt.

"You're not a slave. You're a woman."

"Kael, I'm not free," she stated without any further explanation.

"Am I beneath you?" Kael asked with a half-smile behind his sarcastic words. "Am I beneath the status of the wealthy Dowleys? Were you just playing a game with me before?"

Lara felt as if she'd been slapped. His words were taunting and cruel, so unlike what she'd thought him to be.

"No, Kael. You're not beneath me. I can't explain why, but I can't see you again."

"If that's true, then you'll meet me in two days."

Looking into his eyes, Lara felt herself start to give way. No, she told herself, her emotions were running wild and she could easily give in, but she would not have Kael harmed because of her. Was it only a few days ago that she'd told herself she would do whatever was necessary to find her own happiness? Perhaps finding that happiness meant giving something up.

"I can't," she said finally, her common sense winning out over her heart.

"I will see you in two days," Kael said in quiet, confident tones, but Lara had seen the hardening of his face as she had spoken her refusal. She turned then, and started walking back toward the waiting Crimmonses. Both Lara and Kael forced smiles upon their faces.

John had awakened a half-hour after Kael and Lara had left for the island. When he saw they were gone, he had questioned his wife.

"They went to the island," Constance had informed him with a smile. Seeing the sudden frown that he could not hide quickly enough, Constance asked what was wrong.

"Nothing," John replied, "I'm just surprised that Lara would go off alone with a man she's just met."

"Oh, John. Sometimes I think you men are so stupid. It's as plain as that handsome nose on your face that she's fair smitten with Kael."

"Smitten is she? Why, she's just a babe," John had replied with fatherly concern. Ever since Angela had brought Lara home, he'd felt almost like her father.

"She's a year older than I was when you nearly stole me from my mother!" retorted Constance with a smile.

"Stole you? Why, your father was terrified for fear I'd not have you. He was so afraid he'd have to start looking again to marry you off that he doubled your dowry to make sure I'd stay with you."

"Ho!" Constance had said with a wide grin that denied the anger in her voice. "Doubled my dowry, did he? And what if I'd told him that you'd already had your way with me, even before you'd asked for my hand?"

"Why, luv, he would have patted my back, and smiled handsomely for saving him so much food and clothing between the time we'd made love and the time we were wed," John replied with an innocent look on his face.

"Oh!" Constance yelled as she flung herself at him, carrying both herself and John to the ground. Their commotion had awakened Angela, who had fallen asleep just after Kael and Lara had left.

"Are you two fighting again?" Angela asked with a soft smile on her face. Her parents never quarreled. They had fights, and they loved. She knew that they were playing now.

"Right you are, m'luv," John admitted. "Your mother's been acting right fancy, throwing your friend Lara at your cousin Kael."

"Mother!" Angela yelled, but she could not hold back her smile. "I thought I was supposed to do that!"

"I don't believe my ears," John said as he threw his hands up.

"Papa, I only wish there was another man like Kael around. I can't stand these groveling fools that are always calling on me."

"One day you'll find a fine man for yourself, I promise you that," John said, his face serious.

"There aren't too many *fine* men around here, Papa," Angela said with a sadness in her voice that tore into John Crimmons's heart.

"There will be one for you."

But not one like you, or Kael, she thought silently. Growing up as John's daughter, Angela knew that she would be unable to accept any man who was less than her father. The first that had met her standards was Kael, and he was her cousin.

Just then Angela saw Kael and Lara walk into sight, and stop to face each other and talk. "Mother," Angela called in a whisper, "look at their faces."

Constance saw what Angela saw, but John Crimmons saw nothing unusual. Just two people talking.

"You're right, Angela," said her mother with a secret smile.

"Right about what?" John asked, bewildered by the feminine secret.

Mother and daughter looked at each other knowingly. "You wouldn't understand, John, not right now."

He let out a grunt of frustration. He had his own idea what his wife and daughter were talking about, but it couldn't be, John told himself, as he saw the mask of anger that suffused Kael's face when he and Lara had stopped talking.

Like the rolling salt water of the incoming ocean tide, Kael Treemont rode inexorably toward his destiny. The gray Andalusian that had carried him almost two thousand miles on his quest moved as swiftly and as strongly as it had the first day he'd left Philadelphia.

Only now the powerful stallion was taking him to a different destiny, one that was causing confusion and turmoil within Kael.

Cresting a small, grass-covered hill, he reined in the horse and stopped to survey the land before him. He quickly found the landmarks described to him.

In the distance, as far as the eye could see, were the gray-brown shimmering mountains that surrounded the ranches and farms of Valley City. Rolling green pastures, intermixed with desolate patches of rocky earth that even the spring thaw waters flowing from the mountains could not help to grow life on, blended into a strange tableau of harsh beauty.

Turn back, Kael told himself, even as his heels dug into the horse's flanks. *I can't*, he admitted as his face fell into set lines of determination.

It had been two days since the picnic. Two days since he'd told Lara that he would see her. Two days that had been filled with conflicting emotions of desire and self-duty. Two nights of tossing, unable to sleep because of the memory of burgundy hair and soft skin upon his lips. The feel of Lara's body against his, waist deep in water, heat pouring freely between them, had tormented him past the point of logic.

By the time Lara had mounted her horse and left for home, Kael had known that he would go after her. Never in his life had he felt so strongly about a woman.

For the past two days, Kael had pried the knowledge of Lara's habits from Angela. By the time he'd said good night the previous evening, he'd learned of Lara's morning rides, and what the blue-eyed woman did with her days.

Angela also supplied the warning that Martin Dowley would let no man other than the one he chose court his daughter. Kael had smiled mysteriously, already secure in the knowledge that he would have this woman who had affected him so deeply.

Hoofbeats echoing in the air alerted Kael to a rider's approach. Still sitting in the dark leather saddle of the gray stallion, Kael turned his eyes in the direction of the sound. About a quarter-mile away, he saw the roan mare and its rider. Patiently, Kael waited.

Holding Camilla back from a full gallop, Lara tried to use the horse's rhythm to soothe and calm herself as her mind attempted to put together the disturbing things she'd learned. In the back of her mind, another warning issued. It had been two days since she'd seen Kael Treemont.

Unbidden, the memories of the burning kisses that had set her body and mind aflame returned. Lara had never felt like this before. At strange moments, staring into mirrors, brushing her hair, tending the garden, Kael's face would float up to haunt her. Golden eyes, filled with desire, moist lips, inviting, strong arms, and a powerful chest taunted her. Lara could again feel his body as it pressed against hers, making her weak with need and desire.

What was she feeling? Was she in love with Kael Treemont? She'd only just met him, seen him but three times, and only once did their meeting last for more than a few fleeting moments. How could she be in love with him? Thinking about Pennsylvania, and the boy she had planned to marry, Lara again questioned the very depth of her emotions. With Jason Grumman, she had felt secure and in control. Jason's kisses had been chaste, and soft; Kael's had been hard, hot, and demanding. Lara had felt a certain warmth and fondness with Jason; with Kael, her body had reacted instantly, and her mind had ceased to function. Why? What was it about Kael Treemont that called her so strongly?

Lara was used to command. The only person she'd never been able to control was her stepfather. Although she did not fear him, she knew that Dowley could do whatever he pleased with her and she would be helpless to stop him. No, Lara wasn't afraid of Martin Dowley the man, but she knew the power that he had and what he could do with it.

Pushing the thought away, and the thoughts of Kael, Lara attended to her newest and most pressing problem. She had known since that night she'd overheard her father and Setterley talking, that her fate was almost sealed. That next day, the one she'd spent with Setterley, had confirmed her fears. His words to her were no idle boast. It was just a matter of time before she would be wed to her stepfather's friend.

Yesterday she'd heard Lew Cross and two other hands talking about a shipment of cattle that was arriving. The largest single herd of cattle to come to the Dowley ranch. Separately, six breeding bulls would follow.

She hadn't needed to hear anything else. Her father, as wealthy as he was, could not afford the stock. Only one man could, and that man was Johnathan Setterley.

Martin Dowley's ambitions were coming to fruition. Together, Setterley and he would control the cattle industry of the western territories. Lara's stepfather would have exactly what he wanted; wealth, status, and control of everything and everybody around. He would supply the vast needs of the army, as he had bragged he would to Lara many times. Dowley, because of his government position, was privy to much information, and he knew the army was planning to open and protect more and more territories so that the thousands of settlers heading West would not fear the Indians.

Yes, she thought, her stepfather was a smart man. When they'd first arrived here, he'd gone to the Indians, to the Shoshone and Arapahoe, and made truces with them. Protection against attack for himself and the rest of Valley City in exchange for cattle and other supplies. Martin Dowley had been empowered to make these treaties, and the government even reimbursed his expenses.

Lara could not fault her father for what he did, because he'd achieved both a peace and a working relationship with the Indians that no one in the territories had ever accomplished before. The Shoshone had proven the most honorable in keeping faith with the treaties. The Arapahoe were not as trustworthy, but did not usually attack residents of Valley City.

From the corner of her eyes, Lara saw a figure on the crest of a hill to her left. In the flash of a heartbeat, she felt a stirring fill her body. Kael! Lara slowed her horse as she neared him, her mind emptying of all its worry and concern as her heart began to race.

When she was within six feet of him, she stopped the mare. Lara's eyes accepted the full impact of the man who sat on the stallion. Kael's dark hair was covered with a wide-brimmed hat, his shirt fell loosley around his chest. But not loosely enough to hide the power that Lara knew it contained. Once again, Kael wore his army pants, tight fitting and tucked smoothly into the tall black riding boots that were now gently pressing against the stallion's flanks, moving the horse to her.

Reaching her side, Kael stopped and smiled. "Buckskins again?"

"I thought you didn't object?"

"I don't. I told you once that I like to see what I look at."

"Kael. . . ." Before she could complete what she started, he leaned over and, stretching out a strong arm, pulled her close. His mouth covered hers, hungry and demanding. The heated spear of his tongue probed into her mouth, searching for her own. Lara went weak as she tasted him. The kiss lasted forever, and when he finally released her, Lara felt herself ready to explode. Her breasts began to ache, and the fire that he had ignited began to wind its way deep into the very core of her womanhood.

"I've waited two days to kiss you. I don't like waiting," Kael said in a voice filled with want.

"Kael, no. We can't."

"We can't?" he replied, tightening his grip on her narrow waist, ignoring the pressure of the mare's flank against his leg. "We can!" he stated as he pulled her against him, holding her body in a grip of iron.

Suddenly, Kael kicked the gray stallion's flanks. Feeling herself pulled free from her saddle, Lara tried to fight him. Before she could prevent it, she was being carried, held tightly against Kael's side as her mare followed meekly behind.

Kael rode over the crest of the next small hill, and then stopped on a plateau covered by buffalo grass. Bending from the side, he lowered Lara to the ground.

"How dare you?" Lara yelled at him in outrage as he dismounted. Then Kael smiled.

"No!" she said in a hushed voice as Kael advanced on her. Stepping back, she tried to fend him off. Lara was unsure of herself, afraid of her reactions to him, and terrified that another kiss would end her resistance.

Taking two large strides, Kael reached her. His mind was inflamed, as was his body. The first time he'd seen Lara he had known desire, and since that first kiss by the river, he'd wanted the blue-eyed woman who stood before him as he wanted no other.

As quickly as she had started, Lara ceased her retreat. Her

eyes locked with his. She felt his arms go around her. Kael stared at her for a moment before he crushed her against him.

Kael felt the heat of her lithe body against his, and felt the softness of her firm breasts as they pressed against him. Blood pounded in his head, turning his every thought to her.

Lara looked up into his eyes and the last shred of resistance fell away. All thoughts of how she should act until she was wed disappeared. She knew the desire and need she saw in his eyes were only reflections of her own.

"Kael," she whispered. The word was more than the calling of his name.

Kael's mouth formed a soft smile as he bent his head and covered hers with his. Lara opened her lips to him, her arms circling his back, her fingers digging into his tight muscles.

Lara felt herself being lifted, then gently deposited on the grass. Covering her body with his, Kael pulled his mouth from hers and lowered it to the pulsing vein on her neck. The touch of his heated lips on the tender skin drew a low, throaty moan from her. Her hands began to run along his back as her eyes closed and she responded freely to him.

Kael shifted, then his strong hand cupped her breast. Her breathing quickened as fiery lances of pleasure engulfed her. His lips were at the base of her throat, and she could feel her blood rush past them. Suddenly, Lara was aware of his hands on her flesh, as they slipped beneath the buckskin top. She felt the first contact of his fingers on the skin of her stomach as his fingertips caressed her. Unable to stop the shudder of pleasure that shook her, Lara's hands went to his face, pulling his lips back to hers and pressing them fully against his.

Lara felt sensations she'd never before known as his hands continued to explore her body. Her hands, too, became pioneers, roaming the length of his back, following the flow of hard muscles until her palms traced Kael's taunt buttocks to press briefly before returning to his head to tangle her fingers on his thick, dark hair.

She stopped breathing as she gazed into his face. What she saw there calmed her, and all fear left. Tenderness filled his eyes. Kael's lips were no longer smiling, and she felt his hand caress her cheek.

"Will you let me love you?" he asked softly. Lara's breath returned as she nodded her head slowly.

"Please," Lara heard herself reply. She felt as if she were watching two lovers, rather than being one of them. It was as if she were two people, one watching, the other wanting. Kael's mouth covered hers again, and the two Laras became one.

Gently, Kael untied the thin leather laces that held her buckskin top together. Then she felt the sun on her pale, bare skin.

Kael's indrawn breath exploded like a hammer in his chest as Lara's breasts were freed. His eyes feasted on their beauty and fullness. The firm but not large peach-tipped mounds called to him. Lowering his mouth, he tasted one already taut nipple. Above his head, Lara's moan filled the air. Kael tasted the satin of Lara's skin, as his hand covered her other breast, caressing it tenderly until his mouth blazed a hot, burning path to the peak of the other breast.

With the first touch of his lips on her breast, Lara felt a lance drive downward, sending little pinpricks of need to her core. She felt the heat of his mouth and hands as he kissed and caressed her, fueling the fire that raged within her to uncontrollable heights. His mouth left hers as his hands trailed downward. Then Lara felt his lips return to trace a blistering path between the valley of her breasts and, without pausing, continue to cover the sensitive skin of her stomach.

Kael's hands and lips stopped at the feel of buckskin pants. The very touch and taste of Lara's skin was pushing him past the breaking point when he suddenly realized that she was wearing both pants and boots.

Slowly, he sat up. Smiling softly at Lara, Kael turned. Then he pulled the leather boots free from her feet. He turned back again and paused. Kael watched Lara's face, her eyes closed, her breasts lifting and falling, bathed by the morning sun. It was true, she was the most magnificent creature he'd ever seen.

Lara sighed silently. Keeping her eyes closed against the glare of the sun, she waited. Only the slightest hesitation at what was to come teased her mind. With the touch of Kael's hands on her waist, even that hesitation flew as she followed his urging and arched herself off the ground. Lara felt the thin leather breeches slide along her thighs and off to join her boots on the grass.

"You are truly magnificent," Kael said, voicing aloud the thoughts that had filled his mind only moments ago. Opening her eyes as he spoke, she saw him standing above her, his torso bare, his boots lying next to hers.

Lara wanted to cry as she gazed at him. She wanted to tell him that standing there, his muscles rippling above her, he was more than handsome, he was beautiful. Lara knew now that what she was doing, what was happening to her mind and body, was right. She knew deep within her heart that this was meant to be.

Not for the first time since they'd met did she compare him to a powerful mountain cat, his graceful movements, strength, and confidence all blended togther in an aura of feline majesty. Now, with the tall, broad-chested man standing above her, his entire body naked and his manly power thrusting forward, Lara felt desire rise anew within her.

Lifting her arms, she beckoned him to her. Kael seemed to flow as he came to her. His body once again covered hers, but this time hot, bare flesh met and melted together as their arms entwined.

Lara felt Kael's lips cover hers, felt his hardness against her and lost herself in the sensations of their bodies. He pulled away slightly, and his mouth again ran a blazing trail from her lips to her breasts, kissing each pliant globe softly before licking her skin with a rasping tongue. Again Kael pulled away, only to return and take her tender skin between his teeth and bite it gently. By the time his lips drew in her stiffened nipple, a thrilling pleasure consumed Lara. At the touch of his tongue against the sensitive tissue of her breast's tip, she could no longer hold her body still. Her back arched, pressing her breasts forcefully against his mouth.

One strong hand dipped to her belly, then began to trail lower, stopping to play at the downy softness that was the joining of her thighs. Kael's fingers lingered for endless moments before they resumed their exploration.

Silky skin met his fingertips as his hand stroked Lara's inner thigh. Kael's blood sang through his body. His breath pushed fiercely against the wall of his chest, and his hardness pressed achingly against her other thigh. Slowly, he moved his fingers and felt the moist warmth below her downy covering. As his fingers caressed her innermost place, Kael heard Lara's voice grow throaty as her moans filled the blue sky.

Pulling forward again, Kael raised himself slightly and fitted himself between her legs. He paused as he looked down at Lara's face, and found her gazing back at him unashamedly. Her eyes seemed a deeper blue now as he saw the trust she gave him. Slowly, he brushed his lips against hers, then lightly kissed each of her now closed lids. Returning his lips to hers, Kael lowered his body, forcing control along every inch of himself as he gently began to enter her.

When Lara stiffened momentarily, Kael stopped his inward movement but did not leave. Gradually, she relaxed again, and only then did he continue.

Lara felt a burning rod against her, tearing into her with pain and pleasure. Her body became rigid, and involuntarily Kael stopped. Her hands were on his back, and Lara knew that her nails were digging into his flesh but she was powerless to stop herself. Slowly, she forced the small degree of pain to flee. Her fingers loosened as she accepted the hot pleasure that was beginning to return.

Lara felt Kael move again. Suddenly, a sharp, snapping pain filled her insides. She called out, and Kael pulled her closer, holding his body still once again. Slowly, with neither of them moving, the pain left, and the first soft tendrils of pleasure begn to wind throughout her body.

Kael moved again, and she felt herself pulled along with

him. His hardness filled her, becoming an almost unbearable, throbbing need that controlled her entire being. She felt his lips kissing hers, felt his body begin to move faster as hers joined him. Waves of pleasure began to flow through every inch of her being. The touch of his chest against her taut nipples, now damp with heat and love, lifted her higher and higher. Kael's thrusting deep within her demanded and received her own body's response, which matched his every movement. Suddenly, Lara tightened around him, felt herself grow weak and strong at the same time. Her voice cried out, but she heard nothing, as his body moved within hers. Lara exploded with rapture, again and again, her mind dissolving amid waves of love, pleasure, and release, which threatened to overwhelm her. She was unconscious of the fact that with each wave of sensation, she cried out Kael's name.

Kael's mind swam in pleasure and awe. From the first instant his hardness had touched her, he began to lose himself within her. With the last vestiges of control, Kael forced his body to obey him, and prevent his losing himself completely inside her warmth. After he felt himself pierce the barrier of her virginity, Kael once again forced himself to stop moving, forced his body to obey him, as he waited for Lara's ache to subside.

Hearing Lara's cry of pain, then feeling her loosen again around him, Kael began to let himself free. The moist heat that sheathed him drew him further inside. Suddenly, he could no longer control himself. Desire and need filled his mind and body as his lips crushed hers. With the twin stiffness of her breasts against him, and Lara's nails in his back, Kael gave himself over to her womanly warmth.

His body became a driving machine that dominated them both. Moving faster as her legs wound themselves around his hips, Kael rode her with every bit of skill and love he could summon. He reached his summit as Lara's legs tightened around him. He heard her call his name, and felt her muscles grip him and pull him deeper.

With his name filling his ears, and his body within hers,

Kael felt himself explode, driving even deeper within her, trying to force his body to mold completely with hers.

After an eternity of love, Lara felt Kael slow, then finally cease. The deep, ragged breathing that came from both of them filled the air. Lara trembled helplessly, unable to stop herself. Slowly, Kael began to untangle himself from her legs and arms. Reluctantly, she released him. Once again, Kael was poised above her, his eyes gazing softly down at her, his smile speaking more than any words. Gently, Kael rolled free of Lara, and once on his back, pulled her into the crook of his arm.

Feeling the glow of passion that her first lovemaking had produced, Lara curled against him, her head resting on his shoulder, her hand open on his chest. Kael's lips pressed against her forehead, tenderly, and she felt his hand cup her breast. Flowing sensations of warmth and pleasure filled her and made her smile.

"It had to be," Kael said as his lips brushed her forehead. "From the first moment I saw you, it had to be."

Lara had known it also, and found herself crying silently. She had done what she'd promised herself not to do. She had given herself, and would now lose the man who had won her. Blinking back her tears, Lara let her hand roam across his chest. Suddenly, she felt a scar beneath her questing fingers.

Lara traced the scar from beneath Kael's left nipple to halfway across his side. She didn't understand why she hadn't felt it before.

"What's this?" she asked.

"In the war. A fragment from a heavy ball," he told her quietly. Lara sat up, ignoring her nakedness as she traced the path of the scar with her eyes. It should have been ugly, but it was part of him, and he was beautiful. She bent, and touched the old wound with her lips.

"I won't let you go," he said.

"Kael. . . ." He silenced her with his finger.

"I can't take you away, not just now, but I will," he promised. Then, as he looked into her eyes and noticed the moisture that was there, Kael told Lara the reason he was in Wyoming. When he was finished, Lara nodded slowly.

"Your father must have been a good man," she said softly, as her own thoughts returned again to the real father she had never known.

"He was," Kael replied, his voice deep with emotion and memory.

"My father," she began, about to tell Kael the truth of her birth, something that no one else in her new home knew of. Before she could go on, Kael leaned forward and brushed her lips lightly.

"I've heard much about him. You have reason to be proud. But, the morning is almost gone, and you'll have to leave me soon."

"No . . . I. . . ." But again, he cut off her protest with a kiss, and suddenly there was nothing in the world that mattered to either of them except each other as their bodies came together again, and joined once more on the summer grass, with the hot sun bathing them in happiness.

Lara felt hard hands dig cruelly into her breasts, as she smelled sour, tobabbo-laden breath in her nostrils. Struggling to get away, she swung her hand upward.

Her open palm met the sallow skin of Johnathan Setterley's face, and a loud cracking sound reverberated in her ears.

With the sound, Setterley's face shattered into a thousand pieces, and Lara began her trip back to the real world. Conscious of her sweat-bathed body, she lifted the multihued Indian blanket off to let the early morning breeze that filtered through the windows cool her.

Pulling the damp material of her light cotton nightdress away from her breasts, she sought relief from her dream in thoughts of Kael Treemont. Her mind was a bubbling cauldron of confusion and despair. Lara knew she was lost. She had been lost since that first kiss by the Popo Agie River. Every time Lara had met Kael since, she fell deeper and deeper into a trap she knew was inescapable.

Lara had tried to warn Kael, to tell him that she could

never be his. But Kael's own words, filled with self-confidence, had stopped her before she could explain.

Lara had always thought that love would mean freedom. Now she realized that to her love, meant only more fetters. In order to protect the man she admitted loving, she must give him up. Her stepfather's legal rights over her, and the archaic rules that governed men and women, would prevent their union. Martin Dowley would never agree to this match, which would be profitless for him. He would do whatever was necessary to rid himself of Kael Treemont. That was the reason she had not mentioned his name once in this house.

With those saddening thoughts came pictures of the too few times she'd had with Kael: swimming together in the rock-bed mountain pool, ducking beneath the downpouring waters of the small falls that fed from a high stream, and holding each other's naked bodies close as the water cascaded over them. Making love on the large, sunwarmed rock that sat above the pool as if it were the altar of a god.

Riding together through the foothills of the mighty snow-capped Tetons. Feeling the wind and smelling the scents of the flowers and trees that grew in abundance along the fertile base of the great mountain chain. Lying in the grassy plains, their horses grazing contently, as they kissed and caressed until neither could hold back, and desire brought them together in another emotion-crested wave of love.

Noises began to intrude on Lara's thoughts as the workday began at the Dowley ranch. She closed her eyes again, and her ears, to anything outside her mind. She smiled as her tongue moistened her lips, and her mind replayed her last meeting with Kael three days before. Two weeks after the first time they had made love.

Lara was near Fox Butte, looking for a heifer she knew was due to birth. Although it was something that was normally left to the experienced hands, a problem had kept everyone busy at the opposite end of the ranch.

Lara wore her buckskins, but this time she had on a white

blouse of light cotton, with a camisole under it to absorb the perspiration the heat of the day would bring.

Riding up the butte, her eyes searched carefully. Off to the right, she spotted the familiar brown and white markings of the heifer. She rode to it, but before she reached the lazing animal, it saw her and lifted its head.

Lara laughed as she saw the cow look at her and snort. Then she watched in amazement, sure that she had seen the cow shrug as it turned its bulk to face her.

"Come on, girl, you have to go home now," she said. The words meant nothing, but her lilting tone seemed to impress the disproportioned animal. The cow began to walk slowly toward Lara, its belly distended with the nearness of the coming calf.

As the ungainly animal passed her, Lara laughed again and began following the cow. By the time they were off the butte, the cow had picked up its pace and was ambling toward its home pasture.

Stopping the mare, Lara let her eyes roam freely. As always, the multicrested and far-reaching Wind River mountains stretched on until they disappeared in a haze of distance.

"Do all your animals listen as well as that one?" asked a rich voice out of nowhere. At his first word, Lara's breath caught in recognition.

Turning to him, Lara drank in the maleness he exuded. "Are you sure you're not a Shoshone?" she asked. Kael's puzzled frown urged her to explain. "I never hear you approach, you just appear. I thought only Indians did that."

"Indians, and men with evil purposes in mind," he added with a smile. Dismounting swiftly, Kael went to Lara and helped her down. Even when her feet were firmly on the ground, he did not release her. He pulled her close and covered her mouth with his. They stayed like that, drinking in the taste, and love, that each gave the other as the sun beat down on them.

"I want you," Kael said in a husky voice that sent shivers of anticipation along Lara's spine.

Without waiting for her response, Kael lifted her into his arms and searched for a comfortable place.

Spotting a small, grass-covered area, Kael brought Lara to it, and gently laid her down.

"You presume much," she said with a radiant smile. Kael looked down at her sparkling blue eyes and held them with his own.

"Do I?" he asked in a low voice as his hands paused at the neck of his shirt.

"You do, but you presume correctly." Suddenly, Lara's expression became serious as Kael pulled off his shirt. He bent and swiftly removed her clothing, and then the rest of his.

Kael gazed at her nakedness, unashamedly absorbing her beauty as an artist preparing a painting would do. Kael feasted on her body. His gaze, roaming everywhere, was followed by his hands, and then his mouth.

Lara watched Kael's dancing gold and brown flecked eyes as they caressed her. She watched their amber turn into a deeper shade, and luxuriated in the pleasure that was so plainly visible.

Just his eyes were enough to fan the flames inside her body and send fiery lances of desire shooting to every part of her. The dark hair that covered his chest and tapered into a narrow line that dropped past his flat belly drew her gaze. Lara followed the furry path until it ended in the shape of an arrowhead. When her eyes fastened onto the already hardened spear of his manhood, her breath rushed from her in a long, deep sigh.

Lara felt his hands caress her breasts, sending even more bolts of lightning to explode within her. Lifting her eyes back to his, she saw his head framed by the sun. Flashes of light beamed through the wavy hair, making Lara catch her breath again as her heart filled with emotion.

Kael lowered his mouth to hers and, pressing her back, covered her smaller body with his. As her palms traced the muscles of his back, her body responded with tingling vibrations of pleasure. Lara's legs opened as her hand encircled him and urged him to her. She felt him enter her slowly, drawing the moment out, prolonging the first exquisite rapture until neither could bear the sweet torture of it, and he plunged deep within her moist softness.

Lara felt his heat and male hardness penetrate into her very soul. Welcoming him eagerly, her body rose against his. Within a breath's time, Lara felt herself explode, felt her inner muscles clench around him as rippling waves of pleasure rolled along her body.

Above her, Kael paused as he, too, felt her fast and intense ecstasy. Then, slowly, he began to move again, growing even harder within her as his lips roamed along her neck.

Gently, Lara pressed her hands on his back, calling him to stop. His eyes rose to meet hers in question. Kissing his lips with gentle bites, Lara forced them to roll over, freeing her of his weight, and at the same time trapping his body below and within her.

For the first time, Lara felt the warmth of the morning sun on her back as her body began to move slowly on Kael. Jolts of pleasure radiated upward, bringing her an all-encompassing sensation. Looking down at him, she felt herself grow stronger as she drank in his male beauty. Kael's eyes burned up at her, amber circles of fire that held her in thrall. Lara found deeper emotions grow within her as she gave herself completely to bringing him to the apex of his pleasure. Arching her back and letting her hips rotate as her body directed, Lara rode Kael as if he were a mount, dissolving in the glow of their passions.

Lara's glossy hair moved freely about as her breasts rose and fell above him. She saw Kael pull himself upward to grasp and bring her against him. Her legs braced against his waist, her hard-tipped breasts pressed against his chest, and her lips went to his neck. Locked together, holding each other as if they were one, they let the sensations of their joining build higher and higher until nothing could hold them back. Lara felt Kael burst within her as his body racked with the forcefulness of his climax. Lara's teeth sank into the muscle of his shoulder as she peaked with him. Both were carried to the farthest points of the heavens.

Minutes later found them still locked together, refusing to acknowledge the end of their lovemaking. Their hands continually smoothed each other's backs, and each tried to still the tremors that flowed and ebbed in waves for an endless time.

"Kael," Lara whispered, her voice low, her head still buried on his shoulder. She felt him move, felt his fingers wind in her hair. Kael grasped a handful of hair and gently pulled her face from his shoulder. Tenderly, he kissed her.

"I love you, Kael," she said, blinking away the moisture pooling in her eyes. Again, his lips found hers and held them for a long time.

A loud bleating broke the silence of the day and made both of them jump.

"The heifer," Lara yelled, instinctively reacting to the sound. Pulling herself free from Kael, she stood and looked around. What she saw rooted her to the spot. Moving quickly, Lara grabbed her cotton blouse, pulling it on as she ran toward the cow.

When Kael reached her side, the calf had been born. As the mother began the job of cleaning her newborn, he drew Lara close.

"It never fails to make me cry," Lara said in an emotion-filled voice, lifting her wet eyes to his. Smiling, Kael placed his finger beneath each eye and gathered the moisture that had fallen.

"You're a picture, my love, standing next to a newborn, calf, under the blue Wyoming sky, half-naked." Blushing, Lara pushed herself away from Kael, and raced back to her buckskins.

Sobered, Kael joined Lara and they dressed, kissed deeply, and parted. Kael, for the Crimmons ranch, Lara for her home.

* * *

While Lara lay in bed and relived her short but wonderful time with Kael, he awoke to the morning sun and went out to speak with his cousin.

Kael found John standing by the corral fence, looking westward at the distant line of mountains. Walking up to his cousin, Kael stood beside him but kept his silence.

Several minutes passed as both men stared outward, enjoying the freshness of the day and the awesomeness of the view.

"Every morning I come out here and look. It's been three full years now since I built this house, but every day before I start work, I must look around." John paused for a moment, using the time to control the emotion that filled his voice. "Lad, I find it hard to explain what the difference between this land and England is to me. I loved England, but I could not grow there. Everywhere I turned, there was someone else. Even in the country, there was nothing left for me. Everything seemed to be taken.

"Look out there, lad. As far as your eyes can see, and a thousand miles farther, is open land, waiting for people like us. There's nowhere else in the world that can give you what you have here."

"John," Kael began.

"No, lad, just let me prattle on. I know you must have heard what I've said a hundred times. 'Tis just an old man's talk."

"If you're an old man, then I must be well past my prime. John, you're only ten years older than I," Kael stated.

"There you go again, ruining my practice for my old age." With that, both men laughed heartily. "What brings you out so early?"

"I'm going back to South Pass City for a few days. I want to see if I can find out anything more, and there may be some letters for me," Kael said. When he had started his odyssey of vengeance, he'd left word with his lawyers that he could be contacted at South Pass. He'd also gone to the Pinkerton Agency and explained his situation, asking if they had means to trace the man who had used the name Malcome Dupont.

After he'd explained the circumstances of his father's death, the detective agency had agreed, with a stipulation that they would spend a year tracing, and if they found nothing, their job would end, but Kael would still be billed. He had agreed. The year had ended while he had been en route to Wyoming. He was hoping that they might have found something.

"I had a feeling it was just a matter of time," John said as he gazed into Kael's eyes. "We had hoped Lara Dowley might have tempered your thoughts."

"No," Kael said with a shake of his head as Lara's image swam up in his mind. "If anything, John, I want this over with so that I can go to her father. I want to marry her. But I won't until I've done what I have to."

"Dammit, Kael, are you going to throw away everything to chase a phantom?" John argued, feeling a sense of sadness grow . . . and, a warning ring in his mind. Angela had told him of Martin Dowley's plans for Lara. He'd hoped that Kael was the man to prevent it. John had seen the love in both their faces.

"I can't stop you, but, Kael, if you can't find the man soon, think about ending this obsession. Your father would be sorely hurt to know you've given up your life for revenge."

"It's more than revenge, John," Kael said as he looked first at John, then around the ranch, and out again to the mountains. "If this man can get away with killing my father, with stealing most of his money, and never pay for it, how many others will fall victim to him? How many people will die because of the greed and callousness of others? You came to this country because of the promise of a wonderful new life. If this man, and others like him, can do whatever they want, then you've chosen a poor place to call home."

"Kael, what you say makes sense, but 'tis merely a rational excuse for continuing your obsession. Mark me well, lad, what you're doing will destroy you. Temper your thoughts, apply them in general, and maybe what you say will inspire others. You can't do it by yourself." As John spoke, he saw the uselessness of his words. Kael's face showed no softening.

It will take time, and love, he thought, before Kael will relent. "All right, lad, enough talk. When are you leaving?"

"Tomorrow. I want to speak to Lara before I go."

" 'Tis Saturday, she'll be in town. You'll be able to speak to her then."

"No, I'll ask Angela to give her a message. I'll see her tonight," Kael stated.

John wisely maintained his silence. He didn't think it would be as easy as that.

The Valley Café was filled with its usual Saturday customers. Small groups of friends were clustered around tables, eating and catching up on events that had occurred since they'd last seen each other. A low hum filled the air as the voices went on, ignoring conversations that were only a few feet distant.

Near the rear of the small restaurant, at a table under a window framed with lace curtains, sat two young women who epitomized the small but growing Wyoming territory. They sipped tea from floral-decorated porcelain teacups and took random bites from the pie wedges that sat before them as they delved deeper and deeper into their conversation. Suddenly, the auburn-haired woman's face blanched. Lara stared open mouthed at Angela Crimmons.

"He can't!" Lara whispered desperately.

"He can't? You can't possibly mean Kael Treemont. If you don't know that by now. . . ." Angela let her last words float off without finishing. Both women knew what she meant. If Kael said he was going to do something, then he would do it. It was a trait that Lara had seen and accepted in the handsome man. The first time he had told her he would do something was at the picnic. Two days later, he had followed up his words with action.

In an effort to quell her growing fear, Lara questioned Angela. "Why?" she asked in another urgent whisper.

Angela looked at her friend with innocent blue eyes. Her smile formed softly as she explained.

"Kael's leaving for South Pass City. He doesn't know how long he'll be gone, and he wants to say goodbye to you himself. Privately," she added. Both knew that Valley City was as far from private as possible.

"Oh, Angela, he just can't. If my father finds out. . . . If he sees him, he'll—"

"Kael can take care of himself," Angela cut in defensively. The pretty young blonde was picking up Lara's fears, and felt them within her. She knew that Lara was in love with Kael, and she felt that Kael loved her friend also. Angela didn't want Lara to lose this chance.

"Kael would be a suitable match for you. When your father learns of his background, his stature, and the lands he owns back East and in California, he'll accept him."

"No, he won't!" Lara declared. Color flowed back into her cheeks as she spoke passionately. "My father doesn't want land. He has all he wants. He doesn't want money, he has that, too. He wants cattle, horses, and the power that those things will bring him! Don't you see that's why I've never spoken of Kael to him? Kael can't trade cattle for me, and that's all my father will accept." Lara paused for a moment to regain her breath. Her hands were on the table, balled into white-knuckled fists. Lara's eyes fastened onto her hands and she slowly opened her fingers. A moment later, she looked at Angela. "If my father finds out about Kael and me, I'm afraid he'll send me to Kansas City immediately," Lara prophesied sadly.

"Why haven't you told this to Kael?" Angela asked suddenly.

"Why? He's your cousin, isn't he?" Lara snapped.

Angela flinched at the intensity of her friend's words.

100

"Angela, I'm sorry," Lara apologized quickly. "I've tried to tell Kael about it several times, but he always seems to think I'm saying something else. He just stops me and tells me I'm not to worry, that he'll take care of everything once his own business is finished with."

"Kael will," Angela said fervidly. Lara saw her friend's expression of . . . idolatry. Lara realized that Angela, too, did not understand what she was saying.

"This cursed trail of vengeance that Kael is following will never bring him and me together. It will destroy us," Lara stated honestly. Intuitively, she felt the depth of her own words. Tears began to well in her light blue eyes, and she fought them.

"You must have faith. Please, Lara, he loves you. I know he does." Angela reached across the table and took Lara's hands, gripping them tightly within her own. Lara spoke then, in a voice so low that it took Angela several seconds to believe what she was hearing.

"If my father finds out that the woman he's sending to Johnathan Setterley for marriage is no longer a virgin, he'll destroy us both! That's why I can't let Kael come to the ranch. I know my father. I don't care about myself, but if something were to happen to Kael because of me. . . . Please, Angela," Lara pleaded, "please stop him."

Recovering her wits as quickly as she could, Angela tried to digest what she'd heard. Although she hid her reaction well, Lara's words came as a shock. Kael and Lara had been loving! Unexpectedly, there were a thousand questions that Angela wanted to ask. She wanted to learn of the mysteries and the thrills, but she knew she couldn't, not now.

"I'll try," Angela said in a hoarse whisper that matched Lara's.

Kael had spent Saturday alone. He had stayed at the ranch while the Crimmonses had gone to Valley City. Spending his hours in thought, Kael had come to a major decision.

Knowing he was at the crossroads of his life, he had struggled to settle the war that raged within his mind. Although John thought Kael unreceptive to his words of warning and caution, Kael had heard everything that his cousin had said. But he had pushed the words to the back of his mind, to hold there until the right time. Now, it appeared, was the right time.

He wanted to marry Lara. He'd known it since their first touch. And he decided that no matter what her father's objections might be, he would win her. But when? The reality of that question, combined with the now well-digested words of his cousin, forced Kael to think.

When John, Constance, and Angela had left this morning, the silence of the empty house had driven Kael from it. After saddling Major, his stallion, he rode the rolling miles to the bend in the Popo Agie River and dismounted at the spot where they'd picniced two weeks ago.

Sitting under the sun of another cloudless day, Kael had let his mind run free. For hours, he withdrew into himself, barely conscious of his surroundings, unresponsive even to the small animals that had bravely, and curiously, come near him.

When he returned from his voyage of introspection, his mind had been calm and his decision was made.

Tomorrow's trip to South Pass City would be the last of his searching. If he learned nothing to lead him to the identity of his father's killer, he would put his revenge to rest. John had been right. It would not do him, or the memory of his father, any justice if he destroyed his own life.

Kael stood, stretching his cramped muscles and feeling the power of the midafternoon sun pour down on him. He looked at the inviting water with eagerness. Pulling his shirt off and quickly removing his boots and pants, he ran naked across the grass. When he reached the river's edge, he flew outward, stretching his muscular body to its limit. As gracefully as an antelope, Kael cut into the cool water.

He swam in the waist-deep eddies, enjoying the feel of the

fresh mountain river that surrounded his body. After several minutes, Kael reluctantly left the water to lie on the grassy bank and let the sun dry him.

Resting there, his mind again roamed. His thoughts returned to Lara, but now they were different. It was as if his swim had washed away the doubts that haunted him, making his mind and body clean and receptive. In his thoughts, Kael visualized the future. He saw Lara as his wife, and as the mother of the next generation of Treemonts.

Lew Cross had been standing near the bunkhouse, hidden in the dark, smoking a small cigar. He cupped its burning end as he saw the front door of the main house open. Quietly, Cross watched Lara, dressed in a buckskin shirt and long skirt, descend the steps and begin her familiar walk to the corral. Cross's surprised eyes watched her bypass her nightly visit with the roan as she continued along the road. He realized that she was preoccupied with something, and Lew Cross wondered what.

Please, don't come, Lara pleaded silently as she waited to intercept Kael. He'd have to pass this way if he were to come. Angela had promised to try and stop him, but Lara could not take the chance that Kael would stubbornly ignore the warning.

To compound her predicament, her stepfather had decided to return home rather than stay in Valley City as was his usual Saturday night custom. He'd come back at sundown, looking tired and in a foul mood. As soon as she saw her father, Lara realized that if Kael did come tonight and Martin Dowley saw him, everything would be lost.

Please, don't come, she pleaded again, even as she tried to deny the hoofbeats that echoed on the hard-packed dirt of the road that led to the ranch.

The pinpoints of the star-woven night were Lara's only illumination. Listening to the hoofbeats come closer, she tried to see into the darkness. The moon was not yet up, and the night sky seemed to dip down to the earth. Lara saw a shadowy figure come closer, until the gray stallion seemed to fill her eyes.

Kael stopped Major before her, smiling as he started to dismount.

"No," she said quickly, her hand pressing his thigh to stop him, "bring me up." Kael reached down and pulled Lara into a sitting position across his lap, then swung the horse around and started back down the road.

About a quarter-mile from the ranch, Lara asked him to stop. He lowered her to the ground and then joined her. The large stallion whinnied once, feeling the lightening of his load, and turned, surprising both Kael and Lara as he faced them. Major inched forward and nuzzled Lara's arm. Kael reached quickly for the bridle.

"No," Lara laughed as she opened her palm. Her mind had been so filled with worry that she'd forgotten to give Camilla, her mare, the oats and molassess. The stallion had smelled it and was now waiting. Lara let the Andalusian take the treat, then turned to Kael to explain. When she did, he laughed with her.

Seeing his laughing face illuminated by the moon that had finally risen above the mountain peaks, Lara felt herself grow sad. She reached up and stroked his cheek. Kael took her hand and pressed it to his lips.

"I love you, Kael, but why couldn't you listen to Angela?" Hearing the sadness in her voice, Kael released her hand and started to pull her close. She stepped away quickly and spoke again. "Why?"

"If I knew what you were talking about, I could probably answer you. I haven't seen her since this morning." And Kael hadn't. After his swim in the river, he had returned to the ranch. An hour before sundown, Kael had shaved and prepared himself both to see Lara and leave for South Pass. When he'd left the ranch, his cousin had not returned from town. He'd left John a note, and started the ten-mile trip to the Dowley Ranch.

"Oh," was Lara's only reply. Suddenly, Kael's arms encircled her slim waist and he pulled her to him. His lips devoured hers, starting the now familiar but unslackening fires of desire within her.

Lara held Kael tightly, trying to draw from his strength, to build her courage up to send him away before it was too late. Finally, after the agonizing kiss was over and she'd fought her breathing until it was under control, Lara spoke again.

"You must leave," she told him. "My father is home. Please, Kael . . ." she urged. She knew her words were coming out like the firing of a rifle, but she couldn't help herself. Lara watched him as his smile twisted, and his eyes became beacons that bore into her heart.

"That's good. I think it's time I met him," Kael said quietly.

"Then you've found the man? You finished your business?" Lara asked, her heart filling with hope at his words. At that moment, she made up her mind. If nothing else, she would leave with him, that very instant. She would not even bother to look back at the Dowley ranch, at the unhappy life she had led there. Those hopes were dashed with a shake of Kael's head.

"Not yet. But I came to tell you something. When I'm finished, we'll go to your father."

Lara stared at him. Her heart seemed to pound so loudly, she knew he must hear it. Slowly, Lara nodded.

"I'm leaving for South Pass," he began.

Lara nodded. "Angela told me. Tonight?"

"Yes. I've decided that I must try once more. If I find nothing, I'll be back, and we'll be together." When he finished speaking, his eyes had softened and his face was relaxed.

"You're not going to look anymore?" Lara asked in a hushed voice. Again, she felt hope rise within her. Smiling, Lara felt the love she so desperately wanted to share with Kael, forever.

"When I return from this trip, it's finished," Kael promised. "Now, do I have to drag you back to the house forcefully, or will you take me to your father?" he asked in a bantering tone.

The expression that filled Lara's face erased Kael's smile.

"No," she said as she shook her head. He started to protest, but Lara cut him off. "Please, will you just listen to me" she cried.

"Go ahead," he replied tersly.

"I must tell you something. I've tried to tell you before, but you would never let me." Lara paused for a moment as her eyes searched his face, trying to memorize once more every line on it. When she spoke again, her voice was husky and low. "If you go to him now, you'll never have me. My father has arranged a marriage for me. I'm not supposed to know of it yet, but I do."

"No!" Kael denied, his mind disbelieving his ears, a red rage building within him.

"Yes. Oh, Kael, it's not something I want, you must believe me. I love you. Only you. But he has control over me, you know that," Lara said bitterly. "It's not fair," she cried. "It's not fair that a woman has no free choice if her parent does not accept her wishes."

Then you'll come with me tonight," he declared. Kael's body shook as he tried to control his anger.

"No," she stated firmly. "Only when you've finished your searching. When you're free to take me away. Kael, I'll not trade one type of prison for another, no matter how much I love you."

Kael gazed at her for a long time, his eyes raking over her face and her body until they finaly returned to the pale blue pools that were the windows to her soul. Slowly, he nodded his head. What she said was true.

"When I return," he agreed finally.

"When you return, and if you're ready for me." Lara paused. Her breath caught in her chest as she looked at him. Fear filled her, sending her mind reeling. Lara was afraid that she might never see him again. Please, she prayed silently, let him find nothing.

"When is this marriage supposed to take place?" Kael asked in a gravelly voice.

"I don't know," she answered with a shake of her head. "Father doesn't guess that I know of it."

"Wait for me."

"I will," Lara promised rashly. "Trust me, Kael, I will." Then, without warning her tears came. She knew the foolishness of the promise she had just made—if he were gone too long, if her father made his decision too soon. . . .

Kael pulled Lara back into his arms, gently kissing away her tears. They stayed like that for a long while, neither wanting to end the moment, neither wanting to part with a cloud of uncertainty hovering over them.

After another long kiss that drained them both, Lara and Kael parted. But they continued to gaze into each other's eyes.

Kael, standing high above her, smiled. "Shall I take you back?" he asked foolishly.

Lara shook her head. "I need to walk," she replied in a halting voice.

"No one can take you away from me," Kael swore as his hand cupped Lara's chin, pulling her eyes back to his. "You're mine!"

"I know," Lara admitted. She was his, totally.

Kael drew his fingers away slowly, then turned and mounted Major. He sat tall as he looked down at her. Without speaking, he turned the stallion and rode away.

Lara felt her tears begin again. "Kael," she cried, "don't leave me. . . ." But the words were barely a whisper, and he didn't hear them. She stood there, watching as her lover turned shadowy, fading into the night that had brought him. Wiping the tears that traced their way down her cheeks, Lara began her long walk back to the house.

Off the side of the narrow dirt road, a pair of lust-filled muddy-brown eyes watched her walk away. Gradually, victory crept into his eyes. After she passed from sight, Lew Cross came slowly from behind a tree and followed her back.

* * *

Martin Dowley's study was illuminated by the glow of oil lamps. He was seated in a large leather chair. A cigar burned absently between the second and third fingers of his pudgy hand, while a snifter of brandy sat ignored on a side table.

Across from him, Lew Cross sat in a matching chair. The foreman seemed completely at ease within the study, smoking his own cigar and holding a brandy snifter. As the silence deepened, Cross took another sip of the liquor.

Dowley's face held a vacant look, but Cross knew the man was thinking hard. Lew had come in a few minutes ago, when he saw through the front window that Lara had gone upstairs to her room. Then, after he saw her silhouette through the curtains of her bedroom, the foreman had knocked softly on the door, and was then brought into the study by the half-breed housekeeper.

After receiving a glass of brandy, Cross began his narrative, uninterrupted by Dowley. When Cross had finished, his employer remained silent. Cross was now waiting patiently.

Dowley's anger rose again. This entire day had been one disaster after another. First, the army captain who had guaranteed the beef contract had found himself transferred. Now he had to start again with a new man. Then, as was his usual habit, he would have dinner at the hotel, before going to the saloon. At the saloon, Martin Dowley would choose one of the three available women and share her bed for a price, until he was satisfied.

But this afternoon, Johnston, the owner of the saloon, had come to pay his monthly note. Dowley had loaned him the money to start the business. When Johnston paid, he told Dowley that he was worried about tonight. There were a lot of people in town, and his three girls were sick. One of them had come down with fever on Thursday. This morning they all had it. Business would suffer. Dowley had been angered, his own desires thwarted.

And now this!

"You're positive?" Dowley asked. His umber eyes narrowed,

almost disappearing within the folds of flesh that surrounded them.

"I'm sure," Cross answered, accenting his words of condemnation with a flume of gray smoke.

"That little bitch!" Dowley's anger turned his face red. "You say this man," he started, trying to remember the name, "this Kael, was leaving for South Pass, but would be back to take Lara away?"

"That's what I heard. He told her he wanted to see you before he left, but she told him to wait until he got back. Something to do with business."

"And when is he coming back?"

"I don't know, I don't think he does, either." As the foreman looked at his boss, he began to relax. When he had joined Martin Dowley two years ago, he'd realized that the easterner was different from most of the settlers. It wasn't just Dowley's money. Cross had known that if he wanted to become someone one day, that Dowley was the man to help him. He hadn't been wrong. After many jobs that no one else knew about, Lew Cross was certain he would one day become rich through Martin Dowley.

"Do you think he's had her?" Dowley asked, his eyes now locked with the foreman's.

"I wouldn't know," Cross said with a shrug. He didn't know for sure, but he would bet his last dollar that they'd lain together. Yet Cross had reasons for not saying so. "I don't think so."

"Then it's not too late," Dowley said with a nod. He closed his eyes and sat quietly for a moment, his mind whirling in thought.

Dowley was positive that one of the reasons Setterley wanted his daughter was because she was not only young and beautiful, but she was also a virgin. Certain men preferred an inexperienced woman. It gave them power over the chit, and made them secure against comparison. Martin Dowley could never think like that. His pleasures were all-consuming, and he cared not what anyone thought of him.

"I'm going to send Setterley a letter. Have one of the men take it to Fort Bridger tomorrow. The cattle should be there by then. If the herd's what it's supposed to be, have him send the letter to Setterley." Dowley paused to relight the cigar that had been forgotten. "The letter will tell him that Lara will be leaving for Kansas City in three weeks for her marriage to him."

Lew Cross maintained his silence. As much as he desired Lara, as much as he wanted her, Cross would not jeopardize what he envisioned for his future. Slowly, he nodded his head.

Dowley looked at him again. When he had hired Cross, he'd done so because he recognized something in the man. As soon as Cross had spoken a half dozen words he knew that Lew Cross was the same as he. Cross would do whatever was necessary to get what he wanted. Dowley had used that knowledge several times, and would continue to use it.

"I also want your most trusted man to stay around the house. I want to make sure that my daughter doesn't leave. Not the house itself," Dowley added, "but she is to be watched whenever she's outdoors. You have someone?"

"Me," Cross replied.

Dowley shook his head. "I have something more important for you."

"Then I'll have someone watch her."

"Good. I want this Kael person taken care of. You say he's John Crimmons's cousin?"

Cross nodded.

"Well, I don't want to upset my good friend John, so perhaps you can persuade this man to continue westward?"

Cross nodded slowly. "But if not?"

"If not?" Dowley returned the question to the asker.

"If not," he began, "he would most likely meet up with an Arapahoe war party. . . ."

"A shame. . . . But John Crimmons would understand. It's a hard country, and the Arapahoes are uncontrollable, almost!"

Dowley said with a smile. "You'll need a few more men. Pick them carefully."

"I'll only need two, but we'll get the job done."

"Make sure Lara doesn't learn of this," Dowley cautioned as he took a sip of brandy and slowly let it wash across his tongue.

"Naturally," Cross replied as he drained his snifter and stood.

"Take care of it for me, and I'll take care of you."

The foreman smiled, nodded his head, and left the study. Lew was satisfied with what had happened, and in his mind, he'd already disposed of the tall man. He also knew that he would be charged with taking Lara to Kansas City. Between here and Kansas, he would find out if she was a virgin.

Cross was so engrossed with his thoughts that he did not see Anna standing near the door to the study. She watched Cross leave the house, then silently turned to go to her room. Before taking five steps, she heard Dowley shout her name.

Anna froze. It had been almost a year since she'd heard Dowley call her on a Saturday night. She heard the liquor in his voice, and the evilness that joined it. Turning slowly, Anna went into the study. She stood in front of Dowley, her black eyes looking at the floor.

"I thought you'd still be up. Get me another drink," he ordered. As she crossed the room, Dowley's small umber eyes followed her. After the saloon had opened, and the younger women had arrived, he'd found little use for her. Dowley looked at her as she picked up the brandy bottle. No, he thought, he now preferred the women at the saloon. After she poured the drink, she started to return the bottle to the shelf.

"Leave it." Anna placed the bottle on the small side table. As her finger let go of the bottle, she felt him grab her wrist and pull her cruelly.

"How long does Lara ride in the mornings?" he asked.

"She always go ze same time. She back in ze afternoon at

same time," Anna replied, knowing she must protect the girl. Anna had overheard everything, and she was afraid for Lara.

Suddenly, Dowley's grip hardened, and he twisted Anna's arm until she fell to her knees. "How long does she ride!"

"Same time," she replied without any acknowledgment of pain on her face. Finally, Dowley let go of her wrist.

"If you see my daughter leave the house, if you see her ride away without one of the hands going with her, you get someone and tell them to go after her. If you don't, you will be punished!"

Anna continued to stare expressionlessly at him.

"Get out!" he ordered. She stood and walked from the room as Dowley picked up his snifter.

Sunlight, unfiltered by curtains, woke Lara. Surfacing through the multitude of sleepy layers that held her captive, she forced her eyes open. She'd been sleeping for only a few hours, but her mind cleared instantly as she remembered the long, hard night.

She recalled standing at the window, watching the star-filled night and wondering what Kael would find in South Pass City. A gentle knocking at the door had pulled her back, and as she turned, Anna slipped quickly inside.

"What?" Lara began, but Anna signaled silence by placing a finger across her lips. When she crossed over to Lara, she spoke in a low whisper.

"No want you fazzer to hear."

Lara nodded, and waited.

"'E know! Cross man see you and you man tonight. Cross man tell you fazzer."

Lara felt herself grow cold with the words. She felt gripped by a paralysis of terror.

Anna, mistaking her silence for something else, went on.

113

" 'E say you go in three weeks. You marry in three weeks.

" 'E send Cross after you man. 'E stop you man from come back."

"He's sending Lew Cross after Kael?" Lara echoed, forcing her voice to work. She saw Anna's head nod once. Lara felt her world fall totally apart. She knew she had to do something.

"Anna, thank you."

"No thank me. Anna like you. Anna hate you fazzer. 'E do bad things to Anna." Then, for the first time in Lara's memory, Anna smiled. The smile softened her hard, broad features and comforted Lara. It was then that Lara knew Anna was, afterall, a friend.

"I'll stop him," Lara said strongly. "I'll stop my father."

"No. You fazzer tell me. Tell Cross you no leave ranch. 'E have somebody watch you all ze time now."

"I'll find a way," Lara said. Anna looked at the younger woman, and saw in the icy blue eyes the truth of Lara's words. The housekeeper nodded her head and turned to leave.

When Anna stood at the door again, she turned back to Lara. "No let fazzer sell you. Eez no good. . . ." Lara saw the woman's eyes begin to glisten, and knew she was about to cry. Before she could say anything, Anna was gone.

Alone then, Lara forced herself to face the truth. She had been willing to go along with Kael, to place her faith in him and not worry about the future. Although she was not about to let go of that faith, she knew that she could no longer stand idly by and wait for Kael to do something. Lara refused to accept marriage to Settlerley, and revolted even more against what her father had in store for the man she loved.

No more crying, Lara swore silently. I'll not play the child any longer. Determination welled up within her as she decided on what she must do. She could not ride after Kael. He was too many hours ahead, and there were too many different trails to South Pass.

It was dangerous to be a woman alone in the mountains. But she must warn Kael. Pacing around her room nervously,

Lara tried to figure out a plan. She stopped at the dressing table to stare at the small miniature of her mother.

"What would you do?" she asked the portrait of Kristen Fairwald. "Help me, Mother." Her mother's blond hair and blues eyes gave Lara the answer. Angela!

Lara accepted Anna's warning that she would be watched, and knew that she had only until daylight to be free. Tomorrow she was to meet Angela Crimmons, and together they would go hear the traveling minister who called on Valley City every second Sunday of the month. Angela was to meet Lara near Little Eagle Butte. From there, the two women would go to the church service.

Lara sat at her dressing table and opened the narrow drawer that held her writing paper. She withdrew a sheet, and dipped a pen in the small ceramic ink bowl. With swift strokes, Lara explained the situation. Somehow, Angela or John would alert Kael to his danger.

When that was done, she pulled her nightdress off and changed into her buckskins. Leaving her room, she saw a faint light on the stairs, but silence pervaded the house.

Lara went down to the main floor, and walked carefully to the study. Slowly, she peeked inside. Martin Dowley sat in the leather chair, his double chin nestled on his chest and his hands resting limply on the arms of the chair. Lara noted the almost-empty bottle of brandy, and knew he would sleep soundly.

Quietly, she left the house. Outside, Lara breathed deeply of the cool night air. She crossed the space between the house and corral at a slow run, and opened the corral gate. Camilla, scenting her mistress, came forward and nuzzled Lara's shoulder.

"Good girl," Lara said as she stroked the mare's face. Looking around, she spotted a bridle left carelessly on the rail. She slipped the bridle onto the mare, and debated getting her saddle from the tack room only to disregard such a move as too noisy.

Lara led the mare out of the corral and walked her for

almost ten minutes before grasping the long mane in her fingers and swinging up onto the horse's bare back.

Once mounted, she bent low, her face almost touching the mare's neck as she forced Camilla into a mile-eating gallop. The brisk air felt good against her skin as she and the horse melted into one.

In less than an hour, she was at Eagle Butte. Even in the darkness, she was able to make out the miniature mountain that looked as if someone had chopped off its peak. Slowing the mare, Lara looked around for the best place for Angela to find the note.

A small creek, fed from an underground stream, ran along one side of the butte's base. Several tall cottonwoods stood alongside the water. That was the spot where she and Angela usually met. Lara walked over to the first tree, and decided it would do. Pulling free the hat pin she had slipped through her buckskin shirt for this purpose, Lara pinned the letter to the bark.

Stepping back to observe the results, she nodded. Angela would not miss it.

An hour and a half later, Lara closed the corral gate and walked back into the house. The large clock in the foyer showed the time to be four o'clock. With a smile on her lips, she looked into the study to see her stepfather still asleep. Her smile broadened at the sight, until anger overcame her. Quietly, Lara left for her room.

As the memory of last night receded, Lara rose and made her toilet. When she finished, she chose a soft blue dress that had a high, closed collar, and full but not puffy sleeves. Its long bodice would accent her breasts and show off the slimness of her waist, but the entire picture would be one of demureness. If she was to play this game, she must do it right. Lara would dress to go to church.

Slipping the soft camisole over her head, Lara tugged it down over her breasts, and then pulled on the long silk petticoat. Next, she sat on the edge of her bed and put on her kidskin boots. Before stepping into her dress, Lara went to her vanity table and brushed her hair. Staring at her reflection, she was pleased to see that her lack of sleep was not apparent. Her eyes were clear, and there were no dark, telltale rings under them. She'd held her emotions in check, and had managed to keep from crying.

Lara replaced the brush on the dresser, then lifted her hair and twisted it into a bun atop her head. She secured the knot with a crisscrossed pair of matching longpins, then stood to finish dressing.

When the dress was on and buttoned, she stepped to her mother's full-length mirror and scrutinized herself carefully. The overall effect was modesty combined with soft beauty.

Only one thing was missing. Lara turned back to the dressing table and opened the small ivory jewel box that held all her most important items. A small cameo brooch, black onyx with an eggshell silhoutte of a woman, caught her eyes. It had been the very first piece of jewelry that her mother had given her, and Lara decided that she should wear it today to remind her of who she was. On the pin's gold back were the initials J.C.F. Lara's mother had told her that it had been her father's, handed down to him by his mother, Jennifer Claremont Fairwald. He, in turn, had given it to Lara's mother. Now it nestled securely above the left breast of the original owner's granddaughter.

With the brooch in place and her confidence holding strong, Lara prepared to go down for breakfast and brave what must happen next.

Entering the dining room, Lara saw Martin was already seated. He wore his usual finery—a short, lightweight waistcoat, a low-collared shirt and small tie, accented by the high-buttoned vest and gold links of his watch chain. He was eating breakfast, and when Lara entered, he stopped to look at her.

"Good morning, my dear," Dowley said with a sickly sweet smile on his face. "You look lovely today. Are you going someplace special?"

"Thank you, Father," Lara responded pleasantly, but it took all her willpower to say the words. "It's the second Sunday. Angela and I are going to the church meeting."

"Oh, we'll see," he said with a strange smile. Lara felt the first realization of his intentions in the pit of her stomach as she sat down.

Anna entered then, carrying the plate that held Lara's meal. The scent of warm biscuits and meat reached her, and she was surprised to find herself hungry. Her eyes met Anna's and held briefly. A flash of warmth passed between the two women as the half-breed set Lara's plate down, then quickly left.

"It's been so long since I've been home on a Sunday morning that I thought we'd spend the day together. Don't you think that would be nice?" he asked.

Although Lara had promised herself to remain calm, she felt a little of her resolve slipping away.

"Why?" she asked. "You've never wanted to spend time with me before. Besides," Lara said, fighting to regain her fragile balance, "I've promised Angela I would meet her. She'll spend all morning waiting for me. She'll be worried."

"I'll send a man to tell her you'll not be there. It's time for us to discuss your future," Dowley declared in a cold voice.

"You mean you'll actually discuss it with me?" Lara said sarcastically. No! she told herself, control yourself.

"Do not use that tone with me!" he ordered.

Lara's eyes dropped to her plate.

"I think you'll like Kansas City," Dowley said with a leering grin as his words brought Lara's face whipping up. He felt pleasure, watching the color drain from her face.

"Please, Father, don't do this to me."

"I like it when you plead with me. Even when it's useless." Dowley shook his head slowly as he continued to speak. "Really, Lara, you ought to be thanking me. You should have learned years ago that what I do is best for all those around me."

"But it's my life your deciding about," she replied in a low voice.

"You should be grateful for that. Listen to me well. You are about to become a great lady. You're marrying one of the wealthiest and most powerful men in the country. You will become one of the leading women of Kansas society. I almost envy you." Martin Dowley's eyes seemed to take on a vacant, distant look as he spoke.

"You must consider your upcoming marriage in a certain way. Think of yourself as a princess, and myself and Setterley as kings of neighboring countries. Johnathan and I are only doing what royalty has done throughout the ages. Daughters of kings were married to other kings, forming alliances that kept the monarchs strong, powerful, and safe from those who would dethrone them. What's happening now, in this country, is that men like myself, and Johnathan, are growing into the ruling class, we are becoming the royalty of the West. And you, dearest Lara, are the means to unite this royalty."

"You're despicable!" Lara snapped, interrupting his insane oratory.

Before Dowley's temper burst, a loud knocking at the front door interrupted them. A few seconds later, Lew Cross stood in the dinning room. Seeing him there, Dowley forced the anger from his face.

"The man is ready," Cross said.

"I'll be right out." As Dowley rose, he reached into the breast pocket of his coat. Lifting out an envelope, he smiled wickedly. "This is your marriage contract. It will arrive in Kansas City three weeks before you do. Wait here for me, I have more to say to you."

Lara had no intention of waiting to continue this pointless conversation. Martin Dowley had made up his mind, and she would not accept being ruled over any longer. She stood and began to leave the room as she heard her stepfather return to the house. She had her foot on the first step when she felt her hair gripped, and her head pulled back.

Trying to fight her unseen foe, Lara lashed backward with

her hand. She felt her hand caught in a damp, wet grip, and felt herself spun around.

"How did you find out?" Dowley demanded in a hate-filled voice. "How?"

"Find out what?" Lara asked, trying to ignore the pain in her arm, which Dowley was twisting cruelly.

"Lying little. . . ." His free hand swung in an arc that ended against Lara's cheek. As pain shot through her, and the sound of the slap echoed in the hallway, she fell to the floor.

Fighting to hide the hurt, Lara bit her lip and tasted the saltiness of her blood.

"Find out what?" Dowley screamed in an insanely loud voice. "Find out enough to try and warn your lover!" he yelled as he held up the note she had pinned to the tree last night. "You were followed," he stated with a cruel smile.

Lara felt hopelessness and defeat crowd around her, and almost gave in. Almost.

Dowley stood above her. His round shape no longer looked funny to Lara, it looked menacing. His face was fixed in cruel lines. As he spoke, Lara felt a chill run down her spine.

"From this moment on, you will prepare for your wedding. You will see no one other than myself or the people that work here on the ranch. You will not dress in pants. You will behave and dress like a lady. If you desire to go outside the walls of this house, you will have an escort. You will not be permitted to leave the property until Mr. Cross takes you to Kansas City, and your new husband."

"Then I'm no better than a prisoner," Lara stated.

"You are my property, and I will do as I please."

Without a word, Lara rose. She stood in front of Dowley and stared contemptuously at the creature who dared call himself her father. The hatred and disgust she felt flowed from her eyes. Turning, she walked up the stairs. The only voice she heard was her own, and she spoke but within her mind. I will not go to Kansas City. I will escape somehow, and I will be free, and I will find Kael.

* * *

Angela Crimmons waited for over an hour, sitting on the seat of her carriage and daydreaming. Eventually, she realized that Lara would not be coming. At first Angela was worried, but then she remembered that Martin Dowley had returned home last night. In fact, she and her parents had ridden with him until he reached his ranch.

This morning her father had voiced his doubts that Lara would meet Angela, because of Martin Dowley's presence at home. Angela knew her father felt that Dowley would want to spend the day with Lara. John Crimmons always thought that fathers and daughters loved to spend time together. He wasn't wrong, except that Angela knew Dowley did not care about Lara.

Shrugging her shapely shoulders, Angela lifted the reins and started the carriage off toward the Holmes ranch where Sunday's service would be held. Her parents were already there. Angela would talk with Lara next Saturday to find out what had happened today, and what had transpired last night with Kael.

As Angela drove off, she did not notice the blue-tipped hatpin sticking out from the bole of the cottonwood tree.

Ice-blue eyes stared down at him.

Kael felt the heat from Lara's body as she lowered herself upon him. Her body covered his smoothly, molding each soft, womanly curve against every lean inch of him. Kael held his hands on the velvety softness of the skin of her back, and pressed her even tighter to him.

In the distance, a haze of mountains framed Lara's head of wild burgundy waves. Seeing her eyes drift close, Kael watched her face as she gave in to his demands.

Suddenly, a dark and menacing voice filled his ears, followed by a muffled shot. Then Kael, once again, saw his father bent over the desk, and felt the ripping pain burst in his head.

Slowly, Kael opened his eyes. It took him only a second to realize where he was. Pushing away the images and the passions that Lara Dowley's face and body had summoned, and forcing the continually repeated visions of his father's death to the back of his mind, Kael's labored breathing returned to normal.

The sounds of the real world, the noise of civilization, filtered through the thin walls of the hotel's room. Wagons rolling down the street, people calling out greetings to each other, combined to urge the tall, dark-haired man to greet the day. Kael stretched, easing the tensions that his dreams had brought. As he lay in bed, his thoughts raced.

The utter exhaustion of his ride had not stopped the battle that raged in his mind. Even with his decision made, his own logic fought him. He could not deny his love, could not fight the desires that had consumed him since he'd met Lara. Kael had never before felt the depth of emotions she'd brought out in him. Whether asleep or awake, he could feel, taste, and see Lara.

Kael was cognizant of the fact that Lara was the reason he was determined to end his search. And for the first time since his father's death, he almost hoped that there would be nothing except the Pinkerton's final negative report. He wanted Lara that badly. Kael took a deep breath as he thought of his trip here.

Eighteen hours of riding through the winding mountains that separated South Pass City from Valley City. Saturday night and all day Sunday had been spent in the saddle. Kael had slept little, a few short hours at the tail of the Popo Agie River as he waited for daylight to arrive. From the edge of the cottonwood-lined river, he had followed his own inner sense of direction as he left the better-traveled wagon trail and cut directly across the short, peaked mountains. Kael angled southwest until he reached the point that signaled his nearness to South Pass City.

As Kael crested the peak of a low mountain and saw his landmark below him, he felt his breath give way as it had the first time he'd seen it.

Red Canyon.

The canyon spread out below him was one of the most powerful sights he had seen in Wyoming, and a good part of the West. It was different from the sweeping strength of the Rockies, or even the high, mighty mountains that surrounded him now. The solid wall of rock that was one side of the canyon went on for miles. Red earth and rock rose in strictly sectioned layers, with a deep red-rust color permeating throughout. The depth of the red reminded him of the Georgia clay he'd fought many battles in during the war. Intermixed with the red, in separate and distinct bands, were slate gray and brown. Even bands of deep green vegetation seemed to have their own zones on the high, vertical wall. On the half-mile-wide base of the canyon grew a lush green carpet. Tall stands of spruce reached upward toward the heavens, dwarfing the plushness of the buffalo grass. The far wall of the canyon was composed of intersecting slopes of the surrounding Wind River Mountains; some slopes were covered with trees and buffalo grass, others with brown dirt and rock.

Kael pulled his eyes from the awesome beauty and, getting his bearings, urged Major onward. As he rode, he wondered who would be the first to try and tame the canyon, to build a home within its protective walls, and to use the water from the mountain slopes to irrigate and grow crops.

From Red Canyon to South Pass City was a three-hour ride, and Kael finished it uneventfully. The sun was dropping below the western mountains when he crested the top of another rise and saw South Pass City below him.

Descending slowly, Kael's eyes swept over the mining town. About twenty buildings lined both sides of the main street; many more were in the process of being built. In the surrounding area were several small holding ranches that were used to keep livestock available for passing wagon trains. Only three of the pens held stock, and Kael knew that a train of settlers had passed through recently.

South Pass City's only hotel stood proudly, its second story rising above its nearest neighbors. The wood siding was clean and recently whitewashed, contrasting sharply with the other buildings' rougher exteriors. A sward of deep green grass spread out behind the town, and the dark pencil line of the small creek that ran through the grass seemed almost invisible in the growing dusk. He would be tasting the creek's sweet water soon.

Before completely descending, Kael let his eyes roam the countryside. Small campfires dotted the slopes, indicating that the hordes of gold hunters were beginning to prepare supper before retiring for the night.

Riding into town, Kael went directly to the livery stable. After paying for three days' feed and stable in advance, he walked to the hotel. When he had wearily finished his supper of tender steak and potatoes, he went to his room, undressed and, with a grateful sigh, lay down on the mattress. Before his head had sunk too deeply into the pillow, Kael was asleep.

He could no longer stay in bed. It was Monday morning, and soon everything would be open. Kael sat up, letting the blanket fall to his waist, exposing his bare chest. Absently, as his index finger traced the familiar path of the scar from his wound, his eyes glanced around the room. He'd been so tired last night that he hadn't bothered to look it over.

It was small, as were most hotel rooms in frontier towns. This one was just large enough to accommodate a bed, a rack for clothes, and a small bureau and mirror, with barely enough space to walk between the furniture. The walls were paper covered, and he saw the sheen of the small, round nail heads that held the seams of the flower-painted paper together. He shook his head sadly at this pretention; the unnecessary use of the paper when smoothly planed wood could have given the room real warmth, and made up for its minute proportions.

Finally, Kael rose to shave, dress, and find some answers.

After a hot breakfast in the dining room, possibly the largest single room in the hotel, Kael stepped onto the wooden sidewalk. He walked until he was across from the small building that held both the assayer's office and the post office. The town was alive with people and he saw that South Pass City was populated mostly with men, like all the new mining towns. Crossing the street, Kael stood at the door.

He hesitated. With a deeply drawn breath, Kael reached for the door handle. One way or another, today would determine his future.

He opened the door and entered. To his left stood the assayer's area, its counter covered with papers and a brass scale. Five men were standing while two others lounged on the hardwood bench under the window. All of them were waiting to have their finds assayed, hoping against all odds that they had hit paydirt.

Kael stepped fully inside. Straight ahead was the post office; a narrow counter with one man behind it, and a wall filled with hanging bags, boxes, and a portrait of a dead man. He hadn't really looked at the portrait on his last trip into South Pass, but then he hadn't really noticed much of anything. The mail clerk had been sick, and the assayer had been in a hurry when he'd helped Kael out. Abraham Lincoln had been assassinated over two years ago. Why, wondered Kael, was his portrait still hanging?

Noticing the stranger's eyes on the painting, the mail clerk smiled. "Everyone agreed that they'd rather see Abe's picture starin' at 'em then Johnson's, since that pompous jackass of a President tried to veto statehood for Nebraska last March," the man explained.

"I don't blame them," Kael replied as he looked at the clerk. "Name's Treemont. I'm expecting some letters from back East. General delivery."

"Yes, sir, if I remember rightly, saw something come in with the last batch. Got a delivery last week," the clerk replied, more to himself than to Kael, as he turned to a large cabinet and started looking through it. "Here 'tis. Captain Kael Treemont?" he asked with his eyebrows raised over thin, wire-rimmed spectacles.

"Retired."

"In the war?"

"Seventh Pennsylvania."

"Atlanta?"

"Missed that one," said Kael. "Wounded a month before."

"Not that I'm unfeeling, and I'm sorry about your being wounded, but I'm sure glad you weren't there. Nasty job."

Kael only nodded his head. He wouldn't get involved in the ongoing argument of Sherman's deed. Besides, he wanted those envelopes that the clerk was holding.

"Plan on living in the territory, or just passing through?"

"I'm not sure," Kael replied thoughtfully. "I've been up in Valley City, sort of like it, but I've got my doubts. Seems to be one man in control of everything. Don't know if I'd like that," he said carefully, trying to feel out the clerk without being obvious.

"I'll tell you one thing. Those people living in Valley City owe everything to Martin Dowley. That's one fine man. If it wasn't for him, there'd be no Valley City."

"Really? Everyone I talk with says how great he is, but I'll tell you something," Kael said, lowering of his voice. "It bothers me when all I hear is good about someone, and nothing bad. Makes me think."

"No need to. Martin Dowley's a good man. Still, he's not just doing good for the territory without doing good for himself, too," the clerk said in a matching lowered voice. "I know for sure he wants to own lots of land. May end up as the biggest landowner in Wyoming. Make him rich as sin when we get acknowledged by the government."

"I sort of figured that, but no one wanted to say so."

"I don't see anything wrong with it myself," the clerk agreed as he finally surrendered Kael's letters. Before looking at them, he decided to take a chance.

"Have you been here a long time, Mr. . . . ?" Kael asked.

"Rhinehart, Claude Rhineheart. Well, Captain, I've been here for four years. Since the first building was added to Brown's trading post."

"Well, perhaps you can help me, Mr. Rhineheart. A friend of mine came out here about two, three years ago—man named Malcome Dupont." Kael watched the clerk wrinkle his brow in concentration, then he shook his head.

"Sorry."

"Thank you anyway," Kael said, as his eyes went to the letters, his mind dismissing Rhinehart. Suddenly, he wanted to be alone, to see what the letters brought, and to know his destiny. With the letters finally in his hand, Kael started out. The envelopes felt like burning embers against his fingers, and his breathing was strained. As he crossed the room, his eyes went to the letters, and his hand trembled slightly.

Because of his intense concentration, Kael did not notice the burly man who entered the building as he stepped onto the sidewalk. Lew Cross looked away from Kael as he neared him, then walked quickly into the building. Cross went directly to the postal clerk and spoke in a low voice.

"What did he want?" Cross demanded.

"Lew, he just came to pick up some mail."

"Damn! Five minutes too late."

"Who is he?" Rhineheart asked.

"Someone who's not welcome back at Valley City."

"So that's why," the clerk mumbled. Cross stared at him with menacing brown eyes until the clerk cleared his throat nervously. "When you get back to Valley City, tell Mr. Dowley that a man named Kael Treemont was askin' 'bout him, and about Malcome Dupont. But I guess you already know that," he finished lamely.

"What'd you tell him?"

"Nothing, Lew. Nothing except that Mr. Dowley was a great man, good for the territory. When he asked about Dupont, I figured I'd better keep quiet."

"You figured right," Cross replied as he smiled at his brother-in-law. "But we don't need to worry, he won't be bothering anyone in Valley City."

Kael wanted to be alone to read the letters, to see if his search was over, or if it would start again. Maybe I'm afraid, he told himself as he crossed the street and entered the hotel. Or maybe I just don't want to look any longer. Toying with the idea of not opening the envelopes, he ascended the narrow steps to the second floor. He stopped before his door, staring at it with unseeing eyes. Kael felt muscle tremors in his hand from the pressure he was exerting on the letters. Slowly, he forced himself to relax and open the door.

Inside, he sat on the edge of the bed and opened the first letter. On the inside of the envelope, in finely printed script, had been the name of his attorney.

> Dear Kael,
>
> I hope that this correspondence has reached you in Wyoming, and finds you in good health and spirits.
>
> In accordance with your instructions, I have sent notification to the foreman of your ranch in Santa Barbara, Manuel Mendoza, telling him that you are traveling westward, but are uncertain of when you will arrive.
>
> As you requested, all properties that were left to you by your father, with the exception of the house in Philadelphia, have been sold. All funds have been deposited in your account.
>
> Once again, I must sadly inform you that I have found nothing further concerning the whereabouts of Malcome Dupont.
>
> Kael, again I urge you to free yourself of your obsession with Dupont. Go to California and enjoy both health and good fortune for the remainder of your life.
>
> Sincerely, I remain your friend and advisor.
> James Arlington III
>
> P.S. I forwarded a parcel to you in care of the South Pass Hotel. I found your dress uniform and sword in your house and thought you might want them.

Kael reread the letter, then let his mind drift to thoughts of California, wondering what life would be like there, with Lara, in the mountains of Santa Barbara. For some reason, he found himself hesitant in opening the Pinkerton envelope, and thought about his lawyer sending his dress uniform to him. Why would James think he might have a use for it? Kael wondered. He'd check with the hotel's owner later to see if it had indeed arrived.

No longer able to stave off his need to see the investigator's report, Kael carefully slit open the envelope and withdrew several sheets of paper. Slowly, he began to read.

The first page was a summary of what had transpired since he'd left Pennsylvania—a month-by-month report. Kael's eyes followed these reports until he reached the last.

I am proud to say that in my final effort, before the year's time was up, I have found something significant. On April 9, 1867, I went to the Department of the Interior, Office of Land Grants, and researched the Dupont case.

I found the name, Malcome Dupont, listed as the purchaser of five thousand acres of land, situated from the fork of the Wind River to the edge of Little Eagle Butte. This land is adjacent to a government grant of five hundred acres issued to a Malcome Dupont.

Because of the strange circumstances in the use of the name Malcome Dupont, I decided to take all the names that were listed as owners of property adjacent to Dupont's and research them. I discovered five more of the names, like Dupont's, were men long deceased. All had purchased between three thousand to seven thousand acres.

Puzzled as to why dead men would purchase land, I investigated forward to see if there were any transfers of deed holdings. I can now inform you of my findings.

I must warn you that my conclusions are not provable without further, and much harder, evidence. But I believe that what I have found is correct and is also the method that Malcome Dupont used.

The seven tracts of land, two owned by Dupont, five by the other deceased men, totaling thirty-nine thousand acres of prime land, have been deeded by registered bills of sale to a Mr. Martin S. Dowley of Valley City, Idaho territory, Wyoming district.

Mr. Martin S. Dowley is also the agent of Indian Affairs for the Department of Interior, and also, if I am not completely mistaken, a very clever man who used the name Malcome Dupont to his advantage! Please take under advisement that there is nothing that can be proven legally without further evidence. With this letter, I formally close my investigation.

Robert C. Cosgrove, Agent
The Pinkerton National Detective Agency

Martin Dowley! The name burned into Kael's mind. He sat frozen as the letter slipped from his numb fingers to float to the wooden floor. Kael's eyes saw nothing. Martin Dowley— Malcome Dupont!

The last weeks of Kael's life flashed through his thoughts. From the first moment he'd seen the unconscious form of Lara Dowley, to the dream he'd woken from this morning.

Was Dowley the same person as Dupont? Had Lara been playing him for a fool—the daughter of a swindler and a murderer? Was that why Lara would never take Kael to see her father? Was that why she used the excuse that her father would separate them if he knew? She had been protecting him, hadn't she?

Kael had poured out his heart to Lara. He had told her of his grief, his hurt, and of his need for vengeance. He'd told her every detail of the murder. Had she already known?

No! Kael's heart told him. The feelings she'd given to him, their lovemaking, were real. Kael had sensed her hatred of her father, even through her words of admiration for what he had done in Valley City.

Wait, Kael cautioned himself, as he fought another battle within himself. Perhaps Dowley was not Dupont. Perhaps he really did buy the land from different people. The only way Kael would be able to judge for himself would be to hear that terrible voice, the one voice he would never forget, the voice of his father's killer. And now, with even more knowledge to aid him, he would find out if Dowley was that man.

Rising slowly, Kael bent and picked up the letters, then placed them with all the others he'd accumulated over the past three years. When that was done, and the leather satchel that held the papers was closed, Kael walked to the door.

Although he'd learned much, he still had a full day ahead of him. He wanted all the information he could obtain about Dowley. Then, and only then, when he had a complete picture of the man, would he return to Valley City.

As the door clicked shut behind him, Kael also closed another door, sealing Lara Dowely from his heart.

Glinting off the red rock, in a breathtaking spectacle of nature's raw power, the sun unveiled a sight of strength and might. Kael's eyes again swept along the sheer height of the south wall of Red Canyon. He saw the multihued striped canyon, which was now the landmark that sent him back on his final confrontation.

The intensity of the wall reminded him of his own mind. How it had become layered with things; each new layer hiding what was below it. Only rarely was he able to open his mind and see it as clearly as he now saw the rock wall. Searching deeply within himself, Kael understood what was happening to him.

The good and the bad were layers, and intermixed between them were the other events in his life. The uppermost layer was Lara Dowley, and she had obscured what had been his mission for years. Her beauty, and his love for her, had covered over what had been most important.

And like Red Canyon, it was a long trip to the bottom of his mind to see what had built the walls. But now Kael's vision was clear. He'd let his emotions for the blue-eyed woman overshadow his logic. For the first time in years, he'd allowed someone to become entrenched in his heart. It had been a mistake.

Although he fought against it, Kael knew with dreaded certainty that Lara's purpose had been to divert him from his goal; to prevent him from exposing Martin Dowley as a murderer.

But she was a virgin, Kael's heart shouted to him. The daughter of a murderer! reason shouted back. Like her father, Lara would use whatever means necessary to achieve her own desires. Virginity was unimportant to people like the Dowleys, it was a false offering of innocence, to protect her father and herself.

Kael thought about their last talk. Lara telling him that her father had promised her to another. How convenient, he thought. A perfect way to dismiss him.

Her tears that night were so perfect. She would need to be a good actress if she were following in her father's footsteps.

Looking down into the depths of Red Canyon, Kael felt the weight of her betrayal and hurt descend upon him. The darkness of despair filled him, washing away the fullness of his love for the slim, auburn-haired woman.

Wait! his heart pleaded, do not condemn her so fast. Perhaps she isn't guilty. Perhaps Dowley is not Dupont. Wait, wait until you know, before you sever your heart to satisfy your vengeance.

Alone, sitting upon the large gray Andalusian stallion, high above the canyon floor, Kael nodded to himself. He pushed the closing waves of darkness away and promised to wait, promised to hear Martin Dowley's voice before he condemned his love to the fires of his vindictive hatred.

Loosening his grip on the reins, Kael signaled Major on. He decided to take the regular wagon trail to Valley City rather than cut through the mountains. He was in no hurry now. Martin Dowley would not be leaving anytime soon. With the power and wealth he had stolen from Kael's father, Dowley would feel secure.

As Red Canyon receded behind him, Kael again envisioned Lara and himself, and traced their beginnings, their loving, and their joining of heart and body.

"When do we take him?" asked one of the riders flanking Lew Cross.

"When he makes camp. If he doesn't, we take him when the sun sets," he replied. Watching the tall man as he rode below, Cross's dark eyes followed carefully. Cross had had a chance to speak to him when they sat across from each other in South Pass's saloon. But Cross had seen no recognition in Treemont's eyes, and he decided that he would not offer the man another opportunity. He would wait until Treemont was on the trail, and then he would be done with the man. It wouldn't be the first time. . . .

Now, with the sun almost touching the highest tips of the Wind River mountains, Cross felt alive with anticipation. It would be easy to fake an Arapahoe attack. All they had to do was kill him, then scalp him. The eastern Shoshone never fought or scalped the white man. To do so was to incur the wrath of the great Chief Washakie.

All that Cross had to do was to leave behind a small piece of buckskin with an Arapahoe marking. Then he could take the body into Valley City, and no one would disbelieve his tale of coming across the dead man on the trail. The gray stallion would be reason enough for an attack. Rarely was such a horse seen in these parts. To own one would give a warrior much prestige.

As the sun dropped, Cross and his two aides watched Kael continue on. When double bands of gray lined the eastern sky, Cross knew that the lone rider would not make camp tonight. Silently, Cross pointed to a side trail that would intersect Treemont's a mile further on. The three men pushed their horses faster as they readied themselves to intercept him.

Riding into the path of the setting sun, Kael's mood dropped along with the orange ball of fire. He'd been able to fight the apprehension and despair of what might meet him in Martin Dowley's office; but with the signaling of the day's end, his mind again dipped into his own living cauldron of darkness.

Suddenly, Kael halted the stallion. A low echoing had penetrated his thoughts. It took him only a second to recognize the sounds. Hoofbeats. Kael turned the horse and waited to meet his fellow travelers. He did not mind traveling alone, but if there were others on the trail tonight, he would accept their company.

His only warning was one that had never failed him. An inner sense that had kept him from death before.

Kael felt the familiar lifting of the hair at the nape of his neck and his muscles tensed expectantly. Danger was near. Pulling his rifle free, Kael dropped the reins. Major had been his war mount, and was trained in battle. The lightest pressure from Kael's heels would tell the horse how to move.

As the noise of the other horses grew louder, Kael's blood began to run swiftly through his body. Then, the hoofbeats stopped.

The sun was gone, and dusk filled the sky. Visibility was low, and the treelined trail that Kael was on grew darker by the second. It was a perfect spot for someone to attack him, but the element of surprise was gone.

Using his left heel, Kael wheeled the stallion around and charged the spot at which he sensed the presence of the other riders. He screamed loudly and at the same instant fired his rifle.

Without hesitating, he reloaded the rifle and raised it again. Suddenly, his ears were filled with return fire. Riding low on Major's back, the bullets missed him, and Kael knew where his attackers were hidden. Wheeling the gray about again, Kael charged through the spruces that covered the mountain slope.

Another rifle flash pinpointed their location. Without consciously thinking of what he was doing, or that he did not have a full complement of troops behind him, Kael stormed ahead.

He fired again, at the exact spot he'd seen the powder flash and, through the sound of his own rushing blood, heard a man cry out. Rather than continue his suicidal advance, Kael kept the advantage of surprise and pushed Major through the trees, away from the ambush. As much as he wanted to know who had attacked him, he admitted the stupidity of fighting an unknown number.

Fifteen minutes later, Kael slowed the stallion and listened for the sounds of pursuit.

Only the night murmurs of the mountain greeted his ears.

With a smile of satisfaction that soon changed to question, Kael turned Major northwest again and began the final miles that would lead to Valley City, and the end of his quest.

"What the hell do you mean he got away?" Martin Dowley yelled. "I told you to make sure he did not come back. Instead, you brought me one of your own wounded men."

"Mr. Dowley, we couldn't stop him. He must've heard us behind him. When we came through the trees, ready to shoot him, he turned right at us and started firing. It was too dark to see clearly, and by the time he'd shot Moss, he was into the trees and gone." The foreman stood shamefaced, knowing that he'd lost a lot of ground with his boss. "But I'll get him, Mr. Dowley. I promise I'll get that bastard!"

"You damned well better," Dowley threatened as his face lost some of the red that suffused it. "I don't ever want to see that man. Ever! Now, see what you can do for your man. I don't want anyone to know what's happened."

"It wasn't bad. Moss only has a flesh wound, it was a lucky shot."

"Don't let Treemont stay lucky too long," Dowley said in a voice that was so filled with venom that even Lew Cross felt fear.

"We'll take care of him," Cross repeated, anxious now to leave.

With a wave of his hand, Martin Dowley dismissed the foreman. Several minutes later, Dowley rose from his leather chair and walked to the stairs.

Lara had heard the men return to the ranch. The echoing of hoofbeats pulled her from her thoughts, stole her away from the only peace she had known for a week. They took her from Kael's arms and lips, and brought he back to the reality of her prison. Watching from her window, she saw Lew Cross and another man pull a third man from his horse and carry him into the bunkhouse. Five minutes later, Cross came to the main house, and Lara heard her father open the front door to greet him.

Muffled voices filtered up to her, but Lara was unable to discern what was being said. Suddenly, her father shouted angrily, and Lara breathed easier. If he was upset, that meant Kael was still alive. Unbidden, tears began to flow from her eyes. She didn't stop them now, and for the first time since that awful Sunday morning, Lara gave in to their release. Moments later, she forced herself to stop as footsteps approached her door and she returned to her bed.

The scraping of a key turning in the lock brought back to Lara the reminder that she was now a prisoner in more than just words. Ever since Monday night, when she'd tried to sneak out of the house, her father had kept her locked in her room. She was only allowed out during the daytime, and only when Dowley was home.

The glowing light from the hallway was diffused by her tear-blurred vision. Turning her face from the candle, Lara wiped her eyes. She would not give her father the satisfaction of seeing her cry. She lay silent for several minutes, as Dowley stood above her.

"I know you're awake. Face me!" he ordered.

Lara turned toward him without bothering to hide the hatred that marked her features.

"Your young man is resourceful. He's still alive, but that will not last."

"Why bother telling me?" Lara asked in a controlled voice.

"Because I want you to understand the results of your foolish actions. Your rebellion will cost him his life. I want you to remember that it was you who killed this man. It is you who force me to wipe away this blot on my character."

"On your character? He has done nothing to you!"

"But he has," Dowley replied with another grimace. "He has tried to take something that is mine. For that, he will pay. For your own duplicity, you will suffer, too." With those words, Dowley stepped closer to Lara, and before she knew what he was doing, his arm moved in a blur, and his hard palm slapped her face.

Lara felt the blinding pain, and tasted the saltiness of blood on her tongue. Filled with a red rage, she lashed out maddeningly. Her hands had balled into fists as she leapt from the bed to attack her stepfather. She felt the softness of a jowley cheek as her fist hit it. Suddenly, an explosion of pain slammed into her chest. She wavered, then fell to the floor.

"That was stupid," Dowley said as he rubbed his face. "That was stupid."

"I hate you! I hate you like nothing else in this world," she declared, ignoring the pain that shot through her with every breath she took.

"Good. Remember that hate. Remember that there is nothing that you can do. You leave in two weeks. Your lover will be dead before then. Remember that, also!"

Lara didn't move as Dowley left the room. Nor did she move when the lock of the door clicked.

"I love you, Kael . . ." she whispered quietly.

Lara did not sleep for the remainder of the night, but sat on the edge of her bed, staring out the window. Gradually, the mountains began to awaken with the pinkish-gray glow of the coming day. She walked to the window and breathed in the scents of the morning. Then, with purpose, Lara went to her bureau and dipped her pen in the ceramic ink bowl.

Five minutes later, the letter was done. She folded it neatly, then began to dress for the day. Breakfast would be the first

step of her week-old charade. Today she would wear the silk
daydress that Dowley had recently brought home, along with
many others. Part of her trousseau so she would arrive in
Kansas City a woman of substance. Every meal that Lara
took with her father meant a complete change of clothing.
Martin Dowley was determined to make sure Lara acted the
part of a great lady.

Today's daydress was lavender silk, with a high lace collar
and a buttoned bodice that sloped gently over the swell of her
high, firm breasts.

Lara put on her camisole, and then the long petticoat,
stepped into her matching lavender slippers, and sat again to
await Anna's arrival. The new dresses required a maid to
adjust them properly. That was the reason for the letter. Lara
would not be allowed to go to the general store to purchase
the food supplies today. Anna would go. Anna would also
deliver the message to Mrs. Smithers, and Mrs. Smithers
would give it to Angela. Everything, every hope Lara had,
was in that letter, and it had to get to Angela.

With that last thought bringing comfort to her mind, she
heard footsteps in the hall. She stood, prepared to begin her
day.

Kael had spent Friday night at the small tributary of the
Wind River, and with daylight he had washed and changed
into a fresh shirt. He did not want the dirt of the trail on him
when he entered Valley City. He wanted no attention called
to him.

It was Saturday morning, and it would be a busy day in
town. A week had passed since he'd left for South Pass City.
Kael had been there three full days, learning and thinking,
before he rode out on Thursday afternoon. He had devised a
plan that should allow him to find out, today, if Martin
Dowley was the man he was searching for.

He would go to the café, have a meal at one of the front
tables by a window, and watch the main street for Martin and
Lara Dowley's arrival. When he saw Dowley enter his office,

he would go around back, avoiding Lara, and get in Dowley's office through the rear. There, he would be able to listen to the man, and would find his answer.

At ten o'clock, Kael was sipping strong black coffee, his stomach filled from the breakfast of steak and biscuits he'd just finished. Throughout the meal, his eyes had not once left the window.

"More coffee?" asked Mrs. Fletcher, the proprietress of the café.

"Thank you," Kael replied with a relaxed smile. "Looks like it's going to be a busy day."

"Saturday always is. Why, in another half-hour you won't be able to find a seat in here for love or money," she informed him proudly. "Valley City will be a big place soon. Lots of important people are going to be living here."

"As important as Martin Dowley?" Kael asked in a smooth voice, betraying no emotion.

"I hope so. Why, if it weren't for Mr. Dowley, there wouldn't be a Valley City, only a trading post." As the woman talked, Kael saw the devotion with which she believed. Suddenly, he found himself hoping he was wrong about Dowley. It would be a sin to bring down someone that everyone held so high. As much of a sin as having given love to someone who did not deserve it.

"Why there he is," Mrs. Fletcher said as she bent lower and looked out the window. Dowley's wagon had stopped in front of the general store, and a dark-haired, widely built woman stepped down from it.

"That's funny," Mrs. Fletcher said, "Miss Dowley always comes to town on Saturdays. I hope she's not feeling sickly. That woman is their housekeeper. She's a half-breed that Mr. Dowley took in when she was abandoned. Good thing for her. She might have ended up with the Indians."

Kael heard the comments, but only as a whisper in the back of his mind. His first sight of Martin Dowley went against everything that he'd heard. Dowley was an unimpressive figure, shortish and round, with a slack-mouthed, unintelligent face. Kael saw nothing in Dowley's features that reminded him of Lara. Then the woman's words penetrated his thoughts.

Could Lara be ill? A wave of sadness spread within him as he hoped Mrs. Fletcher was wrong. Then his eyes followed Martin Dowley as the man drove his carriage passed the café to his office.

Kael stood and went to the counter. He paid for his meal, then slowly walked out of the café. On the wooden sidewalk, he paused and glanced up. The sky, so blue and clear earlier that morning, had clouded over. The gray clouds looked ominous. Putting on his flat-brimmed hat, Kael began to walk toward Dowley's office. When he reached the stables, halfway between the café and Dowley's, he went in and checked on Major.

The gray greeted him with a whinny. Kael patted the horse's muscular flank, then walked to the rear of the stable and out the back. His amber eyes made a thorough survey of the street.

No one.

Carefully but confidently, Kael began to make his way to Dowley's office. He had already checked it out, having circled the town on his arrival, riding in from the north end instead of the south.

Quietly, Kael's fingers closed on the handle of the back door. Slowly, testing for any noise from the hinges, Kael began to open the door. It moved freely, and Kael breathed a sigh. When it was ajar enough for him to slip through, Kael spent another few seconds listening. Then he stepped inside.

At the same moment, the front door opened, and Kael heard someone else come in. Flattening against the wall, he froze.

"Mornin', Mr. Dowley, got a few minutes?" a voice asked.

Dowley grunted, and Kael heard the footsteps start again. Then another door closed. Quickly, he moved. The wall ended and his eyes took in the office.

Benches lined two walls, a waiting room much like those back East. Peering around the edge of the wall he leaned against, Kael realized that it was part of Dowley's private office. Voices filtered through the wooden partition, but not clearly enough for him to distinguish one from another. With no one else in the waiting room, Kael silently turned the corner. He saw the office door had been left slightly open, and gave a silent thanks that the door itself had no glass in it. Apparently, Dowley liked his privacy. Carefully, making sure his boots would not betray him, Kael inched closer and listened intently.

"Mr. Dowley, you've got to give me more time. I'll pay my note, please just give me a few more months," the man pleaded. To Kael's sensitive ears, it was plain that the person was begging for his life. Kael waited for Dowley to speak.

"You've already had a six-month extension, Blair." came the cruel, mocking words. "Six months to make good your loan. I'll be expecting you Monday morning at ten. Either have the money, or you'll have to deed over that thousand acres on your north quarter."

"That will leave me with only five hundred acres. I can't survive on that. . . ." Kael did not hear the last pleading words.

He was transfixed. He felt the sound of Dowley's voice explode within his mind, felt the white-hot heat of three and a half years erupt within him.

"You'll never get my land!" screamed the voice in the office. "That's what you wanted all the time, wasn't it? That's why you were so damned generous. You wanted my thousand acres to add to your own. You're a greedy bastard, Dowley. You'll have to kill me and my family to get it!" the angry farmer declared.

Suddenly, Kael's muscles unlocked. His mind started to work again, and a cold, deadly feeling took over his thoughts.

No, not here, his inner self warned.

Slowly backing around the corner, Kael slipped out the back door.

Once outside, he forced himself to take deep breaths of the sweet air in an effort to cleanse himself. The bitter taste of bile slowly disappeared as his mind began to function properly. When he was fifty feet from Dowley's office, Kael stopped.

Any doubts were gone. The trail that had taken him from Pennsylvania to Wyoming had ended in this fertile frontier valley. Martin Dowley was Malcome Dupont. The voice Kael had listened to only seconds ago was the same voice he had heard just before his father had been murdered. Martin Dowley was the man who had killed his father. Kael Treemont's three-and-a-half-year search had ended, and shortly, Martin Dowley's life would end also.

In his mind, a key locked another door, securely preventing Lara Dowley from returning to haunt him. He had waited until he knew. Now, he would not let his emotions interfere with his task.

PART II

July–August, 1867

Lara Dowley spent Saturday in her room. She had no choice. Before her father and Anna left, he locked her in again and told Lew Cross to keep watch on the house in a voice loud enough for her to hear.

Rather than lie on the bed or sit on the stiff-backed chair of her dressing table, like some caged animal, Lara began to use her mind. Today marked her first full week of imprisonment. Kael had left a week ago, and because of her father's rage at not being able to stop him from returning, Lara's hope was renewed.

Once Angela received the note and gave it to Kael, freedom was only a few miles away.

But she must still find a way, if all else failed, to get away from Martin Dowley.

A wandering thought beckoned Lew Cross. Lara had always been aware of the foreman watching her, aware that he had never acted on his lust because he feared her father.

Gradually, a plan grew. Her knowledge of Cross might be her key to escape. Flirting and teasing, she would begin an attempt at seduction. She could surely do that. After all, Lara reasoned, she'd read a great many books. She would make him want her so desperately that he would do anything to get her. She would insist on being out of the house, that he take her for a ride, and then, Cross would receive his reward. Before he could claim what he believed to be his, Lara would ride away. Lew Cross would be too afraid of her father to reveal the truth.

Perfect, Lara thought, with a poor attempt at humor. And just how would she overpower Cross if he tried to stop her, let alone prevent him from taking what he wanted? No, if she used seduction to escape, she would have to pay the price. Was it worth it? Lara asked herself.

She gave up that idea, knowing the only thing she would gain by giving herself to Lew Cross would be her own shame.

But with that thought, Lara felt a change within herself. It was subtle, and she could not really understand it, but she found herself thinking more clearly, with more common sense and determination than ever before.

Feeling a strong resolve build within her, combined with the frustration of being imprisoned, Lara began pacing around her room. Her blue eyes flicked everywhere. The walls, the floor, the window, and the furniture were all inspected minutely. Searching for something—anything—to help her, Lara continued to pace. Her gaze fell on the small portrait of her mother, and she paused.

Fool, Lara scolded herself. For almost three years, she'd been a fool. She'd sat around and let Martin Dowley run her life. This past week has been no different than any other since she had arrived here. She's spent every day since her mother's death as a virtual prisoner, under Dowley's authority. Stupid! Lara told herself. She had been vain, stupid, and romantically foolish to wait for the rescue of true love. . . . It's the West, she told herself. It's a new land with new rules, not the East with everything prearranged in an orderly manner.

"You don't own me, Martin Dowley!" Lara screamed at the top of her voice. "You don't own me!"

With the outpouring of rage, calm eased over her. The nervous energy and powerless feeling had fled and she relaxed.

Thoughtfully, Lara decided what must be done. She would leave at night, after her stepfather was asleep. Anna would have to help, but Lara knew she would. Anna would have to have Camilla ready where she could be reached without anyone hearing.

Lara glanced around the room again, but this time her mind directed her eyes with a purpose. Going through the drawers of her bureau, she began to withdraw garments. No dresses. She would wear her buckskin pants and shirt. If she were leaving at night, even though it was summer, she did not want to be cold. She would bring one other pair of buckskin pants, and two cotton blouses. The three items of clothing would fit in her leather bag, and would leave room for a few personal items.

All the jewelry her mother had left her, and of course her mother's portrait, would go. That was all Lara felt would be necessary to start a new life. That, and money. Opening the third drawer of her bureau, she reached to the back and grasped the small pouch.

As she slowly withdrew her hand, a tremor passed through her. Lara's eyes went to the soft pouch, and rested on the crest that was engraved on it. Three seagulls floated over a large sailing ship, and the letter "F" rose above it all. Inside were twenty gold sovereigns. She remembered vividly both the time and the story her mother had told her when she gave the pouch to Lara. It had been on her tenth birthday.

"You are old enough to understand what I am going to tell you," Kristen Fairwald Dowley began, as she sat across from Lara. "Your father was the last of his line, the last male Fairwald. When he died, there was no one to follow a tradition that had been going on for over two hundred years."

Lara sat silently as she listened. It was rare that her mother spoke about her real father, and Lara dared not interrupt. She did not know why she found it difficult to swallow, but she sat quietly, watching the moisture that filled her mother's eyes.

"For ten years before your father was born, the Fairwald Shipping Company was having problems. By the time your father was born, the once mighty company had been reduced to three ships. By the time your father was ten, there was only one ship left. But that single ship, under the command of your grandfather, continued to keep the Fairwald business at a certain level.

"When your father reached the age of twenty-two, your grandfather took his final voyage as captain. Returning from that voyage, he gave command of the ship to your father. At the same time, he gave your father this purse containing twenty gold sovereigns."

As her mother paused, Lara's eyes went to the small pouch she held aloft. For the first time, she saw her family crest, and saw the proof that there was indeed a heritage she could call her own.

"This pouch and its contents have been passed down from father to son for seven generations. After your father died at sea and you were born, I put it away for you. There would be no more Fairwald men to receive the legacy."

"But what of my grandfather?" asked Lara, with a choked voice. She saw her mother blink away threatening tears, and take a deep breath.

"Your grandfather was an old man, and when his son died, a good part of him died, too. The only thing that kept him alive was awaiting your birth. Your grandfather awaited the next Fairwald heir to rebuild the family fortunes, and to pass on the legacy to." Kristen paused a moment to look away from her daughter and dab at her eyes with a lace-trimmed linen handkerchief. When she turned back to Lara, her face was once again composed.

"When you were born, and your grandfather was told you were a girl, he could not face the news. He died that night."

"Oh, Mother," Lara cried as she went to Kristen's arms and felt herself held tightly against her mother's breasts.

"It was not his fault, Lara. He had wanted something that could not be. I believe he knew that. I believe he knew that even if a boy had been born, he could not have lived long enough to teach him about the sea. He was only waiting to see the next Fairwald before he left this earth."

"But?"

"There are no buts, there is only reality, my little one. Reality is what you must always see in life. Reality is the reason I married your stepfather. To make sure that both of us would not want for anything. I have loved, deeply, and that will satisfy me until I can rejoin your father in heaven. As long as I stay on this earth, I will pretend be the proud wife of Martin Dowley. Now take this pouch, it is your only inheritance from your father. Put it away safely, and when you are older, you must decide what you will do with it. You can spend it foolishly if you want, or you can keep it as a reminder of your father, or you can start a new legacy to be handed down to your own children. Whatever you decide, remember, it is yours and yours alone."

The memory of that day faded as Lara turned from the bureau and placed the purse of sovereigns with her clothing.

The gold coins could mean the difference between life and death once she escaped, and if it were necessary to spend them, she would make sure that her father's legacy was not wasted. Although he would never know it, her father may have saved her life.

Satisfied that she would be able to survive after her escape, Lara packed the leather bag that would be attached to the saddle and placed it against the far wall of her closet, hiding it behind several dresses.

Only then, with the physical items prepared, did she feel better. Less caged. On her dresser were three books that she had taken from her stepfather's shelves yesterday. She picked one up, sat in a chair, and became lost in a world of words and descriptions that were far from the wild mountains of Wyoming.

"I just can't believe it," Constance Crimmons declared for the tenth time since she'd read Lara's letter. The first time had been when the three Crimmonses had left Valley City, at Angela's request. Now, nearing home, Constance again spoke her disbelief.

"It's true," Angela swore. "Mother, you know it is! Poor Lara told us often enough. Why else would she not be in town? Why didn't she meet me last Sunday?"

"Slow down, Angela," John cut in. "You've only Lara's word that she's being confined. That she's being sent off to be married. Besides, 'tis the usual way of things for a father to arrange a marriage."

"We're not in England any longer. Things are different here," his daughter cried.

"Angela, we know how you feel, and we agree. 'Tis better to marry for love, and have a happy life, but most arranged marriages work out well. If that were not so, don't you think the custom would have ended long ago?"

"It should have anyway. Papa, what about Kael? What of Lara's note that says her father tried to have Kael killed because he was courting her?"

"Angela, I don't know, but I think we had better wait to see Kael, whenever he gets back from South Pass."

"I agree," Constance said as she put her arm around her daughter. "I don't know what's happening right now, but I can't imagine anyone as good and fine as Mr. Dowley doing as Lara says."

"I can," Angela whispered.

Ten minutes later, the Crimmons carriage turned onto the narrow road that John had built himself. As the sun set, the wagon passed the small corral, and Angela sat up straighter. Her eyes saw Major, and her heart began to beat faster.

"He's here, Papa. Kael's back!"

"I've eyes in my head girl, I can see," John replied with a smile. As the carriage stopped, the front door of the house opened, and Kael stepped out.

"Oh, sweet mother of God, he's found him," John whispered in a choked voice. Both women stared at Kael, neither daring to speak. The handsome angles of his features seemed to have changed. Gone was the full-lipped smile that had seemed ever present. His usually glowing eyes seemed dull, as if they were someone else's. It was more than obvious that Kael Treemont had indeed found out who had killed his father.

"Welcome back, lad," John offered as he stepped down from the wagon and walked over to Kael. "I take it that you've learned a good deal from your trip?"

"I have," Kael replied as his eyes went to the two women who had remained seated in the carriage. "Can we talk alone?"

"You two go ahead," called Constance. "Angela and I have unpacking to do, then we've supper to prepare."

The two men walked silently to the corral. John wisely waited for Kael to speak. When he did, John Crimmons felt thunderstruck.

"Martin Dowley is the man who murdered my father!"

After leaving Dowley's office, Kael had taken his horse and ridden from town in the vise of ironlike self-control. When he was clear of Valley City, Kael released the rage within. Kicking the stallion's flanks harshly, he gave the horse his head, loosening all restraints.

Bending low with the tautness of the Andalusian's neck against his cheek, Kael let himself become part of the powerful muscles, flesh, and bone of the thundering stallion.

Kael blocked out everything and everyone except for the land and the air that rushed by him. He lost all mooring in time, returning to his surroundings only when Major began to slow.

Sitting up, Kael looked around. He did not know how long the horse had been running, for he did not know how long the black rage had controlled his mind. But as he surveyed the countryside, he saw he was near the Crimmons ranch. Kael smiled, realizing the horse's instincts had brought him here. Rather than follow the trail to the ranch, Kael turned Major toward a low-rising hillock, and climbed up onto the grazing pasture. Then he began to canter toward the ranch house. In the distance was a small flock of sheep.

Kael took in the strange sight of grazing animals surrounded by the mountains and wondered about his cousin's venture into sheep raising in the West. Sheep and cattle ranchers did not usually get along, but here, in the new territories, wool would be welcomed by all, including those who raised beef.

Slowing Major, he skirted around the thirty-odd balls of fluff. He stopped the gray stallion near a small stand of spruces. Dismounting, Kael dropped the reins and gave his horse the freedom to graze. He seated himself at the base of a tree from where he watched the stallion nuzzle the buffalo grass. Then his eyes went to the sheep, watching them eat contentedly, secure in their own little world.

Removing his hat and placing it near him, Kael rested the back of his head against the bark of the tree and closed his eyes. He let his mind begin to wander, trying to sort out his confused emotions. Suddenly, one of his past conversations with John returned with a crystal clarity.

"Dowley is a good man," John had told him. "He's helped everyone in the area. Why, the man's responsible for bringing in most of the stores and businesses in Valley City."

"Responsible?" Kael had questioned.

"Yes. Either by loaning them money to get started, or by convincing them to stay here and not continue to California or Oregon. Martin Dowley has brought the beginning of prosperity and civilization to the area."

"It also makes him richer, doesn't it?"

"I'll not be denying that. If a man's willing to invest now and wait until there is a true town around him, then he has every right to profit from his efforts," John had replied thoughtfully after he had gazed at Kael for a moment.

"I agree with you, but something's bothering me about Dowley and I don't know what it is," Kael had said. "He's just too good, and I've yet to meet anyone that has something bad to say about him. That is not normal."

"You're wrong, lad. Lara's not overflowing with praises for him."

"As a father, not as a citizen. She thinks well of him when it comes to his contribution to the territory."

"All children have a different picture of their parents than do outsiders. Kael, Martin Dowley is destined to become one of the greatest men in the territories. He alone has done more to assure the existence of Valley City than anyone could ask. You know that Dowley was the first white man to secure a total peace with the Wind River Shoshone. The great Chief Washakie himself agreed to the treaty. And because of that, Valley City is the only settlement in two hundred miles that can live peacefully and never fear Indian attack."

Martin Dowley is a great man! A great killer, Kael thought as the memory of the talk faded away. Then, hearing the bleating of a lone sheep and feeling the warmth of the sun on his face, the logical part of Kael's mind began to function; the part of his mind that had made him leave Dowley's office rather than barge in and kill the man.

Because Martin Dowley had spent three years building himself an image, a public accusation would not be believed. Kael had no hard evidence. Yes, he could seek him out and kill him, but to what purpose?

To extract his vengeance through the man's death would not be enough. Humiliating him, taking something from him and then exposing him, would be a punishment that Dowley would never recover from. It had to be something important. It had to be important enough to destroy him. The people must know that Dowley was not the saint they pictured him to be.

Only one other man in Wyoming dared admit what Dowley truly was. Kael pulled the name from his memory, the name he'd heard this morning—Blair! Blair would be one of those who would cry out willingly against Dowley. How would he implement his revenge? Kael pondered.

Unwanted, but refusing to stay locked away, Lara Dowley's face formed in his mind. Her smile, once so perfect and beautiful, now seemed false. Her soft hands, so wonderfully caressing and gentle, now seemed to take on the scales of a snake.

Lara! his mind screamed.

Screwing his eyes shut tighter, Kael concentrated on the face of the woman of deception. A plan grew boldly. But even as it developed, Kael's heart and mind fought another kind of Civil War.

Part of him claimed her as the beautiful woman that he loved, while the other recognized her only as a deceiving witch who constantly changed from lover to liar, from virgin to whore. . . . And just for those reasons, his method of vengeance would work.

As the sun reached its zenith, he stood with it, ready to move on to the ranch.

"Martin Dowley is the man who murdered my father!" Kael repeated as he turned to look at his cousin's face.

"I heard you the first time, lad," John said in a low voice.

"I know how much you respect him, but you must believe me, it's true."

"Do you, lad? Do you really know how much I respect Martin Dowley? Do you know that I feel about him as I did your own father? I've looked up to him as our leader. He is a man I could go to with my problems, and return with a solution. Now you're asking me to believe he killed your father. I suppose you have irrefutable proof?" John asked, his gaze never wavering from Kael's, even though Kael saw the moisture that filmed his cousin's eyes with a fine sheen.

Kael nodded slowly, then pulled the letter satchel free. He took out the Pinkerton report and handed it to John. John read it quickly, then gave the paper back to Kael before he looked out at the sunset.

"The man says it's all speculation, he can't prove the charge.

He can't prove murder, or the use of false names to purchase the land."

"That's true."

"Then what do you plan to do?" John asked, still looking toward the western hills.

"I'd like to call him out, face him with his deeds, and kill him! But—"

"But," John cut in swiftly, "everyone in Valley City will cry for your blood. He owns the largest amount of land, and nearly half the businesses in town. If you kill him, the people will hang you before you can defend yourself. To them, Martin Dowley is not just a man. He's the lifeblood of the entire territory."

"John, I'm not stupid. I'm angry. I want justice, but I am not stupid!"

"Then I think you'd better tell me what you have in mind, for it's definite that you've already an idea." With those words, John turned to Kael. The Englishman's face was set in hard lines of control, and Kael knew that John's very foundations of belief in himself, in his ability to judge others, and in his adopted country, warred within him.

"I won't kill him," Kael said slowly. The lines of tension in John's face eased, and he nodded. "I'm going to hurt him. I'm going to humiliate him and force him to come after me. When he does that, I'll confront him and prove to the world that he is not what everyone thinks."

"And how will you do that, lad?" John asked in a husky whisper.

"With your help."

"Go on."

"I want your word that you'll help me, and that you'll not mention one word of this to Constance or Angela."

"You're askin' for a lot, just on faith," John replied.

"Did my father ask for any more from you?" Kael said cuttingly.

"Your father never asked for anything that was not right."

"John, the man's a killer and a thief. What I'm asking is

159

right. If you don't want to do this for me, or for my father, then I'll do it myself."

John Crimmons studied Kael, feeling a sadness spread through him. He loved his younger cousin, as he had Kael's father. John owed it to Ryan Treemont to try to stop Kael from destroying himself needlessly. If necessary, John would help Kael, but the help would also be aimed at Kael. Slowly, John nodded his head.

"First, do you know a man named Blair?"

"Carl Blair, a farmer. His place is about fifteen miles south of here. I showed him how to make mortar."

"Talk to him, John. Talk to him tomorrow. Dowley's going to take his land if he doesn't pay his note on Monday."

John felt the disbelief he'd been unwilling to relinquish start to leave him, replaced by acceptance as Kael recounted the conversation he'd overheard this morning.

"Is there a way that he can raise the money?" Kael asked when he finished. Another piece of his plan slipped into place.

"There's no one in these parts, except Dowley, with that much cash."

"Then find out how much money Blair owes," Kael told him.

"Why?"

"Because I'm not a pauper. I'll assume Blair's mortgage, and give him enough money to pay Dowley. I will not let that bastard destroy anyone else."

"Robin Hood," John said with a smile.

"Who?"

"Robin Hood, a fine and noble man of Sherwood Forest. 'Tis a story that was written long ago, I believe Constance has the book. I'll see that she gives it to you."

"John. . . ."

"All right, lad, now out with the rest of this foolhardy scheme."

"I'm going to marry Lara." The intense outpouring from

160

John's eyes, at Kael's words, did not cause Kael to hesitate. "I'm going to marry her and take her away from Dowley."

"Because you love her?"

"Because she is Dowley's daughter, and he's using her."

"You'll destroy her!"

"If she's part of Dowley's charade," Kael agreed. "But if not, she'll be loved."

"No, Kael. In your father's name, I ask you not to," John pleaded. "She's a good child, a good woman. Don't do it, don't hurt her. She'll not be understanding, or forgiving, either."

"John, she's deceived me. She may not know she was used by her father, but she deceived me badly."

John felt Kael's words physically, felt the force of them as surely as if Kael had hit him. "And what will you do once you've married her, and your vengeance is finished? You'll be married. Have you thought about that?"

"It's a sacrifice I'll have to make," Kael replied quietly. He'd thought about it, but that was all. He refused to allow his mind to go further than today.

"Don't be so quick to condemn her, the father is not the daughter." Even as he spoke, John knew his words would bounce off the steel doors that Kael had erected around his heart. "Well, lad, I've a bit of news myself."

Kael waited silently.

"Angela received a note from Lara today," John started. Then he told Kael about the note, and Lara's problem.

Kael digested every word. Once the danger had passed, a warning proved nothing. If he had been killed, no blame would fall on Lara. If he were alive, Lara had tried to warn him and would be thought innocent. Perhaps she hadn't known at first, or perhaps she just hated her father enough to use Kael to escape him. Perhaps. . . .

"Here's what I intend to do," Kael began, outlining his plan to the minutest detail. When he was finished, John looked at him sadly.

"Your mind's made up?"

"It is," said Kael quietly.

"I don't think your father would appreciate what I'm doing for you," John observed in a sad voice of acceptance.

Lara had lost herself completely in the book she was reading, and had been startled to realize she needed to light a lamp to continue. The sun had set, and the afternoon was gone. But Anna and her father had not returned. She also felt pangs of hunger that the cold bread Anna had left did not assuage.

Then, as she looked out her window, she saw her stepfather's carriage roll in. When it stopped, she watched Anna go to the rear and begin to bring the supplies into the house. Lara returned to her chair and picked up the book. Soon she heard Dowley's heavy footsteps as he ascended the steps.

A moment later, the key turned in the lock and her door opened.

"You are free to join me downstairs," Dowley said.

"You are far too kind, Father," Lara replied sarcastically.

"Anna will have dinner ready within the hour," he said, ignoring Lara's words. "Change into something appropriate. Since I am forced to miss my usual Saturday evening company, I would prefer to have a properly dressed woman as my dinner companion." With that, Dowley left, but did not lock her door.

Lara's first thought was rebellious. She'd wear buckskins and be damned! But she changed her mind quickly. Thinking about her chances for escape, Lara realized that complacency was her best camouflage. With that thought, Lara began to prepare for dinner.

Later, standing before her mirror, Lara eyed herself critically. The usually unruly mass of her hair was under control; the long waves fell smoothly, and she had pulled the front and sides back, using two shell combs to secure it at the crown. The hair pulled away from her face, making Lara's eyes look even larger.

Another of the new dresses that her father had given her was reflected in the mirror. This one, a white evening gown, had the short bodice that was becoming fashionable around the world. It barely covered Lara's shapely shoulders, and the sleeves extended down for only a few inches. The material of the voluminous skirt was gathered and held by lace and tassles at strategic points so that the overall effect was selectively revealing of Lara's shapely figure. The tops of her breasts bobbed enticingly above the thin strand of lace that finished off the bodice's top. A double sash of blue ribbon criss-crossed under her breasts and fell in soft folds to the hem of the skirt, caught every few inches by darker blue tassles.

Lara's feet were encased in slippers of the same satin material as the dress, but were not visible when she stood.

Doing a pirouette, Lara watched the skirt's movements. Satisfied that she looked both the fancy woman and the obedient daughter, she started to the dining room. She had no fears that the time it had taken her to dress, almost two hours, would rekindle her father's anger. Dressing oneself in this type of clothing was time-consuming, and Lara knew she could not ask Anna to stop cooking in order to assist her.

Entering the elegant dining room, Lara accepted the unvoiced praise of her father, who stared at her as if he owned a priceless object of art that was for his eyes alone. True to habit, Martin Dowley was dressed finely also. His dark gray waistcoat, with its matching vest, complemented the fine linen stiff-collared shirt he wore.

"I'm sorry it took so long, Father, but I thought you would not mind the wait," Lara said, smiling sweetly.

"You please me," Dowley agreed as he lifted his glass and drank. "Even if you took an hour too long, you please me. Turn around." Lara complied. "Good. You are learning. One day you will thank me. One day, when you understand the power that you will wield, the power that your husband has harvested."

Wisely, Lara kept her silence. Dowley forced his bulk from the chair, and walked to the head of the table. "You may call Anna," he told her.

Lara picked up the silver bell and shook it once. Then she went to the wine bottle that was already opened. She poured her father's wine first, then waited for him to taste it. When he was done, she filled her own glass and sat at the opposite end of the long, oval table.

Throughout dinner, Lara began to implement her strategy. Cautiously, she asked questions. How did Jonathan Setterley live? Was his house large? Did he have many servants? Each inquiry was designed to make Martin Dowley think she was beginning to accept her fate.

By the end of the meal, Dowley was slightly drunk, and in better spirits than Lara had seen him recently. When her father walked her to her room and held the door for her, he spoke slowly, as if trying to control his tongue.

"I see you have spent your time alone wisely. Continue to do so and you will find your future husband very beneficial to your life. Remember, Lara, you are about to become royalty." Dowley paused for a moment, concentration etched on his features.

"Perhaps tomorrow, since you've learned to behave yourself we shall take a ride in the carriage."

"That would be very nice, Father. Good night," she said with a forced smile that she hoped he would not notice.

"Good night," he responded as he closed the door. A moment later, Lara heard the lock click.

Alone, Lara began to undress. Every item of clothing she removed she threw from her with charged anger. When she was finished and stood totally naked, her breasts heaved with both freedom and exertion. Damn him! Halfway through dinner, she had realized something.

Martin Dowley was insane. She could hide from it no longer. He was insane. Queen Lara, indeed!

That night, Lara's dreams were filled with visions of Martin Dowley, dressed in the robes of royalty, a golden crown upon his head and a staff of silver in his hand. His jowley face hovered above her, his finger pointed at her as he spoke, over and over again.

"Queen Lara . . . Queen Lara . . . Queen Lara."

Then Johnathan Setterley joined her father. He, too, wore royal robes, but his crown was of bull horns, and his staff, a snake, was alive and wiggling.

"Come to me, my queen, come to your king. . . ."

Over and over, the dreams came, washing her in waves of sadness and horror, until finally, the gentle rays of the morning sun bathed her face and called her to the new day.

A gentle knocking at her door alerted her just as it opened. Anna stepped in and smiled a rare smile. She closed the door and walked to the bed.

"I give note to Mizz Angela 'erself," Anna said.

"Thank you," Lara cried as she rose from the bed and put her arms around the housekeeper. "Thank you, Anna. I was afraid Mrs. Smithers might mention the note to my father. You know how she and everyone in Valley City looks up to him."

"Anna know. You like bath?"

"Oh, yes."

"Good. Ees ready."

"My father?"

"I tell you fazzer zat you ask for bath yesterday. 'E say you wait for today. Bath water outside. I bring een." Anna went

166

back to the door and returned with two large buckets of hot water. Within minutes, Lara was seated in the tub and luxuriating in the warmth of the water.

"What if he won't let me see Lara?" Angela asked as she fidgeted on the seat next to her father.

"He will, love, he will," Constance said as she patted her daughter's hand. Angela looked at her mother with thanks. But she was still worried. Her mother always looked for the best in everything, and although she somehow managed to find it, Angela knew that with Martin Dowley it was only superficial.

Angela was frightened that Dowley might suspect she knew he was keeping Lara confined, but she had a job to do, and she would not let Kael or Lara down. Kael had left with them this morning, but was not going all the way. Halfway between the Crimmons ranch and the Dowley land, he had left them. He'd been mysterious as to his destination, but no one tried to question him. Angela had her job, and that was to deliver a note to Lara.

John was timing his arrival at the Dowley ranch to coincide with breakfast. Martin Dowley, when at home on Sundays, always ate breakfast at the same time. Lara had told them that more than once. If Lara was required to eat with him, then she would not be hidden during their visit.

The sound of a horse and carriage interrupted the lecture that Dowley was giving Lara at the end of breakfast. With a look of annoyance, he stood and went to the window. When he turned, anger was on his face.

"It's John Crimmons and his family," he said. Lara felt a rush of hope surface, but kept her face expressionless. "Do I have to send you to your room?"

"What do you want me to do?" Lara asked wisely.

"Will you behave? Will you do what you're told?" he demanded, his dark eyes staring deeply at Lara.

She knew that she would not have to do anything. Her

friends were here because of her note, they would do nothing to cause her harm.

"I'll do whatever is necessary, Father, but let me at least say goodbye to Angela. She'll never understand if I don't."

"I'll warn you only once. If you do anything at all to try to avoid this marriage, you will suffer greatly. And so will anyone else who interferes."

"I won't do anything wrong, Father," she promised.

The knocking at the front door stopped further talk. Anna went to the door, and a moment later the Crimmonses entered the dining room.

"Lara, please tell Anna to bring more tea for our guests," Dowley said.

Lara went into the kitchen quickly and relayed the request to Anna. When she returned to the dining room, everyone was seated.

"I was just telling John and Constance that you were feeling poorly last Sunday, and that Angela had already left when I sent one of my men to tell her."

"Yes," Lara agreed with a smile, "I woke with a fever, but it passed the next day."

"I missed you yesterday," Angela said with a smile.

"I know, but Mr. Cross had some work that had to be done, and I didn't want to spend the entire day waiting for Father to be finished with business," Lara lied.

"What brings you by?" Dowley asked absently.

"We're going to Carl Blair's for the church meeting, and we thought we'd stop by to see if you wanted to join us. It's become a regular thing now, even when the minister is not here," John said innocently. It wasn't a lie, but not the truth, either. He wanted to see Dowley's reaction to Blair's name. There was none at all.

Before anything else was said, Anna came in with tea, small biscuits, and a crock of honey. Carefully, she poured each cup, and offered the biscuits to each person. She started with Mrs. Crimmons, and then went around the table. Angela was seated next to Dowley, and when she served the young blond-haired woman, Anna's wide body blocked Dowley's view completely.

Realizing the opportunity, Angela quickly slipped a folded sheet of paper onto the tray as Anna poured. When she was finished, Anna placed the dish of biscuits over the note and left.

Lara, holding her breath as she watched, released it slowly when she saw that her father had not observed the ruse.

"Are you going to tell your news?" Dowley asked with a smile.

Lara looked at him for a long moment, forcing calmness on herself.

She nodded once and turned her lips into a smile.

"I'm going to be married," Lara said in a low voice.

"Wonderful!" John exclaimed with a wide smile.

"Oh, Lara!" cried Angela as she left her seat and went to her friend, pulling her tightly against her. "Tell me," she demanded in a voice that sounded almost too happy.

Lara told the Crimmonses about her marriage, and although she felt she would choke with every word, she managed to get through it. Then, looking over at her father, she was rewarded with a benign smile.

Ten agonizing minutes later, the Crimmonses left. Lara, desperate to see the note that had been slipped to Anna, asked her father if she could be excused.

"Of course, my dear. And, Lara, your performance was very good. I almost believe you are beginning to look forward to this marriage now."

"I . . . I don't know, Father. Perhaps one day I'll learn to love Johnathan Setterley, I just don't know." With that false admission, Lara left for her room, feeling her stepfather's eyes follow her as she walked up the stairs.

Love, how stupid, he thought, as he watched her. Money, power, that was worth something. Love . . . that was worth nothing.

Inside her room, Lara saw the note on her dresser. With

her heart beating wildly in her breast, and her fingers trembling with hope and anticipation, she lifted the paper and unfolded it.

Dearest Lara was all that she could read before her eyes flooded at the sight of Kael's handwriting. Then, wiping away the tears, she began to read.

Fourteen sunrises. Fourteen sunsets. With each rising and setting of the sun, Lara felt her freedom draw closer. Fourteen breakfasts. Fourteen suppers. Twenty-eight meals with Martin Dowley. Each one progressively harder to face than the one before. Each one harder, except the fourteenth supper; the twenty-eighth meal.

Fourteen nights filled with dreams of Kael Treemont. Fourteen nights of burning amber eyes, and strong hands caressing each part of her body. Fourteen nights of wishing for the reality of his gracefully muscled body lying next to her.

The note Angela had slipped on the tray had been explicit. Kael would come for her the night before she was to leave for Kansas City. Just thinking about the note gave her the same reaction she'd had when she read it. Her heart pounded, and her eyes misted. Kael had written that he would come, to take her away and to marry her. She was to be ready to leave at any instant after her father was asleep. If possible, Lara was to arrange to have her horse in the corral. If she could not, Kael would get another mount. They were going to California.

They would be married before they left. It was being arranged. "Be ready, my love," he had signed the note.

And she was!

Lara thought about the route she would not be taking to Kansas City. Of the wagon, now waiting for her, and the ten men who were to be her escorts. The small band would go East in stages during the course of the twenty-day journey. They would ride from army post to army post through Wyoming, Nebraska, and finally into Kansas. They would stop only for meals and sleep.

The schedule of the trip, although hard, was nothing like her original journey West. Also, Lara had grown into a strong woman, with no resemblance of the fifteen-and-a-half-year-old Eastern woman-child who had been on the wagon train.

The only change in the plan, and the only possible complication, was that her stepfather had decided to accompany Lara on the first leg of the journey, which ended at Fort Hallack. There, he would join more of his men, who were bringing Dowley's new, large herd to the ranch. At Fort Hallack, Martin Dowley would say goodbye to the daughter he had sold for his own ends. He would be one step closer to the control he wanted over the Wyoming territory, and Lara would be on her way to her marriage to Setterley.

A smile curved her lips. It will not be that way, Father, she vowed. She would be married and gone! Looking out her window, Lara gazed at the star-filled night. The moon was not yet up, and the darkness of the heavens, with their myriad of sparkling dots, looked more comforting and inviting than frightening.

"Soon," she whispered to the stars, "soon I will ride beneath you."

Lara had followed all of Kael's instructions. She would be ready to go with him, and to marry him. She had already told Anna, who had promised to bring Lara's saddle to the spot she instructed.

Using every feminine mannerism she could, Lara had seductively coaxed Lew Cross into exercising Camilla, and leaving the mare in the corral.

Cross had agreed, and as he let his hand go to Lara's shoulder, the veil of control had fallen from his eyes as he looked at her. Within those dark depths, Lara saw his naked desire. She forced herself to smile at the foreman. Even now, Lara shuddered at the memory of his touch.

It had worked. Every day for the last two weeks, Lew had excercised the mare, and Lara had watched from her window. Each time she saw Lew Cross, she felt a chill of revulsion pass through her body.

Never again, Lara told herself, never will I have to see him.

The one part of Lara's plan that had not worked had been the way she had tried to make her stepfather think she had surrendered to the idea of the marriage. Dowley accepted this change in her, but had still refused to let her free when he was not home, or when he slept.

Hearing her stepfather's footsteps on the stairs, Lara left the window and went to bed. She wore a nightdress with a satin robe over it. Lara knew she seemed ready for bed, and that was what she wanted.

Lara's breath caught in her throat as the lock clicked and the door opened.

"I wanted to say good night, my dear. Tomorrow is waiting for you eagerly." Lara heard the liquor in his voice, and saw the taunting expression on his face.

"Good night, Father," she replied with what she hoped appeared to be a sad smile.

"Such sadness does not become you, my dear, but I'm sure Johnathan will change that look. You have a wonderful fate ahead of you. I'm glad to see that you've begun to accept it," Dowley said as his eyes swept the room. All her baggage and personal possessions were gone, awaiting her in the wagon below. Only the dress she had worn tonight and the traveling dress she would wear tomorrow remained.

"Do not forget the dress you wore tonight. I'm sure Johnathan will like it."

"I won't forget," Lara replied in a monotone, wondering why he was doing this to her. Was he just trying to draw out his own enjoyment?

"I do believe it will be lonely here once you've gone. I'm surprised," he said foolishly. Lara knew it was the whiskey making him talk like that. "Perhaps I should remarry?"

Lara suppressed a shudder at the thought. She knew, too well, how he had treated his first wife. The second would receive the same, or worse.

"If we were back East, it would be easier. There are few women around here that are unmarried," Lara said in a sickly sweet voice filled with commiseration.

"No, my dear daughter, again you are wrong. There is one. . . ."

"Who?" Lara asked, feeling a tug of fear within her.

"I'm surprised. You, of all people, should know. After all," Dowley said, as a grotesque grin spread across his face, "she's your friend."

"Angela?" Lara whispered with fearful incredulity.

"Of course, my dear. She's of age. She would look perfect sitting at my table."

"Her father will never permit it!"

"John is not a stupid man. By giving me his daughter, he will become secure. He, too, will be a part of the royal family. And as an Englishman, he understands what that means," Dowley told her knowingly.

"He will never let you have Angela," Lara repeated.

"As you would never marry Setterley?" her father asked with a mocking laugh.

"Don't do it, Father, please."

"Do not tell me what to do!" Dowley took a step forward and raised his arm. Lara stood her ground, refusing to move, daring her stepfather to hit her. "Be careful, Lara. I would not want you to arrive in Kansas City with your face marked." Then, suddenly, Dowley seemed to regain his senses, and his face lost the red hue that had risen with his rage. "Do not be foolish on your last night here. Go to sleep, Lara."

Again, she used the self control that she had taught herself during these weeks of captivity. She nodded her head. "Good night, Father," she said as the door closed and the lock bolted into place.

"And goodbye!"

Ten minutes later, Lara left her bed and removed the robe. Then she took off the nightdress, leaving on only the light camisole and silken undergarment that would prevent her buckskin pants from chafing her. Moving as silently as she could, lest she make noise to attract her father, Lara dressed again. The soft pants flowed over her calves and thighs, and were cinched at her waist by drawstring thongs of leather. Lara slipped the buckskin blouse over her head, and felt excitement and tension mount within her. When her boots were on, she was ready. She had at least an hour before Kael would be here, but she was ready. Moving one candle to the window, Lara placed it on the sill and gazed out.

"Come, my lion, come to me with your eyes of golden fire," Lara whispered as she looked up at the pale brilliance of the now rising moon.

Silently cursing the midnight moon, Kael tied the gray Andalusian to a small sapling and began to work his way to the main house of the Dowley ranch. Only one light was visible, and he knew it signaled Lara's presence and her acceptance. Kael had spent the first week since telling John about Dowley in the Wind River mountains with Painted Hawk and his people. There, Painted Hawk had told him of the different trails that cut across the mountains, and which of them would be the easiest for him. There were several, but Kael wanted one in particular. He knew he would have a head start of three to five days on Martin Dowley, depending how long it took him to figure out which passes Kael used. But for insurance, if Dowley did not start after him within three days, an Indian would seek him out and tell him of the two white people he saw alone in the mountains.

Kael hoped it would be only three days because of the way

he'd orchestrated everything. Carl Blair was now his ally. The farmer had blessed Kael for his help and had promised to be the first to decry the name of Dowley.

The wedding would take place in Blair's home. The minister, Jeremiah Bluetriech, would perform the service. There would be at least twenty people to witness the marriage. Everything was planned to the closest minute. No one would question Dowley's absence at first, as things would move too swiftly. By the time Kael and Lara stood before the preacher, only a minute would have passed since their entrance. After the newlyweds left, John Crimmons and Blair would tell the guests the truth about Martin Dowley.

But only after Kael and his wife were gone. Kael expected Dowley to pursue them to South Pass. He smiled in the moonlight as he coaxed Lara's mare to him, and then led her from the corral to the tree where he'd tied the stallion. Saddling the mare quickly, Kael's smile broadened. While Dowley chased them to South Pass, they would be going to Union Pass. But word of their whereabouts would reach Dowley.

He would come after them. Kael would be ready. When it was over, he would bring Martin Dowley back to face the people, and to extract his final justice.

Ridding his mind of these thoughts, Kael began to concentrate on what he must do now. He must show love for Lara! He must not let her know, not yet, that he knew about her. Let her think that love had blinded him. Moving with the stealth of a mountain cat, he started to the main house. Passing the loaded wagon, he heard something move.

Kael froze.

The footsteps continued until he felt a presence behind him.

"Isn't the horse enough? Or is there more that you want?" Lew Cross asked as he put the barrel of his pistol against the small of Kael's back.

It had taken Kael's war-trained body only an instant to analyze everything that was happening. He'd heard no telltale click of a cocking hammer, and he knew he had a chance. As soon as the gun rested firmly against his skin, Kael unwound like a spring.

He turned siftly, his elbow knocking away the gun barrel as his hand, balled in a fist, flew at Cross. Kael felt a jarring along his arm as his fist connected with the foreman's chin. Instantly, Kael's other fist crashed into Cross' mouth with a dull thud. The power that was transmitted along Kael's arms, fed by his need for speed and silence, was more than enough to knock the man out. As Cross fell to the ground, Kael grabbed the gun. Bending over the foreman, Kael dragged him to the wagon, lifting him effortlessly and dumping him inside.

Kael joined the unconscious man and, searching in the darkness, found the rope he knew would have to be there. Working fast, he tied Cross securely, then opened one of Lara's trunks. Taking whatever material came to his fingers first, Kael pulled it out and quickly tore two strips from it. The small one he used as a gag. The second was larger, and Kael made a hood of it and covered the man's face. The longer he stayed in darkness, hoped Kael, the longer he would stay asleep.

Then Kael made his way to the front of the wagon. There he took an envelope and placed it on the front seat. To make sure it would not blow away, he pulled the long, thin nail that he had hidden inside his hatband, and pressed it through the paper and into the wooden seat. When he finished, he stepped from the wagon and paused.

Looking up, Kael saw Lara silhouetted in the window. It was the first time he'd seen her since he had left for South Pass, and although he could not see anything but a dark form, he froze.

Lara heard Camilla's low whinny. Her breath caught in her chest as she saw a tall figure lead the mare away. Moments later, she saw him return and begin his walk to the house. Then fear shot through her. Lara's hand flew to her mouth to stop the scream that hovered there. Another shadowy figure had emerged from the rear of the wagon and was coming behind Kael. With the aid of the moon, Lara was able to make him out. Lew Cross.

As if watching a dance unfold below her, Lara saw Kael knock Cross out and take him to the wagon. Then he lifted Cross in before going in himself. Moments later, she watched Kael emerge at the front of the wagon, hesitate for a second, and then jump down and begin his walk to the house.

Three steps later, she saw Kael stop and look up. Lara knew it was too dark to see clearly, but for some reason she could see his every feature. The strong, well-rounded chin, the full, soft lips, the straight nose, and the glowing eyes were all revealed to her. Then his face went dark as he bent his head and started to walk again.

By the time Kael had reached the front door, Lara had her bag in hand, and a small Indian blanket around her shoulders.

Vainly, Lara listened for Kael's footsteps on the stairs. She was finally rewarded by the sound of a key in her door's lock. She breathed a sigh of relief. Everything had gone as planned: Anna had been able to let Kael in, and had given him the key. The door opened, and Lara's breath left her as she stared into his face for the first time in three weeks.

"Kael," she whispered as she stepped up to him. She felt his arms go around her, felt his mouth against hers for only the barest of seconds before he pulled away. With a finger to his lips, he motioned Lara to silence. She nodded her head and began to follow him.

When they were outside and the front door was closed behind them, they half-walked, half-ran to the tethered horses. Kael took Lara's bag and tied it to her saddle. Then he turned slowly, and she went into his arms.

Lara felt a tide of emotion flood her as her lips sought his. She pressed herself against his chest as she kissed him, and felt his hands pull her harshly nearer.

"I love you, Kael," she said as she drew her lips from his for only a second before kissing him again hungrily. A moment later, their lips parted, and Kael's hands went to her small waist to lift her into the saddle.

"Wait," she whispered. He held his hands tight around her. Lara gazed into his face, her eyes wandering over every feature until they rested on his eyes.

Kael felt the emotions with which she gazed at him, felt them pull at him, felt them reach into him with a tearing, rending pain. Slowly, he forced himself to gain control, to remember what he must do.

"I love you," he said. His voice carried no further than her ears. He felt Lara sigh, and then saw her nod. Quickly, he lifted her up to her saddle, then went to Major. Silently, he led both horses away until he felt they were far enough. Then Kael mounted his stallion and they began to ride toward their destiny.

Behind them, in the very spot they'd just left, a long figure stepped from behind the trees. The half-breed housekeeper walked into the path and watched the two receding figures. Then, slowly, she made her way back to the house.

Instead of going to her room, Anna climbed the stairs and went to Lara's. Once inside, the housekeeper closed the door and moved the large dresser, slowly and silently, to barricade the door and allow Lara and Kael more time before Martin Dowley discovered his daughter was missing. Anna hoped he would waste time breaking into the room.

Anna realized that she would be beaten for this, but she also knew that the lovers must get away. Anna, too, would leave, as soon as she could. She no longer wanted to stay in the white man's world. She would return to the village of her mother, to the Arapahoes.

Patiently, Anna began to wait for dawn.

Cool night air washed across Lara's face, giving reality to her freedom. Feeling the mare's movements beneath her, and occasionally glancing to her side to make sure she was not dreaming, she began to believe that she would make it, that she and Kael would be married and would leave for their new home.

Family. That, more than anything else, was what Lara wanted. Kael, husband and father to their children. She, mother and wife, lover and mistress, would make sure that their life would be long and happy.

Breathing in the combined fragrances of heartleaf, mule's-ears, wild onion, horsemint, and wild roses, carried aloft by the night breezes, Lara felt the last chains of her bondage released.

As Kael rode next to her, Lara felt another wild racing of her heart. The moon had dropped behind the mountains, and although the night was dark, she needed no light to know his handsome profile.

Free, and with the man she loved, thought Lara, as the

horses continued their canter. They had been riding for two hours, and she was content with the silence that they had fallen into.

A short time later, Kael motioned Lara to slow her horse. There was a carriage waiting in the road. Lara and Kael rode up to it, and when they were abreast of it, her heart quickened again. Standing by the side of the wagon was the Crimmons family.

Angela's smile was brighter than any sun, Lara thought as she dismounted and went to her friend. Hugging each other tightly, both young woman began to talk at the same time. Angela won out.

"Lord, you look lovely," she finally said.

"I'm going to make a fine-looking bride in these buckskins," Lara laughed. Again, the two women hugged.

"That's why we're here."

"Why is why you're here?" Lara asked, puzzled.

"For your gown. Do you think we'd let you be married without proper clothing?" Angela asked with a smile.

Lara, her features set in a questioning look, glanced back at Kael, and saw his grin. Then she heard John walking from the rear of the carriage.

" 'Tis a grand sight you'll be this morning if we let you wear your pants. Why, people will talk about it for years. But," John said, a smile spreading wide across his face as he continued, "we want everyone to talk about you for even longer." To accent his words, John lifted both hands high, and yards of material unfolded.

Lara's eyes went wide when she saw what was hanging from John's hands. Shimmering in the fading starlight was a wedding dress of white silk. Lara stared at the gown as John spoke again.

" 'Tis the same dress that Constance married me in, and it will be the one Angela wears when she marries. Since the day Constance put it on and we were wed, our life has been happy. I pray that yours will be the same."

"Enough, John," Constance interrupted. "Lara, you'd do us much honor if you would wear it today."

"And if you don't, Lara Dowley, I'll never forgive you!" Angela warned with tears trailing along her cheeks.

Lara would not trust her voice, so she nodded, feeling tears begin to well in her own eyes.

"Good!" declared Constance, as she motioned for John to hand Lara the dress. "Now we'd better get moving, she said as she pointed to the East, at the faint lightness that was now showing there. "I know for a fact that the gown will have to be pinned if Lara's going to make use of it."

"Lara, I'll take your horse, you go ahead with the ladies." Lara nodded at Kael and started to the carriage. Stopping for a moment, she turned to look back at him. Over his shoulder the first band of gray framed the Eastern mountains, and Lara realized again, that with the light would come her freedom, and marriage to the man she loved.

Kael nodded at Lara, then urged the stallion next to the carriage. He bent, taking her into his arms. His lips covered hers, and she felt the power in his arms as they crushed her to him. Suddenly, Kael released her and backed the horse away. He and John watched as the carriage started down the road until it disappeared from view.

"Kael," John began, as he held the mare's reins, "can I not talk you out of this foolishness?"

"It's not foolishness, John. It's something that must be done."

"You'll be hurting an innocent girl. Don't you see that? Don't you understand the cruelty of what you do?"

"I've told you before, if she's innocent, she'll not be hurt."

"What do you call marrying someone to achieve vengeance? Marrying a woman who loves you as deeply as Lara does! Do you not call that cruel?" John asked, unable to mask the bitterness in his voice.

Kael hesitated. His mind was back to an earlier hour, when he had seen Lara silhouetted in the window, and his heart had begun to pound. It had been easy, while he had been with the

Shoshone, while he had been anywhere but near her. His mind had been made up, and he knew what he had to do. But when he'd seen her, his heart had ached.

"John," Kael began, choosing his words carefully. "I know you think what I'm doing is wrong, but I want you to know that I love Lara. Whatever happens, I do love her. But I must finish what I've started."

"Don't try to ease your guilt with statements of love. Do as you must, but I'll not willingly accept a lie. . . ." With that, John mounted. He turned again to Kael.

"Lad, I saw the love that woman has for you. And I saw the love you had for her before you knew who Martin Dowley was. Whatever happens after this morning, you're going to have to work hard to salvage what you've set out to ruin!"

Kael sat on the gray Andalusian and watched John begin to ride toward the Blair farm. He felt a twisting in his stomach but forced it away. Pressing his heels into Major's flanks, Kael rode after John.

The Blair farmhouse was like most of the homes in the area. It was small, well built, and warm, comfortably housing Carl Blair, his wife, and their three children. The main room was filled with furniture that Blair had made since his arrival. Hand-hewn chairs and stools that were simple and useful furnished the room nicely. But today, like almost all the Sundays of the past year, the main room was a crush of people. Fifteen people were milling about, with six women sitting in available chairs. There was just enough space, barely, for the minister and the wedding couple to stand, and for everyone else to see the ceremony.

A sudden hush fell as one of the bedroom doors began to move. Kael took a deep breath and stepped into the main room. He looked at the sea of faces, and with another breath began his walk to the minister.

As Kael made his way forward, his six foot height resplendent in an army uniform of blue, his wide shoulders and long arms accentuated by golden braid, there were audible sighs.

The dress sword at his side gave a solemnity to the morning that would be remembered for a long time. Weddings were rare in the territory, and weddings with a groom as handsome as the retired army officer even rarer. The tale of this marriage would be retold again and again to the young girls who would eventually become brides themselves.

Reaching the minister, Kael stopped and waited. The low hum of voices began again, until suddenly the room fell into total silence. Kael heard the door of the other bedroom open, and he turned.

Angela Crimmons stepped into the main room first. She was dressed modestly in blue, her wheat-blond hair in a bun. Her deep blue eyes found Kael's, and she smiled nervously.

Angela stepped to the side and waited.

A moment later, a vision of white stepped through the door. Lara's burgundy hair and blue eyes were covered by a sheer white veil that fell over her face. The gown fit her magnificently. Its tight bodice flowed over her breasts, revealing the soft rise and fall of her chest. Her flesh was hidden by a delicate white lace that reached from the tops of her breasts to the high collar of the dress, which accented the elegance of her neck. It draped over her shoulders, blending into silk sleeves that molded the length of her arms, ending with laced ruffle cuffs at her wrists.

The skirt flared over her hips in graceful lines. When Lara walked, it seemed to Kael that she was floating, and behind her, both Angela and Constance held the billowing train that added to the effect.

Halfway to the minister, John Crimmons came to Lara's side and took her arm. When they reached Kael, she stopped. Her heart hammered and her stomach churned as she looked into his eyes. Slowly, she forced herself to regain a certain calm, aided by what she saw in his eyes. With a deep breath, Lara smiled behind her veil and stepped next to Kael. Together, they turned to face the minister.

*　　*　　*

"Lara! Open the door!" Dowley shouted as he pushed against the barricaded wood. "Dammit, open this door or you'll feel my anger on your skin!"

The obese man rammed his shoulder against the hard door. His face was suffused with scarlet, and a single purple vein throbbed dangerously at his temple.

Dowley stopped his futile banging and turned to get help. As he walked down the stairs, he heard raised voices. Quickly, Dowley ran through the house and out the front door. Several of his hands standing behind the wagon were untying Lew Cross. Dowley barged through the men and demanded to know what was going on.

"We found Lew tied up," one of the men said.

"Obviously," Dowley replied sarcastically. "What happened?" His eyes were on the foreman's.

Cross was rubbing circulation back into his wrists as he looked at his boss. "I heard someone out here last night, and I went to check on it. Before I knew it, someone hit me and knocked me out," he lied.

"Who?"

"Your daughter's lover!" Cross shot back.

"And you let him get away?" screamed Dowley. Again, his face turned scarlet, and the vein at his temple stood out fiercely.

"He had help. I saw him take the mare away, and then I saw him come back. I was about to take him when someone knocked me out!"

Dowley looked at the foreman, then glanced back at the house. In Lara's window, he saw the wider shape of Anna.

"Here's something," another ranch hand called as he pulled an envelope from the seat of the wagon and walked to Dowley, who was surrounded by a dozen silent men.

Dowley took the envelope, but before he opened it, he looked at Lara's window. "Two of you go upstairs. Get that half-breed out of the room and bring her down!" Then, when two of the men left to carry out the order, Dowley opened the envelope. As he read the letter, his hands began to tremble, and the vein throbbed wildly.

When he finished, his face was the color of a whitewashed house and his dark eyes were glazed. "I want everybody mounted. We're going after that bastard. I want him dead!"

When the ranch hands went for their horses, Dowley again held up the letter. His hands shook visibly with effort as he read every word again and again.

> Mr. Martin Dowley, also known as Malcome Dupont:
>
> Know that I have found you out. I have taken your daughter and will stop the plans you have made for her and yourself.
>
> We are to wed at the home of Carl Blair, who will not welcome you. After your daughter becomes mine, we leave for California. Do not bother to follow us.
>
> Accept defeat as I have had to for almost four years. Accept the loss of your daughter. I have taken her as payment for your debt. You, Malcome Dupont, or Martin Dowley, have taken a life from me. I now take one from you. Remember, you are alive. Ryan Treemont is dead.
>
> Kael R. Treemont
Philadelphia, Pennsylvania
July 27, 1867

Treemont! Why had he not connected the names before? Dowley knew the name well. Ryan Treemont was the man who had made his desires possible. But when the old man had found him out, Dowley had killed him. And that fool boy who had come barging in . . . Dowley had been positive that young Treemont had not seen him. How had he been found out?

Dowley shook his head as his anger built again. It didn't matter how he'd been discovered. All that mattered was that he get Lara back. Without her, his empire would face a serious setback. He was not going to allow that to happen. It had taken too many years, and too many lives, to lose now. One more life meant nothing, especially this man's.

"Everyone's ready," Cross called. Dowley nodded, then turned to see Anna being dragged between two men. When they reached him, they threw the woman at his feet. Glaring down at her, he saw the defiant set on her features.

"Stand," he ordered.

Anna rose slowly, pulled her shoulders back, and faced him.

"Did you help them?"

She did not reply.

"Did you help them?" Dowley repeated, but for once he did not raise his voice. He stared at her, his eyes narrowing until they were lost in fleshy folds.

Still Anna did not respond.

Slowly, Martin Dowley smiled. Anna felt revulsion flood her, but she did not allow it to show.

He lifted his hand.

Anna kept her eyes locked on his.

Dowley's arm and hand moved quickly as he slapped her. He hit the housekeeper three times. Each time the echo of the slap reverberated loudly in everyone's ears. When he stopped, the woman was still standing, her eyes boring into his.

"Kill her!" he ordered, and turned away. Several of the men looked at each other. One of them took Anna's arm and began to lead her away. The rest mounted their horses and waited until Dowley did the same. Suddenly, a shot rang out.

The twelve men waited for the hand who was now walking from the barn. When he reached them, and sat his horse, Dowley turned to Lew Cross.

"Blair's." With a loud thundering of hooves, Martin Dowley and his men began the pursuit of Lara and Kael.

No one had questioned the man who had taken Anna away. The men who worked for Martin Dowley were not settlers. They were men who never built homes, married, or raised families. They worked for whomever they wanted, and never asked or answered questions. They were a new breed, one that had grown from the war, hardened to death and living for whatever desires they wanted fulfilled. But not all were bad.

In the barn, Anna waited until the dust settled from the departing riders. When everyone had gone and she knew she was alone, she smiled. The hand had not even tried to scare her. He had motioned her to silence, then fired into the dirt floor.

Anna left the barn and went to her room. She gathered together those few things she called hers. Then, without any show of emotion, she left the house and began her walk to the Owl Creek mountains, and the village of her people. The Arapahoe would take her in. They hated the white man as much as she.

"I now declare that you, Kael Treemont, and you, Lara Dowley, are man and wife. You may kiss the bride," the minister said in a resonant voice. Kael smiled, lifting Lara's veil slowly. He turned the gauze over her head, and let it fall behind her. Lara looked up at him, her breath catching in her throat as she saw the desire that filled his face. She knew it matched her own. She watched him gradually lower his lips to hers, until her eyes closed and she lost herself in the depth of the kiss.

The excitement that held the small crowd in its power was now ending, and with it came an audible question. Where was Martin Dowley? For some unexplained reason, everyone had been too caught up in this joyous event to wonder.

Before anyone could pick up the question, the minister congratulated the newlyweds. Then he turned to the assembled people and spoke. As he held their attention, Kael, Lara, and Angela slipped away unnoticed.

The carriage was ready. In it was Lara and Kael's clothing. Camilla and Major were tied to the back, and everything was waiting. Quickly, Kael helped Lara and Angela up; then, taking the reins, he started the team. They drove for only a mile before turning off the main trail and riding into the foothills.

Eventually, Kael slowed, pulling to a halt by a stand of lodgepole pines. Angela and Lara jumped down, and Lara almost fell, caught in the long train of her dress. Laughing, the women ran into the woods so that Lara could change into her buckskin pants and a light cotton shirt.

Kael switched clothes, too. He took the fresh uniform off and put on his faded uniform pants and his light shirt. The day promised to be warm, and it would be at least one more day before they would enter the higher mountains and have need of heavier clothing. When Kael was finished dressing, he folded the dress uniform neatly, and placed it in the carriage. Upon it, he rested his saber. He would leave them in John's care.

Within a few minutes, he heard the women coming back. As he turned, he felt as if the past were coming with them.

Lara was attired as she had been when he first saw her, lying on the ground, in the light buckskin pants and shirt. Her hair, now free of the veil, tumbled past her shoulders, sparkling warmly in the sun.

Angela stopped in her path, and Lara ran to Kael. When she reached him, she went into his arms. "I love you, my husband," she said in a whisper. "I'm ready."

Looking down at her, Kael felt a tightness in his throat. For the first time, the reality of what he was doing held him in its torturing grip. Forcefully, he pushed away the thoughts as he smiled at her.

"And I love you, but we must wait for a few minutes."

"But my father must be coming for us," Lara protested. "He'll scour every inch of the valley until he finds us."

Kael smiled at the fear in her voice as he cupped her chin in his hand. "He won't find us. We're waiting for our guides," he explained. With that, Angela's eyes widened, and he knew they were no longer alone. Slowly, Kael turned, and as he did, he felt Lara stiffen.

"Welcome, Painted Hawk."

"It is time, Treemont. You are ready?" the Indian asked.

"We are ready. Painted Hawk, my wife, Lara Treemont."

Painted Hawk walked up to Kael and Lara. Stopping before them, he smiled warmly. "I have seen you often, when I have hunted. You ride and dress like a man. I do not know that I would have a squaw who would do such things."

Lara felt herself redden, but realized that the Indian's words were a compliment rather than a condemnation. Also, the realization that she had been watched, often, by others began to dawn on her. As Lara was about to speak, she saw Painted Hawk's impassive face freeze as he looked past her.

Both Lara and Kael turned, and saw Angela Crimmons standing behind them. Her eyes were wide, and her face flushed. The modest blue dress did not conceal the heaving of her full breasts as she stared at Painted Hawk.

"Painted Hawk, this is the daughter of my cousin," Kael said.

"Cousin?" Painted Hawk asked, as he slowly turned his face from Angela to Kael.

"The daughter of my mother's brother. Her name is Angela, she is the daughter of John Crimmons," Kael said pointlessly.

Painted Hawk had already turned back to Angela. After a long moment, he again returned his eyes to Kael. "We must leave now," he said as another sort of veil slipped into place, hiding behind it whatever Kael thought he saw in the Indian's eyes.

At a signal from Painted Hawk, three Shoshone warriors rode up. With them was Painted Hawk's cream and brown spotted horse, and a packhorse loaded with supplies. "We must leave."

"We're ready," replied Kael as he turned to Angela. "Tell your father everything will work out well." Angela came to him, and Kael pulled her close.

"I'll miss you, Cousin," she said as tears again filled her eyes. He kissed her forehead, then stepped back. Angela moved to Lara and they embraced. "Lara, I'll miss you most. What will I do now?" she asked. Suddenly, Angela turned and ran to the carriage. As she climbed up, Painted Hawk jumped onto his horse's back and went over to her.

He sat straight, his sinewy body clad only in a buckskin loincloth, his long black hair falling loosely behind him, and his black eyes gazed deeply into Angela Crimmons's dark blue ones.

"Crimmons's daughter. Your father man with small white cattle?"

It took Angela almost a minute to control the feelings that raged within her. Then, for the first time since she had seen Painted Hawk, her lips formed a smile. "Sheep."

"Sheep?" Painted Hawk echoed, his voice puzzled but his expression still unchanged.

"They're called sheep," she explained.

"You tell father, your family never fear anything. Painted Hawk always protect woman with sun-color hair." Then he wheeled his horse toward the waiting group. Angela stared at his retreating back, the smile gone, replaced by open-mouthed surprise. Slowly, she turned the carriage and began her short ride back to the Blair farm.

As Angela drove away, Kael, Lara, and the Indians silently began to ride north.

Carl Blair stood as the minister turned away from the assembly and walked to John Crimmons. Blair began speaking softly at first, and then with more power. Crimmons and Reverend Bluetriech huddled in one corner, listening to Blair, knowing what he would be saying.

While Blair spoke, the minister removed two papers from his pocket.

"These are the certificates of marriage, one for the territory, the other for the church. I will register the legal certificate, you should keep the other for Mr. Treemont."

"I thank you, Jeremiah. We asked a lot, and you had every reason to refuse."

"I think not. It was more than obvious that those two are in love, and after what you've told me about Martin, I could not, in good conscience, send Lara to what her father sought."

Perhaps you should have, John thought, as his mind envisioned what Lara would soon be facing. "Looks like Carl has everyone's attention," the minister observed.

John looked at the crowd. Their expression ranged from

out-and-out disbelief to the nodding heads of those who had felt Dowley's hand in their businesses. John began to listen attentively.

"I don't believe that Dowley was going to take your land because he decided to call in his note. I'll bet there's more to it than that," one of his defenders challenged.

"Let me answer," John called as he stepped to Blair's side. John looked directly at the man who had spoken. "Nathan, you and I arrived here together. We came on the same wagon train. You, myself, and five other families, including Dowley, were the first settlers here. Now, I'm going to tell you all the truth." John paused, seeing everyone's eyes were on him. Constance smiled softly at her husband and nodded her approval.

"Martin Dowley did try to foreclose on Carl Blair. He wanted the property that is adjacent to his. That was why he loaned Carl the money in the first place. Dowley knew that Carl couldn't pay him back when he was supposed to. Dowley is sly. Although he dated the note for when he wanted, he told Carl not to worry. He would extend the loan for whatever time was needed. Martin Dowley called in that loan three weeks ago." A disapproving murmur swept the room, and John waited for silence.

"We know that we are all cash poor. Our lands, our property, our possessions and family are what make us wealthy. Only Martin Dowley is cash rich. We must all go to him if we need money. Three weeks ago, Carl was prepared to fight for his land. He was prepared to kill whoever came after him. But the man who was married here today, my cousin Kael Treemont, loaned Carl the funds to pay Dowley off. That is the only reason we are standing in this house today!

"Now," John continued after a long pause, "everyone here must assess themselves. You must prepare for the day Dowley calls in his notes. He wants to rule this territory like a king. Be warned. Be prepared."

"He's coming," Angela cried, bursting through the front

door. "Dowley and his men are almost here. I saw them as I drove in."

"Everyone! Listen to me. We must give Lara and Kael time to get away. Don't tell Dowley that they've left for the South Pass." Almost everyone nodded their heads in unison. Some might not believe what they'd just heard about Dowley, but they would give the newlyweds a chance.

Within moments, the thundering of horses' hooves announced Dowley's arrival. Everyone watched the front door open again as he burst inside.

"Where are they?"

John stepped forward, but felt the minister place a restraining hand on his shoulder. Jeremiah Bluetriech walked up to Dowley.

"They've left, Martin. We're all sorry you missed the ceremony. It was lovely," the minister said in a low voice.

"How dare you marry them without my permission? I'll see that you pay for what you've done. Do you hear me?" Dowley screamed.

"Now, Martin, please control yourself. Lara's of age, and Captain Treemont will make a good husband. Why, I do believe she'll flower in California."

"How long ago did they leave?" he demanded.

"What difference does it make, Martin, you won't catch them," the minister said calmly. "They're at least an hour ahead of you, and their horses are fresh."

"I'll get them, and this marriage will be annulled. You're fools. Do you realize what you've done? Do you?" Dowley raged. The faces that looked at him mirrored their disbelief. The kindhearted man they had always looked up to was gone, replaced by a screaming madman. Several of the women looked away, unable to accept their loss of respect.

"You'll be sorry when I've found them. Every last one of you will know what it is to make an enemy of Martin Dowley. Every last one of you!"

"You're on my property, Mr. Dowley," Blair said in a flat, cold voice. Dowley's face jerked toward the voice, and his small eyes widened. "I don't have any obligation to you anymore," Blair said as he cocked the rifle that was aimed at Dowley. "I want you and your men off my property, and if you come back, I'll kill you!"

"You'll never survive here, Blair, not without my aid," Dowley said, his calm apparently restored by the man's threat. Dowley's eyes went to John Crimmons. "You, too, John? I thought you knew the ways of life." Then Dowley's eyes moved to cover Angela Crimmons. They lingered on the young woman for several seconds before he turned his back to the crowd and stalked out.

Angela watched him leave, trying to stop the shivering his lascivious look had brought on. She felt her mother's arm go around her protectively, pulling her close.

"He really is insane," Angela said in a low voice. Everyone within earshot nodded their heads. A heavy silence hung over the room as people began to gather into smaller groups.

The sound of the departing horses lightened the air. Several families began to leave, and within ten minutes the only people left were the Blairs, the Crimmonses, and Jeremiah Bluetriech.

"I wish Kael and Lara safely to their destination," the minister said.

"With God's help and yours, they'll make it," John said with a smile he did not feel. "South Pass will put them three days behind."

"If you're right," the minister agreed. "But I pray you're wrong about your neighbor's greed."

John knew that of the twenty-odd people present when the minister asked them not to reveal Kael and Lara's destination, several owed Martin Dowley great sums. He would learn their supposed destination.

An hour later, Dowley and his small army were riding south. Cross had suggested that they look for trail signs once they passed the more populated area. South Pass City had been his guess as to the couple's destination. But Dowley wasn't sure. He was about to order Cross to split the men in half, one group to head toward South Pass, the other to scout the outlying areas, when he saw a lone rider cutting across a grazing pasture. Cross halted the men and waited.

Dowley smiled when he saw who it was.

"So, Nathan, you've decided to be smart," Dowley stated. Nathan Peck nodded his head slowly. "Well?"

"Tell the truth, Mr. Dowley, I heared some talk this mornin'. Before I tell you what you want to hear, I'd like somethin' in return."

A smile formed on Dowley's face; he knew what the farmer wanted. "I could foreclose on you, Nathan."

"Then you'd never know what I could tell you, would you?"

Dowley kept the smile as he lifted his hand and snapped his fingers. Lew Cross's pistol was now a foot from Nathan Peck's face.

Although the farmer paled, he did not back down. "Look up'n that rise," he said.

Dowley and Cross looked. Peck's twenty-year-old son and the boy's wife sat on horses, watching.

"What do you want?" Dowley asked.

"M'note canceled. Call it payment for information."

"You'll have to trust me until I get back. I'm not going to Valley City now to get the papers."

"'Tain't necessary, have'm right here," Peck said as he handed Dowley the note. Dowley took it, and also took the quill that Nathan extended with a smile.

"I suppose you have ink?" Dowley asked sarcastically. Nathan withdrew a chicken bladder and held it out. Angered, Dowley jabbed the quill's tip into the bladder, and watched with satisfaction as it poured its dark stain on the farmer's hand. Without looking at the document, Dowley signed it and noted that it had been paid in full.

When Dowley handed the paper back, his dark eyes glowered at the farmer. After Nathan Peck examined the signature, he smiled and lifted his hat to Dowley.

"They're going through the South Pass. 'Afternoon, Mr. Dowley." With that, Nathan Peck turned his horse and rode away.

"Stupid fool. He was better off before. Now I'll starve him out."

Lew Cross knew what Dowley was talking about. Peck's farm was next to Blair's. Dowley wanted them both. When Martin Dowley came back to Valley City, Peck would find all his credit at the stores gone, and the prices for whatever he needed too high to afford. Dowley would win, no matter what.

"Split the men up. Take the mountains. If you find them first, kill Treemont, then find me."

"Yes, sir, it'll be my pleasure," declared Cross.

"Don't miss them," Dowley warned. Lew Cross knew as he called the men to him that he had better be the one to find Kael and Lara. His future depended on it.

Coming down the north slope of the mountain, Lara reined the mare to a halt as her eyes filled with the spectacle below. It was at least ten or more miles away, but the awesome beauty was fully visible.

It was a butte, possibly the largest one Lara had ever seen. It stood tall and spurlike, at least a mile away from the nearest of the Owl Creek mountains to which it should have been attached. Its sheer face reflected the afternoon sun, its solitary beauty was impressive.

Painted Hawk dropped back to join Lara and Kael. "That is Crowheart Butte. We make camp there tonight."

"Why is it called Crowheart? This is still Shoshone land, isn't it?" she asked.

"Tonight I'll tell you the story."

Lara watched the Indian speed up until he was once more in the lead. She felt strange being surrounded by Indians, two in front and two behind. She also wondered about Painted Hawk. Since leaving home, she'd become aware that the

Indian was an unusual man. He spoke English more fluently with each passing mile.

When they had left this morning, Kael had explained that Painted Hawk would take them on the first leg of their journey, but would not accompany them further. The Indians would protect them, even after Kael and Lara reached the mountains, by guarding their rear against her father's pursuit.

They had been riding for hours when Lara had asked to stop so they could eat. Kael had gone to the packhorse and taken something from it. When he returned, he handed her a piece of jerky. With an apologetic smile, he explained that they could not rest, that they must reach the first campsite before dark. It was important for their escape. Lara had nodded as she looked at the dried piece of meat.

Seeing her expression, Kael had felt another stab of guilt. "I'm sorry," he'd begun, "I know a wedding day should be special, filled with friends and family, feasting and enjoying life."

"Oh, no," Lara had replied, "this is the happiest day of my life. I'm free for the first time. I wouldn't trade this ride, this meat, for the finest wedding feast in Wyoming. I love you, that's all I care about." And when he turned away from her, she saw the sadness in his eyes and felt bad. He wanted to give her what he felt she should have, Lara had reasoned.

"In California, my dear husband, you may give me a wedding feast. In California, you can make this wedding day return."

Kael had turned back to her, his eyes alive again, and a smile played on his lips when he spoke. "When we reach California, I'll give you a feast the likes of which you'll never forget!" Kael had declared in a voice louder than he had intended.

They were in the valley as she pushed the earlier part of the day behind. Kael rode several yards ahead of her, and Lara watched him as she rode. His back was straight, and his head high. He moved as one with the large stallion. The giant Andalusian suited Kael perfectly. She could see the muscles that covered his back through the damp material of his shirt. But she would feel them later, she knew. Lara was waiting for tonight, and she hoped the Indians would not be sleeping too close.

Feeling the wetness of perspiration as it rolled down her chest, Lara gave a silent thanks to Kael for the hat he had packed with the rest of the provisions. The afternoon sun was broiling in its intensity, and Lara felt she was its prime target.

Two hours later, with the sun almost hidden by the western peaks, the small party stopped at the bank of the Wind River. Here, the large river was narrower, and Lara realized that they were further away from Valley City than she had thought. The rushing water looked fresher, and she saw small trout swim past.

"Lara?" Kael called. She turned to look at her husband. He was still mounted, his horse standing quietly next to Painted Hawk's. "Painted Hawk is taking me to the butte. Would you make a fire so that we can eat when we come back?"

"Of course," she said with a smile. "What would you like me to cook?" Even as she spoke, Lara felt a flash of panic. The only dish she knew how to prepare was sweetbreads, which had been her mother's favorite. Since she had been a child, Lara had always had a cook. Even on the wagon train, cooking had been someone else's job.

Seeing her stricken expression, Kael smiled. "Kaniwa and Smooth Feather will catch trout. Why don't you just start the fire. When I get back, we'll bathe," he added with another smile, then watched Lara look at the Indians. Rather than add to her discomfort, Kael nodded to Painted Hawk and they forded the water and started toward Crowheart Butte.

Watching him go, Lara felt part of herself go also. When the two men became more distant, she turned to see what the Indians were doing.

Speechless, Lara watched as two braves strung their bows and slotted their arrows. The two stood motionless over the bank, statues carved of flesh. Suddenly, Lara heard one bow twang, and saw the Indian jump down to retrieve the arrow.

When he returned, a large trout with multicolored scales shining in the light wriggled helplessly on the arrow. As the Indian pulled the fish free, the other brave let loose his arrow, and followed, as it, too, impaled another trout.

Seeing the Indians in action, Lara forced herself to do her share. She turned and saw the third brave taking everything off the packhorse and tethering him. Lara began to forage for wood. There was much around, and soon she had a pile high enough to last several hours.

Lara laid out the kindling, covering the dry buffalo grass she had put down first. She remembered the many times she had watched the cooking fires prepared on the wagon train as she assembled the smaller pieces of wood, then built larger pieces over them.

When she was finished and satisfied, she realized that she had nothing to start it with. Going to the supplies that were on the ground, Lara began to search for the flint and striker. It was getting dark now and what she had been doing had kept her busy for over an hour. She knew she must find the flint quickly, or they would have no fire tonight. As she searched, her hand fell on a small leather satchel, which she held up. She saw Kael's intials engraved into the leather and began to open it. When she lifted the flap, she saw it was filled with papers.

"There!" Painted Hawk stated as he pointed northwest. "There, Treemont, is the path you follow. You see the river, how it winds like a snake?" Kael nodded slowly. "Near the headwater is the trail you seek. By the edge of the river, between two large mountain peaks, is your way. It is marked with five boulders, each one smaller than the one below it. That is where you turn into the mountains."

"I thank you, Painted Hawk," Kael said solemnly. The view from the top of the butte had been worth the climb. Kael could see the hazy tips of the Rockies in the distance. He saw, and memorized, as much as possible of the land between the butte and Union Pass.

"When you reach the first of the high mountains, do not follow the easy trail. That is the dangerous trail. The Crow, Arapahoe, even the Sioux call it their hunting grounds. Be careful, Treemont. Be wise."

"I will," Kael promised.

Painted Hawk stared at his white friend for a moment, then nodded. "Good. Look at map," Painted Hawk ordered as he pulled an arrow free from its quiver and knelt in the loose dirt of the butte's top. Slowly, he drew a map. Kael studied it, absorbing every line the Indian traced.

"When you cross into the high mountains, the first water you find will be at Fish Creek. Do not mistake a smaller stream. Fish Creek goes so." Kael watched the warrior trace a small "u" as he detailed the river.

"Why can't I cut across?" Kael asked, questioning the need of extra miles when the shortcut would save him time.

"Bear likes man!" Painted Hawk stated.

"Bear?"

"You call him grizzly!"

"We follow the water." Kael did not see the smile that creased the face of Painted Hawk as he completed the map.

"Follow Fish Creek until fork. Follow larger water until lake. Follow water from lake until it meets second river. Then you follow that to Snake River. You follow Snake River to its end!" Painted Hawk said as he stood.

"Again, I thank you."

"No. You are friend. You are on the blood path and I help. In two sunrises, warrior will go to Dowley. Tell him he saw man and squaw near Union Pass. Then you must be ready."

"I will," Kael said as his eyes went back to the distant, snow-covered peaks of the Rockies. "I will."

"What are you doing?" came Kael's angry voice as his hand pulled the satchel away. "Why are you snooping in my papers?"

Lara turned and saw the fury that filled his face and felt a shock run through her. "Kael, I'm sorry. I was looking for flint," she explained. "I didn't mean to pry."

Kael's face softened, and he drew Lara to him. "No, forgive me. I'm tired, and I'm not used to sharing myself and my belongings with anyone." Then, before she could say anything, Kael bent and brushed her lips.

She felt little shocks run from her mouth and begin to flame within her. She pulled back from Kael, and smiled.

"If you tell me where the flint is, I'll forgive you."

Kael bent, and opened a leather bag that had been next to the satchel. He pulled out the striker and handed it to her.

"Start the fire, woman," he ordered gently, "and when it's lit, join me over there." Lara followed Kael's finger to a bend in the river. The river itself was shielded by several high rocks.

"Yes, my husband," Lara softly replied. As she walked away, Kael's fingers went to the satchel. He opened it and looked inside. He knew he'd been in time, barely, and as his fingers touched the papers, he gave a silent prayer of thanks that he'd caught Lara before it was too late. Pulling his hand free, and watching Lara as she struck the flint to the kindling, Kael secured the satchel and put it inside another of his bags. Then, as he saw small flames begin to lick upward, he took a blanket and walked to the river.

Lara noticed him go and her heart raced in anticipation. Putting one final piece of wood on the fire, she stood, but waited until Kael had disappeared from sight. She was bothered by his sudden outburst. Why? Was he hiding something, or was it what he had said? Shrugging, she decided that he would have to get used to her soon. With that thought, Lara started walking toward the spot where she had last seen Kael. The Indians were moving to the fire, and Lara knew she and Kael would have privacy.

Twilight was peaceful as Lara removed the last of her clothing. She stood on the low bank and watched Kael standing waist deep in the river. As Lara entered the water, she felt small bumps begin to form on her skin in protest to the chill. By the time she reached Kael, her nipples were hard and she was shivering.

Kael drew her into his arms, pressing the heat of his body against hers. Lara reacted immediately. Hungry lips pressed against hers, fiery lances shot through her as she felt him harden against her. Slowly, Kael's body glided down, and his lips traced a burning path along her throat until they stopped at her breasts. Gently, Kael took each nipple into his mouth and kissed it. Lara felt his hands on her back, massaging gently, pulling her harder against his mouth.

Eventually, he released her and stood. In the darkening night, she saw him reach over to a jutting rock and lift something. Then Lara felt the slipperiness of caked soap being rubbed on her stomach. She smiled as she fought down her desires and let him wash her.

As their eyes adjusted to the dark, all Kael and Lara saw was each other. He lathered Lara's breasts, made her turn, and then washed her back. His hands roamed all over her, dipping into the soft, tender folds of her womanhood, and then moving upward to stroke her belly. When he was done, Lara took the soap from him.

"My turn," she said in a low, husky voice. Slowly, maddeningly, Lara began to wash Kael. She started at his shoulders, first rubbing the soap over them, and then moving her hands in small circles to clean him. Lara felt the power of his muscles with every touch of her hands. His chest, and the soft, furry mat that grew there, soon glistened with suds. His lean, hard stomach felt the lightness of her fingertips as they, too, traced lazy circles, freeing Kael from the grit of the day. Lara's hands dipped below the water, and Kael felt her grasp his hardness, exploring and learning more of her husband. As she felt Kael throb within her grasp, Lara slipped on the rocky river bottom.

Kael caught her, and they both went under, but Lara knew

she was safe as soon as she felt his arms around her. Standing, he lifted her and started toward shore. As he stepped from the water, he bent and kissed her. Without taking his lips from hers, Kael knelt as he lowered her to the blanket.

Feeling the softness of the wool beneath her back, Lara released her arms. Kael stood above her, a towering giant, with water cascading from his body. Opening her arms, she called to him.

Lara felt his weight descend upon her, felt his lips again on hers and all his male strength against her. Moving her hands along his back, she parted her legs and welcomed him into her.

Everything around them disappeared. There was no one, nothing in the world, except for them. Lara felt him deep within her, felt herself grow stronger with love, until she began to moan unknowingly. She felt Kael's chest against her breasts, and marveled at the sensation. Her hands dipped onto his buttocks, feeling their strength and power as he moved within her.

His lips against the skin of her neck was like the touch of a gentle fire. And all at once, Lara knew that it was more than just the lovemaking. Suddenly, she knew that she had chosen right. Loving Kael Treemont had been her destiny since the day she was born.

With a sigh of contentment, Lara let herself free. She felt Kael fill her fully, then felt herself begin to rise and move in perfect harmony with her husband. Opening her eyes, she gazed into his face.

"I love you," she whispered as her body peaked, and she felt Kael join her, filling her even more with his love.

Slowly, their bodies stopped. Kael remained atop her, supporting himself on his elbows. Lara moved her hands lightly along his back until they joined, and she pulled him tightly against her, uncaring of his weight.

She felt his lips kissing her eyes, cheeks, ears, finally stopping at her lips, where their tongues touched and tasted of each other.

Gradually, Kael lifted himself from Lara and rolled to her side. Lara turned, molding herself against him. "I love you, Lara. No matter what our future brings, never forget that."

A cold chill ran along her spine at his words. Kael felt it also, and he rose quickly and wrapped her in the blanket. As Lara lay within the warmth of her man-made cocoon, she watched her husband dress. She could not help the misting of her eyes as she marveled at his grace and handsomeness.

"Dinnertime," Kael announced with a smile as he handed her her garments.

"Kael . . . I can't wear those . . ." she said, wrinkling her nose. "Would you get me fresh clothing while I wash these out?" Kael smiled at her and left. When he was gone, Lara lifted the blanket and carefully wrapped it around her shoulders. Then she cleaned the shirt and camisole in the mountain water. When she was finished, she stood and turned, the clothing dripping water everywhere.

"Kael!" she screamed as she saw him standing behind her, watching in silence. "How long have you been there?"

"Long enough to enjoy what I saw," he answered as he reached for the wet attire. Taking the pieces in one hand, Kael gave Lara her dry clothing.

"Turn around so I can get dressed," she requested.

"What?" Kael replied as he stared at her.

"Turn around. It's improper to watch a woman dress."

"After what we've just—? Lara, we're married. Get dressed."

"Turn around!" she ordered again. Kael looked at her for a moment, deciding whether to humor her or not. "Kael, either you turn around or I'll walk back to the camp naked!"

"You'll do what? If you're embarrassed to dress in front of me, how could you parade naked in front of four men?"

"Kael, being naked and getting dressed are different. I like being naked for you. But when I dress, I like it to be private." As Lara spoke, she began to walk toward the camp. As she reached him, Kael put up his hands.

"Okay. Get dressed." He turned his back to her and laid

out her washing to dry. Lara dressed quickly, slipping on the buckskin pants and a heavier buckskin shirt. Even though it was summer, the night air was becoming chilly.

"Thank you," she said simply when she was through. Kael nodded. Another lesson learned.

Finishing the last of the fish, Lara sat back, contented. She had to admit it was the best meal she'd eaten since she'd left Philadelphia. Thankfully, Lara also admitted to herself that if she had cooked rather than Smooth Feather, no one would have eaten. But Lara had watched and she had learned. She only hoped her first attempt at cooking would be half as good.

The six people sat around the campfire, all enjoying the silence. The darkness was broken only by the stars.

"Tell me how Crowheart Butte earned its name," she said into the quiet, and seeking out Painted Hawk.

"Woman of Treemont, I will tell you the story, but you must promise to tell me what I ask of you." Lara looked at Kael for explanation. He only raised his eyebrows and shrugged. She turned her attention back to the chief.

"Agreed."

"You know Washakie, great chief of all Shoshone?" Painted Hawk asked. Lara nodded. "Not long ago, many Crow warriors, led by a warrior chief, came onto the hunting grounds of the Shoshone. They were not content just to kill elk and deer, but also stole many of our horses.

"Washakie was angered that the Crow would steal our ponies, and called together a small but brave band of warriors.

"Washakie chased the Crow for two days, until the cowardly Crow reached this butte. Here, Washakie challenged them to fight. But after a short battle, the Crow ran to the top of the butte. Washakie, a great warrior and a great thinker, ordered half his braves to gather the horses and take them and the animals the Crow had slain back to the villages of the Shoshone.

"Then Washakie and the warriors formed a circle around the butte, and waited." Painted Hawk paused for a moment as he looked from Lara to Kael. He saw comprehension on his friend's face and nodded.

"Three sunrises later, the chief of the Crow stood at the top of the butte. He knew his warriors would die without food or water, and knew also that if they came down, the Shoshone would kill them.

"The Crow chief stood tall and shouted mightily. He challenged Washakie to send any warrior he chose to fight him. The one who remained alive would decide the battle.

"Washakie is a great chief. He would send no man in his place. Angered that the Crow had taunted him, Washakie climbed the butte and met the Crow in battle. When it ended, Washakie stood above the Crow. The warrior was not yet dead." Painted Hawk paused again as he looked deeply into Lara's eyes.

"With his knife, Washakie cut into the Crow's chest. Then he held high the still-beating heart of his enemy. When everyone's eyes were upon him, Crow and Shoshone alike, Washakie ate his enemy's heart."

Lara's stomach knotted and she thought she would lose her dinner. But from the corner of her mind, another memory came forth.

"Washakie is not a young brave. How long ago did this happen?" she asked. Painted Hawk looked at Lara, and for the first time since she'd met him, she saw his lips form a smile.

"Two summers maybe. . . . Maybe one," Painted Hawk answered. "Washakie is brother of my father. Washakie has many years."

"If I am correct, Washakie is older than my father. Washakie has sixty years or more," Lara said.

"Washakie is a great chief. He has sixty winters, or more," Painted Hawk agreed.

"Were you there?"

"No."

"Do you believe the story?"

"This butte had no name until the battle," Painted Hawk replied, not answering her question.

"Do you believe the story?" she repeated.

"Every Indian nation believes it. That is what is important. No Crow, no Blackfoot, no Sioux come to Shoshone hunting grounds," Painted Hawk finished.

Lara maintained her silence.

"Now, I ask you," Painted Hawk said, reminding Lara of her promise.

"I will answer, perhaps truthfully, but I ask for something in return."

Painted Hawk glanced from Lara to Kael before he spoke. "Treemont. You be careful of woman. She not hear well. She think she can remake bargain in middle."

"Kael!" Lara appealed to her husband.

"You made the bargain, now live up to it," he said with a full-faced grin.

Painted Hawk studied Lara intently for a moment before he spoke. "Crimmons's daughter, Ang . . . Angela," he said, trying to pronounce the unfamiliar name, "she have brave?"

"No," Lara replied, as the smile that was on her face froze.

"She is very beautiful. Will her father sell her?"

"Sell her? Civilized people do not sell women. Women marry because of love, not because they are bought and paid for!" Lara declared in icy tones. If it had been daylight, Painted Hawk would have been warned by the hardening of her eyes, but it was too dark to see clearly.

"Your father sell you, no? If I make bargain with Crimmons man, Crimmons sell daughter to me!" Painted Hawk stated confidently.

Anger flooded Lara at his words. She didn't bother to think out what he'd said, and how right it must look to him. Starting to rise, Lara felt Kael's hand on her shoulder.

"Wait," he whispered. "Painted Hawk, my wife does not understand."

"I understand!"

"Be quiet," Kael ordered her, then spoke to Painted Hawk. "It is rare that a white man will trade a woman. Lara's father is not a good man. That is why he has tried to do this thing. But John Crimmons would not sell his daughter. If Angela loved someone, that man would receive her without payment."

"The white man's way is strange, and hard. It is easier to trade. Do you think Angela would find me unpleasant?" the Shoshone asked.

"I don't know," Kael replied honestly.

"Oh, no," Lara whispered. Both men turned to her.

"You think she not like Indian?" asked Painted Hawk.

"I don't know," replied Lara, "but I do know something. Kael, I forgot. . . . Oh, I'm sorry . . . I wanted to warn John. Last night, Father told me he was going to talk to John. He wants to marry Angela." The haunting look in Lara's eyes hurt Kael deeply. Was this another of her innocent acts? he wondered. Everything she did was at odds. She seemed to know everything, but it was always after the fact.

"John will not agree to that," Kael stated.

"My father has ways," Lara reminded him.

"Your father want to buy Crimmons's daughter?" Painted Hawk asked.

"Yes," Lara replied, "but he will not be able to."

"I will not allow!" declared Painted Hawk. Lara believed him.

The fire had almost died when they finished talking. Kael rose, pulling Lara to her feet. "We must sleep," he said softly.

Lara nodded, then turned to Painted Hawk. "Will you answer my question?"

"Ask."

"Do you believe the story?" Lara queried again.

"I am a Shoshone," Painted Hawk answered as he walked from Lara and went to his blanket.

"Kael," she said, "he's insufferable!"

"No," Kael said as he drew Lara into his arms and gazed down at her, "he's a Shoshone."

"*Ohhh!*" yelled Lara as she tried to pull away from him. Once again, Kael held her imprisoned within his grasp. Slowly, he lowered his mouth to hers, and tasted again of her sweetness.

"Come to bed, wife." And that night, under the star-clustered Wyoming sky, on the valley floor that separated two mountain ranges, Kael and Lara slept as man and wife for the first time.

Kael took the lead, Lara followed on the mare, and the packhorse brought up the rear. They rode at a fair pace as Kael picked out the trail through the heavy stands of trees that covered the mountainside. This was the third day of their journey; the third day of their marriage. It was the day after leaving Painted Hawk and his braves at Crowheart Butte. Last night they had camped near the headwaters of the Wind River. When the sun had risen today, Kael and Lara began their odyssey into the heart of the Teton Range of the Rocky Mountains.

Starting from Union Pass, they traveled westward, and by midafternoon were deep within the mountains. Kael was attempting to gauge how far they had come, and how much longer it would take to reach Fish Creek. He wanted to spend the night there, and also wanted to arrive with enough light left to fish for their dinner.

Because of the terrain, which forced them to ride in line rather than abreast, Kael was able to think without having to make conversation with Lara. For that, he was thankful. His mind was still a warring mass of thoughts. For three days, he'd called Lara his wife, deceiving not only himself, but her. For three days, Kael had been trying to temper his emotions, and use the logic that dictated the course he was now on. For three days, the weight of his guilt had ridden heavily upon him. Each hour that passed, each day that fell behind them, whispered to Kael that he was wrong.

This morning when he'd awakened and looked at his wife, his heart had almost stopped. Sleeping peacefully in the breaking dawn, Lara had seemed vulnerable and almost ethereal. Gazing at the woman his heart told him he loved, Kael began to feel a loosening of the restraints he'd forced upon himself.

Perhaps John was right; the daughter does not have to be like the father. He thought of all the evidence he had amassed against her. She had known who he was. If Lara had told her father, would not Dowley have gone after Kael immediately? Wouldn't he have tried to silence Kael, kill him before he reached South Pass? The foolish attempt near Valley City did not have the authority of someone desperately trying to kill him.

What of her warning? Lara had said that she tried to get a message to Angela. She had tried to warn John about Dowley's plan against Kael. For her efforts, Lara had been imprisoned. Had Kael, in his own way, dismissed that imprisonment, relegating it to Martin Dowley's fear of losing Lara before her marriage? Suddenly, Kael realized an even deeper truth. If Lara had told her father about him, would it not have been easier for him to have her lure him to a spot where Dowley's men could take him?

Why would she marry him? If she was what Kael thought, Lara would have been calculating enough to get away from him as soon as she was free from her father. Was she waiting until they reached California?

No, Kael reasoned, the ride across the mountains was too dangerous. If Lara wanted California, all she would have had to do was reach South Pass City. Hiding from her father, no matter how powerful he was, would be easy with her beauty. No, he decided, it was all in his mind.

While one part of Kael fought its battle, another part went back to that morning, and he again saw the sleeping form of his wife.

The sun had not yet risen, but the land was bathed in honey-hued shades of gold. Lara's shimmering hair was spread out beneath her head, and her lips held a faint smile.

He watched as she slept, watched the even rise and fall of her breasts through the cream material of the nightdress she had slept in. The skin of her face was smooth, and glowed in the early light. Kael felt his passion mount again, and lowered his head to gently kiss her closed lids.

The touch of her delicate skin against his lips sent a shiver of desire through him. Forgetting the need to break camp and start their ride, Kael began to trail his lips along her cheek, stopping momentarily at her mouth to brush against it lightly before continuing downward to her neck. He felt her stir, and saw her turn her head. His eyes fastened on the even pulse of the blue vein beneath her skin, and his tongue traced along its path until he reached the joining of her neck and shoulder. Kael's hands had begun their own movements, running lightly across Lara's stomach, rising up to caress her breasts, and feeling her nipples harden beneath the nightdress.

A low sigh reached his ears and he lifted his head to see Lara looking at him. "Good morning, my love," she said with a soft smile.

As their eyes held, he saw hers fill with a desire as urgent as his own.

They made love slowly, gently, keeping pace with each other until neither could halt the rushing tide that swept them to completion. When their lovemaking was over and Kael rested on Lara, held against her by her slim arms, he searched her eyes and was again reminded of the magnitude of what he had done.

* * *

"Kael, it's magnificent," Lara said. Her emotion-filled whisper pulled Kael from his thoughts. "My Lord, I've never seen anything like this before."

Neither had Kael.

Then he felt Lara's hand grasp his as they sat immobile on their horses. Spread out before them was a panorama few white people had ever seen.

Faraway stretched the mighty snow-capped Rockies. Their spectacular height and endless distance was overwhelming. Kael and Lara had ridden to the crest of a flat-topped mountain that was still below the timberline. All around them, and below, was lush, ripe, vegetation; spruces, lodgepoles, cottonwoods, pines, and white barks. Wildflowers, some that Kael and Lara could recognize, others that they'd never seen before, grew with uncontrolled abandon. Reds, yellows, pinks, and lavenders complemented the multishaded greens and gave a startling beauty to the land that surrounded them. The power, strength, and beauty of the Continental Divide's peaks, and the land that spread out before them, brought their own frailty into focus.

"Kael, I feel so. . . ."

"Beautiful," he finished for her. Then he kissed her quickly. "This is a gift, what you see around you. A gift given to few. What you see is beauty, freedom, and it is yours, for now and as long as we're here. It's a gift that will return whenever you close your eyes. You mustn't feel insignificant. Nature is a part of us, and because we can be awed by it, we can love it."

Looking into Kael's luminous eyes, hearing his words, Lara felt the overpowering vastness of the land lessen.

"Lara, deep within you, you have strength. These mountains require you to use it. Don't fear them. Give yourself to the land, to nature, and it will give you back a better understanding of yourself, a new and different strength," Kael said solemnly.

"You believe that," Lara stated in the same low whisper she'd first spoken with.

"I do. Once we've gotten through these mountains, we'll never be the same. We'll learn about each other and we'll need each other to survive. These mountains aren't cruel, but they'll be a hard taskmaster."

Lara watched him as he spoke, and felt the depth of his words. Their effect was sobering and she slowly nodded.

Two hours later, with the sun still above the western peaks, Kael and Lara reached the south fork of Fish Creek, and slowly wound their way along its banks until Kael found a protected site to make camp.

They were now deep in the mountains, and although Kael did not fear an Indian attack, for Painted Hawk had said that it was usually the early fall that found the hunting parties out, he wanted protection from beasts of prey. Cougars, bears, wolves, and many other animals could be dangerous to them, and their horses.

The campsite was almost cavelike, with two high rock sides that reached, trianglelike, to the edge of the creek. Approving the spot with a smile, Kael nodded to Lara as he dismounted and pulled his rifle free. Kael would fish, but not with bow and arrow. The shallow creek was fertile with large trout. Its very shallowness would allow him use of the rifle at a range that assured he would be able to make a clean kill.

As Kael walked to the water's edge and found a good spot to shoot from, he saw that Lara was already freeing their equipment from the packhorse. She had insisted on doing her share, and he was willing to let her. They both had to work hard if they were to reach their destination. Again, a smile played on Kael's lips. His thinking had changed drastically since the start of their trip.

Although the sun had not dropped, a cool breeze tugged at Kael, and he knew that the evening before was the last of the warm summer nights for a while. Beginning tonight, and until they crossed the Divide and reached the lower lands of Oregon, darkness would bring the cold.

* * *

Kael woke instantly on the morning of the fourth day. His mind was clear and alert as he listened intently for what had broken his sleep. His quick movement as he sat woke Lara, too.

"What?" she asked.

"Nothing," Kael replied. "Just my imagination. I must have been dreaming that someone was coming after us."

"I'm glad it was a dream," Lara replied, shivering in the cool morning air. She could not believe the difference in the temperature between her home and the mountains. It was close to frost this high up.

Kael stood quickly, pulling the blanket back over Lara. Then he put on his buckskin serape. "You rest. When the fire is ready, we'll eat."

She smiled at his words as she closed her eyes again. Five minutes only, she promised herself.

Kael bent over the wood, arranging it so that it would catch quickly, but his mind was still bothered by his waking reaction. He knew what it had really been. Every day since they'd left Painted Hawk, Kael had left obvious markings. A bold trail that could be easily followed by someone with experience. A trail that Dowley and his men would pick up and follow. But Kael had realized, after his deep introspection yesterday, that his vengeance was done. That he no longer had the burning need to face Dowley and destroy him personally. Dowley had been hurt, his punishment for his crimes had started, and Kael knew that it would not stop. The loss of his only daughter was just the beginning. Dowley would lose much, in his business dealings with the cattlebrokeer from Kansas City, and with the community that was learning who and what Martin Dowley was.

At the same time, Kael also realized that what he really wanted was to share his future with Lara.

He struck the flint.

Watching the first tendrils of smoke rise from the tinder, Kael decided that he must tell Lara the truth. He would accept whatever anger and hatred she would turn on him, and promised himself that he would prove his love and win hers back again.

The first red tongue sprouted, and as it did, a wave of dizziness engulfed him. Closing his eyes, Kael willed it away. It passed slowly. Then nausea rose: this too, he fought. Slowly, Kael stood. *I will not be sick!* he told himself, *I will not!*

That was Kael's only fear. Sickness in the wild would condemn both him and Lara to death. Alone, Lara would not stand a chance of finding her way out, and he knew she would not leave him to die alone.

He must cover their trail, Kael told himself as another wave of dizziness surged through him. When it passed, relief was etched on his features and he was glad that Lara was still in their blankets.

Lara was worried. Kael had been unusually quiet, and she did not like the way he looked. His eyes were slightly glazed, his face drawn. When she'd asked him, he had told her it was a headache. But he was not sitting the way he usually did as he rode the stallion, and his customarily graceful movements had been slow and awkward.

Lara decided to maintain the silence that Kael had wrapped himself in. She did not want to disturb him, but she still fretted. On top of that, he had insisted on stopping every half-hour in an effort to hide their trail.

"In case your father and his men find our starting point," he had explained. Lara questioned that remote possibility, and he had reminded her of her father's close association with Chief Washakie. Kael had said that Washakie could give her father a brave who would be able to track them. She understood the logic, but was puzzled by Kael's turning from her when he spoke. Intuitively, she knew Kael was holding something back.

But now, an hour later, Lara had decided that it was his headache that had made her feel that way. She knew several people who suffered from severe headaches; some gave in to them and hid from light for days, while others ignored the pain as best they could, going on with their work and life. She knew Kael was like that. He would disregard the headache, but she was determined that he should rest.

When they stopped for lunch, she would insist on making camp to enable Kael to rid himself of the headache. Lara would brook no argument today, and he would be wise to listen. With a smile, Lara nodded her head confidently.

By midday, they reached the fork created by the joining of the north and south branches of Fish Creek. Kael then started to follow the main body of the creek, which was now a frothing, bubbling rapid.

"When do we stop?" Lara asked plaintively.

"Hungry?"

"Starving," lied Lara. She was hungry, but it was becoming even more important to get Kael to take care of himself. She also realized that he was driven because of the pain, and any protest she made would fall on deaf ears. Once they came to a halt and his willpower was low, she would insist they make camp.

"We'll stop soon," Kael told her. Lara watched his back after he turned away. His eyes were heavily glazed and his face flushed. Alarm rose within her. Lara pressed her heels into the mare's flanks and rode next to Kael.

"We stop now!" she declared.

"Not yet," he insisted in a tight voice. "We need more distance."

"You can't ride any further. Kael, please. . . ."

"No!" He snarled the word, his face turning hard as he shouted. Before Lara's horrified eyes, Kael's amber eyes closed, and he slipped from the saddle.

Rushing panic filled Lara. She was frozen to the saddle, her eyes wide and her mouth open as she watched Kael drop to the ground. The sound of his body hitting the earth broke Lara's trance.

She shed the fear that gripped her as she jumped from Camilla's back to go to Kael's side. Turning him over, Lara saw his face was flushed bright scarlet by the fever that ravaged him. Setting her legs wide, Lara bent and slipped her hands beneath his shoulders.

Breathing deeply, she lifted and pulled Kael away from the horses. She half-carried, half-dragged him to the bank of the creek.

Quickly, Lara went to the packhorse and pulled a large blanket free. Then she ran back to Kael and spread the blanket out next to him. When that was done, Lara rolled him onto it and knelt next to him.

The horses would stay nearby. Major and Camilla were well trained. The packhorse was still tied to the mare and would follow her wherever she went.

With that knowledge, Lara's mind calmed, and she began to assess the situation. She lifted Kael's head and cradled him against her. Then she began to look him over.

Headache!

Now the word seemed to burn deeply into her consciousness.

First the headache, then the fever. No, Lara prayed, it was too late in the summer! No, please, no. . . . Fighting down a rising wave of hysteria, she began to examine Kael's scalp. Her fingers trembled with fear as she searched. When she had covered half the dark mass, she began to relax. The calm lasted only for a fleeting breath as her fingers touched something soft.

The blood drained from her face, and her breathing became ragged. Closing her eyes tightly and twisting Kael's unresponsive head further, Lara parted his hair and looked.

Biting her lower lip, she tasted the saltiness of her blood. She had found what she had prayed she would not.

Scooping some of the loose earth under the blanket, Lara formed a cushion for Kael's head. Only then did she gently lower him down.

Lara forced herself to regain control. Methodically, as she stroked Kael's feverish brow, she decided what she must do. She went to the horses. First, she removed their supplies from the packhorse and tethered him. Next, because she would be caring for Kael, and because she could not risk the horses wandering, she secured Major and her mare, attaching a rope to the stallion so that his grazing would be limited. Then Lara began to lay out their supplies. She worked quickly, everything she did accentuated by low moans from Kael's fever-racked body. When everything was unloaded and she knew the location of each piece of equipment, Lara gathered wood for a fire.

While the flames built, she searched for a suitable tool. Her eyes fell on Kael's hunting knife. Lifting it carefully, she inspected the blade. The shining steel reflected the bright afternoon sun. Its sharp point was needed. Bringing the knife to the fire, she rested its bone handle on a rock, letting its tip be licked by the fire.

As the knife heated, Lara checked on Kael. The tall man lay still, and she felt a lump rise in her throat. Her eyes filled with tears as she turned to look up at the blue sky.

"Please, don't let him die. . . ."

Lara wiped her eyes. She must remember what Kael had said yesterday. She must draw strength from the mountains that surrounded them. Lara's eyes were clear again. She walked to the fire, and to the knife that awaited her.

The headache should have warned her. And Kael's eyes. But Lara had not connected them. She knew that it wasn't her fault, and even if she had known what it was, she could not have prevented it. It had started days ago. Probably at Crowheart Butte. That would be an area that would hold them.

With the fever running rampant through his body and her worst fears now confirmed, Lara knew what had stricken Kael. She had seen it many times in the past three years, and she knew that only a few survived the fever. But Kael was strong and young, and those two things would help.

Carefully, Lara withdrew the red-tipped blade.

Once again, she lifted Kael to a half-sitting position, and then lowered him so that he was on his side, with his head securely on her lap. The glowing knife sat on another rock within her reach. Slowly, she parted his hair and found what she must destroy.

"It will be over soon, my love. Don't fight me," she whispered as Kael started to move. The sound of her voice soothed him, and he lay still again.

Picking up the knife, Lara brought it near his scalp. Carefully, she touched the brown-gray growth that was protruding from his skin. The smell of burning hair assailed her nostrils, but she held the knife steady. Suddenly, Lara saw the brownish body contract and she pulled the blade away. Swiftly, using the nails of her thumb and index finger, Lara pulled it out.

She held the small tick between her nails and searched for its head.

Wiggling at the top of the sac, the tick's head and small body showed it was still attached. Lara dropped the insect onto a rock, and placed the hot metal to it. Then she lifted Kael's head from her lap and returned it to the blanket.

Looking down at his face, Lara realized the fever was worsening.

Spotted fever was dangerous. But at least he was free of the tick that had caused it. It would help that his body would have one less battle to fight. The hours between now and tomorrow morning were crucial. If Kael survived them, he would live.

But the fever must be broken!

Again, she stood above him, her feet widely braced as she began to tug. Without hesitation, she dragged Kael into the cold mountain stream and sat, letting his head rest on her thighs as the creek's water began to draw the fever from his body.

Loud howling pulled Lara from her semi-sleep.

She was under the blanket, next to Kael, as she tried to sense how far the sound had traveled. Again, the loud and haunting call of the wolf shattered the night.

Lara rose and went to the fire, placing several more branches on it. When she saw the bark begin to smoke, she returned to Kael's side.

Darkness covered the sky.

For the first time since Lara had started her ride to freedom, she feared the night. Her only light was the orange glow of the fire. She had lost track of time while tending Kael.

She did not know how many times during the long afternoon she had dragged him into the cold waters of Fish Creek. With each submergence, his body had cooled, only to have the fever return again. Each time Lara had pulled him from the stream and dried him, she had done more around the campsite.

The high pile of wood resting a few feet from them would last until morning. Their supplies were close at hand, and Lara's eyes sought the rifle.

Kael's low moan sent a chill through her. She turned to him, and saw him shivering. Ten minutes ago, he had been bathed in sweat. Now his skin was covered with goosebumps. Once again, Lara opened the Indian blanket that was around her shoulders, revealing her nakedness.

She knew what must be done. She had been doing it since darkness and the cold night air had come. Lara covered Kael with her body, using her flesh to warm his and regulate his temperature.

The nighttime calls of wolves echoed in her ears, but did not sound any closer. Pushing everything from her mind, Lara concentrated on Kael. Soon she was rewarded as his body stopped its shaking and she felt his skin begin to warm.

When he was calm again, Lara drew away and covered him with the blankets. Wrapping her own small covering around her, she stood. They were extremely vulnerable, and she must not only tend Kael but keep the camp safe.

She walked to the horses and checked them. Then she took their only pot, filled it with water, and placed it on two of the burning logs. When it reached a boil, Lara took a small packet from their supplies. She smiled. Kael had thought of everything. Although there had not been much room, he had packed things that would be treats during the trip. The packet of dark teas had been one. Now, the tea was a necessity.

She put several pinches of leaves into the pot, and when she saw the water change color, she picked up two small, triangular-shaped leaves and dropped them in also.

The horsemint would be good for Kael's chest, and the tea would help warm him. Several minutes later, Lara removed the pot from the fire. Before forcing him to drink the tea, she poured some for herself and sipped it.

The sky was cloudy, and Lara shivered. Tonight was so different from yesterday. So many things had changed. Last night she had felt secure, loved, and protected. Tonight she was the one protecting, as she fought to keep herself strong, and Kael alive.

Lara wanted Kael's arms around her. She wanted to feel his

warm, hard body against hers. She wanted to hear his voice telling her of his love.

"Please, please, Kael, don't leave me," Lara whispered through welling tears. It was the first time she had allowed herself any emotion since Kael had fallen from the horse. It was the first time she had thought of herself. She would let herself cry now, and when it was done, she would go on.

Slowly, as her tears fell, she cursed the man who had forced this upon her. Martin Dowley was responsible for whatever happened tonight.

Several minutes passed before Lara regained enough control of her emotions to pour the tea.

Propping Kael against her chest and holding his head with her free hand, she put the cup to his lips. Patiently, Lara waited until Kael sensed the heat at his lips. Then, as his head moved away, Lara spilled a few drops of tea into his mouth.

Holding his head tightly, Lara let him cough. He seemed to awaken slightly as he drank the mint-flavored brew. It took a while, and by the time Lara had forced him to drink it all, the tea was cold. Again, she laid Kael on his side and pressed her body to his.

Exhaustion was overtaking Lara's willpower, and her eyes began to close.

"No! No! Father, no!" Kael cried. Lara jerked awake as the screaming words pierced her ears. Kael was writhing in his sleep. Even in the cold night air, he was sweating. He screamed aloud, crying and cursing. Lara felt his brow. It was hot to the touch.

The fever had returned and, with it, delirium. There was little Lara could do now except force Kael's protesting body to stay covered; the cold nighttime air would not do what the cool water had done earlier.

She moved to his head, lifting it so that it rested on her lap. She stroked his hair. She could do nothing else. Lara understood that Kael was reliving the murder of his father. Holding him, comforting him while he relived, over and over, the horrible tragedy that had robbed him of the parent he loved, Lara began to understand the depth of his loss.

She cradled his head in her lap until the first bands of light filtered into the sky. With the coming of day, two things had happened. Kael had stopped raving, and his fever had broken again. He was sleeping peacefully.

By noon, she knew that Kael would recover. As soon as she had seen the rash of red dots appear, she had breathed a sigh of relief. Almost always, if the person lived through the first day or two of fevers, he had a good chance of recovering. The onset of the spots signified the second phase of the sickness. Kael would be weak, and would have more sieges of fever, but none would be as severe as yesterday's.

It was time to get him to eat. He must get his strength back as soon as possible. Some people recovered quickly, in a matter of a few days; others took weeks.

On the fire was their single pot, its outside blackened from contant use. Water boiled and pieces of the dried beef floated within. She had searched the area around them and had found wild carrots and onions. Although neither would stand up to a housewife's scrutiny, Lara had put them in the broth. The onions were almost dry; another week would have found them withered and dead.

Lara tasted the food and wrinkled her nose at its ripe flavor. But it was better than anything else she had. It was liquid, and it had substance. Kael needed all of that.

While she let the broth cool enough for him to eat, Lara went to the creek and wet a piece of cloth. She returned to Kael and wiped his face. When she was done, she was rewarded by his slowly opening eyes.

He blinked several times before he could focus. Lara smiled as she watched his tongue moisten his lips, and heard him try to speak in a cracked voice.

"Sshhh," she whispered, "you'll be all right. You've been very sick." Kael nodded slowly.

"Headache's gone," he said in a gravelly voice.

"Can you take some soup?"

"Nothing . . ." he replied. Lara smiled again.

"You have to eat," she stated. Then she stood and walked to the pot. As she poured the soup, Kael tried to struggle to a sitting position. His body failed him, and he fell back.

"Here," Lara ordered gently, as she returned and sat next to him. She started to lift him but felt him struggle. She stopped and looked at him. "Please." Kael nodded his head.

Sitting, Kael smiled at her. His eyes were dull, but no longer glassy. She lifted the spoon and brought it to his lips. Slowly, Kael opened his mouth. It took her almost ten minutes to feed him. By the time she was done, Kael's eyes started to close. Gently, Lara lowered him to the blanket.

It was the only time Kael regained consciousness that day. The fever came and went in cycles, and by nighttime, Lara was completely exhausted.

Before allowing herself to give in to fatigue, she forced herself to eat more dried meat and several of the large, wild strawberries she'd found that afternoon.

Each foraging excursion Lara had taken had been close to the camp. She was never out of earshot, lest she miss a call from Kael. The strawberries had excited her, and she ate them with pleasure.

When Lara finished eating and fed Kael more broth, she knew she must sleep. Again, she removed her buckskin shirt and lay next to Kael, pressing her warmer body to his. As her eyes closed, she saw Kael awaken for a moment, stare at her, smile, then close his eyes. Seconds later, Lara slept deeply.

The second night of Kael's sickness passed quickly. Lara woke several times, and each time she checked him. Four times she had brewed tea and forced him to drink. Only once did Kael fall into a delirious fever, and that had passed quickly. By dawn, Kael's fever seemed gone, and his breathing was much improved.

By midmorning, she knew the worst was over. Kael would sleep for another day, and then would need at least two more days to gain strength. There had been only one brief episode, after she had fed him, when his mind had wandered and he'd spoken. It wasn't delirium, he just seemed to be carrying on a conversation with someone in his sleep.

Now that Lara was relaxed enough to rest on the bank of the creek, Kael's words came back.

"He's the one. He killed him. It took me a long time, but now I've found him!" Kael had said. Then he'd fallen silent. Seconds later, Kael had spoken again. "She had to know. She had to know about Dupont. She had to. . . ." Again, silence had followed this utterance.

"You owe it to me. You owe it to my father! I'll take her from him. . . ." After those last words, Kael had fallen silent, but this time no words followed.

Now Lara wondered if Kael had meant that he'd found the man who killed his father. A sudden thought occurred to her. Kael had not spoken of his father's death, or of his own need to find the murderer since that night he'd come for her. Why?

Had he found him in South Pass City? Had Kael killed him? Turning, Lara looked over at Kael. His face was smooth, and his chest rose and fell rhythmically. He was sleeping peacefully.

Who was Kael going to take from whom? Lara wondered. Then her eyes went past Kael, settling on their supplies. She had been so involved in tending him that she did not know what they had left, she was unsure what she'd used during the past two and a half days. Standing and stretching, Lara decided that she should take inventory.

The midafternoon sun warmed her, and another cloudless afternoon stretched out above the Rockies. Lara smiled as she walked to the supplies and began to check them.

First she determined how much food remained and saw that they had less than half of what they'd started with. Then she began to check each of the bags. As she opened one of Kael's, her eyes fell on the leather satchel that had his initials on it. Shrugging, Lara put that aside and went on with her inspection. When she was finished and had a good idea of the remaining supplies, Lara decided that she would wash their clothing.

An hour later, with the wash spread out to dry, she brewed more mint tea. She woke Kael, and in his half-stupor, he drank the tea without argument. Next, Lara prepared the ingredients for more broth for Kael's dinner. When that was done, she rested again.

The sun was still up when Lara awoke from her nap and automatically checked Kael. He was sleeping peacefully. She watched him, sitting at his side, and felt her heart quicken. Even with his face and chest covered with the red spots, there were few men who could match her husband's good looks. In sleep, she thought, Kael was beautiful, although she knew if she told him, he would be embarrassed. Men. . . .

Standing, her heart momentarily satisfied with the enjoyment of watching him, Lara went back to the fire. She placed the pot on the flames and started the soup. Then she looked around.

Her eyes fell on the satchel, and she reached for it. She did not wonder why, and was almost surprised as she opened it. It was as if the forbidden bag called to her.

Curiosity did the rest.

Feeling that it was time to learn more of her husband, Lara began to read the letters. By the time she had finished the third, she was trapped. She knew what she held was a detailed history of the last four years of Kael's life.

Letter after letter detailed his unflagging search for Ryan Treemont's killer. Letters from the government, letters from lawyers, and letters from the Pinkerton National Detective Agency.

They all seemed to say that Kael's money and efforts were being wasted. Lara paused in her reading to check the broth, and to wonder why the people that he hired had not seen the dedication that Kael had for what he was doing. Twenty minutes later, only two letters remained unread.

Lara opened the first one, and read Kael's lawyer's final letter telling of the sale of the Pennsylvania properties, and of the his failure to locate Malcome Dupont. A smile played on her mouth as she now realized where Kael's dress uniform and sword had come from.

The last letter was from the Pinkerton Agency. And as Lara scanned the report, she shook her head sadly. Then she saw the name Malcome Dupont, and began to read every word carefully.

Lara felt herself turn cold. She drew in her breath sharply as she read the last part of the report. When she finished, Lara's mind darkened.

Eleven riders reined in their mounts on a signal from the twelfth. They watched the bulky foreman and the Indian dismount to inspect the area.

When the Indian was finished, he looked at the dark-eyed man. "This called Union Pass by white man," he said in his best broken English. "Three horses go there," he stated as he pointed almost due west between two tall peaks.

Lew Cross looked at the same ground the Indian had. It had been a while since the others had passed here.

"How long ago?" Cross asked.

"Three day. Maybe four. They not make fast time from here. Trail hard. Not open land."

"Good," Cross said with a smile. Then he looked up at the sky. The midday sun beat down on him, but rather than be bothered by the heat, Cross knew they had five or six full hours of riding left.

With the Indian tracker in the lead, Cross knew they would make good time. His small army traveled light. They hunted game wherever they stopped, and the few supplies they carried would see them through. That, and the fact that they were not hampered by a pack animal, or a woman, made a big difference between his men and the two they sought. Cross knew they should have them by tomorrow night, or the morning after, at the latest.

Cross mounted again, and with the Indian in the lead, began to head out. Lew Cross felt good. He would have them both soon; Lara Dowley would be returned to her father, and Treemont would be dead.

Opening his eyes slowly, Kael felt as if a great weight were lying across him. His arms seemed leaden, and his legs refused to obey his commands. His vision was blurry, but he was able to make out different shapes in the fading light of the day.

Sick! Kael realized he was sick. Lara! He tried to move, but couldn't. Then his memory began to return. Kael tried to sit up, but a rush of dizziness swept over him and he let his head fall back.

His first memory was arguing with Lara. She had wanted him to stop and rest. He'd gotten mad, yelled, and then? Nothing. . . . Looking above him, Kael thought he must have been unconscious for several hours.

Slowly, and with great care, Kael raised himself up. In the dim light, he saw Lara, sitting near the fire, her back outlined by the orange glow. He waited until the dizziness passed before he tried to call to her.

"Lara," he said, but the only response was a strangled gasp. She had not heard him. "Lara," he called again, forcing strength into his voice, and was rewarded by seeing her stiffen slightly.

She stared at him for a moment before standing. Watching her as she walked toward him, Kael felt himself grow warm. Although he was weak, his mind was clear, and nothing of the headache that had dominated him earlier was left. His eyes played over her, and he wanted to tell her that he loved her.

As Lara bent over him, Kael smiled up at her. Immediately, he noticed her tight, drawn expression. The dark circles under her eyes told him that he'd been sick for longer than he had realized. It couldn't have been only hours ago that he'd passed out. Not with the way she looked.

"How long?" Kael asked.

"Two days," she replied as her hand went to his forehead.

After a moment, he felt her hand press more firmly on his head, and he let himself fall back. Her voice had seemed distant, and Kael thought it was from tiredness.

"I'm sorry," he apologized.

"Sorry?" A startled expression momentarily crossed her face, then disappeared as she spoke again. "For being sick?"

"For not being strong enough to fight it."

"You're only a man, Kael, men get sick," she said in a low voice. Her face eased, and her voice seemed warmer. "I didn't even know until this morning if you would make it."

Her words chilled him. "That bad?" he asked unnecessarily.

Lara nodded, then rose. "I'll be right back," she told him as she walked to the fire. A minute later, she returned with broth and sat by his head. She lifted him and let him lean on her.

Resting on her softness, Kael took comfort in her closeness as he tried to eat. His arm and hand would not obey him, and he was forced to let Lara feed him. Throughout the meal, he felt as though Lara were far distant from him, her mind on other things.

"Lara," he began after he had finished the broth, "thank you."

"Thank you? For what?"

"For caring for me."

"Isn't that what a wife is for? To care for her husband when he's sick? To make sure he's happy and does not suffer?" she asked. Kael was taken aback, not by the words themselves, but by the fierceness with which she spoke them.

"Then thank you for being my wife," Kael offered in a soft voice as he turned to see her better. He felt emotion almost choke him as he looked at her face. She had been crying when she'd answered him, and he'd not known it. Even in the darkness, he was able to see the glistening path the tears had left on her cheeks. With a determined effort, Kael forced his hand to her face.

"Why?" he asked, puzzled by her outburst and tears.

"I'm sorry, I guess I'm just tired," Lara explained. Then

she smiled and held his head as she moved away. Gently, she lowered him to the blanket. "Get some more rest," she said as she brushed his brow with her lips.

Kael heard her words as a faint echo. The effort of eating and talking had drained his weakened body. Slowly, Kael felt himself slip into darkness.

Walking quietly away, Lara tried to stop her tears. Damn him! she thought as she reached the fire. *Damn him, my stepfather, and all men!*

When Lara had finished the letter from the Pinkerton Agency, she'd felt her world turn dark. All her hopes and dreams, her faith and trust, had vanished with the last of the written words.

Martin Dowley was the man who had killed Kael's father. Martin Dowley, her stepfather. Again, Kael's earlier words, when he was delirious and when he talked in his sleep, resurfaced in her mind. Yes, Kael had learned who the murderer of his father was. And the woman Lara had wondered about, the one Kael said must know. It was she! Kael had been talking about her. He thought that she had known about his father's death.

Clarity filled Lara's mind, a crystal clarity of understanding. Everything fell into place. Kael had only married her to hurt Martin Dowley! Their strange trip northwest instead of southwest, Kael's certainty that her father would come after them, all added up to something that he'd planned. Kael wanted his revenge on Martin Dowley, and Lara knew she was part of that revenge.

White-hot hatred shot thorugh her as she finished analyzing what she had learned. Of course Kael had been angry at Crowheart Butte when he found her searching the satchel. Kael knew that if she'd learned the truth then, she would have left him as fast as she could.

Then she calmed. Two could play this game. Lara promised herself, then and there, that she would not return to her stepfather, nor would she be the bait for Kael's vengeance. A bitter laugh was torn from her throat at the thought of Martin

Dowley. Kael did not know that Dowley was not her true father. Lara had never told him. Would that have made a difference? Not any longer, she decided.

Occasionally, Lara stirred the broth as she developed a plan of her own. She would leave Kael and find her own way back. Not back to Dowley, but to South Pass City. There, with the gold sovereigns, she would buy passage back to the East. Back to Pennsylvania, and to the life and friends she had been forced to abandon.

Another thought rose, unbidden. She could not leave Kael until he was strong enough. Yes, Lara admitted that she loved him. No matter what she had learned today, Lara loved him fully. She had given him her heart, her soul, and her body. She knew it was real. She also knew she could never forgive him for his dishonesty, and especially for his lack of faith and trust. If he ever loved her, it had been before he'd known who Martin Dowley was.

Did he ever truly love her? Forcefully, Lara built her defense against Kael. She would care for him, not say anything to him until he was stronger. Hopefully, it would not be too long.

She would tell him when he was well. Kael Treemont would not dare prevent her from reaching her freedom and a new life.

Lara lost all track of time as she thought of the deception Kael had played on her. At one point, she had seen the broth boiling over, and had pulled it from the fire. Shortly after that, she heard Kael call her name. Fighting to control the raging hatred for his killing of her love, Lara had risen and gone to him.

Now, as the tears stopped again and Kael slept, Lara began to wonder if she could hold out. If she could stop herself from telling Kael that she knew about him. . . .

She must! Lara realized as she turned back to check on the husband she could no longer trust.

✳   ✳   ✳

Waking slowly, Kael opened his eyes to the first hint of a new day. His mind was alert, and his body felt lighter. He had slept peacefully through the night. Turning his head sideways, he saw Lara's sleeping form a foot from him, her back to his chest, her hair covering her face.

Slowly, he began to leave the blankets. Carefully, testing the strength in his muscles and trying not to awaken Lara, Kael stood up. This effort brought little dizziness, and he breathed a sigh of relief. He walked to the fire where several embers still glowed. He nodded and smiled. As tired as Lara had been last night, she had not let the fire die. Kael moved about easily, testing himself to see how weak he was. Then he went to the pile of wood and took several branches to put on the fire.

With each step Kael took in the cool morning air, he felt strength flow into his limbs. Next, he went to the supplies, taking fresh clothes and a cake of soap. Without disturbing Lara, he removed a single blanket from what had been his bed, and went to the creek.

Twenty minutes later, he walked back to the campsite. His eyes were sparkling and he felt healthier. With his bath, Kael had washed away any remaining doubts about his future. Today he would tell Lara the truth. Today he would put the past behind him, and be done with lies.

He owed that to Lara, that and much more. He owed Lara his love, his honesty, and his life. Reaching the supplies, Kael froze. A small rabbit stood on its hindquarters, not twenty feet away, fascinated by the leaping flames of the campfire. The rabbit was far enough away not to be frightened, yet close enough for Kael to see plainly.

Kael moved slowly, bending to reach for his rifle. Carefully, he aimed the barrel and began to ease the trigger back. The echo of the shot rang loudly through the mountains, and in its wake, Kael walked to the dead animal.

The sound of the gunshot startled Lara awake. Jumping up to see what had happened, she saw that Kael was across the fire from her and bent over something. She watched as he straightened and turned. She saw the game he held by its ears. Smiling broadly at her, Kael walked back to the fire.

"I thought you would be pretty tired of jerky," he said. Lara smiled at him, feeling a rush of excitement as her eyes took in his again-graceful movements. Kael was better, she said to herself. With that thought came the memories. Although the smile stayed fixed on her lips, the sudden rush of warmth that filled her left, and Lara turned cold again.

Lara concentrated on the taste of the rabbit. She had not realized how hungry she'd been for real food rather than the dried beef. Occasionally, she would glance at Kael. He was eating slowly, holding back what must have been a desperate need to eat solid food, so that his stomach would not rebel at the unaccustomed filling.

Finishing her meal and using her lips to remove the grease from her fingers, Lara went to the fire. She lifted the pot, and poured the last of the tea into two cups. It had bothered her to use the last of the tea leaves, but they had served their purpose well, and it was time for her to enjoy one cup without worrying about Kael.

"Thank you," he said as Lara placed his cup next to him. She answered with a smile. Then she sat and, sipping the drink slowly, watched Kael finish eating. When he was done and lifted the cup, he smiled at her.

"I love you," she heard him say as she watched his amber eyes glow softly at her. "Until this morning, I'd not realized just how much." Lara sat, almost mesmerized, as he stood and walked to her. With his words, her mind had gone blank and her body felt frozen. Fighting desperately to retain control, Lara watched him come closer. When he reached her, and put a hand on her shoulder, she could not hold back. She could no longer control the conflict that stormed within her. Searing anger flashed through her, wiping away his words of love as her hand threw his from her skin. Quickly, she stood and stepped away.

"Don't lie to me!" she screamed. "No more lies!" Lara watched his face change from tenderness to incomprehension. Trembling with rage, she waited for him to speak.

"How did you—"

"How did I find out?" Lara cut in. "I have ears. I have eyes. I'm not some stupid animal you found that follows you blindly. Or am I wrong, is that what you think? How could you do this to me? How could you?"

"Lara, let me explain," he asked in a low, steady voice. Lara saw he had recovered from his first shock quickly. She should have expected that.

"No. I don't want to hear your explanations. You used me to get even with my father. You lied to me when you told me you loved me."

"It was the truth!"

"No! You told me we were going to build a new life in California. You lied about that, and everything else." Lara ignored the tears that flowed down her face as she spoke. Her voice had gone from an accusing scream to a whisper filled with icy rage.

"I married you!"

"You lied about that, too! You married me to take me from my father. I heard you say so yesterday. 'I'll take her from him' was what you said. You said that I knew about my father. But you were wrong, Kael. You were wrong. I'm as much a victim of Martin Dowley as your father was, and you are!"

"Let me speak," he demanded, as he closed the space between them.

240

"There's nothing you can say, or anything I want to hear, that can change what you've done. I want my freedom. From you, from my father, and from anyone else who would use me."

"You're my wife," Kael said in a loud, hard voice. "Remember, you are now my wife!"

"In name only. I will no longer be your wife for anything else," she insisted.

"You can't change what's been done," Kael said softly. "You married me willingly, you took your vows and you will keep them."

"You lied to me. Your vows were lies. I will not honor a marriage born of deceit. It's over. When we break camp, I leave alone," Lara said in a hushed voice.

Swiftly, Kael closed the distance between them and grabbed her. He pulled her to him, and stared into the glacial pools of her eyes. His own eyes glowed with anger as he began to speak.

"You're my wife. If you don't want to hear what I have to say in my defense, then I won't waste breath on an explanation. But," Kael said in a steel-tinged voice, "you are my wife. You will not leave me!" Before she could prevent him, Kael crushed his lips on hers. She fought him, keeping her mouth in a tight, ungiving line, ignoring the sensations that flooded her, that threatened to weaken her resolve. Twisting away suddenly, Lara was able to break free of his grip. Only the fact that he was still weak from the fever that had ravaged him enabled her to escape.

"Don't ever touch me again!" she spat. Kael looked at her silently for several long seconds. Her breathing, ragged from her anger, returned to normal. Anger was her enemy, too, and Lara was determined not to lose control again.

Then he smiled and stepped back. "We'll break camp now. We've been here too long. It's dangerous now," he said as he turned to pack the supplies.

Defiantly, Lara glowered at him without moving to help.

"You can't go yet, you're too weak," she informed him triumphantly.

"There's no choice. Your father and his men will catch up with us soon."

Lara did not question his certainty, she was sure it had all been part of his plan. Kael glared at her menacingly as he waited for her to join him.

When he realized she would not, Kael grabbed her arm. Lara felt his fingers close cruelly. Although she tried, she could not break his grip.

As his hand closed even tighter, he said quietly, "You will listen to what I tell you, and you will do what I say." Forcefully, he threw Lara down on the blankets. "Pack them!" he ordered.

Her eyes shot lances of anger as she twisted on the blanket to look at him through wildly disarrayed hair.

After another minute of glaring, Lara began to move. She was filled with rage, but she was also powerless. Now her mind was made up. At the first opportunity, she would escape. She would avoid both Kael and her father, and become free. Slowly, Lara stood up and began to pack.

"What's wrong?" Cross asked as the Indian walked back toward him.

"They hide trail. Harder to find."

"You lost them?"

"No lost. Trail take longer to find. I no need tracks, plenty of sign tell where they go. We close." Without speaking further, the Indian went to his horse and mounted it. Although his expression remained unreadable, the scout was puzzled by what he'd found.

As he started his horse forward, Smooth Feather thought about what he was seeing. Painted Hawk had told him that the man wanted to be found. That a plain path would be left, an easy path for a white man to follow. The markings were being hidden now, and he wondered why.

Smooth Feather was the best tracker of his village, and the hidden trail he followed was easy to read. Although he could have gone faster, Smooth Feather had a feeling that the white friend of Painted Hawk needed more time before he faced his enemies. Acting on intuition, Smooth Feather kept the group moving at a slow pace, ignoring the anger in the dark eyes of the leader. They were at least one full day behind, but Smooth Feather did not know exactly how close, since the dry weather kept markings and tracks fresh for a long time.

Lara watched Kael's back as he rode in front of her. They were following the main body of Fish Creek, and because there were no big mountains to climb, they were making good time. Patience, Lara cautioned herself, patience. Let him relax, let him drop his guard. With a smile Kael could not see, Lara nodded her head.

When they stopped to rest the horses and eat their midday meal, the pall that had hung over them continued. When they started out again, and throughout the afternoon, the silence went on unbroken.

Lara knew that Kael must be tired, but this time she did not ask him to stop. Let him decide when, let him decide where, she thought.

But she was tired herself. They had ridden for another five hours after eating. Now the sun was dropping, one edge of the red ball was already behind a tall peak as they came through a thick stand of cottonwoods.

After they broke clear, Lara's eyes saw a lake before them. It was wide and long, with streaks of red from the setting sun reflected in long fingers across the surface of the still waters. The blue lake looked deep and inviting as they rode to its edge.

Twisting in the saddle so that he faced Lara, Kael spoke. "We'll camp here for the night." Then he slid from the gray stallion and went to her. He untied the packhorse's lead, and walked the laden animal to a small tree. After securing the horse, he began to unload their supplies. Several minutes later, Lara joined him.

"Gather wood and start the fire," Kael ordered. "I'll see what I can find for dinner." She looked at him, then nodded. She was surprised. They had ridden all day, and she knew Kael was tired, but his strength had returned. He seemed fresh as he moved easily through his chores.

"Whatever you say," Lara said in a flat voice, "husband!"

Kael accepted the word the way he would a slap. His eyes flared, and she saw the muscles in his neck bunch.

"You seem to have made up your mind to hate me. Although that's your right, remember, Lara, that we still need each other if we are to survive out here. Hate me if it suits you, but do not fight me."

"Whatever you say," Lara repeated in the same dull, flat voice. Watching Kael walk away, she saw that his anger made him walk stiffly, his back held ramrod-straight. She watched as he took his rifle and disappeared into the nearby trees.

Shrugging her shoulders, Lara began to forage for wood. As she did, her anger diminished and the emotions she'd held back throughout the day began to break free. Shoring up the determination within her tired mind, Lara forced them away. She would not weaken. She would not!

The darkness that was descending on Kael and Lara had also stopped the twelve men who had reached the campsite that Kael and Lara had left that morning. Smooth Feather examined the ashes of the dead fire and looked at the evidence that surrounded him. The man and woman had been here for several days, and had left today. Perhaps it was his primitive senses that told him, but Smooth Feather knew one of them had been sick. Now he understood why the trail had been covered. The man had, indeed, needed time.

"Well?" came the rough voice of Lew Cross.

"One day. They leave here today." Smooth Feather would not lie. It was too plain to see. "Tomorrow we catch them. They follow creek to lake. It only way," he explained to the

244

foreman. And tomorrow, when Smooth Feather led them to the white friend of Painted Hawk, he would blend into the trees and be gone. The white men would fight without him. Painted Hawk had ordered that. One more day and Smooth Feather would be rid of the men he did not like.

As the Indian went to his mount, Cross's eyes were on the night sky. Soon I will have you, he thought. Since this afternoon, when the idea had hit him, Cross knew what would happen. Martin Dowley's fine daughter would no longer be a virgin, and Lew Cross would have no fears. He, too, would have her.

Kael had hunted well. Lara finished the last of the meat, and sat back to stare quietly into the fire. Earlier, Kael had returned with three rabbits he had killed for dinner. Lara had prepared them, after he had shown her how, and then she watched him cook them. Everything had been done in a deafening silence, accented only by the calls of birds, insects, and wild animals. As the night progressed and their silence continued, the sounds of nature seemed to grow louder with every passing minute.

Keeping her eyes on the dancing flames, Lara heard Kael stand. He would check the horses now, she thought, after which he would add more wood to the fire. Then, finally, he would go to sleep.

She felt rested, sitting on the soft earth. The chill of the night air was balanced by the fire. The weighted tiredness that had plagued her in the late afternoon was gone; although she was tired, she also felt restless.

Turning, Lara watched Kael bring the horses nearer and tie each to a different tree. She realized he was taking no chances with the animals. Next, he went to their supplies and packed most of them away, leaving only the essentials for the morning.

"Is it necessary to do that tonight?" she asked.

Straightening, Kael looked at her. "If your father and his men are near, we'll not have much time." Then he continued working.

Lara stood and stretched. She walked over to the blankets she had laid out earlier, and picked up her nightdress. Although she had slept in her buckskins during the past nights because she had to care for Kael, Lara was uncomfortable in them and preferred her regular sleeping garment.

Walking far from the fire, Lara quickly shed her leather clothes and put on the long nightdress. When she returned, she saw that Kael had added more logs to the fire, and now moved to the blankets. Once there, he turned and saw Lara walking toward him.

"You look lovely tonight, wife," he said with a strange smile on his face. Rather than answer Lara moved past him, bent, and picked up a blanket. She stood straight, staring defiantly into his glimmering eyes.

"Where are you going?" he asked in a low voice.

"To sleep."

"Standing?" he asked with another smile.

"I'll sleep where I want, and how I want," she informed him in frigid tones. Then, turning from him, Lara walked closer to the fire and spread out the blanket.

"You are my wife," Kael said as he came up behind her, "and you will sleep by my side."

"I sleep where I please," she retorted angrily, refusing to face him.

"Lara," he said, his voice filled with unexpected tenderness. She turned then, fighting the moisture that filled her eyes. "Lara, come to me, my love. I love you as I have never loved another. You must believe that."

"You lied to me from the first. I never know when you speak the truth," she said in a subdued voice. Lara fought a battle again, deep within her, a battle of heart against mind. When Kael had spoken her name so softly, and when he told her he loved her, her already unsteady defenses threatened to crumble. But she understood what was happening within her, and understood also that if she gave in it would be for the moment only. She could never trust someone who had deceived her as Kael had.

"Lara," he called again in a deep but gentle voice. She shook her head quickly.

"No, Kael." Then, without looking at him, she lay down on the blanket and stared into the flames.

Kael watched her, his sadness and anger combining to make him ache for the woman he loved. He feared he was losing her, even though he knew she loved him. He had been wrong, and he had tried to tell her. She wouldn't let him, and that made it worse. Quietly, Kael went back to his blankets.

He sat watching Lara for a long time, studying the silhouette that he knew was not sleeping. Although his body had been weakened by sickness, he had regained most of his strength. With it had come a resurgence of the desires that had been flooding him since he first set eyes on her. Had not two months passed? Kael asked himself. He felt that he'd loved Lara for years. He fought against the desire, but as his eyes continued to trace the soft blanket-covered curves that were outlined by the fire, his body cried out for her. When he'd promised himself to tell Lara the truth, he'd also vowed that he would win back her love.

Could he, or would Dowley and his men find them first? He had wanted to meet Dowley on his own terms, but had rejected that plan in favor of reaching California with Lara. Now, neither might be possible. He did not want to lose her, he did not want Lara taken from his life.

With a desperation born of love and need, Kael rose and walked toward Lara's reclining form.

She heard his footsteps, although he wore no boots, and she closed her eyes, feigning sleep. She sensed him standing above her, gazing at her. Then she felt the heat from his body as he knelt behind her; his knees on the ground, his thighs against her back. A flash of desire flooded her, but she forced it away. Then she felt his warm breath near her neck and knew he was going to kiss her.

Moving with all the speed that anger and uncertainty lent her body, Lara rolled away from him and stood. She stared down at the kneeling man and saw the surprise on his face.

"Stay away from me, damn you!"

"Why? You love me," Kael stated confidently as he rose.

"No!"

"You love me," he said again as he, too, stood, towering over her.

"No!" she vehemently denied again. Turning from him, Lara began to run. A heartbeat later, Kael caught her in one of his iron-strong hands. She turned suddenly, her hand flying upward. The feel of his face against her open palm was painful, and she gasped at what she had done.

He stared at her with no change of expression. It was as if he'd not felt it. Then she saw the desire that radiated from his eyes.

"No, damn you, no!" she screamed at him. She tried to pull away but could not. Slowly, Kael drew Lara into his arms and closed off all escape.

"Lara, you're my wife," he said as he brought his lips against hers. She fought him, ineffectively kicking him, hitting him with small, balled fists until she realized the futility of it.

She felt herself lifted as Kael began to walk to the blanket. He lowered her tenderly, all the while gazing into her eyes.

"Stop fighting me," he ordered. Lara lay still, her breasts heaving from her exertions. Hatred filled her eyes, the loathing within them making the light blue orbs even lighter. Kael did not care as he began to pull his shirt over his head.

Seeing the shirt cover his face, Lara reached for the rifle that Kael had left next to the blanket. By the time he had the shirt off, Lara had the barrel raised, and he faced the barrel of his own weapon.

"Will you shoot me?" he asked with a sad smile.

"If you come one step closer, Kael Treemont, I will blow your head off!" she answered defiantly.

"Only one step? A condemned man is given a full walk before he's executed," he said as he took a step closer to her.

"Stop!" Lara screamed the word. He stopped. Then, before Lara's stunned eyes, Kael began to remove his buckskin pants. "Stop that!" she commanded again.

Kael ignored her command as he continued to undress. When he again faced her, he stood naked. She stared at the tall, muscular man who was standing before her, his magnificent body alive with the reflected light of the fire. She felt her mouth go dry as she watched him.

"Why did you do that?" Lara asked in a wavering voice.

"I want you to remember me, not my clothing, after you've killed me," Kael answered. Suddenly, she realized he was moving again.

"Please don't make me shoot you," Lara pleaded as her finger began to pull on the trigger. Kael only smiled at her.

Lara felt her strength begin to ebb. "No!" she shouted, and took a deep breath. She saw him dive at her. His hand grabbed the barrel, ripping the rifle free. Then he was on her, covering her body with his, as his lips sought hers.

Lara was trapped beneath him. Her breath left her as his body pressed on hers. His lips were against hers, and his tongue pushed passed her teeth. Fighting desperately, she began to hit his back.

Kael ignored her ineffectual blows as his desire mounted higher. His tongue forced itself into her mouth, searching for hers and finding it.

Burning, lancing heat pressed against Lara's skin, and she realized her nightdress had ridden to her hips. She felt Kael's skin against hers, felt his male hardness pressing against her thighs and his lips searing hers.

She grew weak, and her resistance ended. She began to cry quietly, the tears running from her eyes and trailing into her hair. The tears stopped as she realized her own body fought her as strongly as Kael. Slowly, Lara relaxed and let her mouth mold against his. She felt him pause before darting his tongue inside her mouth again.

The weight of his body lessened on hers as he shifted slightly. Her own hands began to stroke his back, and her hips pressed against his in desire.

Kael pulled his lips from hers and traced them along her neck. Soon his mouth was on her breast and she felt its moist heat through the nightdress. His hands roamed freely, caressing her skin, rubbing it lightly, darting everywhere. Then he moved again, and Lara felt his lips and tongue on the tender-soft skin of her belly. Daggers seemed to pierce the skin, hot flashes ran rampant through her, and her mind lost all thought except for the touch and feel of him.

Feeling her nightdress move upward, Lara lifted her arms and shoulders. Kael slipped the gown off but did not let her lie back. He pulled her to him, crushing her breasts against his chest, kissing her deeply as his hands ran over her back. Then his mouth again trailed along Lara's neck, dipping lower until he let her drop back slightly. Kael took one of her hard nipples in his mouth, and Lara moaned with the pleasure of it. Her back arched, and he pressed his face between her breasts, breathing deeply of the scent of her skin. Gently, Kael lowered her to the blanket.

He was kneeling above her, gazing down at her, and she saw the desire and love that filled his eyes, that controlled every handsome feature on his face. She opened her arms to him, and Kael smiled.

"I love you," he said as he bent, avoiding her arms, and tasting her breasts again. Never had she felt such raw desire surge through her. Every nerve ending screamed for Kael's touch. Every inch of her body craved him, needed him, wanted him. She moaned loudly again, as Kael's mouth drew a path from her breasts to the downy softness that was the covering of her womanhood. Lara felt her thighs tremble as his lips ran across them, she felt his hands go under and lift her to him. She felt the hot tip of his tongue as it tasted of her deepest treasures. Then, slowly, his mouth began to trace its way upward, biting and caressing along her stomach, breasts, neck, until it returned to her mouth. As he kissed her, he eased between her legs. Lara felt him enter her, felt his hardness penetrate, and felt herself push against him, trying to pull him completely within her. There were no easy movements, no pacing, no soft and gentle lovemaking. Lara moved with Kael, moved against him, felt him cover her, felt herself grow tight around him.

Her head moved from side to side, as sharp, staccato moans of pleasure filled the night. She heard Kael's voice join hers as they drove each other past the point of restraint, and reached the climax of their lovemaking together.

Lara's legs wrapped around him, Kael drove deep within her and then stopped. Their breathing was loud in their ears. They lay still, locked together, muscles trembling against each other until their breathing returned to normal.

Slowly, Lara unwound her legs and let Kael free. He kissed her tenderly, letting his lips barely touch hers as he lifted himself and lay next to her. She turned from him, pressing her back to his stomach and chest.

"Lara. Love. Listen to me." She turned her face further into the blanket to hide her tears of shame. She had reacted to him instead of fighting him. She had let her body betray her. Her heart had controlled her, and that was wrong.

"I love you, Lara. You know I'm speaking the truth." And she realized he was. But she also knew how she felt about him. She loved him, but that was no longer enough.

"I know," she admitted, "but it doesn't matter. It's too late."

"Damm it, woman! Nothing is too late."

"Some things are," she said in a sad voice that contained a final acceptance.

"As you will," Kael said gruffly. "But if that's the truth of it, then there's something you should know."

"I'm not interested."

"You should be," Kael said as he grabbed her shoulder and turned her to face him. Lara saw that his rifle was in his other hand, but felt no fear. "The next time you mean to shoot me, or anyone else, cock the hammer!"

Lara stared at him, then at the gun. She'd been so afraid of him, and so afraid that she might shoot him, that she'd forgotten to pull back the mechanism. Relief flooded her.

Although she'd actually tried to fire the weapon, she'd not been able to. Tears rolled from her eyes as she stared at the rifle. Her shoulders shook, and her sobs grew louder.

He pulled her against him, letting the weapon fall to the ground, forgotten, while he tried to comfort her. Eventually, Lara's sobbing stopped, and Kael pulled slightly away.

"Lay back, my love, it's time for sleep."

Lara nodded as she lay down. She turned her back to Kael when he rested beside her. But she could not stop his arm from circling her, nor could she find the strength to move his warm hand from her breast. Slowly Lara felt her eyes grow heavy, and she slipped into a world of dreams.

The lake was two hours behind, and Lara had yet to break the silence she had imposed since leaving. She could not dampen the rising sense of defeat because of her weakness. Lara had awakened before Kael this morning, and had bathed in the cool lake water to try and wash away the memory of last night. When she had returned to the camp, she'd gathered what few things of hers had not been packed already and secured them within the bags. She was aware of Kael's eyes on her as she went about her duties, but was thankful he'd not spoken.

Before starting, Kael had brewed tea from local herbs he'd found in the woods. When he handed the cup to Lara, she took it without comment and drank. The licorice flavor of wild anise rose from the misting steam to greet her nostrils, and at the same time, she tasted the horsemint that had been added. But when Kael had given her some of the cold rabbit meat, her stomach convulsed. Shaking her head, Lara turned from him.

"Lara," he said in a quiet voice, "we need to discuss what happened."

"I don't wish to discuss it," she whispered.

"I do!"

"Then discuss it with your horse!" Lara had declared as she stalked away. Standing on the dark, soft earth of the lake shore, Lara had looked out over the water. Mountains, high, bold, and powerful, loomed close—the last wall of the Continental Divide. Until she'd awakened this morning, the mountains had been a hazy, wavering line in the distance. Lara had realized that she and Kael were almost there. Once into the rugged mountains, she knew she would not be able to return. She would have to go on, and then?

She should have felt the thrill of excitement to be finally near the edge of freedom from her father, to be with the man she loved and had married. But it wasn't real, and the wall of mountain that had stood before her was only another wall of a prison.

Feeling the mare break stride, Lara was pulled back into the present. Her eyes were again filled with Kael's back, until they finally moved past him. Drawing in a deep breath, Lara almost gasped. The rocky mountains of the Continental Divide had grown even nearer. By nightfall, they would be at the base. The sheer power, height, and menace of the forbidding mountains chilled her. Her eyes went to one of the mountains, then trailed upward along its face. Up past the timberline of green, following the red, gray, and brown rock until her eyes reached the line of white. Lara's eyes continued traveling along the snow until she saw the peak itself, faintly showing through a billowy cloud.

Determined, Lara looked away. They would stop in a while, to rest the horses and to eat. Her stomach growled at the thought, chastising her for having refused breakfast. Her body did not follow the dictates of her mind, she realized, with the first trace of humor she'd felt since yesterday.

"They leave today!" Smooth Feather stated as he shifted through the dirt that had been used to put out the fire. It was midday, and the Indian and the eleven men who followed him had ridden hard. They'd covered the distance from last night's camp to this spot at the lake in less than five hours.

Lew Cross stooped down to feel the ashes for himself. "Today," he agreed with a smile. Smooth Feather looked into the man's face and then away. Rarely had the Indian seen such hatred.

"They camp at foot of mountains when sun go down," said Smooth Feather as he glanced toward the towering rocks.

"Why stop there today?" Cross questioned, his eyes locking with the Indian's black ones.

"They camp before dark. Need rest, must be strong when enter high mountains. Must not be tired."

"Then we'll get them tonight," he said. Smooth Feather knew the man was not speaking to him or the other men, only to himself.

Cross waited until his men had eaten their jerked beef, and the horses had drunk their fill. Then, with a triumphant grin, he signaled his small army forward. Everyone was ready; they knew their job was almost over.

Kael and Lara followed the small river that flowed from the lake as they made their way to the mountain base. By midday, he'd known they would reach the first part of the Divide by late afternoon. Knowing that he must move fast, lest Dowley catch them, Kael continued on for another hour. By midafternoon, he knew they must stop to rest the horses.

Signaling to Lara, Kael halted the stallion. He dismounted and loosened Major's cinch so that the horse could drink and graze comfortably. Then he did the same for the packhorse, while Lara saw to her mare.

The tall, well-muscled man, and the smaller, long-haired woman, sat by the edge of the narrow river and ate their meal of dried beef. Kael's eyes swept over Lara, and only occasionally did he glance back in the direction they had come from. After an hour, he stood.

"It's time," he said. Lara rose, too, and watched him go to

the stallion. He took his and Lara's canteens, and went to the
river to fill them.

Watching him kneel by the water, Lara realized this might
be her one chance. looking around, she saw a tree branch
lying nearby.

Swiftly, Lara picked it up. Quietly, she walked up behind
Kael.

Lifting the limb as high as she could, Lara let it swing
downward, using all the strength she could summon.

The branch's arc ended on Kael's head with a loud, thunking
sound.

Lara stared, horrified, as she watched him fall to the ground.
Reacting immediately, she dropped the branch as Kael's face
sank into the river. Grabbing his booted feet, she dragged
him back onto the ground.

Kael was unconscious. The water had not revived him.
Now, another worry assaulted Lara. Had she hurt him badly?
As she bent forward, she gave a sigh of relief, seeing Kael's
chest rise and fall slowly. Then she checked his scalp, and
found the rising lump. He was alive. He would be all right.

Using all her strength, Lara dragged him to a tall cottonwood and propped him against it. Then she brought his gray
stallion to the tree and tied him to it. Working swiftly, she
took enough of the dried beef to last her five days, one
blanket, and a small bag that held some of her things. She
attached all of these to Camilla, and mounted the horse. She
sat in the saddle, ready to leave, but could not put her heels
to the mare's flanks.

Gazing down at the unconscious figure, Lara began to cry.
"I'm sorry, my love. I truly am. I love you, but I must have a
life of my own with someone I can trust. Goodbye, my love.
Be safe. . . ." Sobbing the final words, she dug her heels into
the mare's sides. Moments later, she was loping eastward.

It was close to a full hour before Lara felt the clean air of
freedom. It had taken her nearly twice as long to calm the
aching in her heart and to almost accept the decision she'd
had to make. Trying to push away invading thoughts of Kael,

she concentrated on the job ahead. Traveling five days through unpopulated territory, avoiding animals, trappers, Indians, and her father was paramount in her mind. The immensity of the task did not prevent her from thinking it through.

She would not stop at last night's camp, but push further along during the twilight hours. She could even ride by starlight if she had to, because following Fish Creek would guide her out.

When she reached Crowheart Butte, Lara wondered what she would do. The logical part of her mind supplied the answer. The Crimmonses would hide her from her father until passage East was arranged. Suddenly, another thought struck her. She could not go to the Crimmons's ranch. They were Kael's kin! They had to know what he'd done, and why. Or . . . did they?

Vividly, Lara remembered her wedding day. Angela had been radiantly happy for Lara and Kael. No, Lara was certain that Angela had not known what Kael was doing, and she was equally certain that Constance knew nothing, either. John. Perhaps John knew . . . If either of the women had known, they would not have allowed the marriage to take place.

Lara's mind cleared as her final solution presented itself. She slowed the mare, her eyes looking around to see how far she'd come. Lara felt uneasy for some reason. She stopped her horse.

Silence.

The usual noises of the mountain country were gone. Lara heard nothing—no birds, insects, or animals.

Nothing.

She felt a chill run the length of her spine as she looked about her, nervously. Suddenly, a horse's whinny broke the silence.

No! Lara's mind screamed as she spun the horse around, kicking Camilla's flanks hard. As she did, Lara saw a group of men pour from the woods. Pressing Camilla into a gallop, Lara tried to make her getaway. Less than a hundred feet later, she saw four men in front of her, blocking her path. Swerving her horse sideways, Lara made a break for the woods. Before she could enter the small stand of trees, two riders caught up to her. An arm went around her waist, lifting her from the saddle. Striking out blindly, Lara fought her captor.

The man's grip tightened cruelly, and she could not breathe. Seconds later, she was released and fell to the ground. Looking up, Lara saw the smirking face of Lew Cross.

"Where is he?" he demanded harshly.

"Who?" asked Lara defiantly.

"Don't play games with me. You have no one to protect you now. Where is he?"

"I don't know."

Cross dropped to the ground, glaring down at the woman beneath him. He swiftly grabbed a handful of her hair and, pulling hard, jerked Lara's head up.

"Did he leave you? Did he tire of you so soon?" mocked Cross. "I wouldn't have tired so quickly." Lara noticed the threatening drop in Cross's voice when he'd spoken the last words. She knew that she alone had heard him.

"You wouldn't dare!"

"Don't be so sure, we're a long way from anywhere. Now, where is he?"

"I don't know. I left him hours ago. He was riding into the higher mountains when I ran away," she lied.

"Ran away?" Cross echoed foolishly.

"Yes! He's the same as my father! The same as you!" Lara almost spat the word into the foreman's face. She was rewarded with another of his cruel smiles before Cross turned his head from her. He called three men over and issued orders.

"Simmons, you, Taylor, and Garner, take the Indian and get Treemont. I don't care if you have to go to Oregon. I want Treemont dead!"

"Lew, the Indian's gone," Simmons said. He was the same man who'd taken Anna into the barn.

"Where?"

"Don't know. When we were hiding in the woods, waiting for her, he disappeared."

"The hell with him. Just get Treemont." The three men looked at each other uneasily, then back at Cross. "Go!" he ordered, "and don't forget the bonuses."

They nodded. Quickly, the men mounted and started westward. Cross could not know that these men and several others had already discussed leaving the foreman and Dowley. They had been in the army during the war, and had hated the discipline. Working for Dowley and Cross was just like the army to them. Silently, when the three had ridden out, they had made their decision. They would not be back.

"Up!" Cross ordered Lara as he pulled her to her feet. He tied her wrists together and lifted her onto her saddle. Cross's hand lingered on her thigh as he smiled at her. "You will be seeing your father soon."

The first thing that Kael was aware of was tree bark against his back. The second thing was the localized pain in his head. Gingerly, he tested the soreness and winced as he touched his head. She got me good, he said to himself with no anger; just a hopeless feeling of loss. The feeling was not for himself, but for Lara. She was strong. She just might survive the Tetons, but she would not be able to hide from her father. Dowley was too close! Kael had felt the closeness of their pursuers since yesterday, and he felt it with the same inner sense that had guided and saved him, time and again, on the battlefield. He could almost taste his enemy's proximity.

"Easy, boy," he cooed as he gripped Major's mane in an effort to stand. Kael had been waiting for Lara to make a break, but he'd thought she would do it tonight. But because he was confident that he could prevent her, Kael had let his guard down. Smiling ruefully, he admitted that he hadn't expected her to knock him out. That hurt his pride more than his head. The smile disappeared as he realized how much Lara's own pride had suffered because of him.

Tightening the cinch, Kael looked up. The sun told him that he'd been out for only a short while, not even an hour most likely. He pulled his rifle free from the saddle holster and checked it thoroughly. With slow deliberation, he loaded the chamber before sliding the gun back into its holder.

Next, he went to the packhorse and removed several items. First, the satchel of letters, then one of his leather bags, his hunting knife, and the remainder of beef. When that was done and the items secured to the stallion's back, he took everything else off the packhorse and freed the animal. Slapping its rump, Kael sent it toward the mountains. He knew it would never go into the Divide, but wherever it went, its hoofprints would help to lead Dowley astray.

Kael mounted the stallion, drawing a deep breath, as he began to ride eastward after Lara. He did not gallop, but rather moved at a ground-consuming pace that also allowed his ears to listen for anything that might be important.

A half-hour later, he felt his inner warning call. Following his intuition, Kael guided Major into the concealment of a stand of spruces.

Seconds later, Kael heard the sound of approaching horses. Tying the stallion to a tree, he began to work his way toward the trail. Soon three riders loped passed his hiding place. Strangely, all three were looking ahead, no one was checking the ground for hoofprints. Stupid, Kael thought. The men did not seem to be tracking him at all. Then another thought occurred to him, sending a cold, twisting sensation to his stomach. As Kael watched the riders go by, he knew that Lara had been caught.

Darkness blanketed the mountains. Cross had decided to camp at the same spot that Lara and Kael had used the night before. A large fire roared, and over it a quarter of elk roasted. Watching the men who cooked it, Lara sat with her hands tied. Cross was taking no chances, but she would still try to escape.

Irrationally, considering her position, Lara was angry that

these men had shot the magnificent bull elk. Angered because they could not carry it back, angry because they would leave the bulk of it behind for scavengers. Rabbit would have been better, she thought, feeling proud of all the times Kael had bypassed the larger game rather than kill an animal for just one small meal. But these men cared nothing about things like that. They were hungry, and that was all that counted.

"Real treat tonight," Cross said as he brought her some of the roasted meat. Lara looked away from him. "It was foolish, trying to get away. Did you know that your so-called husband left a note for your father? He bragged that he took you for revenge." Lara's glance at Cross was filled with disdain. "I can make the trip back more comfortable," Cross smirked.

"And I'll tell my father the price for the comfort," Lara replied in icy tones.

"After what you've done, he wouldn't believe you. He doesn't give a damn for anything except his land, cattle, and the power he'll be gettin' when you marry Setterley." Sadly, Lara knew that every word he spoke was the truth.

"Maybe," she replied, "Maybe not. But touch me, and I promise that one day I'll kill you!" Cross almost backed away from the deadly sound of Lara's voice. Her face and eyes told him that she, too, spoke the truth.

"Afterward, you'll feel different," he said quietly. But he quickly turned and left her alone. As he walked back to his men, Cross thought about the three he'd sent after Treemont. Had they caught him yet?

Lara, her hands bound, ate only a little of the meat while she listened to the men talk. Then she watched as they began to drift to their blankets to sleep. She heard Cross issue orders, assigning watches for the night before he returned to her.

Bending over her, Cross checked the bindings on her wrists; then, with a satisfied grunt, he picked up another strand of rope. He tied Lara's ankles before winding the twine up and around her waist. Then he connected the end of the rope to her wrists. There was just enough play to allow her slight movement, but it was secured in a way that prevented her from reaching her ankles. Cross then spread out a blanket for her.

"Go to sleep," he ordered. Rather than argue or glare at him, Lara lay back on the blanket. She was sure that she would be unable to rest tonight, but her body betrayed her. Soon she slept. But she was haunted by dreams of a handsome, amber-eyed mountain lion that crouched above her, watching her, protecting her.

In the rolling land that separated the Wind River Mountains from the first ridge of the Continental Divide was a man whose eyes glowed with reflected moonlight. Kael Treemont was higher up than the group that camped by the lakeside, and he had an unrestricted view of the fire that burned below.

Kael knew he would not be able to free Lara tonight. Her guards would be too alert. Tomorrow might be risky as well. Everything depended on how far they rode during the day. By the third day, they would not be as alert. They would be more relaxed and unsuspecting of being trailed. Kael sat against the hole of a tree, his shoulders and torso covered by a blanket. He let himself doze. He knew he would need all the strength he could muster when the time to act came.

On the third morning of her captivity, Lara awoke to a cloud-filled sky. For the past two weeks, the weather had been perfect—clear, warm midsummer days had been their company. Today she knew that the high mountain chill of the night would stay with them throughout this sunless day.

Today would be the last day, tonight the last night in the mountains. By tomorrow afternoon, they would have reached the eastern slopes of the Wind River Mountains, and her future would be sealed.

Shivering, Lara pulled the blanket around her. Although she knew she would spend an uncomfortable day in the wet, she prayed hard for the clouds to open so that the rain would slow them to half their pace.

The precipitation that Lara had prayed for came an hour after they began their ride. By midafternoon, the day had turned into a shroud of misting drizzle. As she had predicted, their pace had decreased and they had covered only half the distance that they should have. Lara and the men had eaten in the saddle. Cross had decided against wasting the time in stopping. The horses had been walking and so were not tired.

Lara's back and buttocks hurt and her wrists were chafed from the rubbing of the rope, but she ignored it all. In fact, Lara kept her wrists and hands free of the blanket, letting them become drenched. The rope was soaked through, and Lara knew if the weather stayed the same until tonight, she would then be able to loosen her bonds. The afternoon passed slowly in the constant rainfall.

For the past two days and one night, Lara had watched Lew Cross carefully. She was waiting for him to make his move. He hadn't on that first night, nor the second. It probably was because too many men had been on guard duty. Throughout the long nights, Lara felt Cross's eyes on her. Throughout the days, she thought of two things; Kael Treemont and escape.

Fervently, Lara prayed that Kael had eluded the three men.

With the onset of darkness, Cross, Lara, and the others camped within a stand of trees that offered some protection from the elements. The horses were a short distance away in a small clearing within the center of tall pines.

Lara noticed that the men were tired and sensed that tonight they would be less watchful. A fire blazed mightily in their midst, kept high to prevent the wet night from putting it out. They had all eaten dried beef again tonight.

A short time later found Lara feigning sleep as she rested against a tree. When the drizzle finally ended, she felt Lew Cross approach her. She continued pretending to sleep as he checked her bonds.

"Are you tired, little lady?" Cross said in a low voice. "Sleep well, for I'll be waking you later. I want you," he said in a hot, breathy whisper.

Lara couldn't stop herself as her eyes flew open and she stared into his dark pools of filth. "Never!"

In the dimness, she saw Cross smile as his heavy hand reached into the top of her shirt and grabbed her breast. His fingers gripped harshly around the tender skin, but Lara refused to acknowledge him. She stared into his eyes with loathing.

"I'll melt your ice," Lew Cross said with another leer as he pulled his hand away.

She realized that several of the men had been watching. Dawning comprehension filled her mind. They were afraid of Cross. They would let him do whatever he wanted. Their only concern was money.

Trying to cast off the sense of revulsion and the painful feeling that remained on her breast, Lara began to work on her bonds. They gave just a little before she stopped. She would have to be careful to avoid being seen. It might take hours, perhaps most of the night, and she hoped that whatever Cross had in mind would wait until then. He had changed the guard duty tonight. Only one man at a time would be on duty. Lara had heard his instructions clearly. Cross would be the last, three others would go before him. She had to get away before it was his turn. That would be when he would come for her.

Kael waited until the moon had set before he started toward the campsite. As silently as a cat stalking its prey, he led the stallion forward.

Each day, Kael had followed parallel to the group. On the first day, he'd learned that Martin Dowley was not with them. For that, Kael was grateful. He did not know how Lara would react if he were forced to kill her father in order to free her. Strange, he thought, how his thinking had changed. A week ago, all he wanted was to kill Martin Dowley. Now, he was glad that temptation was gone.

As he moved nearer to the camp, his ears took in the

silence that surrounded him. Smiling to himself, Kael began to lead the stallion toward the spot where all the horses were.

Lara suppressed the scream of pain that was almost torn from her throat as she pulled one hand free of the ropes. She knew without looking that her wrist and hand had been badly scraped by the bonds. Taking a deep breath, she loosened her other hand. The soaking that the rope had received today had done what she expected, though it had taken several hours of effort. The still-painful burning of her skin reminded her of the cost.

Ignoring that, and keeping her eyes glued on the watchman, Lara began to untie the rest of the ropes. Soon the task was completed.

She waited as the blood flowed into her freed ankles. When she was certain that she could stand and run, she pulled the blanket from her shoulders.

She hadn't much time. Lew Cross would be the next watch, and she must be gone before that. Her eyes were on the guard, and had been for the last hour. The man had not moved once in the past fifteen minutes. She hoped he was asleep.

Carefully, Lara began to crawl behind the trees. When she reached their relative safety, she stood.

The guard remained still.

Running would be stupid. It would cause too much noise. Walking swiftly and quietly then, she made her way toward the horses, leaving captivity behind her.

Lew Cross lay silent.

The foreman's eyes were open, but it was too dark for anyone to see. His body had not permitted him sleep in anticipation of what would soon be his. Lying on his side, Cross stared through the darkness that separated him from his desire. Throughout the night, he had watched Lara Dowley.

Soon, he thought. Again Lew's blood began to heat and he felt the hardness of his need. Then Cross saw her move.

Instantly, his mind became alert. He watched, unmoving, as Lara shed her blanket and crawled behind the trees. Cross's eyes went to the guard. Asleep! Slowly, a smile spread over Cross's face. There would be no fuss, no fighting, no cries for help if Lara was well away from the camp.

He could get away with taking his pleasure of her. That was all he wanted, once. But he was unsure of his men's reaction. If they wanted their share of Lara Dowley when he was finished, there would be trouble. If everyone else wanted her, too, then she could never be brought back. That's why he had waited. Tonight would be the last night in the mountains. Tomorrow they would be too close to home for his men to risk the chance of being caught.

Cross wanted Lara desperately. His mind filled with the memory of the times he'd watched her, hidden in the darkness, as she'd fed the mare, or walked in the starlight. Again, his lust reared high.

Then Cross heard Lara begin to walk, and he rose to follow her.

Lara passed through the woods and into the small clearing. She saw the dark shapes of the horses milling around, and began to walk within their midst. As she did, she softly called Camilla's name. A moment later, she was rewarded by the mare's muzzle brushing her arm.

"Good Camilla," she whispered. Leading the horse away, Lara went to the pile of saddles and bridles. As her hands fell on the pommel of her saddle, she felt Camilla pull slightly away. Straightening, Lara turned.

"That wasn't too smart," Cross said as he stepped close to her. His hand shot out and he grabbed a handful of Lara's hair. Yanking her toward him, his other hand pressed her against him. She felt his mouth seek hers. Fighting him, Lara tried to avoid his lips.

"No!" she screamed, as Cross's mouth covered hers.

✻   ✻   ✻

Kael secured his stallion to a tree and started making his way toward the horses. He wanted to find Lara's mare and separate it from the others before he went after her. If he couldn't find Camilla, he would take any mount. Once Lara was safe, he would chase the other horses away. If it worked, they'd have at least a half-day lead on the men.

Now, Kael's mind ordered as he saw the first of the mounts.

Suddenly, a voice broke the stillness of the night. It was Lara's! Moving with the speed of a man possessed, Kael entered the small clearing. When he saw the sight before him, he froze. When he moved again, redness tinted his vision.

"No!" Lara screamed again as Cross increased his lascivious attempts. She felt as if she were suffocating as Cross's mouth trapped hers, forcing her to breathe his noxious breath. Her stomach twisted, and she tried to fight him. Lifting one knee quickly, Lara kicked him. Cross was ready for her and deflected the blow with his hip. She felt her head jerk back, and the foreman released her. His hand flew upward, slapping her across her mouth.

"No," Lara screamed again, fright and anger giving more power to her voice.

"Quiet!" Cross ordered as he yanked her hair. She fell backward, hitting the ground hard. Her breath was knocked painfully out of her, and she felt her arms trapped under her.

Before she could recover, Cross fell on top of her. One hand covered her mouth, the other pawed her body. Lara tried to squirm loose, but could not move his bulk from her. She felt the hard, rampaging lust of the man pressing against her thigh, and she was sickened. His free hand was now on her shirt, and the sound of it ripping echoed in her ears. Then she felt Cross's wet lips on one of her breasts, and his teeth biting sharply.

Pulling one of her arms free, Lara turned her fingers into claws and grabbed for his face. Her nails reached the skin of the back of his neck and dug in deeply. Lara raked hard.

Cross jerked his mouth from her breast and, growling with rage and pain, slapped her again. She felt the stinging pain across her face as blankness began to descend. *Fight!* she warned herself. Then Cross's weight lessened, but she could not make her muscles work. Her eyes opened, and she saw him leering at her as he pulled his rigid staff from his pants. Again, blankness threatened to end her sight. Fight! she ordered herself. Fight!

Then, out of the night came a shape, and with it, Lara felt life surge within her.

Kael!

A loud thud sounded. Lara heard the horses begin to rustle nervously as Kael collided with Cross.

In the low light of the star-filled sky she saw them battle. Working herself to a sitting position and pulling her shirt closed, Lara watched, unable to do more.

Kael was filled with insane rage. Every finely tuned sense was aimed at destroying the man who was raping his wife. Nothing else was in his world except the large mass of his enemy. Kael leapt, as a mountain lion would, upon the man's back, knocking Cross to the ground. Then he launched himself again, his arms reaching for the foreman's neck. Feeling the tightly corded muscles beneath his fingers, Kael began to squeeze, to choke his foe. His breathing was ragged, and he knew only the animal that he was, and the animal below him.

Cross slammed a knee into Kael's stomach and knocked him off. Quickly, both men reached their feet and charged each other. Kael did not feel the blows that were raining upon him as he focused solely on his enemy's distorted features. His fist collided with Cross's chin. Once, twice, three times, the powerful fists maddeningly pounded Cross's face.

The foreman dropped like a dead tree.

Unable to control his wrath and hate, Kael dropped on the now defenseless man and continued to pommel him mercilessly.

Lara saw Kael move with the grace of a cat as he weaved through Cross's punches to hit him again and again. She saw Cross fall, and saw Kael dive on him to continue beating him. Lara reacted quickly. The others would be coming soon.

She knew Kael was past hearing, crazed with anger, fighting blindly. Grabbing his arm, ignoring the sound of his fists against Cross's body, she tried to gain his attention. At last, Kael went limp; his hands fell to his sides. Then he turned to her and the anger left his eyes as she saw his recognition of her.

"We have to get away," she whispered urgently. Kael nodded, stood, and pulled Lara gently into his arms. He pressed her close, and both could feel the trembling within their bodies.

"I love you," Kael said. She looked up at him and slowly, her eyes filling with tears, nodded.

"And I, you," she said softly. They kissed, then drew apart.

"Come," he ordered as he took Camilla. Lara lifted her saddle and reins and followed Kael through the woods.

The mare was made ready and Kael lifted Lara onto the saddle. "We'll start again. We'll start fresh, without hatred, only love and trust," he told her confidently. Lara gazed down at him and felt all her barriers melting away. She loved him. She knew that. She loved him and needed him. Yes. They would start again.

"Please," Lara said finally.

Then, turning from her, Kael went to the stallion. Suddenly, he froze as he heard footsteps behind them. Untying the horses, he grabbed the pommel and began to jump up.

A loud, thundering shot rang out, and Kael felt the lance of pain in his head. Then there was only darkness.

Lara screamed as she flew from Camilla's back and went to Kael's still body. "No! No! No!" she screamed as she lifted his bloodsoaked head. "No! Oh, my God, Kael, No!"

Then Lara Dowley Treemont began to cry, rocking back and forth with her husband's head in her lap as Martin Dowley's ranch hands surrounded the couple.

Lara's mind was a whirlpool of anger, hatred, and loss. She sat on the mare, but her eyes saw nothing of the land she rode through, and her ears heard nothing of the talk that surrounded her. After three days, her thoughts were still on only one thing—Kael Treemont.

Crowheart Butte was behind her, but she had not seen it when they passed. Nor did she notice the eyes of Lew Cross as they kept her under constant vigil. Lara did not even see the dark bruises that covered his puffy face.

She had not heard Cross's explanation when his men had revived him. He told them that Treemont had freed her, and he had tired to stop them. Lara had not heard their amazed reactions, nor seen their staring eyes as they took in her torn shirt and exposed breasts.

All Lara could see was the faint light of morning when they had dragged her away from Kael. Lara saw the men who looked at Kael, and heard their voices when they told Cross he was still alive.

Over and over again, Lara heard Cross's final words when

he told the men to tie her husband to a tree—to leave him for the animals to feast on. Her last vision was of Kael, his wrists bound over his head, his lean, muscular torso strapped to a tree. Only his feet were free, and they must hold him up lest his weight pull his arms from their sockets.

When she had last seen Kael, his eyes were closed and his breathing was labored. His face was covered with drying blood.

Oh, Kael, Lara moaned silently.

He was gone from her. Killed by animals that ranged the mountains. Gone from her life but not from her heart. She would remember him always. His death would not go unpunished. Lew Cross, the other men, and her father, would pay as they could never imagine for his death. Yes, thought Lara, they would pay.

Moments later, her eyes began to focus. Glancing around, she pinpointed her location. Crowheart Butte was fading behind her. She would be at the ranch by nightfall. Then Lara searched out Lew Cross.

When she saw him, she smiled.

Cross sat stiffly under Lara's inspection. After a moment, he urged his horse forward until he rode next to her.

"Aren't you going to try and take me before we reach my father?" asked Lara tauntingly. Cross ignored her as he rode silently. "Do you know the story of Crowheart Butte?" she asked.

"I've heard," was his sullen reply.

"Remember it," she said with a wide smile. "Remember it well." Her smile remained as she saw Lew Cross thinking about it, and blanch.

Before night fell, the group rode into the ranch. By the time they were at the corral, Martin Dowley's grotesque face and waddling body reached them.

"Get down!" he ordered Lara. She did. Dowley grabbed her arm and, twisting it behind her back, propelled her forward. He stopped, shouting over his shoulder, "Cross, wait for me in my study," before he pushed Lara toward the house.

Once inside the house, Dowley forced Lara upstairs and into her room. There he flung her to the floor.

"This time you went too far!" he screamed as his rage heightened. His face was dark with anger. "You have defied me once too often!" Twisting her head so that she could look at him, ready to meet his challenge, she noticed his arm lifted high, whip in hand. As Dowley opened two fingers, the whip uncoiled. Slowly, her stepfather let his arm drop lower behind his head

In one blurring motion, the whip flew through the air and bit across her shoulder and back. Though the pain was excruciating, Lara Fairwald Dowley Treemont kept her ice-blue eyes locked on her fathers. With each stroke of the rawhide, she promised herself that she would not cry. She would not give Martin Dowley the satisfaction of seeing her broken.

Again and again, the whip leashed across her body. Soon Lara could not hold her stepfather's eyes as her own closed and merciful darkness stopped all her pain.

In the low-lit study, Dowley met with his foreman. Martin drank from a large snifter, but Cross sat emptyhanded, withering under Dowley's verbal abuse.

Cross had already reported and given his own version of the beating he had received from Treemont. Cross had guaranteed that Kael was dead, and when it was said, Dowley seemed to lose most of his wrath.

"What about the men who went after him?"

Cross shrugged.

"I'll tell you what about them. You'll never see them again. Simmons was one, right?" Dowley waited for confirmation. "He was the one who was supposed to have taken care of Anna. Well, he did. He let her go."

"I heard him shoot her," Cross responded in disbelief.

"So did everyone. And everyone thought she was dead. The only thing that died was a piece of dirt," Dowley said sarcastically. "We're well off with him gone.

"Now we've got some new problems. Crimmons and Blair are shooting off their mouths. We need to stop them. But first I want Lara in Kansas City. Tomorrow I want you to send a man there. This time make sure it's someone you trust." Dowley waited for Cross's slow nod.

"While Lara is being married, I want Blair and Crimmons killed! I don't care how you do it. I want it done." Martin Dowley paused after these fateful orders. He looked at Lew's battered face for a long, heavy moment. "You're sure he's dead?"

"Treemont was shot in the head. We left his body tied to a tree for the animals."

Good. Tomorrow you give the men their bonuses. They earned them. Then we've got some other things to attend to." Dowley stayed seated as he watched Cross leave the house. There were many things that had to be done. The week ahead was needed to take care of any loose ends before Lara left for Kansas City. This time he was going, Martin Dowley decided, and he intended to make sure that Lara reached the altar. The right altar. When the wedding was over, he expected John Crimmons to be dead. Dowley would then have a new wife.

Some time during the night, Lara awoke on the floor. She was aware of the burning pain on her back, and slowly, gently, removed the shirt that was now only tattered rags and dried blood. Then she fought the agony as she removed her pants. Measuring her steps, Lara went to one of her trunks. She untied the soft leather pouch from around her waist and slipped the gold sovereigns into it. Next, she took a dress and pulled it up over her legs. When it was at her waist, she went to the bed. She lay face down and closed her eyes. The sharp lances of pain racked her body beyond the point of endurance, and Lara again felt herself spin into unconsciousness.

A light tapping woke her. Swimming through a veil of wavering images, Lara moved. The searing ache returned, gripping her and tearing a low moan from her lips. She watched the door open.

One of the men that had captured her came in. He seemed embarrassed by her exposed back, and by the blood that was caked on it. Lara recognized him as Jim Logan. He'd been working at the ranch for almost a year. He was also one of the youngest hands. Logan stepped closer to her, standing stiffly under her withering stare.

"Miss Lara, your father's gone to town and I thought you might need some help," he managed to say. She saw the honesty of his words written on his face. She also sensed the shame that seemed to emanate from him.

"Miss Lara, I'm real sorry 'bout what happened. I wish I could've stopped it. There weren't no need to whip you. I brought somethin' for your back, if you'll let me."

Before Lara could reply, Logan stepped forward and knelt at the side of the bed. Tenderly, he moved Lara to the center, being careful not to let her dress fall too low. She felt the gentleness of his hands, and relaxed for the first time since Kael had been shot.

"I'll try'n be easy, but it's goin' to hurt a lot."

Lara nodded as she watched him dip a cloth into a bucket. Suddenly, fire seemed to shoot through her back. Biting into the blanket, Lara tried to block out the pain. She heard Logan talking to her, soothing her as he cleaned her wounds. When he was done, he sucked in his breath.

"God, Miss Lara, your father's crazy. . . ." And, incredibly, she heard the man hold back a sob before he continued. "You . . . your back's goin' to be scarred, Miss Lara, I'm sorry."

She cried then, silently, with her head buried in the blanket. Yet after several minutes, she forced herself to regain control.

"I'm goin' to put some salve on your back. It's goin' to hurt a whole lot more'n the cleaning did. I'm real sorry, but it's the only way to help you."

"Do it, please," she said. As Jim applied the healing ointment, Lara clenched her teeth and tried to block out everything except her thoughts about Kael. At least she could feel pain. Kael could feel nothing. Kael was dead, and her stepfather had murdered him as surely as Dowley had mur-

dered Ryan Treemont and her mother! Those thoughts built a
wall that stopped most of the pain. When it finally broke
through the wall, Lara fainted.

What seemed like years later, she awoke. At first she felt
nothing, but when she stirred, a groan of pain escaped from
her dry throat. Then she realized that the pain had eased.
That somehow it was better.

"Don't move too much," came the young cowboy's voice.
Lara turned her head to see Logan sitting quietly in a chair.

"How long have I been asleep?" she asked.

"Couple hours. You needed it. The salve should've made
your back feel better."

"Yes, it did. Thank you. Would you turn around? I want
to sit up . . ." she said. Logan smiled shyly and did as she
requested. When she slowly eased herself up, she lifted the
front of the dress and covered her breasts. Then Lara realized there was no blood on top of her shoulders. The young
man must have cleaned her while she slept. Wisely, Lara
decided not to mention anything.

"All right," she said, and Logan faced her.

"You won't be able to move 'bout too much, but in two or
three days you'll be feelin' a lot better."

"Does my father know you've done this?"

"No, ma'am," he said.

"He'll fire you if he finds out."

"Yes, ma'am. But I'm leavin' anyway. I can't live with
m'self here, not after what I was a party to. I think I'm goin'
to head to California. Maybe find me some gold."

"Mr. Logan, I don't know how to thank you. I've got a
little money hidden—"

"No," he cut her off. "I didn't do it for money, Miss
Lara." By the hard expression on his face, she knew not to
argue.

"Then my thanks must do."

"That's all I want," he said. Then he stood and walked
over to her. "Be careful. Your father's not right. He's not
right. . . ."

"I know. Mr. Logan?"

"Yes?" he said as he reached the door.

"Could I ask for another favor?"

"If I can."

"Would you go to the Crimmons ranch and tell them I'm here? Someone has to know. Would you tell John that his cousin is dead?"

"I'm goin' to South Pass. I'll try 'n stop by on my way." At the door, Jim Logan paused again. "Miss Lara, I'm real sorry 'bout everything." Then he was gone.

"So am I," she whispered as her eyes misted. Slowly, she turned to lay face down on her bed. "So am I."

Two days later, Lara was able to move without constant pain. On the third day, Martin Dowley had begun to use her as a servant; to prepare his meals, and to clean the house.

He'd returned that first night and informed her that she would leave in six days for Kansas City. Lara had not responded to him, and Dowley did not seem to care. But when he'd seen her back covered with salve, he grew angry.

Lara told him not to waste his breath, that the person who had helped her had left. Ten minutes later, she heard Dowley screaming at Cross. When he came back, he locked Lara in her room.

The first food she ate was the next morning. After that, her father informed her that if she wanted to eat, she would do the cooking. She'd already learned, from the talk that floated up to her window, that Anna had not been killed. That made Lara feel better.

Now, with only three days left before she was to leave, Lara was trying to figure out another way to prevent the marriage. She had the run of the house, whether Dowley was home or not. That had been simple. Cross had posted four of his most trusted men just outside.

She also wondered why John Crimmons had not come to see her. She was positive that Jim Logan would make good his word and tell them. But Crimmons's complicity in helping her to marry Kael would have warned her stepfather. Had he already done something to them?

Since morning, a plan had been forming in her mind. Her father's obsession with power, and his ridiculously royal thoughts, might work in her favor. Also, his earlier remarks about marrying Angela could be put to use.

It was over dinner that she first broached the subject, and was instantly rewarded by Dowley's reactions. She had gauged him right.

"Father, I know I have no choice now, and I must submit to your authority," she began. Dowley looked at her cautiously as he chewed a piece of beef. "Don't think I've forgotten what you've done to me!" she spat harshly, knowing that to give in completely would ring false to him.

"All for your own good."

"And for yours, Father!" She allowed her rage to fill those last words; she needed him off-guard.

He stiffed, and a dangerous glint shone in his umber eyes. "Do you never learn! Dammit girl, I'll whip you again if I have to."

Lara made herself appear to cower, to look frightened by his threat. "No, please, let me speak," she whispered. Dowley nodded, satisfied with his power over her. "Do you think more scars will make my future husband happy?" she said quickly, then went on. "I can't fight you any longer. I can't and I won't. Father, all I am going to ask is that you let me have a little dignity when I am married."

"Dignity?" Dowley asked, surprised at this request.

"Yes, Father. If what you say is true about yourself and Johnathan Setterley becoming the rulers of the territory, then you must not drag me to him like a slave."

"Oh, and what must I do?" he asked sarcastically.

Lara knew that if she said it right, it would work. It had to. "I have nothing left. The man I loved is dead, and you will not have me in your house. Let me go to my marriage as a woman. Let me have the dignity of a real wedding, or at least the appearance of one. Do not make me stand alone," she pleaded.

"And what would you have me do?" Dowley asked, delighted she was pleading with him. He swelled with the pleasure of power over his stepdaughter.

"You once likened yourself and Setterley to kings, and myself as a future queen. Would you bring a future queen to her mate in bondage? Drag her to the man you want an alliance with as if she were nothing more than an Indian squaw?"

"Now you want a court of ladies in waiting?" Dowley asked with a sneer. But Lara detected the interest in his eyes. Now was the time.

"No. I want what you want. You want me to appear happy in this marriage. You want me to accept it so that you will be enriched. Well, Father, you are about to get your wish. I'm tired. Now I want a life for myself. I want power, too! I'm not a little girl anymore. You can drag me to Kansas City, you can force me to marry Setterley, but I can ruin you! I can make Johnathan Setterley's life so miserable that he'll want to erase the name and memory of Martin Dowley from the West!"

"You wouldn't dare!" Dowely stated.

"Yes, I would! But, dear Father, do it my way, and I'll go to Setterley willingly. Do it my way, and you'll have your wish, and possibly even a marriage of your own."

"What are you talking about?"

"I want Angela and Constance Crimmons with me. They'll be my escorts to Kansas City, and stand with me when I wed. It will give you your chance to avail yourself of Angela, to woo her on the return to Wyoming."

And, Lara thought, a chance to warn Angela and Constance of her stepfather's plans before it was too late. Yes, Father. You will think about this, and you will agree.

Lara watched her father's face run a full gamut of expressions before his eyes finally cleared and settled back on her. What she didn't know was that her words had completed the plans he'd already made. If Angela and Constance were with him, then they could not hold him responsible for John's death. When they returned, Dowley would take care of everything. He would become indispensible to the Crimmonses, and save them from ruin.

"Lara, you surprise me. You do have a mind after all. It's too bad you didn't start using it earlier," he said with a sigh. "All right. I agree. Write a note to your friends. Invite them in a way that will make it impossible for them to refuse."

With that, Martin Dowley sat back, a smile spreading across his face as his eyes became vacant.

The hot ball of the sun woke Kael. Its fiery brightness burned his eyelids, forcing them to open. He felt the dizzying ache in his head, and the stiff paint of blood on his cheeks. Then he realized he could not move his arms. As he lifted his head, the pain receded for a moment, and he remembered what had happened. He saw his hands secured to a branch above him. As he took a deep breath, he felt the other bonds that tied him to the tree.

"Nooo!" His scream shattered the stillness of the empty woods. Kael screamed again and again, until he lost consciousness.

When he awoke for the second time, he was flooded by instant awareness. Never before had he been so helpless.

Lara! She was gone now. Taken back by Dowley's men. Gone, to marry the man in Kansas City, but safe from the menace of the man who had tried to take her by force. Kael knew he'd hurt Cross badly enough so that all he would do now was to take her to Dowley.

But Kael could not help her. He knew that he was finished, that he would die soon.

As if to confirm his thoughts, Kael heard rustling in the trees. Seconds later, a small rabbit entered the clearing. For a while the animal sat, studying him. Then it scurried into the underbrush.

The morning passed with agonizing slowness as Kael watched a parade of wild creatures go about their lives. Through it all, he wavered in and out of consciousness. The head wound, although just a grazing shot, had weakened him badly so soon after his bout with spotted fever. By midafternoon, Kael was too weak from the loss of blood and the heat of the day to do more than half-support his body on his weakened legs. If Dowley's men had left him sitting, he could have stayed stronger.

Now there was nothing he could do. Sooner or later, more dangerous animals would scent the blood and death that filled the air.

He passed out again, but woke from the pain in his shoulders. This time his legs had buckled and he had hung for many long minutes. Straightening, Kael forced his aching muscles to support him once again.

Suddenly, he became aware of a deathly silence around him. His eyes searched the area. There! A fuzzy brown and black muzzle. Slowly, the entire animal stepped out of hiding and Kael's blood turned to ice. The coyote moved toward him, sniffing the air all the way. When it was within reach, Kael took a deep breath.

Letting himself hang by his arms, he kicked outward. The coyote dodged the booted foot and slunk away. Kael's eyes locked with the predator's. A loud, wailing howl issued from the scavanger, and Kael knew it signaled his end.

Within a minute, Kael was surrounded by ten of the animals. One at a time, they advanced on him. One came too close, and Kael's toe connected with its snout. With a whimper of pain, the coyote backed away.

Kael fought hard to hold on. He fought all the dark forces that tried to lull him, to call him from this world. Kael Treemont fought with the last vestiges of his life force.

Then another sound penetrated the woods. A deep-throated growling sent the pack of coyotes slinking away. He was alone once more, and again he waited for death.

Gradually, Kael saw the gargantuan head and humped shoulders emerge from the trees. Then he watched as the rest of the gigantic body followed. It was huge! When it reached the middle of the clearing, the nearly black animal rose to stand on its hind legs.

Kael grew weaker as the animal reached its full height. Nine feet from ground to snout; huge paws, with long, curving claws, glinted in the afternoon sun. Sharp, white teeth greeted his eyes.

Grizzly!

Tied helplessly to a tree, Kael faced the most ferocious animal in the West. He stared at twelve hundred pounds of death and trembled. Drawing a deep breath, Kael waited for his end to come. The smell of fear would force the bear to him.

Kael had one chance, a very small chance. If he went limp, if he did not move, perhaps the bear would leave him alone. It had been known to happen.

Closing his eyes and drawing on his inner strength, Kael resurrected Lara's image within him. He made love to her in the small falls of the foothills near her father's ranch. He rode the mountains with her, held her hand, and again made love to her. He lost himself, ignoring the pain in his body, ignoring the fetid smell of the grizzly that was now only inches away, inspecting him curiously.

Then the bear growled a hair's breadth from his face. Kale's eyes flew open, and he stared at the monstrous teeth within the cavernous mouth. Unexpectedly, the bear then backed away.

Kael watched its retreat, and as it dropped to all fours, the bear circled him, then stopped in front of him and growled its challenge. Kael remained motionless. Suddenly, the grizzly reared. Kael saw its curved claws raised, and watched as its paws drew further back. Now he would die.

Waiting for the fury of the attack, Kael could do nothing. Then he heard a strange whistling noise, and a low thud. The bear froze, its heavy paw midway to its target, then turned.

An eagle-feathered arrow stuck out from the grizzly's neck. With a roar, the bear ripped the arrow from its skin. Blood spurted, followed by the loud and terrifying cry of an enraged grizzly.

The bear swung back to Kael, its eyes now surrounded by red. Suddenly, an arrow pierced one of the eyes. Five more arrows quickly protruded from the animal's hulk. Kael was mesmerized by the bear's howl of pain. Slowly, like a giant tree that had been cut in half, the grizzly fell. The arrow that entered its eye had also penetrated its brain. The bear died at Kael's feet, one huge paw raking along Kael's hip as it fell.

In a half-daze, Kael watched five Indians appear from the trees. Seconds before Kael blacked out, he wondered if he'd been saved from the bear only to be tortured by the warriors.

"Your white friend has many troubles," Smooth Feather said as he stood beside Painted Hawk.

"You did not see him cringe from the bear, did you? No matter what his fortune, he is a brave man." Accepting the rebuke gracefully, Smooth Feather joined his chief and helped Painted Hawk free Kael. While they laid him on the ground and examined his wounds, Painted Hawk gave orders to the other three warriors. Ten minutes later, they lifted the unconscious white man from the ground and placed him on a hastily constructed litter. They attached it to the horse they had found two hours earlier, and guiding the Andalusian, they began their journey back to Painted Hawk's village.

Kael never fully awoke during the trip, but he was aware that he was traveling. Two days later, he arrived at the village. The five warriors had ridden day and night in order to get him back as soon as possible. Within minutes, several of the Indian women stripped Kael of his clothing, and the medicine man hovered over him.

Under his direction, the injured man's wounds were cleaned, his wrists and chest covered with a dark yellow salve, and a whitish powder was poured over the path the bullet had made, and over the slashes on his hip. Then the shaman put another powder into a drinking horn, and had one of the women force it into Kael's mouth.

When the medicine man was finished, he signaled the women to look after the white man, and left the tepee to seek Painted Hawk.

"He will live," the medicine man pronounced, as he sat next to Painted Hawk.

"I am glad."

"You care for this man?"

"I do. He is brave and he is strong, and he is also good," the young warrior chief stated.

"Is it because you are half white that you feel that way?" the old man asked.

A flash of anger passed through Painted Hawk's eyes but vanished quickly. "You, old father, know better. I am a Shoshone! No matter what mixture of blood flows through me, my heart is Shoshone."

The other man nodded, then sighed. "I have watched you, Painted Hawk, since you were but a nestling. I have watched you grow into a powerful warrior and a great chief. I watched you as you sat at your mother's feet, learning the language of the whites." The medicine man paused, his eyes hooded in thought. Then he took a deep breath and went on.

"I had a vision many years ago, and in it, I saw you and I saw a white man. The very man that now lies within your tepee. You left with him once, but returned. Then, you left again, not with him, but to seek him where the great salt water begins. The second time, you did not come home. I have waited many years for this vision to be fulfilled. Now it has begun."

"I see no reason for leaving my people," said Painted Hawk, moved by the old man's words but unwilling to accept them. "This is my home. I shall always call it my home."

"That is truth but one does not always live in his home.

Painted Hawk, you are destined to be a great man, to see many things, and to live a life that brings new things to you constantly. It is not bad. Accept what happens in your future so that you will be able to adapt and become the great man that I saw in my vision." The shaman rose slowly, smiling down at Painted Hawk. "You and your white brother, for he will be a true brother to you, will leave in five days. Be prepared. You will take others with you, and your path will bring you back, this time."

Painted Hawk watched the old man walk away. He did not argue with him. Painted Hawk knew better. Although he had been educated by his white mother, he was still a Shoshone, and his respect for the powers of medicine men was great. And Silver Shadow made the strongest medicine. It did not matter that Painted Hawk could speak three languages, and could also read French and English. It only mattered that Silver Shadow had seen his future, and Painted Hawk knew to fight it would be futile. Perhaps he'd known all along he would one day leave his people. Perhaps that was why he had never taken a bride.

Alone, Painted Hawk allowed himself to smile at the memory of the night that he, Treemont, and Treemont's woman had spoken. He almost laughed again at the woman's reaction when he'd asked about Angela Crimmons. Of course he knew the customs of the whites, he was half white himself.

Slowly, with the acknowledgment of protesting muscles, Painted Hawk went to his tepee. Inside, he nodded to the woman who watched Kael, and then, before he lay down to sleep, he withdrew something from a small pouch at his side. He handed these to the woman. She looked at him questioningly. Painted Hawk nodded his head at the peacefully sleeping white man. The woman then spread the sharp objects on the ground before her.

Treemont would have a necklace of bear claws when he awoke. Smiling again, Painted Hawk lay down on his blanket and fell asleep.

* * *

"I won't allow it!" stated John Crimmons as he stood above his wife and daughter. "I will not allow you to go to Kansas City with that man!"

"John, are you to tie us then? Are we no more than your sheep, to do as you bid?" Constance asked in a soft voice as she looked up at him.

"Connie, luv, do you not see the fear I have for you? Can you not realize the hate I have for Dowley?"

"Yes, John, but I have also known the love and compassion you've lived your life with. Are you to condemn Lara to a life of misery, a disowning of her because of her father?" The challenge in his wife's eyes gripped him tightly. "Are you going to do the same thing Kael did? Punish the daughter for her father's crimes?"

"Connie, you know me better than that. It is only my love and care for you and Angela that makes me forbid this trip."

"Do you not want to learn what happened to Kael? How he died?" Angela asked. "Please, Papa, please let us go. Lara needs us. We can't let her go again, not like this."

Seeing the determination on their faces, John realized his life would never again be peaceful if he withheld his permission. Also, Angela might just take it to mind to sneak away. He knew exactly how hardheaded his daughter was.

John relented but received several promises in return. The least of which was that both women would carry concealed weapons. Also, and most important, if they found Lara did not actually want them, but it was another of Dowley's games, they would signal him. He would trail them for a day.

It was settled. They would be leaving tomorrow, and Angela and Constance packed. Shortly after that, John and Constance retired for the night. They lay silent, holding each other closely.

"I've never regreted marrying you, John Crimmons, and I never will."

"You had no choice, nor did I," he said. Then, in the darkness, John kissed his wife. "Take care of yourself and our daughter."

287

"I will," Constance promised as she responded to her husband's caress. Soon everything disappeared from their thoughts as they made love.

After twenty years, John and Constance knew each other well, but neither ever tired of the other. Every time they made love, it was a reaffirmation of their commitment.

Five days later, just as the medicine man had foretold, Kael Treemont, Painted Hawk, and several warriors rode from the Shoshone village. They were headed for the Crimmons ranch and to find Kael's woman.

Around Kael's neck, and dropping onto his bare chest, hung four long grizzly claws; his memento of the death that had loomed over him.

He felt strong again. His wrists had healed, and the grazing wound at his scalp was a thing of the past. The only one of his injuries that had bothered him was his hip. The medicine man had used his herbs, and no infection had resulted, but Kael knew the scar would be with him always.

It was late in the day when Kael and his small band reached the ranch. When they arrived, one of the hands informed Kael that everybody had left that morning, but John was expected back tonight. Kael decided to wait for John before going any further.

The ranch hand eyed the Indians nervously, but Kael told him everything was all right, and the man went about his chores.

When night came without John's return, Kael offered the Indians food. They all laughed, and shook their heads. The warriors took bags from their horses and sat on the ground. They ate the food they were accustomed to.

"You not eat?" Painted Hawk asked.

"And you do not speak well," Kael replied. During the past days, he had learned more about Painted Hawk, and his fluency had shown through.

"It is a habit, when I am in the white man's world."

"There is no shame in speaking well."

288

"There is no trust given to an Indian who knows too much about the white man."

"Stupidity," Kael said. "They felt that way about black slaves. More people died because they wanted to keep one type of man a slave than have been killed in wars for the last fifty years."

"Now you understand why I do what I do," Painted Hawk said as he rewarded Kael with one of his rare smiles.

"I guess I do," he agreed.

"Would you care for some of my food?" the Indian asked.

"Thank you, no. I've no stomach to eat until I see John."

With that, Kael began to walk aimlessly about. His mind was filled with thoughts of Lara, and he knew that he would not stop again until he had her back. No one would prevent that, he swore, as he touched one of the bear claws.

No one!

Sitting silently on the seat, Lara stared out of the coach window. She was upset. Her finely thought out plan had not worked.

Martin Dowley's insane desire to become part of what he envisioned to be the new royalty of the West had once again interfered. Instead of a peaceful and calm ride shared by herself, Angela, and Constance, Lara found herself also with Dowley.

It was crowded with all four of them in one carriage. The wagon that held the trunks and the trip's supplies followed. Eight riders surrounded them, giving the group a distinct air of importance. During the first day, there were no opportunities for her to speak with the women privately.

Her father, by way of explanation, had told them that the cramped arrangements would last only as far as South Pass City, where they would spend the night. In the morning, they would leave in something a bit more comfortable. Then Dowley had smiled secretively, but refused to say anything else on the subject. The only good thing, thought Lara, was that her stepfather was in a rare good mood.

Constance had been their savior that day. She had told them story after story of the Crimmons family's voyage from England to America. But when Constance had spoken so warmly of her and John's love, Lara had started to grieve again. Willfully, she forced the emotion away. It was private, and she would not share it.

That first night, Lara found herself in the room next to her father's, with Angela and her mother sharing another room down the hall. Lara knew that if the three of them got together, so that she could tell them what was happening, Martin Dowley might hear. Wisely, she decided to wait for a better opportunity.

The next morning had been filled with shock. When Dowley escorted the women from the hotel, a large, ornate coach stood waiting for them. Angela let out a gasp when she saw it. Dowley preened himself beside it, his obese body moving in a poor imitation of a strutting peacock.

"It arrived last week. I ordered it almost a year ago. Magnificent, isn't it?" Neither Angela or Lara spoke, but Constance smiled and nodded slowly.

"Why, Martin, 'tis the same style of coach that the gentry use in England." Everyone watched as Dowley's smile grew larger.

"As a matter of fact, it is. Except that it was made in Philadelphia, and designed for use in the West. When I received word it had arrived, I thought it would be a good idea to test it on the trip to Kansas City, and to enjoy its comforts."

Angela had clapped her hands delightedly, and stepped closer to inspect it. At first, Lara had been worried about Angela's reaction, her apparent liking of her father's ways, but when Angela was behind Dowley's back, she turned quickly and stuck out a pink tongue. Even Constance could not help smiling at that.

That was three full days ago, Lara thought, as she continued to stare out at the countryside. And, she had to admit, the coach was more enjoyable than the carriage. It was almost bearable, sitting on the soft velvet cushions, shielded from the sun by velvet curtains. A small cabinet below their seat held wine and a capped bottle of water. All the luxuries of royalty, yet Lara knew the three women were nothing more than prisoners.

During the two nights that had followed their departure from South Pass City, they had slept in the open, making camp along the trail. But tonight, within the hour, they would reach Fort Laramie, and the comfort of real beds and a served meal. And, Lara added, privacy in which she could speak to Angela and Constance.

As soon as they had arrived at Fort Laramie, the women went to their rooms to wash and change their clothes.

They had dined with two of the ranking officers, and when they were finished, everyone, including Dowley, sat in polite conversation.

Following a yawn that was only partially hidden, Lara smiled at the men. "If you all will forgive me, I find myself tired from today's journey. If you will excuse me, I'll leave you gentlemen to your brandy and cigars." As Lara rose, so did the other two women.

"And we, too, must say good night," Constance explained with her own bright smile. Martin Dowley half-rose, as if taken by surprise. He completed the movement as the officers stood.

"I shall walk you to your rooms," he said as he began to push back his chair.

"Please, Father, don't trouble yourself. Enjoy your time with these officers. It's far too rare that you get the opportunity to speak with men of such breeding and intelligence."

Dowley's jaw dropped momentarily, but he knew Lara had trapped him well. "Quite right, my dear, have a pleasant evening. I shall look in on you later."

"Gentlemen," said the three women, each giving a slight curtsey before turning to the stairs.

Once upstairs, on the second floor of the simple hotel that was part of a growing civilian city, and in the relative safety of Constance's room, they all began to laugh.

"Men of such intelligence. . . . My goodness, Lara," Constance gasped, trying to control her laughter. However, when the humor vanished from her face, she seriously probed Lara's eyes. "Will he stay downstairs long?"

"Hopefully. He does like to play the braggart. We should have at least an hour."

"Good. Then I'd suggest you tell us the reason you needed us here. After four days, if I don't find out, I just might scream!"

Lara nodded soberly and began. She talked with a measured pace, forcing all emotion from her voice as she told the tale, refusing to allow either woman to interrupt until she finished. Lara knew that if she let them question her about Kael's death, she might not be able to go on. She spoke in clear and even tones, and felt as if it were all happening again. The tears that fell from her eyes went unheeded.

When she finished, she saw the pale and shocked expressions of her friends. She also sensed that they accepted what she said as the truth but were unwilling to believe it all. Especially when she told of her stepfather's plans to wed Angela, and of her own whipping the night she was brought home.

Angela and Constance had led far different lives than she. Theirs was a life filled with love, warmth, and compassion. Lara's had been void of that since her mother's death. To emphasize the urgency of her warning, she turned from them and unbuttoned the bodice of her dress. When she shrugged the material free from her shoulders and arms, she lifted the silk camisole. Lara heard sharp, indrawn breaths of shock.

"My Lord," Angela whispered. Lara turned to see disgust on Constance's face, and tears flowing from Angela.

Slowly, Constance opened her arms, and Lara fell into them. At last she began to cry as she had never done before, with tearing, wrenching sobs that told of her anguish and loss. After an eternity against Constance's warm bosom, Lara began to recover. Part of what had happened to her had been cleansed, her hurt eased, not gone. But with this sharing, the heavy weight of her grief had lessened. She knew now she could endure the memory of Kael that she had been afraid to live with.

"Angela," Constance said in a soft voice, "go to the stairs and see what Martin is about. Then come back here quickly."

Angela nodded and left the room. While she was gone, Constance continued to hold Lara, whose breathing was slowly returning to normal. Constance knew that grief must have a release, and she was glad that she had been able to let Lara share it with her.

Within moments, Angela returned. "He's still drinking with the captain and the other one. Looks as if they'll be at it for a while."

"Good," Lara said as she pulled away from Constance and wiped her eyes. Then she slipped her arms through her sleeves and rebuttoned the bodice. "I've been hoping, foolishly it seems, that with the two of you along to distract my father, I could escape somewhere between Wyoming and Kansas. That won't work now. You'd both be in too much danger."

" 'Tis certain that your father is not taking the least chance. Although he talks much, I see the way he is always watching you. He listens to every word that you speak."

Lara nodded at Constance's words. "This could very well be our only time free of him," she said with a sad smile. "But even more important than that is to find a way to prevent him from marrying Angela." Lara's expression removed any doubt the women had about what she'd told them.

"John would never permit it," Constance stated with more confidence than she actually felt. The memory of Lara's scarred back was fresh in her mind.

"My father would never let one man stand in the way of what he wants," Lara declared vehemently. "John, alone, standing against my father—maybe. But John, alone, against my father's men?"

"I'll not have anything to do with him! Nothing!" Angela swore.

"Yes, you will!" Lara shot back. As she spoke, both women

heard the warning in her voice. "You must continue to act just as you have, listening to him talk and smiling nicely. You must not let my father know you are aware of his plans."

Angela and Constance nodded silently.

"You must realize the danger I've put you in. My father is mad. He does whatever he wants because he thinks that his money and power allow him to be above everything and everyone. So far it has!"

"We knew you needed us and we came willingly," Constance said. It was true, but for the first time since the start of the trip, Constance Crimmons fervently wished that her husband were here. "And what of your own danger?"

"I'm not sure. At first I thought I could get away somehow. But now I think that the only way I'll be free of my father is to wed Setterley." Lara paused for a moment as she looked from face to face. "I'm sorry that I've dragged you into this. . . ."

"All is not lost, yet. We'll think of something," Constance said with the first genuine brightness she had felt since Lara began her tale. Although she would try to find a way for Lara, Constance sensed the impossibility of success. But she was older, and knew time could be an ally as well as an enemy. Anything could happen between now and the wedding. . . .

John Crimmons rode home in the early darkness of the newly fallen night. His thoughts were on his wife and daughter. He was still angry with himself for letting them go, but he had been powerless to prevent it. His own guilt at his part in Kael's wild scheme had been a burden that needed easing. Constance had known this also, and that was another reason she'd been so adamant.

John had grown to hate Dowley, and although he could not rid himself of a haunting feeling of danger to his family, he realized that Dowley would do nothing as foolish as harming them. Because if Dowley did, he would be ruined.

John turned off the main trail and relief flooded him. He

was tired. He'd not done what he'd promised Constance. Instead of following them for one day, he'd camped outside of South Pass City that first night, and had followed them the next morning. When he'd felt assured that Constance or Angela had not signaled him, he started for home.

Now he looked forward to a hot meal and his bed. Suddenly, John reined in his horse. Several dark shapes sat on the earth near the corral, and too many horses were inside it. Loosening the rifle, John proceeded carefully. Slowly, the forms rose to face him. John pulled his gun free at the sight of Indians. His heart began to beat faster, and his nerves stretched tautly. Then, from the center of the small group, a tall man stepped out. John stopped his horse and waited.

"Since when do you welcome kin with a rifle?" Kael asked.

John Crimmons reacted as if he'd seen a ghost. He flew from the saddle, his gun forgotten in his hand as he advanced. When he was within five feet of the man and saw that it really was Kael, his weapon dropped from numbed fingers as he closed the distance. John grabbed Kael in a sweeping hug, lifting him and whirling him around.

"Dead! You're supposed to be dead!" John shouted, smiling broadly as he finally released Kael.

"I was supposed to be," Kael agreed.

"Would you tell me what in God's name is happening around here?" John demanded. The worry about his family was gone for the moment in the joy of seeing his younger cousin alive.

Kael motioned to the Indians, who once again resumed their sitting positions, ignoring both men. Then, walking John toward the house, Kael began to explain what had happened to him since he'd last seen his cousin.

While he talked, John lit the lamps and brought out a bottle and two glasses. When Kael finished, John poured drinks.

"I'm in dire need of some spirits, lad, and I would be pleased if you'd join me." Both men drank silently. As John refilled their glasses, Kael looked into his eyes.

"Where are Constance and Angela?" John raised his eyebrows, then downed his drink in one gulp. "Well?"

"Yes, lad, you'll have to know." Then, with Kael's stare of disbelief, John told his story.

"We've got to stop them!" he cried as John ceased speaking.

"Well, it's for sure Lara won't be marrying Setterley now, since she's a widow no more."

"There's more to it, John."

"Then let's have it all," the Englishman ordered.

"Were you, or the women, able to speak to Lara before they left?"

"No. The only thing we got was a letter from Lara, asking Connie and Angela to stand up with her at the wedding."

"Did you try to see her?" Kael asked hopefully.

"Yes. Angela tried, but she had no luck. She said that men were posted in front of the house, and they told her that Lara had gone riding with her father. They wouldn't be back until dark."

"Then Lara did the right thing."

"Dammit, Kael, will you try to make sense?"

"The reason Lara asked for the women to accompany her to Kansas City was so that she could warn them."

"About what?"

"Dowley. He's decided he wants to marry Angela."

"What!" John roared as he stood. "Are you crazed? Do you think I'd let that fat obscenity near my girl?" John sat slowly as he realized what he'd said, and what he'd done two days ago. "She's with him now, isn't she?" John finished in a low whisper.

"Right now she's safe. He won't do anything. He can't. This wedding is too important to him. He'll wait until Angela has no choice. That's why Lara did this. So she could warn them and they would tell you. You must protect yourself from Dowley. If I know anything about him, I know he'll try to kill you. You're his enemy. Even if there was no Angela, you helped me."

"I won't pretend to understand how you can be so sure,

but I want you to think about something." John's piercing eyes said more than his words. "It wasn't more than three weeks ago that you told me that Lara was no better than her father. What changed?"

"I did! I was wrong, completely," Kael admitted. He watched John's face, but it remained immobile. "And because I love her!"

Slowly, John Crimmons smiled. "You understand that now, lad, do you?"

"Lara was not responsible for what happened," Kael stated truthfully.

"And how do we get them from Kansas City?"

"Damned if I know," came Kael's reply, "But I'm going to!"

"We're going to," John corrected.

"John, he won't harm Constance or Angela. He can't take the chance."

"It's my wife and daughter you're speaking of. I'll thank you to let me make my own decisions." Kael knew that the gentle tone his cousin spoke in masked an iron will of determination. John's mind was made up; nothing would change it.

"I'll tell Painted Hawk we leave in the morning."

"The Indians are coming with us?" John asked, surprised.

"After what happened to me, Painted Hawk feels I get myself in too much trouble. He's decided to help me out," Kael said wryly. "Besides, he has another reason."

"Another reason?"

Kael smiled as he shrugged his shoulders at his cousin's question. John would find out soon enough.

Kael was glad that Painted Hawk and his braves were going with them. The Indian's guidance and knowledge would enable them to reach Kansas City in time to prevent the wedding. Using trails that were little known, or never used by whites, Painted Hawk could deliver Kael safely to his destination. Even through hostile Indian territory, he knew that Painted Hawk would not fail him.

Lara stood in front of the large, gilt-edged mirror and looked into it. The woman who gazed back was a stranger. She was not unknown, but she was a stranger. Lara knew the woman, she had seen her often in the dreams of her childhood. The woman who was reflected back at Lara, was whom she had once envisioned herself to be.

Dressed in the finest silks, the most modern gowns, bedecked with jewels and finery, servants at her beck and call, was the woman that ten-year-old Lara Fairwald Dowley had yearned to be. Now she was nineteen, and all she wanted to be was Lara Treemont, astride her mare, wearing her comfortable buckskins, and riding next to her amber-eyed husband. Suddenly, her heart grew heavy.

"It is you in the mirror," she told herself. "Lara Treemont is no longer. She is as dead as her husband." The woman in the lavender silk dress stared blankly back at her. Turning away, Lara went to her dressing table and sat on the chair.

Tomorrow, Lara thought, she would be married. Everything that Angela and Constance and she had discussed when they had the chance seemed to fail. Nothing they could do would stop this wedding. But Lara was glad she had been able to warn them about her father. That alone almost made it worthwhile.

They had arrived in Kansas City three days ago, feeling helpless and lost in the bustle of the city. Lara was amazed at the changes in the dress of the women, and at the way the city had grown since she passed through it nearly four years before. Riding through town to Johnathan Setterley's grandiose home, Lara had watched everything. If she were to get away, she must have some idea of where to go.

But even that had been futile. She had not left the house since her arrival. Everything, her wedding gown, new clothes, had been brought to Setterley's home by the merchants. A full staff of servants watched over her. She was as much a prisoner here as she'd been in Valley City.

Her lips curved into a slow smile. She still had one thing

left. Last night, Constance had come to her room, and had given her a small pistol. She told Lara that it was John's, that he'd given it to her for protection. Now Constance wanted her to keep it. Lara had not argued.

Shaking her head, Lara stood again. She had postponed the inevitable for another hour, but now she must go downstairs and have dinner with everyone. She moved to the mirror to check her dress one last time.

The lavender gown was by far the boldest she had ever worn. Dipping dangerously low across her breasts, it stopped a bare half-inch above the nipples. The dressmaker who had delivered it two days ago had told her it was the latest fashion from Paris. Lara could not have cared less.

The corset was cinched tightly, making Lara's slim waist even smaller, and at the same time it pushed uncomfortably upward, forcing her breasts to lift and appear larger than they were. The skirt was wide, and was supported by a crinoline underskirt and two petticoats. The hem brushed gently against her silk-encased toes.

Lara's hand went to her throat, and then dropped to her side. Falling seductively across the tops of her breasts was a long, triple-strand necklace of luminous pearls that Setterley had given her as a betrothal gift. The maid had done her hair up, with a small bun centered on the crown. Several thick strands of wavy hair had been left to drop artfully along her shoulders in an effort to hide the marks of her whiping. Luckily, the worst of the lashes had cut much lower on her back. Only a few faint lines on her shoulders would remain forever.

Lara left her bedroom and began to descend the ornate staircase. The house was a marvel of decorating and architecture. It seemed as if it had been taken from a fairy tale. The furniture was elegant, and the landscapes and portraits that adorned the walls were well done. Although the house was ornate, its flamboyance reflected the man who built it. Johnathan Setterley's ego was imprinted on everything. She would be just another of his possessions.

She heard the voices of her father and Setterley as they entertained the Crimmons women while waiting for her. Taking a deep breath, Lara entered the salon.

In the early hours before dawn, six Indians and two white men rode through the deserted streets of Kansas City. Their arrival had been timed to avoid the talk that would follow this strange band.

They followed Kael's lead, riding down the main street until he turned off. They continued for another quarter-mile, until reaching a small compound of buildings. Passing through the gate, Kael, John, and Painted Hawk read the sign above them. Then Kael slid from the saddle and went to the door of one building and knocked. A few moments later, it opened. A half-dressed man in an army uniform looked into the darkness questioningly.

"Evening, Sam," Kael said in greeting.

"Closer to morning, Captain," replied the sleepy officer.

"I need to speak with you."

Major Sam Bell, commanding officer of the military supply depot, nodded and stepped back to let Kael enter. As he did, he noticed the men that were still mounted. Sam Bell's eyes widened briefly before he shrugged and closed the door.

Once inside, Bell lit a lantern and motioned Kael to a chair.

"Sam, I need a favor, a big one."

"Don't you always," the officer replied. "Who are your friends?"

"Can you put them up for a while?"

"Why not," Bell agreed.

"There may be a reason why not," Kael advised him.

Suddenly, the man's face registered understanding. "You found him!"

"I found him, but that's only part of why I'm here again." Then, quickly, Kael told his story. When he was finished, his friend stared at him strangely.

"If I didn't know you as well as I do, I'd throw you out. That's some tale, old friend."

"Sam?"

"Let's get the men settled. How many are Indians?"

"Six. Their leader is Painted Hawk, subchief of the Wind River Shoshone."

"Special treatment?" Major Bill asked.

"He'd be insulted if he were treated differently than his warriors."

"I like him already," Bell said as he stood. "Let me get quarters arranged for them."

Fifteen minutes later, the Indians were settled, and Kael, John, and Sam Bell were again seated at the major's table discussing what they could do. At one point, Kael's eyes had taken on a faraway expression. When they cleared, he looked at both men.

"I've seen that look before," Sam Bell said in warning.

"I think I've got the answer. It will protect Angela and Constance, free Lara, and destroy Dowley!"

"After your last perfect plan, I'm not too sure I want to hear this one," John observed. Kael ignored his cousin as he began to speak. Bell was mesmerized as he listened to every detail of the plan. Kael spoke clearly and technically, as he'd done before every battle the two had fought together in the war. When he finished, both men were in agreement with him.

Now all they had to do was wait for the right moment.

The next day was a busy one for Kael. The Shoshone stayed within the military compound, as he, John, and Bell went into the business district of Kansas City. Kael purchased clothing for himself, and a plains wagon complete with a team of horses. Then, entering a woman's store, he bought several feminine items. By that time, it was past noon, and as Kael and John ate lunch, Sam Bell left to run another errand for Kael, one that only he could accomplish. While Kael and John were in the small café, across town from them, in a large house staffed with many servants, a burgundy-haired woman was having the final fitting of her wedding gown.

At Bell's returned, he informed Kael that the ceremony had

been set for the following week. Seeing Kael's reaction, he smiled and held up his hand. "However, there was a sudden change in plans. The wedding will be held tomorrow. Most unusual, but not unheard of."

"Dowley's worried about something," John stated.

With the fresh news, the rest of the afternoon was filled with hurried activity. By nightfall, everything that Kael needed had been done. By midmorning tomorrow, with good luck, Kael and Lara would be free of their past, and on the way to their future.

Dinner had been a long and agonizing affair, with conversation dominated by Setterley and Dowley. They spoke of their grand schemes for the future and of their plans to make Wyoming the cattle capital of the West. Between them, it sounded as if they had already divided up the country that they would be ruling. But to the women, several things were apparent. First was that Setterley seemed to talk down to Dowley, as if humoring him. Second was the way Setterley's eyes constantly lingered on Lara. The way he stared at her as he spoke, and the way his eyes always dropped to the swell of her breasts. His lust was so overpowering that it made the women avoid looking directly at him.

When dinner ended and the small party moved to the salon, Martin Dowley had gone to Angela's side, even as Setterley maneuvered Constance and Lara away from them. While Johnathan tried to keep them occupied with stories of his vast business affairs, both women kept glancing back at Dowley.

After another half-hour of listening to his boasts and hearing him extol the virtues of the Kansas City society that he predicted Lara would become the mistress of, Constance bid the cattlebroker good night. She neatly extracted her daughter from Dowley's clutches, and both women swept upstairs.

Lara, too, began to say good night, but Setterley placed a cold hand on her arm and asked her to stay for another moment. Although she did not want to, she agreed. From tomorrow on, unless a miracle took place, she would be spending much time with him, and felt she should accept the inevitable. She would never submit to him willingly, yet she must pretend to do so until she could somehow gain her freedom.

As her friends left, Lara saw Setterley give her stepfather a calculated glance. Dowley smiled and bid them both good night. However, instead of going to his room, he went outside.

"Alone at last," Setterley breathed as he caught her hand within his own. Lara suppressed a shiver at the clammy dampness of his fingers.

"I told you once that you would be mine. You laughed at me. Never laugh at me again," he ordered in a low, menacing voice. Then he pulled her against him, his lips covering hers as his hands roamed her back. Setterley's fingers dug into her pliant derriere, forcing her even closer against him.

Feeling his desire swell against her, Lara tried to extricate herself from his hold. "Why do you fight me?" Setterley asked with genuine puzzlement.

"I am not your property until tomorrow. Until then, you will lay no hand upon me!"

"What difference does one night make?"

Lara noticed that his breathing had become heavier, and his face was flushed. Again, he pulled her against him. His mouth crushed hers cruelly as his hands traveled freely over her. She felt his probing fingers at the top of her bodice, and gasped as he pulled the material down with a sharp jerk. Suddenly, one clammy hand was cupping a breast.

"No!" Lara spat. With all her strength, she slapped Setterley's face and backed quickly away, covering her naked flesh as she did.

"Bitch!" he roared as he advanced, his own hand held ready to hit her.

"Yes. Hit me. Slap me hard," she told him defiantly. "Mark my face so all your guests will see my bruises tomorrow."

Slowly, comprehension registered on his face. Dropping his arm, Setterley stopped and looked at her. A slow smile spread across his face as he began to speak. "Yes, I do believe you're right. Very well, Lara, until tomorrow, and our wedding."

Quickly, Lara fled the salon for the relative safety of her room. When she was in bed, the small pistol that rested beneath her pillow comforted her almost as much as the memories that paraded through her mind during the long, sleepless night.

"Now if only your face matched this gown, you'd be an absolute vision of beauty," Constance said sadly. "Did you not sleep at all last night?"

"I couldn't," Lara replied. "Could you have?"

"I doubt it. Hold still!" she ordered as she adjusted the bodice again. After Angela and Constance had gotten ready, they'd chased out the servants and finished dressing Lara themselves. Before doing so, they'd packed their belongings in a single trunk, and had it brought downstairs in preparation for their return home. When the wedding ceremony and lavish reception were over, they would leave with Martin Dowley.

"It is beautiful," Angela observed in a wistful voice. Despite the dark circles under Lara's eyes, she was in fact the perfect picture of feminine beauty.

The ivory wedding gown, made of silk, satin, and lace, was a magnificent creation. Lara was covered from just below her chin to the floor by the smoothly flowing garment. The high collar of Chantilly lace blended into a long satin bodice. The bodice itself seemed to be molded to her, accentuating her full breasts and narrow waist. From a curving line, set at her hips, it arched to a point several inches below her navel where the satin blended into the silk skirt which flared widely to the floor. The tight sleeves were made of ivory Chantilly that ran the length of her arms, ending in large, soft cuffs that reached to Lara's fingertips. The silk train stretched to a length of more than ten feet.

As Constance made one final adjustment, Angela brought over the veil and set it on Lara's head. The sheer ivory Chantilly fell in smooth folds from the top of Lara's glossy hair to below her waist.

Handing Lara the train, Angela tried to smile. The attempt at cheerfulness failed as Angela turned away, stifling a sob.

"It's time," came the growling voice of Martin Dowley, who stood framed in the now open doorway. "The coach is ready, and Johnathan has already gone to the church."

"We'll be right down, Martin, just a few more slight adjustments," Constance informed him. The three women stared at him until he left.

Dowley wore a full-length waistcoat of brocaded velvet, and beneath it was a matching vest with silken piping. His silk shirtfront raised into a low-rolled collar, with a dark tie fastened by a golden pin. The black trousers were creased sharply, and fell to the tips of his shoes.

"He'll probably die of the heat," Constance commented.

"Not him," Lara replied. Then her voice softened. "I don't know how to thank you," she said to her friends as a wave of sadness swept over her. It was almost done. Soon she would be without them.

"Ssh," Angela said as she hugged her, "we'll see each other often. I'll make Papa bring us!"

"Would you do something for me?" Lara asked. Both women nodded quickly. She went to the dresser. The soft, doeskin pouch rested there, hidden behind the small portrait of her mother. Lara picked up both of them and returned to her friends.

"I would like you to keep these for me."

"Of course," Constance agreed with a tender whisper. "But why?"

"Because when the day comes that I can be free of this marriage. I want these two things to be where I can find them. If I can't take them when I go. . . ." Constance's slow nod of understanding stopped further explanation. Then Lara took a deep breath. "If I die, or I am unable to claim them, I want the pouch, and its contents, to go to Angela's first born."

"What is it?" Angela asked in a quiet voice as she took the pouch.

"Open it."

Angela's deep blue eyes widened as she followed Lara's instructions, and poured out three gold sovereigns. "Lara!"

"It was my inheritance. It was to be given to my child, if I had one. It has been in my family for several generations."

"But the coat of arms . . . 'tis English. And the 'F'? Your family is Dowley," Constance stated as she inspected the pouch. When she'd first seen the purse in Lara's hand, the English coat of arms had caught her eye.

"My father's family is Fairwald. Martin Dowley is my stepfather," Lara admitted for the first time.

Both women stared in shocked silence. Lara was able to read their thoughts. Kael's foolish vengeance had been aimed at the wrong person.

"Lara . . ." Constance whispered as another thought surged in her mind. "What of a child by Setterley? Will you not want that child to have the inheritance?"

"I'll have no child by that man!" she stated.

Constance felt another shock. One thought arose, the memory of the pistol that she had given Lara.

Before anything else could be said, there was a knock at the door, followed by the butler's voice announcing that the coach was waiting. Silently, the three women started from the room, Lara's hand firmly within the warm confines of Constance's.

Ten minutes later, as the ornate coach rolled to a stop before the church, Lara peered between the velvet curtains. She let out a low gasp when she saw the crowd that was gathered in front of the church.

"Why are there so many people here?" she asked her stepfather. Martin Dowley laughed as he, too, looked out the window.

Settling his bulk back into the seat, Dowley continued to smile at her. "It's what I've been telling you. Johnathan is perhaps the most powerful person in the West. His wedding is a special event, and whatever day he decides to marry, the people would come to gawk at the spectacle. Johnathan and I are important people, and soon you shall learn what it is to be one." Dowley paused as he turned to stare intensely at Angela. "Do you envy your friend?"

"My goodness, yes," she replied with false brightness.

After what seemed like an eternity of waiting, the coach door opened and the stepladder was attached. Three liveried servants stood to receive them. Martin Dowley descended first, followed by Constance, and then Angela.

Pulling the veil down, Lara was the last to get out. A hush swept the crowd as it watched the bride being escorted into the church. Keeping her eyes straight ahead, Lara tried to ignore the feeling that she was an animal on display, rather than a bride going to the altar.

Once inside the vestibule, she let out her breath. The doors that led to the sanctuary were closed, and two more servants stood guard. The bridal party waited as one of the servants went into the sanctuary. Moments later, Lara heard the sound of an organ.

The small army troop stopped in front of the home of Johnathan Setterley only minutes after the Dowley coach had left. With the troops was a plains wagon. Dismounting, the officer in charge led his men to the front door, used the brass doorknocker, and waited for a response.

The door opened, and a Negro servant faced the men. His eyes took in their uniforms, and he stood taller. "Yes, sir?"

"Mr. Setterley asked us to pick up his guest's baggage. There's been a change in plans and we're to escort Mr. Dowley's party to Wyoming."

The servant noticed the covered wagon. To his eyes, it looked like the same one that his new mistress's baggage had arrived in. He was also used to the sudden changes of plan that were Johnathan Setterley's way. He led the soldiers to the waiting baggage.

Quickly and efficiently, the luggage was carried to the wagon. Shortly thereafter the group was on the street that led to the edge of town.

Twenty minutes later, the servant who had answered the door went to the rear of the house. There, he saw the plains wagon that he had thought the army men had driven away. "Oh, Lord," he whispered.

The music seemed to strike at her head as Lara walked down the long aisle. The faces of the guests were blurred through her tear-filled eyes. Her arm, resting atop her stepfather's, felt leaden, and she knew all hope was gone. Angela and Constance trailed behind, each holding a corner of the silk train, neither looking anywhere but ahead.

Slowly, Lara closed upon the altar. Then she felt her father lift her arm from his. She stood facing the minister, ignoring Johnathan Setterley at her side. The music ended, and the minister opened the gold-inlaid Bible. For some reason, she saw every detail with a crystal clarity that even the lace of her veil could not soften.

She watched the minister's fingers as they turned the pages of the Bible. When they stopped, she saw his lips form words.

Concentrating, Lara tuned out his voice as she commanded her legs to support her, and her body not to tremble. Her stomach churned, and she knew if she'd eaten this morning, she would have been unable to hold the food down. Then the minister's voice rose, and Lara knew the service was ending. It was then that she began to listen to what he was saying.

"Do you, Lara Dowley, take this—"

A loud crashing of door against wall resounded in the church. The minister stood wide-eyed and open-mouthed. Setterley whirled around, and Lara too, turned.

She felt the blood rush to her head. Her hand flew to her mouth, and she bit her knuckles. Walking down the aisle was John Crimmons . . . and Kael!

No, she cried silently, *a dream, a dream*. Kael is dead. . . .

But his ghostly presence did not vanish. Rather, it loomed larger, as did the cavalry men that followed him. Unable to move, Lara watched helplessly. Kael wore the full dress uniform of a retired military officer. John wore an immaculate suit of clothing, and the soldiers marched in precise steps behind them.

"What is the meaning of this? How dare you interrupt my wedding!" Setterley demanded, outraged.

Kael stopped six feet from Setterley, and stared into his eyes. "Sir, the woman you are about to marry is my wife." The timbre of his voice did not need loudness to carry in the church. Gasps of astonishment filled the sanctuary.

"You are a madman!" Setterley charged. Then the cattle-broker noticed Sam Bell. "Major Bell, please remove this man at once," he ordered.

"I'm sorry, sir, Captain Treemont is correct," he replied as he walked up to the minister, handing the startled man several documents.

Lara decided she must have fainted and this was nothing but a dream. Then she saw the red line of healing skin above Kael's ear, the path that had been left by the bullet, and slowly Lara raised the veil over her head and took one step forward.

"No!" Dowley yelled as he stepped between Lara and Kael. "You're dead," he screamed, pointing a fat, shaking finger at Kael. "You are dead!"

Kael stiffened, and Lara realized the amount of control he

was exercising to stop himself from killing Dowley. "I am here. Your men did not kill me, as you killed my father. Out of my way, murderer. I will take my wife from here—now!"

Moving swiftly despite his bulk, Dowley reached a hand into his coat and withdrew a small pistol. "You will not interfere in my life again," he shouted as he pulled the hammer back.

Before he could complete the motion, John Crimmons grabbed the fat man's wrist in a viselike grip, squeezing until Martin's fingers were forced open. The sound of the gun hitting the carpet was loud in the silent chapel.

"I'll kill you! I'll kill you!" Dowley howled ineffectually. "Do you know who I am?" he shouted. The insanity that held Dowley prisoner was now clearly written on his face. The scarlet that suffused him, the wide, white-rimmed pupils that stared out frighteningly, all showed what he was.

"Mr. Setterley," the minister called as he watched the events unfold before his eyes, "Captain Treemont is correct. I am holding the certificate that verifies his marriage."

Setterley's back stiffened as he faced Lara, his face a mask of hatred that almost surpassed her stepfather's. Setterley's dead gray eyes raked her, and Lara felt ravished. She did not blink, but stared coldly back at him. Then he turned to face Martin Dowley, who was still held by John Crimmons.

"You have brought me shame. You've lied and embarrassed me. I will not forget this. Dowley, I shall destroy you!" Then, without glancing at anyone else, Setterley walked down the long, seemingly endless aisle.

Releasing Dowley with a hard push, John turned to take his wife and daughter within his arms.

Kael gazed at Lara for a moment, then he slowly closed the distance between them. Before he took two steps, Lara moved.

With a cry that tore through the heart of every person in the church, she ran into her husband's arms. They melted together, frozen in an instant of time, alone in a world that belonged to only them. Their lips touched, their bodies blended, and they knew that whatever had happened before was past and their future would be filled with peaceful love and fulfillment.

Finally, the two lovers parted, and as they did, they were surrounded by soldiers. Led by John, Angela, and Constance, Lara and Kael Treemont left the church.

Behind them, Martin Dowley glowered. His face was distorted as his wild eyes watched them walk away. "It's his word against mine," he shouted to the people who remained. "It's his word against mine," Dowley repeated. The people began to leave, ignoring the man who stood screaming in their midst.

"He can't prove anything!"

PART III

Santa Barbara, California
October, 1868

A cool breeze swept off the Pacific Ocean, and reached into the bedroom windows of a house ten miles inland. In the large, wood-beamed room, lying within the canopied four-poster bed, Lara Treemont watched her husband sleep. Kael's breathing was slow and regular, and she felt her love for him wash over her in gentle waves. His eyes were closed, but Lara could still see them as they had looked at her throughout each day, speaking of his love without words.

In the faint moonlight that entered the room, she saw Kael's mouth form a smile. It had been over a year since that terrible, wonderful day in Kansas City, and almost ten months since they had arrived here, in Santa Barbara.

When Kael and Lara had left Kansas City, they'd gone with the Crimmonses, Painted Hawk, and his warriors. The trip to Valley City had been filled with happiness, and the enjoyment of themselves and their friends. When they had reached South Pass City, Kael and Lara had bid goodbye to the people who had helped them. But they had also shared their doubts with the Crimmonses, about Martin Dowley and what he might do to John and his family.

" 'Tis not something the two of you should be worrying about. Dowley will do nothing to harm us. He has already lost most of his standing, and when I tell of the doings in Kansas City, no one will bother with him again," John had declared confidently.

"Perhaps not," Kael had agreed, and then he told John that he had left a sworn affidavit concerning Dowley with Sam Bell, and that the major was going to try and file formal charges against him. Lara had hoped this would happen, but she believed her stepfather's deviousness would win out.

While Kael bought supplies for their trip and John helped him, Lara and the women had said their own goodbyes. Constance had returned Lara's portrait of her mother, and the doeskin pouch of golden sovereigns.

Breathing a sigh of relief, Lara had smiled at Constance. "Thank you for not giving me this in front of Kael," she had said.

"Why?" Constance had asked, puzzled.

"Because I want to wait. Let him love me as Lara Dowley for a while."

"But I'm sure he does," Constance had said with deep emotion.

"I know he loves me, but I feel I must wait until I'm sure Kael has come to terms with the fact that the man he thinks of as my father is still alive, and that he must remember it each day he looks at me."

The next morning, as soon as the golden Wyoming sun had risen, they left for California. Painted Hawk and his warriors rode with them until they passed through the Continental Divide. When the Shoshone left, Lara had felt her unwanted past depart with them.

"Treemont, go with peace, prosper, and make many children," Painted Hawk had said with a rare smile.

"And you, Painted Hawk, my friend, you must do the same," Kael had replied.

"It is not yet time for me. And, Treemont, my brother, we will meet again. It has been foretold." Then Painted Hawk had gazed at Lara for a long moment. "Woman of Treemont," he said in a low voice, "I wish you many years of joy, with bright suns and warm days to fill them." Lara had stared at the Indian as he spoke with the fluency of a diplomat. Her mouth did not close until he and his men had disappeared from sight.

She could still remember Kael's laughter as he'd told her what little he knew of Painted Hawk's ancestry and education. Lara, too, had smiled at the confirmation of her earlier suspicions that the Indian was more than he appeared to be.

The trip West, through Utah, Nevada, and finally into California, had been uneventful, its days filled by passing terrain, and its nights filled with love that Kael and Lara shared beneath the open skies. It was when they had reached California that a new feeling had taken over her emotions. Lara had felt that she was finally coming home.

Before they'd reached Santa Barbara, Kael had told Lara that he didn't want to rush but wished to proceed slowly, so that they could see, learn about and appreciate the people and the land.

Instead of taking the direct route, the couple had taken a longer way that wound through towns and villages as they reached lower and lower into California. Small towns abounded everywhere, and the closer to Santa Barbara, the older the buildings and towns were.

Everything in southern California had a Spanish flavor to it. The churches and missions were the most magnificent Lara had ever seen.

The people had been friendly, and the life most led seemed to be a good one. They crossed green mountains and rode through lush valleys as they moved closer and closer to their ranch. Although most of the mountain ranges were smaller and less imposing than the Rockies, Lara had felt as equally at ease in them as she had in the mountains of Wyoming. Then, after a month of traveling, Kael and Lara had entered the Santa Barbara mountains.

Lara would always remember her first view of Mission, Santa Barbara, and the twin towers that rose to greet the world. They had just started their descent to the populous area when Lara had seen the old church.

Santa Barbara itself, with its Spanish architecture built with adobe, had drawn Lara's eyes with its beauty. Everything about the area made her feel happy and content. The soft, green rolling mountains, the plateaux, and the blue waters of the ocean had all pulled her, and claimed her heart. The warm salt air was wonderful against her skin, and again, Lara had felt glad to come home.

Her initial sight of the ranch had kept her spellbound. Nestled within the mountains, the high Spanish house seemed to stand out, yet blend in. The home was two stories, made of brick and Spanish stucco, with a red-tiled roof that glinted softly in the sun. The high, arching, façade suited the dwelling perfectly. Set off at a short distance from the main house were several smaller ones, modeled after the larger one, and Lara knew that—these would hold the ranch hands and their families. At a modest distance to the rear was a large stable and two barns. Several hundred feet away was a riding corral that finished the layout and completed the harmony that the original designers had visualized. Surrounding it all were the fertile pastures for the herds of cattle that seemed well fed and numerous.

To Lara, this impression of her new home would remain with her always.

Kael had driven the wagon to the main house, and as he slowed to a stop, two riders came in from the south pasture. The lead rider had reined in his horse before the wagon just as a heavyset woman stepped from the front door. The man had taken off his tall hat, exposing a head of black hair. He'd smiled at Kael and Lara, his mustache following the curve of his lips. When he spoke, it was in heavily accented English.

"May I be of service?" he asked.

"You are Manuel Mendoza?"

"I am," the Mexican had replied as he waited for the stranger to continue.

Kael got out the wagon. "Permit me to introduce myself. I am Kael Treemont, and this is my wife."

The man looked puzzled for a moment, but then comprehension changed his expression to one of welcome.

"*Patrón*," Manuel had said as he jumped from his horse to stand before Kael. "Welcome, *Patrón*, to El Rancho del Sol," and as he had finished, Manuel swept his sombrero in wide gesture and bowed.

Yes, Lara thought as she continued to watch her husband sleep, from the moment they'd arrived at the ranch, she'd felt her life begin anew. The ranch became her heaven, set amidst blue water and high green mountains. The ranch hands were all Mexicans who had been born in California, and who had refused to leave when the wars had ended. They were Californians, they stated; not Mexican, not American, just Californians.

Lara adjusted quickly to life as a rancher's wife, but she was more than just that. She and Kael shared everything; the joy of living and the joy of working. Lara did, as she had once done for her stepfather, the record keeping for the ranch as well as overseeing the staff that worked within the house. She had started a vegetable garden, an herb garden, and for her own special delight, a flower garden. For two hours each morning, she joined Kael on his rides to check the work being done on the ranch. Each of her days was filled with many things and many people, but her nights were only for Kael.

Suddenly, Lara sensed eyes upon her. Pushing the memories of her arrival away, she saw Kael gazing at her.

"Can't sleep?" he asked with a soft smile as his hand went to her cheek and stroked it gently.

"Just thinking," she replied as she took his hand in hers and moved it to her lips, kissing its palm. Again, as it always happened, heat welled within her, and she saw the matching desire on Kael's face. Bending over, Lara smiled before she covered his lips with hers.

Tasting his tongue as it entered her mouth, her body draped warmly across his. Then she slid lower on him, as her lips and tongue roamed over his chin and slipped along the side of his neck. Unsated by the taste of his skin, she continued to kiss and lick through the mat of his hair-covered chest. Slowly, Lara took each of his dark nipples into her mouth and caressed them tantalizingly. Leaving the dark circle, Lara's lips traced the path of the scar that ran from below the nipple to his side, skimming lightly over the healed tissue.

Kael moaned deeply. His hardness pressed against her as she continued to slide her lips along his body. She touched each rippling muscle of his belly as her lips traced their way over them. He moaned again, and she grew even more alive with desire. Heat flamed upward, filling her breasts with an aching need to be stroked, and making her loins moist and ready. As her teeth nipped and teased along the curly mat that was the carpet of his manhood, Kael's hands wound through her hair and pulled her to him.

Moving quickly, Lara began to straddle her husband. His hands cupped her breasts for only a moment before he lifted his head and she felt his mouth on one waiting breast. An arrow of need leapt from her nipple and exploded within her. In a heartbeat, she was astride him, letting him fill her completely. She felt vibrant and whole with Kael buried deep inside her as she lowered her breasts to his chest. Kissing him deeply, Lara rode him as she controlled her desires and delighted in their shared love.

Suddenly, she could hold back no longer, and with little cries of pleasure, she urged him to join her in the completion of their ecstasy.

Wave after wave of rapture engulfed her as she pressed herself even tighter against Kael's heaving chest. Although they had finished making love, she could still feel Kael's heat within her and was loath to release him.

They stayed locked together for several minutes as Lara

bathed in the warm glow of their lovemaking, and enjoyed the feel of Kael's lips on her cheek and hair.

Slowly, she began to move again, her lips seeking his as the fires again rose within her. Her hands and lips became demanding as she reached into his heart and mind and brought him hard again within her. Suddenly, she felt herself lifted. She fell from Kael, only to have her lion of a man return, filling her again with himself as he pressed down on her.

She felt fragile, enclosed within Kael's arms. Holding her tightly, moving faster and faster, Kael forced Lara to join him again, as their passion raged out of control. Their voices mingled with the sounds of their bodies, until a low cry was torn from her throat, and her legs and arms wrapped around his muscular body. Trembling from the wild surges of her passion, Lara clung desperately to him.

Later, as she lay against Kael's side with her arm resting atop his chest and her head on his shoulder, she could no longer hold back her news. Kael felt warm moisture on his skin and turned his head at the same time as he lifted her face to his.

"What?" he asked as his eyes probed hers.

"I'm happy," she said as she sniffled foolishly. Kael kissed a salty tear away before he spoke.

"Tell me," he ordered gently.

She smiled. Her husband knew her too well.

"I am happy . . . and . . . we're going to have a child," she whispered.

Kael stared at her, his eyes wide in amazement Then a grin spread across his face.

"Thank you," he said only a second before he kissed her.

It was midafternoon when two wagons stopped at a small ranch in the Santa Barbara mountains. There, a tall, rangy man asked directions. After he'd received them, John Crimmons got back into the lead wagon and started the horses again. Behind him, the other driver did the same. It was only after the wagons rolled past that the rancher noticed it was an

Indian driving the second one. Next to the Indian was a young blond woman with large blue eyes. The rancher shook his head as he went back to his house.

Two hours later, John, Constance, Angela, and Painted Hawk stopped the wagons again. The sun was still in the sky, but it was nearing the horizon of blue water. Painted Hawk stepped from the wagon to look out at an ocean for the first time.

" 'Tis a lovely sight," John observed as he joined his friend.

"I have never looked upon water the color of this," Painted Hawk said as his eyes scanned the beauty of the Pacific.

John smiled and nodded. In the nine weeks they had traveled together, he had grown to like and respect Painted Hawk as both a man and a friend. The Shoshone became one of them, and had helped them reach California safely. A frown creased the Englishman's brow as he thought of what had forced them on this trip.

After their return from Kansas City, life had quickly resumed its usual pace. Yet during those first several days, John devoted himself to speaking to his friends, neighbors, and as many of the residents of Valley City as he could, telling them what happened to Lara and of the crimes that Martin Dowley was hopefully going to be prosecuted for.

But at the same time, Constance had confided in John that she was worried about Dowley. She believed Lara's warnings about him. John did not agree and Constance could not argue with him. Dowley would never marry Angela, John stated with finality. A month passed. Then two, and there were no incidents. Even Constance began to lose her continual doubts.

As fall descended on Valley City, everything seemed to be normal in the growing town that had been born just a few short years ago. But those who lived there sensed a change in the air that was not a change in season. Martin Dowley was seen rarely. No longer did he come to town daily. Since his daughter's defection, no new business or settlers had come to Valley City. The days had become crisp, and the nights cold.

Then, one mid-October night, everything changed. Just before dawn, John was awakened by a persistent hammering at the front door. Pulling on his pants, he went to answer it as Constance rose and hurriedly dressed. When John opened the door, he was met by the smudged and sooty face of Mary Blair, who stared hauntingly at him. In the low light of the lantern that Constance had lighted, John saw the only clear skin on Mary's cheeks was that which had been washed by her tears. Behind her huddled the three Blair children.

"Carl's dead," she blurted. "The farm's burned." Then she began to cry. Constance rushed to her neighbor as Angela joined them. They urged the woman and children inside. When Mary had finally calmed, she told them what had happened.

"We had just gone to sleep when we heard the cow bellow. Carl went outside as I went to the window. I saw him running to the barn, then I saw an explosion of flames. It was awful! I heard that poor, terrified cow. And when I started to go outside, there was a gunshot . . ." Mary's loud sobs tore through the house as John, Constance, and Angela looked on helplessly.

"I saw Carl fall to the ground, just as two riders came from the back of the barn."

"Do you know them?" John asked suddenly.

"No . . . I couldn't see them clearly. Just two men on horses. Then they rode over to the house. I started to wake the children when the first torch broke through the window. . . . They were going to kill us all!" Constance pulled Mary tighter within her arms. Angela took the children to the kitchen to clean them.

"We . . . I rushed the children down to the root cellar. Carl always said if there were a fire, or any danger, that was where we should go. I did," Mary said in a sad, proud voice. "The house burned over us. I don't know how we survived. The fire was so loud, and when the roof caved in, I thought it would break through into the cellar. I was scared even after I saw the floor would hold. The children huddled around me in the furthest corner of the cellar, and for some reason the smoke didn't reach us."

Mary's sobbing tale wrenched painfully at John's heart. He knew who had done this. The anger within him needed the release of action.

"When we came out," Mary continued, "Carl wasn't where he'd fallen. But as I looked at what had been our home, and I walked to the barn, I saw him. . . . They'd thrown him into the burning barn. What was left of him was in the ashes. The animals were dead, our winter stores had been destroyed. I took the children and we walked until we got here. . . ." Now, Mary sat quietly within Constance's arms, and rocked slowly back and forth, not seeing anything around her.

John's eyes met his wife's, and he spoke in a low voice. "I'll go tell the others. I'll be back by noon. Take care of her, Connie," he said needlessly.

"Be careful," she whispered back.

John spent the morning visiting the nearest neighbors, and by late afternoon, six men stood among the blackened remains that only yesterday had been the farm of Carl Blair. When they finished burying him, they stood around his grave and stared at each other, waiting for someone to voice their thoughts. Sensing their reluctance, John took it upon himself to speak.

"We know whose work this was," he stated as his eyes challenged them to deny it. "We must face Dowley!"

The five men looked at John, but only one was able to hold his gaze. "What's wrong with you?" John demanded in an accusatory tone. "Are you willing to let that man kill whomever he wants, destroy whatever is in his way?"

"We can't fight him, we can't stop him," said one of the men. "We all owe him money. If we tried to fight him, we'd be ruined, or worse, we'd end up like Blair!"

"And you call yourselves men. . . . 'Tis nothing but groveling fools that you are! Good Lord, I came full across an ocean to find the very thing I tried to escape. I thought I left behind me the cowards who cringe at people who seek to control them. I'll be damned if I let Dowley get away with this."

"John," Ben Noland interjected. He was a small rancher, and the only one who had not turned from John's blistering attack. "You and I, and maybe a couple of others, are the only ones not in debt to Dowley. You can't ask these men to give up their dreams, everything they've worked for, because of what Dowley did last night."

"Dreams? Slaves don't dream! Can't you," John said as he lifted a long finger and pointed to the men, "can't you see that you're not free men? Don't you understand that 'tis but a matter of time before Dowley gets to you? Before he squeezes you out, and takes your dreams for himself? If he lets you stay, you'll end up working for him and have nothing left for yourselves."

The men shifted uneasily under John's fierce stare. "You must believe me. I've lived with this all my life. I saw it each day I grew from child to a man. The poor, serving their squires and lords. The land they worked on and the animals they raised went to their masters. Is that why you came West?"

"He'll destroy us as he did Blair," another man said in a low voice.

"Then be his slave!" John declared as he turned and mounted his horse. "I'll be going to see Dowley about this, soon. Whoever will join me I'll see tomorrow at my home." John galloped away without a backward glance.

Throughout the remainder of that day, and the next, John Crimmons fumed at his inability to get the people of Valley City to stand up for themselves. But on the night following the burial of Carl Blair, Ben Noland and two other ranchers who owed nothing to Dowley came to the Crimmons ranch. John, Ben, Jim Rivers, and Hal Kendal had talked half the night. When they were done, a partial agreement about what to do had been reached.

They would send a letter, with Mary Blair and her children, to the commander of Fort Bridger. Mary and the children would be going back East from there, with money John and his neighbors had raised for them. But John was not satisfied with this and told the men he was going to face Dowley anyway. Would they come with him? After much silence, and helpless looks, John angrily threw his hands up in the air.

"You must confront him with me!" he shouted. But none would.

That following Saturday, John rode slowly through town until he stopped in front of Dowley's office. As he dismounted, Lew Cross left his post in front of the building to alert Dowley.

While John waited, a small crowd formed behind him. Word had spread fast, as it can only in a small town. In the crowd were the men who had helped to bury Carl Blair.

When Dowley emerged from his office, John stepped forward. He felt himself grow cold with anger as he looked levelly at Dowley. The dark coals of the man's eyes glared at him with insane hatred.

John felt as if he were staring at the devil himself. Dowley looked older, his face puffier, and John could see the red and blue veins that mapped the fat man's cheeks and nose. John also smelled the mixed stench of stale tobacco and old liquor that enveloped Dowley.

"What do you want?" Dowley demanded in a voice that snarled with warning.

"To talk about Blair's murder," John stated in a flat voice.

"Do you?" Dowley asked, as he looked into John's face, and then at the crowd of people that surrounded them. Most of the crowd turned their eyes from Dowley's. Only John held the other's gaze. "Carl Blair died in a fire."

" 'Tis not the story I know," John said in a tightly controlled voice.

"Blair was a fool! Every drifter and trapper in the territory heard he came into money. He bragged in the saloon that he paid me off. In gold! They must have thought he had more," Dowley said as he brushed aside the charges that John was making.

" 'Tis a fact that you're lying, Martin Dowley," John replied in a dangerously low voice. "Everyone knows how Carl got his money."

"You call me a liar? And what are you? A foreigner who raises disgusting animals that destroy the very grazing land that feeds them!"

"Don't try to change the subject, Dowley. We want an explanation about your dealings with Carl."

"I've had no dealings with Carl Blair since the day he paid his mortgage. And I'll have no more dealings with you!" he shouted in a hate-filled voice.

"I've sent for help. I've reported that you murdered Blair!" Ben Noland stated.

"You did what?" Dowley yelled. Then the grotesque mask of hatred and fat changed into a caricature of an obese buffoon as he began to laugh. "You reported me?" he asked incredulously, shaking his head from side to side. "To whom? I control this territory," he stated. Dowley began to walk back to his office. When he reached the door held open by Cross, Dowley turned back to John.

"Don't ever get in my way again. From this moment on, there is nobody in Valley City who will do business with you if they want to do business with me!" Then Dowley laughed insanely as he disappeared inside.

When John returned home, and related what had happened, he would not listen to his wife and daughter's arguments to leave Valley City. Instead, John prepared the ranch for a long winter.

The Crimmons family made several trips into South Pass City to bring home enough supplies and grain to last the cold season.

By early spring, they had started their regular routine, and the hardship of the past winter was beginning to fade from their minds. Then, one balmy spring day, Martin Dowley and his men arrived. John greeted them with open hatred and a loaded rifle.

"I would think that after so many months to mull things

over, Crimmons, you'd not be greeting me this way," Dowley
started. "But I like you . . . and your family. I am a forgiving man. Apologize and it will be as it was. I will bear no
grudges," Dowley said with grave benevolence.

"Get off my property! Murderer!" John retorted. "If I see
you, or your men here again, I'll fire without warning."

Dowley's smile grew wide as his eyes disappeared within
the fatty folds of his lids. Slowly, the smile faded and John
saw the dark eyes look over his shoulder. Turning quickly, he
saw Angela and Constance standing in the doorway.

John pulled the trigger, firing into the air. "You'll be leaving now," he said as he reloaded the weapon, "or I'll be
forced to shoot you." John held the rifle sights on Martin
Dowley's head.

"You can't survive without me," Dowley said as he signaled his men out.

That night, another long argument dominated the Crimmons
home, with John refusing to yield.

Two days later, Amos Stangly, John's only ranch hand, did
not return from the grazing pasture. As twilight fell, John
went to search for him. He found Amos among a small flock
of sheep, lying face down, his head split open. War had been
declared.

A week later, almost half of John's flock was slaughtered.
John knew he must get help. The letter and charges that had
been sent to Fort Bridger had not been answered, and it was
obvious that Dowley's influence had stopped it. Deciding on
what he must do, John readied himself for a trip to Fort
Casper to seek assistance from the territorial administration.

Although he feared for his wife and daughter, John had no
choice. If they went with him, there would be nothing left
when they returned. Instead, he first found their circuit
minister, Jeremiah Bleutriech, who was due to arrive in Valley City in two days. Hearing the situation, the minister
agreed to stay with the women. After that, John rode out.

It was on the second day of his trip to Fort Casper that
John began to sense something strange. Fear and desperation

enveloped him. As he crested a small rise, John stopped the horse. He could not go any further. Intuitively, he knew something terrible was happening to Constance and Angela.

Turning his horse, John rode through the night, early the next day, he arrived home. The silence of the ranch was deafening, and with a fast-beating heart, John entered the house. He called out his wife's name, but there was no answer. Carefully, he searched the rooms.

Empty.

John went to the barn. Inside, he found the minister tied and gagged within a stall. Freeing him, John helped him to his feet.

"Jeremiah, what happened?" John asked in a dread-filled voice.

"I'm sorry. I failed you and your family," he said as he took a few tentative steps.

"Later," John ordered, supporting Jeremiah as they walked to the house. Inside, John poured a glass of whiskey for him. After he drank it, and breathed deeply a few times, Jeremiah began to confirm John's fears.

"Yesterday afternoon, Dowley and his men showed up. It was as if they knew you were gone. I told the women to stay inside while I went out to face them. I ordered them off the property. Martin laughed at me. He waved to one of his men, who rode over and kicked me in the stomach. As I lay on the ground, they broke into the house. I couldn't move, John, the hand who had knocked me down held his horse over me. Another one tied me up while the others dragged Constance and Angela out. They took me into the barn and gagged me, then hit me on the head. I came to last night, but I couldn't get free." The minister stopped talking as he gazed at John's pain-etched features. "I'm sorry I couldn't stop them."

" 'Tis no fault of yours, Jeremiah, only my own stupid, unyielding ways." John went to a large cabinet, took out a box of ammunition, and filled his pockets. When he was finished, he turned to the minister. "Rest here, Jeremiah, then you'd better go into town and see to your hurts. I've got something that I must do."

"They'll kill you," Jeremiah warned.

"Perhaps, but not till I've finished with Dowley." Then John left. What he did not tell the minister was that he was going for another kind of help. Possibly the only help he would find.

That night, John Crimmons rode through the darkened Wind River Mountains. By sunup, he crested a small rise and waited. Within the hour, a small group of riders met him. John spoke a name. The Indians surrounded him, and led him to their village. There, he faced Painted Hawk.

After another hour passed, the pair led a group of warriors through the foothills to the Dowley ranch.

John rode to the front of the main house where he fired his rifle in the air, and was rewarded by having Lew Cross, Dowley, and three ranch hands surround him. Although his heart beat fast, and his blood raced through his body, John maintained a calmness that did not betray the heat of his searing anger.

"Have you come to make your peace, and to give your blessing for my marriage to Angela?" Dowley asked with a smirk.

"I've come for my family, and I've come for you!" John stated. As he spoke, one of the hands drew his pistol, confident the Englishman would not see him.

The soft thud of an arrow entering flesh greeted the movement. Startled, all eyes fell on the man who dropped his weapon and stared at the arrow sticking from his shoulder.

"I want my family!" John stated as Painted Hawk emerged from his hiding place to join John's side. His bow and arrow were steadily aimed as Lew Cross reached for his gun holster. Cross froze as his eyes fastened on Painted Hawk.

Dowley turned to the Shoshone. "You would break the treaty of Washakie?"

"Washakie does not know of this, yet!" Painted Hawk warned. "You release women!"

"Get off my land!" Dowley countered.

Painted Hawk stared at Dowley for a long while, then raised his bow and shot into the air. "Look behind me."

Dowley looked and saw twenty warriors, marked with the paint of battle, lined up not more than three hundred feet away. Dowley blanched.

"Release my family," John Crimmons ordered. Cautiously, Dowley nodded at Lew. Cross went to the house and within moments returned with the women. Seeing them, John felt his heart sink. The expression on Angela's face told him the worst. Slowly, John raised his rifle and aimed it at Dowley.

Dowley trembled as he faced his death.

Then John felt Painted Hawk's hand on his, lifting the barrel. "We cannot, for then I would be breaking the peace my chief has made. If I do that, I must die also."

Slowly, Painted Hawk's words penetrated the wall of hate and anger that held John a prisoner. With a deep exhalation of breath, John lowered his weapon. He dismounted and went to his wife and daughter. He embraced them as Painted Hawk's warriors formed a protective circle around them. Then John put Constance on the horse behind him and Painted Hawk drew Angela up on his mount. They rode in silence from the Dowley ranch.

At home, with Painted Hawk and the warriors gone and Angela finally asleep in her bed, Constance told John what had happened. When it was over, he turned to his wife with tearstained cheeks, and pulled her close.

" 'Tis my fault it happened, and 'tis something that will never be mended. We leave as soon as we can," he said finally. Constance nodded as she held her husband's head to her breasts, giving him as much comfort as she could.

The next day, the Crimmonses began to pack with the aid of a friend. Painted Hawk had not left with his warriors as they had thought, but had stayed to guard the Crimmonses against Dowley if the man should return. When he faced John in the morning, Painted Hawk told the Englishman that he would be leaving with the family if they were going West.

John accepted his help. The journey was made easier with Painted Hawk along, guiding them through the worst of the mountains, and keeping them well fed with game that he hunted. Soon Angela began to come around as the sharpness of the memories of being raped by Martin Dowley faded. By the end of the first month of travel, Angela had become the happy, spirited woman she had once been—almost.

After John had spoken with Angela, and had counseled her as best he could—because he knew that it must be a man who explained why these things happened, and it must be a man to show her that it would not matter to someone in the future—she began to show more life in her eyes.

But it was Painted Hawk who sat by Angela's side, speaking rarely, while he gave her the comfort and nearness of a friend without demands. By the time they reached California, the three former Britons and the one Indian had formed bonds that would never be broken.

Now, as John led the two wagons toward the magnificent Spanish ranch, he wondered how Kael and Lara would react to their arrival. Pulling the brake, John saw the familiar figure of Lara Treemont emerge from the large house, and he smiled warmly.

By dinnertime, the ranch was in a festive mood. Kael had returned in the late afternoon after Lara had made the Crimmonses and Painted Hawk welcome. She had had their belongings brought inside and had shown everyone to their rooms. When they were settled, Kael had ridden in, accompanied by Manuel, and had been greeted by his excited guests.

After the initial shock of seeing his cousins had passed, Kael saw Painted Hawk standing silently off to the side. Letting his hand slip from John's, Kael walked slowly to his friend.

"I am glad to see you, Painted Hawk," he said with more emotion than he intended to reveal.

"It is as I told you, Treemont, my brother, we would meet again at the correct time."

Then Kael pulled Painted Hawk into an embrace, and felt the other's arms go around him and press tightly. When they parted, their eyes held each other's unwaveringly. "My home is yours."

"Thank you, Treemont." Then Kael and Painted Hawk

335

were swept along by the rest and went into the house. The women, deciding to change for dinner, left the men to their own devices. Kael took them into his library. As John looked around, a smile broke across his face.

"This room reminds me of your father's in Philadelphia."

"It should," Kael said with a matching grin. "I had all his books shipped here before I left for Wyoming. They came by ship and were waiting for me. Drink?" he asked both men.

John accepted, but Painted Hawk shook his head negatively. "Your whiskey does not agree with me. I dislike the harsh burning."

"You'll learn," John prophesied.

"It is not a matter of learning, but of tasting," Painted Hawk informed the Englishman.

"No matter," Kael cut in as he handed John a glass and all three sat. "What does matter is why you've arrived here with all your possessions. What happened?" Kael's expression brooked no argument, or delay. John told his tale with no apologies.

"Again, Painted Hawk, I owe you much," Kael said.

"*We*, lad. *We* owe Painted Hawk much," John added.

They looked at the lean, copper-skinned man, and waited for the Indian to speak. Sensing that he must, Painted Hawk said, "There are no debts. Our friendship started with a debt, my brother's return. But, Treemont, John, there can be no debts among friends. My people know that the man they have been dealing with is not honorable, and Chief Washakie, my uncle, is grateful. He has sent an emissary to speak with your government; to make a peace that is fair and just for the Shoshone. What I have done for you can only be seen as a small payment for what you have shown to the Shoshone nation. The peace that Washakie seeks will protect all our people against men such as Dowley. There is no debt," repeated Painted Hawk.

Both men accepted Painted Hawk's words. John took them at face value, but Kael knew that there was more. He would talk with him later.

Now, Kael wanted to change his clothes, and to talk to Lara. Another fence had been broken. Hundreds of head of cattle had gotten loose and were wandering in the foothills. He did not think all of them would be found and he was worried. This time, unlike the last, the fence looked as if it had been torn down deliberately.

Dinner had been wonderful, and Kael had enjoyed watching the Crimmonses eat the meat that had been prepared, along with the vegetables that Lara had grown in her garden. The two biggest surprises had come from Painted Hawk. When the Indian joined the rest at the table, he wore his ceremonial buckskins. The smooth animal skins shone beneath the large chandelier, and he walked with an almost ethereal grace.

When dinner was served, Kael decanted the wine. He bypassed Painted Hawk to pour some for John.

"Treemont, I said I did not like your whiskey. I said nothing of wine," Painted Hawk pointed out.

Kael stared, then returned to the Shoshone and poured the red liquid into his glass.

"Thank you, Treemont."

"Will you call me Kael?" he asked. Painted Hawk nodded and smiled. Kael watched in fascination as the Indian lifted the goblet to sniff the delicate bouquet. With another smile, Painted Hawk sipped the wine. Afterward, he looked up at Kael and nodded.

"I'm glad you approve," Kael said as he finished serving the wine and sat down. Painted Hawk's eyes followed him with a puzzled look.

"Treemont . . . Kael, did I not do that correctly?"

"Do what?"

"The wine."

"Did you do what to the wine correctly?" Kael asked, perplexed at the twist in the conversation.

"Did I not taste it right?" Painted Hawk inquired.

Suddenly, John let out a loud, sharp laugh. "Aye, lad, you tasted it right enough."

"Good," Painted Hawk noted. "It was as my mother said."

Rather than probe any further and get himself even deeper into this mystery, Kael decided to give Painted Hawk time to tell what was fast building into an interesting story.

By the end of dinner, everyone had become more relaxed. It was then that Painted Hawk spoke. "It is time for me to explain something," he began. Everyone stopped what they were doing to listen intently.

He told them the true circumstances of his birth. His mother's capture by the Blackfoot, when she, her husband, and a small group of traders had ventured too far from the West India Trading Post in British Canada. Her husband's death, and her subsequent escape and recapture by the Shoshone. There, she adapted to the Shoshone way of life and fell in love with Painted Hawk's father, Chief Washakie's brother. Painted Hawk and Two Wolves were the children of the union. They were raised as Shoshone. But Regan Sheffield Porter had also taught the boys to read, write, and speak fluent English and French. She taught them, too, about table manners, the history of England, and what to expect in the white man's world. Painted Hawk's mother died when he was fifteen, at peace with herself and her surroundings.

After Painted Hawk finished his tale, a strange silence continued around the table. Kael noticed that Angela's eyes were bright as she studied the Indian.

Painted Hawk spoke once more. "And now you, Kael Treemont, may call me by my first name also. It is Neil. Neil Sheffield."

"I'll be damned," John Crimmons murmured in an awe-filled voice.

"Attention!" Kael called as he stood and clinked a silver spoon against his wineglass. Once everyone had quieted, he smiled.

"It seems tonight, with everyone baring their deepest secrets,

that I shall also. Lara and I have an announcement to make."
Kael paused for effect. "I will no longer be the last of the
Treemont line!"

Angela leapt from her chair with a squeal of excitement,
and went to Lara, embracing her tightly. Constance smiled
warmly before replacing her daughter and kissing Lara's cheek.
John congratulated Kael. Seeing Painted Hawk's questioning
look, John turned to him.

"Neil, Lara's with child," he explained.

The rest of the night was spent in idle speculation about
raising children in California, and with Painted Hawk-Neil
Sheffield answering a barrage of questions. But sitting next to
Lara, Kael's mind was on other matters; the mystery of the
broken fences, and the things that John had not told him.
Kael sensed a void within his cousin's narrative, and he would
not be satisfied until he learned everything.

Later, as Kael and Lara lay in their large bed, he asked her
about his cousin's problems in Valley City. She looked at
him, and he saw moisture build her light blue eyes.

"Tell me," he ordered softly.

"You must not let them know I've told you." After Kael
promised, Lara proceeded to reveal the private talk she'd had
with Constance, just before Kael had returned to the house,
and while one of the ranch hands had been showing John and
Angela some of the grounds. As she told him of Angela's
treatment at Martin Dowley's hands, she felt Kael stiffen
beside her and grasped his hand within hers.

"Why wouldn't John tell me?" Kael asked. "Does he think
I would feel any less for him, or Angela?"

"No," Lara said, wiping her eyes, "I think he's afraid you
would start after my father again, that you would become
vengeful."

"I want to see Dowley pay for what he's done. I want him
to pay for my father's death, for your humiliation, and for
everything else. He's been paid to a degree, by our marriage,
but again he's struck at me and my family. I will find a way,

but it will be the right way. The law and the government will handle it," Kael promised.

Lara kissed him gently. "Thank you, husband."

Before Kael fell asleep, he thought of the charges that he had filed against Dowley. The ones that Sam Bell had taken care of, and the new ones that he'd filed here, at the territorial government headquarters in California. No, he had not given up his desire to see Dowley punished, he had just matured enough to do it a better way.

Three days later, Kael, John, Painted Hawk, and Manuel, the foreman, were inspecting another downed fence. Kael was angry, but relieved at the same time. The herd that had been in this pasture had wandered yet had stayed near by, grazing contently. As the men looked for signs, Painted Hawk called Kael over.

"There were five. They came from the East, and returned the same way." When he stood, clad only in buckskin pants, his coppery-brown chest reflected the noonday sun. "We can track them, Kael. Perhaps they are not far."

"It's too late, Neil," Kael admitted. "We must catch them while they act." Turning to Manuel, he told him to round up the cattle. That afternoon, Kael issued watch orders. The men would begin patroling the fences in pairs, ten minutes apart. Enough hands worked the large ranch to do this, but the real work of the ranch would suffer. Kael had no choice and he understood this, just as Manuel Mendoza and his men did. There were no arguments given to their new *patrón*. They liked and respected him, and they would do what was necessary.

The next days and nights were peaceful, but Kael did not change the watch orders. He, John, and even Painted Hawk, rode with the men, covering the perimeters of the property nightly.

A suggestion of John's helped. For two days, the men herded the cattle into one pasture. They would be moved every couple of days to insure proper grazing. Fewer hands were required on the boundaries when cattle were close together.

Several uneventful weeks passed. Kael and Manuel believed whoever was doing the damages had decided that the ranch was too well protected now. Kael had no intention of giving up learning who it was, but calving time was near, and the men needed their rest if they were to work at their full potential. Kael and Manuel elected to cut the patrols down, using only six men a night, and never the same men twice in a row. For another week, this worked. Gradually, the ranch returned to its regular operating schedules and procedures.

With the Crimmonses and Painted Hawk at the house, everything seemed perfect as far as Lara was concerned. The days were filled with love, friendship, and peacefulness. At long last, Lara knew she'd found what she had always wanted. The new feelings that generated within her body, and the knowledge that she and Kael were to be parents, brought an inner tranquillity that she had never before possessed.

One night as she lay in bed, restless and unable to sleep, she again thought of the one thing she had put off revealing. Lara had not yet told Kael about her father. It must be done soon. Kael would be pleased. With a smile of satisfaction, Lara drifted into sleep.

Although her activities had changed with the arrival of her guests, she still found time each morning to ride with Kael. Today, as they rode the north range, Kael's eyes were distant, and their conversation was sparse.

"Something is bothering you. Do you want to talk about it?" she asked.

Reining his horse, Kael smiled at her. "It seems that I can't hide anything from you."

"Do you want to?"

"No." Kael dismounted. With his hands on her waist, he lifted her from the saddle and let Lara slide along his body until her booted feet touched the ground. Sparks of desire burst through Lara as she pressed against Kael's muscular body. He brushed her lips lightly, then stepped back and took her hand. They strolled beside the fence; the large Andalusian stallion, and Lara's gelding ambled behind.

"You're still worried about those incidents?" she suggested.

"No, nothing has happened in weeks. I've already told Manuel to go back to the usual operation. We have to. There are too many head in the one pasture, calving's started, and we'll lose a lot of new stock that way. No matter, we must return to normal."

"Who do you think it was?"

"All the ranches have been having problems. Perhaps it was just our turn," he said with a shrug. Then he stopped and gazed at the land around him. "Lara, about John and Constance."

She wondered about that also. They were almost penniless, having had to give up nearly everything to leave Wyoming. "Yes?" she asked, sensing that her husband already had something in mind.

"I think they like the area and wish to settle here. I'd like to set them up."

"I'm glad," Lara said as she took Kael's other hand in hers.

"But there's a problem."

"John," Lara said.

"He won't take the money. There are a few thousand acres available, about fifteen miles southwest of here, but John says he'll have to wait until he earns the cash."

"You didn't offer to buy it for him, did you?" Lara asked in a low voice.

"Why not?"

"Oh, Kael, you're so smart when it comes to almost everything, but not when it comes to family money. John has lost everything, and what he lost had been bought with your father's money to begin with. It's not really pride, I guess it's just that he was so close to having made everything work in Wyoming. He wouldn't take anything from you, not after he had to give up what your father's money had gotten him the first time."

"What do we do?"

Feeling good that Kael needed her advice, she smiled softly at him. "Take John to the bank and arrange a mortgage. You can guarantee the loan, and because John refused to see his land go to my father, it is still deeded to him. That, too, can be used as collateral, so John will not feel more indebted to you."

"Common sense, no less," he said as he squeezed her hand within his. "Beauty, grace, and common sense. I'm a lucky man," Kael commented as his love for her showed on his features. "Come, it's time to talk to John."

John agreed. They would go into Santa Barbara next week to speak with the people in the bank. Kael offered to start off his cousin with a small herd, which John would pay for from the profits.

Four more days passed peacefully, until one night, excited screams broke the quiet of the sleeping hours. Jumping out of bed, Kael raced to the window. Licking the darkness were orange-red flames rising from the far stables. The men were shouting in their struggle to fight the blaze. Grabbing his pants as he left the room, Kael warned Lara to stay in the house. Then he was gone. Lara got up and dressed.

By the time she was outside, Constance and Angela had joined her. The women went to the burning barn to see if they could help. As Lara reached it, several men were leading horses out. Quickly Lara went to the water-bucket line. Kael was not there.

Flames shot skyward, and Lara knew the structure was lost. Turning to Manuel, who was urging his men on, Lara ordered him to concentrate on keeping the second barn wet so that it would remain undamaged. Then she ran to the stable.

The front of it was already on fire as John led out two horses, their eyes rolling widely, and their hooves prancing on the ground.

"Where's Kael?" she screamed.

"Inside. He's getting the last horses," John said in a breathless voice that was followed by a racking cough.

Lara stared at the burning door, praying that Kael would get out in time. Her heart pounded violently as she waited. Suddenly, a loud cracking echoed in the air. Lara jumped at the noise as part of the roof collapsed. "Kael!"

As if in answer to her cry, she saw an image appear within the flames. Then she saw the giant gray stallion leap through the blaze with Kael on his back, and another horse pulled behind it. Within a frozen second of time, as her heart stopped beating, Lara saw her husband ride to safety.

Racing to him, she felt relief flood through her. Kael dismounted and pulled her close. After that, everyone watched as the stable disintegrated before their eyes. Their only consolation was that the second barn had not caught fire.

Moments later, Manuel and another hand carried the unconscious watchman to the waiting group. His bloodied face was evidence of how hard he had been hit.

Immediately, Lara gave instructions for the man to be taken to the house. There, she supervised the tending of his wounds, assisted by Carmella, who was part of staff. When the man's injury was cleaned and bandaged, and he'd awakened, Kael and Manuel questioned him. He had not seen who had hit him, and had heard no one before he was attacked.

Later, as everyone sat around the kitchen table drinking hot coffee, they wondered who was behind these terrible events that were plaguing them. After the fire had died out, Painted Hawk searched the area but found nothing. Kael studied those around him, stopping at his foreman as Manuel began to speak.

"I can think of only one thing, *Patrón*. It is more than twenty years since the war ended, but the children of the men who once owned this land are now of age, and must want revenge for their losses."

"Why this ranch?"

"It is the best. You have the best ranges, the most land, and are the easiest to attack. You are deeper into the mountains than the others, and furthest from the nearest neighbor."

"You think the fences were these people's work?"

"I thought so then but I did not want to speak until I had proof. I do not have proof yet, but it must be so," Manuel finished.

"I want the guard doubled," Kael told him. Manuel nodded, then left to implement his new orders. Soon after, everyone returned to their rooms to try to sleep away what remained of the night.

But as Lara and Kael lay in their bed, a strange feeling came over her. Turning to Kael, Lara placed her hand on his chest.

"Asleep?"

"No," he said in a matching whisper.

"Do you think Manuel is right?"

"I don't know," he said with a sigh. "What else could it be?"

"I don't know, either. Kael, I'm worried, but I don't know why." Suddenly, Kael pulled her against him, and she felt the warmth of his flesh against hers.

There were no shooting sparks of instant desire, no rushes of heat that consumed her, just the comfort of his body against hers, easing her mind and making her forget about anything other than themselves.

The next day, Kael and John went into Santa Barbara. When they returned, Lara saw the look on John's face and knew everything had been taken care of. The Crimmonses would be their neighbors after their own house was built. Until then, they would continue to live with Kael and herself. And Lara would have Constance's help when the baby arrived, for which she was grateful.

Smiling ruefully as she watched the men ride up, Lara touched her stomach through the soft cotton of the skirt. She was in the beginning of her fourth month, and she had started to feel the gentle swell of her expanding belly. Last month, Lara had noticed the loss of her waistline and at first had been upset. It was only when Kael had caressed the skin at her waist that her fear of losing the beauty he desired had departed. Now, she felt radiant as her body continued to change, and

Kael watched her with more love in his eyes each day that she grew. Not once had she been sick, and for that, too, Lara was grateful.

That night they had a dinner party to celebrate the buying of the Crimmonses' future home. Everyone was in a light mood as they ate, and afterward they all gathered in the main room to drink, talk, and share a common bond of love and friendship. Only Neil Sheffield-Painted Hawk, did not join in with the rest. He sat in a chair, his face stoic as ever, as he watched the happiness that surrounded him. Then, as the evening drew to a close, Angela left the room. Kael watched as Neil's eyes followed her exit and he saw the longing that Neil tried to hide.

Moments later, Angela returned, and a hush fell. She stopped in front of Neil, a sweet smile on her face, as she took a package from behind her back.

"I, I mean we, have a present for you." Then, as Angela's face flushed scarlet, turning the color of her eyes an even deeper blue, she gave Painted Hawk the gift.

Neil opened the small package slowly. Lara watched as his eyes fastened within. Without hesitation, a copper-hued hand reached inside, to reappear holding a gold circle. His eyes went to Angela's. It was then that Lara was sure of what she'd noticed about Neil since his arrival. He was in love with Angela. Lara thought that she would talk privately to Kael, to find out if he agreed with her.

"It was my grandfather's watch," Angela explained. "We would all like you to have it because you are our friend." Then she averted her face for a moment to wipe the tears her emotions had brought out. When Angela turned back to Neil, she knelt and showed him how to open it. The golden cover released to reveal a clock face with finely etched numerals. Then Angela began to teach Neil how to tell time.

Unable to fight against it any longer, Lara accepted the tiredness that had been a constant companion since she had become pregnant. Wishing everyone a good night, she left for her bedroom.

One by one, the others also retired. Soon, only Kael and Painted Hawk remained. Although Kael was tired, he sensed that his friend needed to talk.

When the silence that enveloped the two men had become comfortable, Kale watched his friend study the watch in his hand.

"Kael," Painted Hawk began slowly, "I will not be returning to the Shoshone."

"I know."

"How?"

"Because you are here. Because when I met you, I realized that you were more than you appeared. Now that I know everything, I also know your mind thirsts for what you have only heard. You have lived as an Indian and now you would see what it is to be a white man."

"There is much to learn, much to see," Neil agreed. "There is also something else."

"Angela," Kael stated. It had been obvious to him that Neil was in love with his cousin.

"You know much. I have never felt the way I do with another. But I also know the way a white woman is treated when she marries an Indian. She is shunned by her own, treated as less than the lowest. I cannot do that to her."

"Not everyone acts the same," Kael responded.

"Enough will, enough will hurt her, and I will not have that happen to her!" Neil swore adamantly.

"Do you forget that you have now chosen the white man's world? You are still thinking like an Indian—a warrior who tells his woman what to do, and how to do it, after he has purchased her from her father. John will not sell Angela to you. You must win her love. Then you can marry her. She's not a fool. If she loves you and wants to marry you, she will accept whatever happens. Do not think for her," Kael advised.

"It will not be easy."

"Nothing that you really want is easy. Neil, my friend, think about what you have said, then speak to Angela about it."

"Do you think she will listen?"

Standing, Kael smiled at his friend. "If you do not speak to her, she cannot listen." With that, Kael left his friend to stare into the fire.

It was well past midnight when a small band of riders halted their horses just out of sight of the watchmen who guarded the ranch. At a signal, two of the men left their saddles and moved forward, as silent as the night itself.

Minutes later, there was the sound of bodies hitting the earth, and the group of men headed for the ranch. At the corral, the leader nodded to his men, and they began their work. They moved carefully among the horses until they separated one from the rest. As the leader watched, his eyes burning insanely, he smiled.

After his men were finished with their grisly work, he gave another signal.

It was some time later that shots woke Kael. Forcing sleepiness aside, he pulled on pants and ran outside. Manuel and two others came to him just as Painted Hawk reached his side.

"Someone's let the horses loose," Kael said as he looked around. He watched Painted Hawk go to the corral and examine the gate. Suddenly, Painted Hawk turned and sprinted to the other side. Everyone followed him. There, against a railing, was the body of one of the ranch hands. He was dead.

"Someone is warning you," Painted Hawk said.

"Warning me?" Kael asked as he stepped next to the body. Kael froze. The man's eyes had been blindfolded, his legs propped into a kneeling position, and his hands tied in front of him as if he were in prayer.

"Lad," John called in a pain-filled voice, "the other guard was killed, also, and . . ." John slowly pointed to the ground ten feet away. Kael's eyes followed his cousin's finger as his numbed mind tried to see through the darkness. Then he saw it, and a new coldness spread through his body. Kael walked to where Major lay on the ground. As he knelt, his hand went to the muscle-corded neck of the horse that had been his companion for over five years. Kael stood slowly and faced the men.

"I don't know who's doing this, but I will find out." The anger that surged through his veins made Kael's voice coarse as he shouted his orders. "Manuel, take care of the men. I want everyone out in pairs. Armed! I want all the horses back. We start after whoever did this in the morning."

"Sí, Patrón, it will be done," the foreman said as his eyes went from the dead men to the dead horse.

Once they returned to the house, the women demanded to know what had happened. After Kael explained, he told them that he would be gone for several days, and that he would be leaving Manuel and several others to stand guard.

At the end of the first hour daylight, the horses had been caught. Kael, along with John, Painted Hawk, and some ranch hands, started out. Painted Hawk took the lead, and soon they were following the tracks of those who had killed. But even as they rode away, John Crimmons was worried. He remembered the last time, months ago, that he had left Constance and Angela alone.

The day passed slowly for Lara. Everything she did reminded her that Kael would not return until he either caught the people responsible, or learned who they were.

Lara had never seen Kael the way he had been this morning. His voice was flat, his emotions nonexistent. Whoever had killed the men last night and destroyed Major would soon face a wrath they would be unable to defeat.

Throughout the long day, Lara realized that she and the other women were constantly under the watchful eyes of Manual, or one of the hands. The men were never far away. By the time darkness fell and dinner was finished, Lara was glad for the privacy of the house. The constant vigil was a painful reminder of the times she'd been a prisoner at her stepfather's ranch. Except for one thing—now she was being guarded to protect her, not to hold her prisoner.

Now the women sat in silence before the fireplace and tried to take comfort from each other's presence. Finally, as Constance looked deeply into the jumping flames, she spoke.

"This may sound foolish," Constance began, speaking as

much to herself as the others, "but I can't help but think that our coming here has something to do with what's happening."

"You're right," Lara snapped, and was rewarded with Constance's eyes meeting hers. "It does sound foolish. This problem started before you came, and it has nothing to do with you!"

"How can you be so sure?" Constance asked. "I don't know why, I just feel that we brought this with us, and I'm afraid for John—"

"Stop it!" Lara ordered, hearing her own fears voiced by the older woman. "They'll be all right. Kael and John and Painted Hawk will be all right. They have to be . . ." she whispered as her hands went to her stomach.

Through it all, Angela had not said a word. When the women stopped speaking, Angela turned her eyes to Lara, and then to her mother.

"Do you think he avoids me because of what happened?" Angela asked in an emotion-filled voice. Not realizing what her friend was talking about, Lara looked at Constance.

"I don't think so, dear. 'Tis only his way," Constance responded. "When Neil looks at you, and you cannot see him, his eyes are filled with love. No, Angela, he's just not sure enough of himself. He's starting a new life, and he needs time. And I don't believe, because you were raped, that it will matter to Neil. He's not been raised the same way as other men. He's more like your father than most, and you haven't seen your own father shun my bed, have you?"

Angela looked at her mother, and smiled softly. Neither saw the expression that crossed Lara's face. It was the one thing she hadn't known. For some reason, she'd thought Constance had escaped that humiliation.

Suddenly, Lara felt Constance's eyes on her, and she saw the older woman nod slightly. "There was nothing I could do to prevent it. Lew Cross raped me! He's much like your fath—like Martin Dowley. But it hasn't affected our love, nor should it."

Lara's heart overflowed with emotion, and a black rage filled her as she thought of her stepfather.

"I'm sorry," she said in a whisper.

"Now look who's talking like the fool. It wasn't your fault, you could not help being part of his family."

Again, a silence enveloped them, but this time the strain and worry were not as heavy.

Seven men stood on the small ridge that overlooked Rancho del Sol. They watched for almost an hour until the leader turned to the rest.

"Can the guards be taken out quickly?" Martin Dowley asked Cross.

"No problem," he said. Without further discussion, he gave orders to the group.

"What about our money?" one asked.

"You get the second half when you've done what you've been hired to do!" Dowley growled, cutting off more questions.

As the men unslung their rifles, Lew Cross shouted, "Let's go."

"It's sleep for me," Constance said as she stood. "All this useless worrying has worn me out. Good night, ladies." As she walked up the stairs, a gunshot rang out, breaking the peace. Constance froze.

Running to the window, Lara stared out. Riders rushed forward, exchanging shots with her men. Abruptly, the firing stopped, but the riders continued to come. Reacting quickly, Lara bolted the front door, then raced to the library. On the wall was a gunrack. Lara pulled down a rifle and loaded it. Returning to the other room, she motioned the women behind her. Lara held the rifle butt against her shoulder and aimed at the front door.

Trying to still the trembling in her body, Lara waited to see if the bolt would hold. Suddenly, there was a loud crash, and the door tore from its hinges to hang sideways in the frame.

Martin Dowley, with Lew Cross behind him, appeared before her disbelieving eyes.

"No!" she whispered as her obese stepfather filled the rifle's sights.

"Did you think I would forget you, daughter?"

"Get out!" She ordered as she began to pull the trigger.

"Would you shoot me? Would you kill the man who raised you, who gave you everything?"

"You gave me nothing!" Lara shouted as she tried to will her finger to move.

"You are mine!" Dowley shouted.

Lara again saw the insanity that gleamed in his eyes. She noticed the coal-dark embers shift momentarily, and then return to her. Instinctively, Lara whirled and fired the rifle. The man coming out of the kitchen staggered as the bullet ripped into his chest. As he fell, Lara turned back to her stepfather.

Too late! her mind warned, as the gun was torn from her grasp. The leering face of Lew Cross stood before her.

"Bastards!" she screamed as she swung at his face. Catching her raised hand, Cross pulled her to him. His free arm went around her neck and secured her tightly against him. The choking grip prevented her slightest movement. In the same instant, Constance launched herself against the man who still haunted her dreams, the man that only John's understanding and love had cleansed her of.

Cross was ready for her. As she reached him, he slammed a fist against Constance's jaw. The Englishwoman dropped, unconscious, at his feet. Then everyone looked at Angela.

Angela stood there, her eyes wide with fright that the sight of Martin Dowley had brought on. In that first moment of recognition, Angela's mind had blocked everything from her. She stood rooted to one spot, unable to move, paralyzed with fear.

Dowley walked to the young woman. Standing in front of her, he smiled. His palm touched her face. She did not move.

Dowley let his hand fall to her breast, and fondled it. Only then did Angela break free of her trance, and scream.

Within the choking hold of Lew Cross, Lara felt Angela's scream tear through her body, galvanizing her to one last effort for freedom. Yet before she could move, Cross covered her mouth and lifted her from the floor. As she was turned from Angela, Lara saw her father slap the younger woman, then grab her hair and pull her after them.

Dowley and Cross ignored the dead man on the floor as they carried the women from the house. Outside, Lara and Angela were tied and put on horses. With Cross mounted behind her, and Dowley behind Angela, they rode from the ranch.

"Something is wrong," Painted Hawk stated. Studying the ground, Neil Sheffield knew they had been tricked. Slowly the lean, copper-skinned man stood and looked at Kael. "The tracks are the same as the others, but they are different. Only one of the horses has a rider. They changed horses."

Staring at his friend, Kael realized what had happened. "The ranch," he said as he turned his horse. Painted Hawk jumped on the back of his Appaloosa, and the five men started back at a gallop.

"Why?" John asked as he caught up to Kael.

"They wanted us away. I don't know who's behind this, but they wanted easy access to the ranch."

"We will be there before daylight," Painted Hawk observed as he glanced at the dark night sky.

"Who?" John asked. Then Kael's eyes met his cousin's, and they both knew the answer.

"He wouldn't," John pleaded.

Kael did not reply.

The rest of the night was spent in short bursts of speed, and long distances covered at a walk to rest the horses rather than stop and waste time. As the vanguard of the day framed the Santa Barbara mountains, the five men rode into the ranch. Kael felt every emotion within him die as he saw the bodies strewn across the ground.

Dismounting, he saw the front door of the house torn askew. Suddenly, Constance came running out. John caught his wife in his arms, and held her until her sob-racked body calmed.

Then the men listened to the horrible story she told. Moments later, Carmella assisted Manuel over to them. The foreman's head was bandaged, but a large, oval spot of blood had seeped through.

"*Patrón*, I cannot forgive myself. We were caught by surprise. They rode at us, firing at everyone. We could not stop them," he said, as his eyes held Kael's firmly.

Placing a strong hand on the smaller man's shoulder, Kael said, "You did your best. We need fresh horses. Have someone saddle them," Kael instructed as he walked into the empty house.

An hour later, the three friends rode out again. Neil Sheffield-Painted Hawk was in the lead, Kael and John followed. They rode hard, with fresh mounts in tow. None of the men spoke, each one's mind on his own private thoughts. But of the trio, only the amber eyes of Kael Treemont betrayed no emotion.

The day had been the longest in Lara's life . . . and the hardest. Held in a cruel embrace against Lew's chest, she had ridden for half an hour. When they stopped, she had been dumped on the ground.

Falling, Lara held her tied hands before her, trying to lessen the shock of landing, the baby uppermost in her mind. Then Cross had pulled her up and half-dragged her to Angela's side. The foreman stood guard over them while Martin Dowley ordered his other men to uncover the wagon that was hidden in the brush.

Thinking of possible escape, Lara studied their surroundings.

But when she looked at Angela, she knew that she could not abandon her friend even if she could get free. Angela's eyes were vacant, and she seemed unaware of what was happening. Angela could not help.

Lara watched the men bring out a wagon. Then they took the women and forced them into the back. Cross bound them back-to-back before unsaddling the horses and hitching them to the buckboard. By daylight, they were rolling East.

Lara listened to what the men said, and realized that she and Angela were doomed. Dowley was a raving lunatic. He had actually given Lara to his foreman. Listening to their talk, Lara learned more of what had happened in Valley City.

Johnathan Setterley had come with thirty men, and had confiscated the large herd of cattle that had been his payment for Lara. After that, Dowley had begun to foreclose on every outstanding debt. Laughing on the seat next to Cross, he bragged that he owned every business and ranch in Valley City. But Lara felt it was strange, the way Lew kept silent.

They stopped at midday, and Lara and Angela were untied. Angela showed a small spark of life, but she still seemed distant. Dowley ordered them to prepare a meal as he, Cross, and the others sat and watched.

While they ate, Dowley began to speak to Lara.

"You embarrassed me. You tried to destroy my reputation, you and your lover." Dowley stared at her, his eyes almost lost in folds of fat. She felt her revulsion toward Dowley, as a sharp rise of nausea threatened to make her sick.

"Now it's my turn. I've lost much because of what you did. Now you will lose. By now your precious husband knows he's been tricked. And he knows who has you. He will come after you, won't he?"

Lara refused to answer. Dowley smiled grotesquely as he lifted his bulk and walked to her. He bent down and began to yell, only inches from her face. "He'll come for you. When he does, he'll die!"

"He'll kill you," she hissed between clenched teeth.

"No, you and my future wife will be in the way. He will

not take that chance. It is I who will kill him. He will come to me, he will beg me to spare you, and then I'll shoot him!"

Unexpectedly, Angela stood and faced Martin Dowley. Her face had become a mask of unconcealed hatred as she moved forward. Hidden in her hand was a long hairpin. Dowley watched as she came toward him, a smile on his face.

"And you, my dear," he said in a softer voice, "will come back to Valley City with me." Then his hand shot out, grabbing Angela's clenched one. With a scream of frustration, Angela fell to her knees.

Without releasing her wrist, Dowley slapped Angela twice, then he shook her imprisoned hand until she released her weapon. "The next time you attempt something like that, I will whip you!"

"I'll not go with you!" she cried.

Dowley laughed in her face. "Cross. Tie them!"

Lew did as he was ordered. Again, both women sat bound together.

"Why?" Lara asked as Cross finished his job.

"Because I'm his partner now. Because I own twenty thousand acres, and ten thousand head of cattle will be mine when we get back."

"If you return," Lara spat.

Cross bent, and covered her mouth with his. "And you will be mine also!"

"In hell!"

"If that's where you want to go," he replied, his eyes devouring Lara. "I've wanted you for a long time. You got away from me once. You never will again."

Defiantly, Lara glared at him.

Cross smiled lewdly in response. "I told you once, after me, you wouldn't want anyone else."

"After you, no one would want to touch me," she threw back at him. "You're disgusting!"

Cross smiled as he put a hand on Lara's cheek and began to caress it. Slowly, his fingertips traveled across her finely etched cheeks, until they dropped to her lips. Quickly, she caught one of his fingers in her teeth.

Lara bit down fiercely.

Lew Cross screamed in pain.

A hand crashed against her head, spinning Lara into darkness.

Painted Hawk melted back into the forest that he had been hiding in. Slipping silently through the trees, winding his way through the brush, Neil returned to Kael and John. "They have made camp. Lara and Angela are tied. There are five men on guard. All are hidden. They wait for us," Neil reported in clipped, precise words.

"No," Kael replied with a shake of his head. "They're waiting for me. This time it's Dowley who seeks revenge. He wants me dead."

"You have an idea, lad?" John asked. Kael looked at his cousin and nodded. John's face was creased in lines of worry, and Kael knew that if they did not do something soon, John would try to free his daughter, regardless of the danger to himself.

"We must wait until dark, then we'll act." Quickly and efficiently, Kael outlined his idea.

Darkness made their imprisonment worse. Lara had watched as each of Dowley's hired killers had come in to eat. The roaring blaze of the fire was a beacon that she knew would draw Kael to his death. Her stepfather had planned well, and Lara was afraid.

Since she had bitten Cross, both she and Angela had been gagged. They could not talk to each other, or do anything else. Now, Lara was beginning to feel the cramps from her inability to move, and the constant pain that centered within her womb. She had to find a way to warn Kael. Nothing else mattered, only the fact that her very presence here would be fatal to her husband.

When the last of Dowley's men had eaten and disappeared into the woods, Martin Dowley came to the women. He removed their gags and unbound them. Lara tried to stand but fell on her side. Dowley laughed.

"Mr. Cross," he called, "I believe your woman needs help." Turning from her, Dowley bent and lifted Angela to her feet.

"No!" Angela screamed as he pulled her against him. Lara could do nothing as her stepfather pawed her friend, and began to drag her to the wagon.

Cross came over to lift Lara but she could no longer wait. She forced her knee high, and hit the soft bulge between his legs. Rewarded by his surprised curse, Lara willed life into her pain-riddled body, and ran to Angela and Dowley.

"Leave her alone!" she screamed as she jumped onto the obese man's back, raking clawed fingers across his face. Startled, Dowley released Angela to spin on his attacker.

Grabbing Lara's blouse, Dowley yanked her to him, and slapped her. Then Cross was there, pulling Lara away and throwing her to the ground.

"Keep her under control!" Dowley ordered, "or kill her. . . ."

She froze. "Bastard!" she whispered as she watched Cross bend over her. His eyes were fastened on the breast exposed by the rent in her blouse.

Ignoring them, Dowley turned back to Angela, who was trying to slip away. One lunge of his fat body brought him to her. Another outreaching of his hand tore open her bodice, freeing her full breasts.

"No!" Angela screamed as she tried to retreat.

"No!"

Kael heard the scream and moved swiftly. The lookout who stood near the tree heard it, too, and immediately became alert. Kael stepped behind him and brought the thick tree branch down. When the man crumpled beneath the blow, Kael took his rifle. Slowly, he began to inch forward.

Before long, Painted Hawk joined him, and nodded. Each had taken care of two guards, and now they were waiting for

John. As Kael watched his wife thrown to the ground, and saw the man he hated begin to attack Angela, an apparition of rage burst through the trees.

John Crimmons was going to his daughter's aid. Moving quickly, Kael and Painted Hawk started in.

Lara heard the noise, turned, and saw John.

"Trap!" Lara screamed. As she yelled, Cross raced for the buckboard where he lifted a rifle from the seat. Pushing herself up, Lara chased after him. He brought the gun to bear on John just as Lara reached him.

Hitting the barrel with her hand, Lara heard the echo of the gunshot loud in her ears.

Kael saw John drop as the shot rang through the night. Forcing himself to stop, Kael raised his own weapon. Lara was falling to the ground as Cross twisted away from her. As Kael sighted on the man, he saw Cross's foot begin to arc toward Lara's head.

Kael had only one shot. Without hesitation, he fired, then dropped the gun and ran.

A third eye appeared on Cross's forehead, and the foot that moved toward Lara's face faltered. Cross fell heavily across Lara Treemont.

A moment later, she was on her feet and in Kael's arms. His eyes burned brightly as he looked at her. Then he spun around.

Martin Dowley held Angela before him, her half-naked body gleaming in the firelight. Dowley held a knife to Angela's breast, and a small trickle of blood had begun to flow.

"Let her go," Kael ordered.

"Don't tell me what to do!" Dowley screamed. "You ruined it all. You destroyed my plans!" he yelled, his voice cracking with each word. "I'll kill her. I'll kill you! You won't win. You won't win!" Dowley's eyes widened as he watched Kael move toward him. White showed around the umber coals as Dowley's fleshy face quivered. Kael saw Dowley's eyes dart sideways at the copper-skinned Indian who was moving toward him. Neil's face was unreadable, every muscle in his body corded tightly.

Dowley used Angela as a shield to face the Shoshone warrior chief. Every muscle quivering tensely, Kael inched forward the way a cat sneaks up on its prey. He must time his actions perfectly with those of Painted Hawk's.

Kael's breathing became shallow as he stalked his prey. Every step that was taken caused his blood to race. Ignoring Angela, Kael concentrated on the fat face in front of him, waiting for the right moment to pounce.

Painted Hawk stepped sideways, forcing Dowley to turn even further from Kael. Painted Hawk feinted left. Dowley tried to move with him. As he did, his grip loosened on Angela, and the knife wavered from her breast.

Now!

Every sense in Kael's finely tuned body ordered him forward. He left the ground in a leap, his hands outstretched, his back arched, his toes pointed. Landing on the man's back, Kael gave Dowley's head a hard twist.

Dowley screamed as Kael pulled him backward. Then Kael felt himself pinned under the fat man's weight, his breath crushed from him. Fighting the darkness that was descending, Kael yelled into the night, reacting to a primeval need. Twisting and rolling, Kael pulled out from under the enormous bulk and reversed himself. His hands gripped Dowley's throat, and he felt his fingers sink into the folds of flesh. Squeezing tightly, Kael began to end the evil life that had haunted him for years.

Suddenly, Kael realized what he was doing. Taking deep, gulping breaths of air, he loosened his fingers.

He would not become another Dowley! He would not kill. Slowly, sanity returned. Dowley's bulging eyes stared helplessly at him. The man's face was blood-red.

"*No!*" Kael shouted as he realized that his years of obsessive vengeance had almost turned him into what he hated most. Standing, Kael stepped away from Dowley.

Angela was being held by Painted Hawk, his strength

comforting her. John, his side bloodied, walked toward his daughter. Lara . . . Kael turned, hunting for his wife.

He saw her standing only three feet from him, her hand still covering her mouth as her eyes searched his face. Kael understood what good this night had brought. He was free from the hauntings of his past.

Opening his arms, Kael pulled Lara against his chest. "I could not have lived, if you had not," he said as he kissed her.

A moment later, Lara drew back. "Is he dead?" she asked in a whisper. Kael shook his head.

"If he is to die, it will be done properly. I will not be his executioner. Justice will."

Lara looked into Kael's eyes and nodded as a smile formed on her lips. The smile was torn from her face suddenly, as her eyes widened. Spinning around quickly, Kael faced Martin Dowley again.

"Fools!" he screamed, every vestige of humanity gone from his face. Only the expression of monstrous evil remained. A rifle was in his hands; his finger on the trigger. Kael blocked Lara with his body as he saw a flash of steel in the air. The gun went off, the bullet flew harmlessly upward as the handle of Neil Sheffield's hunting knife penetrated the side of Dowley's neck.

Martin Dowley died before his obese body fell to the ground.

It took two days for all the details to be settled. The territorial marshal had jailed Dowley's five men, pending trial. The injured hands at the ranch were recovering, and the dead had been buried. John's wound had been judged superficial. Angela had recovered from her shock quickly, and for the past day she and Neil Sheffield-Painted Hawk, had spent only rare moments apart.

Kael had insisted that the doctor from Santa Barbara be sent for to examine Lara. The doctor agreed with her that nothing had happened to hurt the baby, and in four and a half months a healthy child would be born.

Now, lying in their large bed, Kael and Lara talked quietly. They had not really spoken about Dowley's death, but Kael knew it had to be aired.

"I didn't want him dead. That part of me is gone," Kael explained.

Lara stared into the lambent eyes that had won her heart, and smiled. "I know. I saw it that night. I wondered was it because he was my father?"

"No. It was because I've changed. You've changed me," he said truthfully. Then, tenderly, he drew Lara into his arms. He kissed her mouth softly, probing within its warmth with his tongue, until he found hers. Kael forced control on himself as he began to caress her. His hands ran over her breasts, feeling the largeness that her pregnancy had given them. Her nipples responded and he bent to take each between his lips.

Lara felt the slow, rambling sensations of his mouth on her tender breasts. She felt the heat of his lips, and at the same time felt the life that was within her begin to stir. Pulling away from him, she took his hand in hers. His eyes sought hers in question.

"Feel," she ordered as she placed his hand on her taut belly. Lara watched his face as he felt the baby move within her. Then she saw him smile as he looked back up at her. Blinking back tears of happiness, she moistened her lips.

"Love me, husband, gently, make love to me." And as Kael began to fulfill her request, Lara knew that afterward she would show him their child's inheritance, and tell her husband the truth of her birth.